The Cost of One's Decision

A Paramilitary Thriller

Zayne Kulder

Reese Halden LLC

The Cost of One's Decision

Published By Reese Halden LLC

Cover art by aliconart

Copyright © 2022 by Zayne Kulder and Reese Halden LLC

First Printing: October 2024

ISBN 979-8-9909576-0-2 (Kindle e-Book)

ISBN 979-8-9909576-1-9 (Paperback)

1 3 5 7 9 10 8 6 4 2

Reader's Advisory

This novel contains coarse adult language, descriptions of intense violence by criminal gangs and military operatives, suicide, and descriptions of sadistic torture and sexual assault.

It is recommended for readers age 18+.

Dedication

This novel is dedicated to the men and women who tirelessly fight to against, and to defeat the scourge of illegal drugs and human trafficking.

This novel is also dedicated to those who have suffered physical or sexual abuse at some point in their lives, and made the decision to persevere, to strive to be better and overcome, and continue with their lives despite all that they suffered.

Author's Note

This story includes an incident of suicide. It is not the author's intent to glorify or condone it; rather, it is included because it is needed for the narrative.

For many people who struggle with problems – despair, harassment, depression, struggling with one's sexual orientation, being bullied, or whatever it may be – suicide was something that they may have thought about, or even attempted, as a way to make the pain and suffering end.

You are not alone if you have had thoughts of suicide – many people at one point or another in their lives have felt this way, the author included. Thus it is the author's sincere hope that, should you have thoughts of suicide or self-harm, that you confront and overcome such thoughts by seeking help from family, friends, co-workers, your religious leaders – someone, anyone whom you trust.

However, if you feel that you can't talk to any of these, can't trust them, or they're not available to you for whatever reason, there are some excellent, impartial resources that are ready, willing and waiting to help:

Within the United States of America:

- National Suicide Prevention Lifeline: Dial 988

- Crisis Text Hotline: Text **Hello** to 741741

Anywhere in the world:

- Visit https://988lifeline.org/ or https://findahelpline.com/i/iasp

- For Children and Teenagers contact the YouthLine: Text **teen2teen** to 839863, or call +01-877-968-8491

Don't let problems drive bad decisions!
Don't be embarrassed, hesitant or afraid! Use these resources!

For out of the heart proceed evil thoughts, murders, adulteries, fornications, thefts, false witness, blasphemies: These are *the things* which defile a man ...
—*The Holy Bible*, Matthew 15:19, 20

It takes strength to make your way through grief, to grab hold of life and let it pull you forward.
—Patti Davis

Mankind must learn that evil is not power.
—Mary Baker Eddy

Murphy's Law

Anything that can go wrong will go wrong, and at the worst possible time.
—Edward A. Murphy, Jr.

Prologue

"*Jefe,* your car is ready."

Jorge Manuel de Corazón turned his head just enough to make eye contact with Tomas. "I'll be down in a minute," Jorge said curtly, dismissing his *teniente* and turned back to gaze over the land below him. A moment later he heard the faint *thunk* of the door closing, and once again he was alone with his thoughts as he leaned on the stone railing of his bedroom balcony.

I wonder what Raul, Eduardo and father would think of our empire now?

I know what they'd think – they'd all be terribly critical, calling it all "a bunch of nonsense," that's what.

Jorge chuckled sardonically at this truth. His father Carlos had been a low-level enforcer in Mexico's Presagio Cartel, a man renowned for his stout build and stamina as well as for his boxing skill, the latter which he'd learned from his seven years of service in Mexico's Navy, while the former was simply genetic, a trait that his two older brothers had shared—

But not him.

Jorge sighed at that, but then a small smile of satisfaction crossed his lips. He'd turned his father's billion-dollar enterprise into one that was now approaching five billion a year, and all because of his "bunch of nonsense." Jorge swirled the remaining three fingers of Maker's Mark in the tumbler he held, the clink of the round ice cube dulled by the liquid, and then put the glass to his lips to sip at the rich liquor as he reflected and remembered.

Through luck, happenstance and being in the right place at the right time, his father had risen to eventually snatch control of the Presagio Cartel, leaving a trail of blood and gore in his wake to achieve that lofty

1

position. Once he had, Jorge's brothers, Raul and Eduardo, had been ensconced as Carlos's right and left hands, and this terrible trio – so much alike in their abilities, outlook, desires, needs and passions – had morphed the cartel into the most powerful one in all the Americas. It was an enterprise that had its tentacles embedded in everything from large corporations and major governments to local and federal agencies, to corner bodegas and family businesses.

It would have continued this way had the digital age not come. Jorge's father and brothers were all brawn, with little brains – the cerebral requirements of the family business had been relegated to lieutenants that his father had recruited from major business schools in Mexico, Brazil and South Africa. But these men weren't family, and thus could never be fully trusted – and with no formal education himself, and no skill at what he'd hired these men to do for him, Carlos could never be certain that they weren't stealing from him.

Realizing at last that his youngest son's proclivity for math, science, reading books and programming computers wasn't something to be disdained, but rather was something that could correct this problem of uncertainty among his hired financial help, Carlos had finagled a spot for Jorge at Rensselaer Technical Institute. Carlos would take full advantage of his son's less-than-manly abilities, and in doing so correct a nagging worry that his hired help was stealing from him.

Jorge excelled in the university environment. He received a B.S. in Electrical Engineering followed by an M.S. in Computer Engineering, and then pivoted, going to the University of Chicago for a Master of Business Administration degree.

Upon his return home after eight years of university education, Jorge's father had placed him in with his hired accountants and financial advisors, and within two years Jorge was running it all, with the former hired help and their families having been forcibly retired under a section of sand in the nearby *Área Natural Protegida Médanos de Samalayuca*, south of the city of Ciudad Juárez.

Finally, Jorge had found the acceptance from his father that had previously been denied to him. Carlos was the proverbial egotistical, self-centered, misogynistic Latin male – he valued physical strength, dominated everything he saw, valued the code of honor special to the cartels, and was all about wealth and largesse.

His brothers were no different. Together with their father, the three satisfied their desires by murdering any who opposed them and, when this wasn't enough fun, roamed the clubs, festivals and the dark, back streets of Ciudad Juárez in search of their next sexual conquest.

While Jorge enjoyed the wealth and largesse that his family's rulership of the Presagio cartel brought, and he dreamed to rule the cartel in his father's stead someday, physically Jorge wasn't built like his father or brothers – they were tall, brutish and solid, preferring to think with their fists instead of their suboptimal brains, while Jorge was definitely his mother's son in this department.

Like her, Jorge had thick, wavy black hair and wide-set hazel eyes. Jorge's features were more feminine than masculine, with slender eyebrows, long lashes, high cheekbones in a heart-shaped face, and full lips with a tall, slender build that was more like a footballer's – football as in soccer, not the ridiculous American sport – than a boxer's physique like his brothers and father had. While these softer, more delicate features combined to make him very attractive, this attraction was more in the line of being boyishly pretty, rather than ruggedly or maturely handsome.

And there was one more thing that made him less of a man in his father's eyes—

Jorge was gay.

He'd never told anyone of his orientation, but the fact that he preferred to have his nose in a book rather than go out riding ATVs with his brothers, or preferred playing games on his computer instead of shooting guns, boxing, or riding horses – all of it made his father suspicious. Carlos had never confronted Jorge about his suspicions, but how Carlos treated him was an indication enough that he knew Jorge's secret.

The eight years of university in the USA was a turning point for Jorge. He finally worked up the courage to be himself, slowly at first, but then delving right in. He discovered that his intellect and personality, coupled with his slender build, dark good-looks, and accented English, worked like a magnet swept over a bin of steel bolts – he could literally pick up anyone of his choice on a whim, regardless of the location. He'd overdone it at first, having a series of one- and two-night stands, struggling at the start with the mechanics of gay sex, but then after a dozen liaisons, he became adept and then the master of it.

Returning to his family had been bittersweet. He missed the sexual and personal freedom he'd had during his stay in the US but was eager to prove himself to his father in the role intended for him within the cartel. Jorge secretly planned to take his father's place as its head someday – not that he intended to forcibly depose his father, not by any means, but as the youngest, knew that one day the leadership of the cartel would be his, especially if he proved himself to be invaluable on the financial side of the family business.

A week after his return, his father had called Jorge into his study for a conversation. Jorge assumed it was about how he'd start working with the hired help—but it wasn't.

"You like men," Carlos had said matter-of-factly once they'd been seated in front of the fireplace.

The truth was that, while Jorge was gay, he was much more attracted to boys than men. Especially teenage boys at the low end of that scale. He liked their slim smoothness, their innocence, their bright-eyed excitement and *joie de vivre*, but mostly he liked being able to dominate them easily, to make them do whatever he wanted.

No doubt this stemmed from the fact that his father and two older brothers were much larger than he was, much more physical and macho, and had tormented and bullied him throughout his childhood. With no way to fight back against them, now that he was an adult, one who had substantial power and position, he found himself much happier raping, torturing and having total control over those he chose for his sexual proclivities and self-aggrandizing needs.

For Jorge, there just was nothing like having his way with an athletic, slender, 13-year-old to make him feel *alive*....

Of course, he wasn't *ever* going to tell his father any of this. It was bad enough that his father was confronting him now, outing him, and in that moment, Jorge struggled with how to respond.

Thankfully, his father saved him from the need.

"No need to deny it," Carlos had told him as he settled back into his chair and regarded his youngest son with hooded eyes that were as dark and lifeless as a cobra's. "And, honestly, ten, twenty years ago, I would have taken you out to the *Área Natural* an given you a permanent home there."

Jorge remembered finding it difficult to breathe after that pronouncement.

"You need not worry," Carlos had continued, waving his hand dismissively. "We live in modern times, no? Your... different needs are something that's not so... so uncommon anymore. Am I correct in this?"

Jorge wasn't able to speak; all he could do was nod.

"It is of little consequence," Carlos had then said casually, but then he had leaned forward, his eyes widening into dark, glowing coals of intensity. "As long as you do not flaunt it! As long as you do not let it cloud your mind! Do you understand me in this?"

"Yes," Jorge had managed to croak out.

"The little head always wants to make the decisions," Carlos had said then, his eyes becoming hooded once more as he pushed back into his chair. "Don't let it drive your... needs... and all will be fine between us." Then he snorted and added, "And don't bring any of them home with you! I don't want to see them!"

Funny, coming from a man who had more mistresses and whores than days in the year, and basically flaunted this fact in front of everyone, including his wife, Jorge mused as he took another sip of his Maker's Mark. *Carlos was a man who let his lusts drive more decisions than anyone.*

Well, it doesn't matter anymore...

He's gone, and my brothers too – yet more casualties of the cartel life.

Jorge stood, and looking out into the waning light of dusk, offered a silent toast. "To you, father, and my dear brothers – rest in peace knowing that your Jorge has everything in hand and our legacy will last for a thousand years! *Saludos!*"

He consumed the remaining liquor in one swallow and stood musing as he lowered his gaze to the brand-new community that was arrayed below his family's hilltop mansion.

My legacy, he thought as he looked upon it.

Not 'our'...

Just mine!

Chapter 1

In His Prime

Jorge had done what his father and brothers could never have done, let alone understand or even conceive of the possibility.

The biggest stumbling block of the drug, prostitution, human trafficking, and gun-running trades were that many of the transactions were done in cash. That had been acceptable in his father's day, when the USA and the European countries hadn't yet enacted strict money policies, anti-counterfeiting technologies, and had advanced artificial intelligence computer systems tracking, evaluating and nosing into every aspect of their business. Even before Jorge had been sent off to university, he'd seen that this way of doing business was becoming as dangerous as it was obsolescent. The digital world was their best bet for continuing their business with a minimum of law enforcement and government interference – essentially fighting fire with fire.

The exclusive, new community of *El Cielo Escondido* – The Hidden Heaven – was Jorge's answer to the cartel's continued success and longevity into the next century.

Built on 500 hectares (2100 acres, or about 3.3 square miles) of semi-arid land southwest of the town of La Escondida in the state of Chihuahua, it was a private enclave for the upper-middle- and upper-class elite of Mexico and Central America. A total of 42 plots of between 10 and 20 acres were available for purchase, upon which homes that had been designed to blend ergonomically with the beautiful semi-arid landscape would be built to the buyer's specifications – anything from traditional Mexican to nouveau colonial to chalet-style, all of them offering a balance of privacy and luxury.

Common features included an indoor and outdoor pool, sauna, whirlpool hot tub, multi-car garages, air conditioning, restaurant-grade kitchens, shooting ranges, bowling alleys, art galleries, solariums, libraries, smoking rooms, entertainment centers, and spacious bedrooms.

For those living in the community, there was an 18-hole golf course designed by the renowned Robert Trent Jones II and its accompanying clubhouse that featured a restaurant run by a Michelin-rated chef. Nearby was the recreation center, featuring play areas for children, a community pool, and a number of additional amenities, including a day spa, ballrooms and meeting rooms for hosting gatherings, and a full-size movie theater.

All of it was encircled with security fencing and protected by a state-of-the-art security system. Armed guards – ex-Mexican Marines who found his rate of pay to be significantly more generous than working for the Navy – provided a human presence at the entry points, to monitor the AI of the security system, and for emergency response. These men and women were equipped with the latest in gear and weaponry, including armored 4WD patrol vehicles and drones.

The community received several international eco-awards for its use of renewable energy to provide all its power needs. A geothermal system, banks of solar panels, and several windmills on the western edge of the community provided more than enough power for its daytime needs, with the excess being shunted into banks of Tesla batteries for providing power during the hours of darkness or when there was insufficient wind or solar. In case of emergency, there were also two natural gas-powered generators that would come online automatically.

The two-billion-dollar price tag for *El Cielo Escondido* had been footed by cartel money channeled through dozens of front companies, which in turn had shunted it through various offshore banks that then provided funding to legitimate construction companies. Even though this had enabled Jorge to launder almost a year's worth of cartel profits, without his name or anything to do with the cartel tied to it, this wasn't the real purpose of building *El Cielo Escondido*.

The whole purpose revolved around the two houses at the base of the hill below Jorge's family's mansion.

From where he stood, Jorge could clearly see these two homes and the areas adjacent to them in the light of portable tower fixtures. Workers were putting the finishing touches on each property, planting the last shrubs and fauna around the mansions, or in carefully sculpted sections on the property. Within the hour they'd be done and gone, leaving two stately, multi-million-dollar homes ready for their new owners.

What the owners didn't know was that, in sub-basements deep beneath each of these homes, were huge temperature- and humidity-controlled rooms in which thousands of servers were racked. These isolated rooms were accessible only from well-camouflaged access points and, being beneath someone else's home, couldn't be traced to or connected with Jorge or the cartel in the extremely unlikely event that law enforcement discovered their existence.

Each server was a cryptocurrency miner, and this was what would enable the Presagio Cartel to grow and evolve over the rest of the century.

No longer would cash be king. Transactions would occur solely in the digital realm, funneled securely and out of sight of law enforcement to and from his cryptocurrency servers. No more duffel bags of cash, with the associated temptations of absconding with it; no more tracing of individual bills, or risk of receiving counterfeit money.

Crypto solved so many problems. The one drawback was the power consumption – law enforcement had discovered one way to track such operations was to monitor power usage, and several criminal crypto banks had succumbed in this manner. The other drawback was the need for high-end graphics cards and CPUs to power crypto mining; these were only manufactured by a few dozen companies and thus were another bottleneck that could be monitored.

Jorge had addressed the first of these potential problems by making the community self-sufficient from the state's power grid. The geothermal, solar, wind, batteries and back-up gas-powered sources were overkill for the needs of the community, but with no way to measure consumption by someone on the outside, this fact wasn't easily determined. And even if someone eventually discovered that the power generation at *El Cielo Escondido* was more than it could ever need, the simple explanation would be that it was there to support any future, additional homes or amenities.

The second was even easier – he purchased a manufacturer of high-end computer graphic cards through a series of cut-out corporations, assuring that he'd be first in line for whenever he needed this critical crypto-mining component.

It was a perfect arrangement, Jorge mused as he strolled back into his bedroom, went to the sideboard and poured himself another two fingers of Maker's Mark. *And I control it all!*

He tossed back the liquor, set the empty glass on the sideboard, and turned to look at himself in the full-length mirror.

He was in his prime. At 32 years old, he was still fit, slim and boyishly attractive, with no hint of gray in his jet hair and still possessing an unlined face, due to a combination of his mother's genetics and a strict regimen of spa treatments and the occasional plastic surgery nips and tucks.

Satisfied with his look, he pulled a charcoal sports coat over his open neck, starched white dress shirt and pulled the sleeves of the shirt down so they settled properly below the line of the sport coat's cuffs. Unlike so many cartel men, he didn't wear any gaudy necklaces or rings – his only nod to adornment was a red and black Breitling watch that hung around his slim, left wrist. Double checking his look one final time, he smiled to himself and left the room.

In the circular driveway four SUVs stood idling, with a dozen of his most trusted men standing around them, forming a perimeter with their focus outward, searching for threats – not that there were any here in his hilltop stronghold, but his men had been trained to never assume anything. One held the rear door of the third Chevy Suburban open for him, and once Jorge was inside, the guard closed the door with a heavy *thunk* that bespoke the fact that it was armored.

"The Oasis, *jefe*?" the driver asked perfunctorily – he knew that was their destination, but it was his ritual to confirm it on the off chance that Jorge might have decided on something different in the intervening time.

"Yes, Raimundo," Jorge answered and settled into the plush captain's chair.

Once the bodyguards got into their respective chase SUVs, and Tomas took up the shotgun position in Jorge's Suburban, they moved forward, slowly negotiating the gravel driveway until they began the long descent on the paved switchback that led to the base of the hill and the main road. Here at the bottom were two guard stations, reinforced concrete pillboxes set to either side of a steel bar gate. These stations were manned 24/7 and had an impressive array of weaponry, from 7.62mm miniguns to grenade launchers and M4 assault rifles. The steel gate barrier was augmented with pop-up steel wedge barriers that would stop anything up to and including a main battle tank from getting past.

As they approached, a guard came out, saluted, and nodded back toward his compatriot in the right bunker. Seconds later the steel gate parted, and the pop-up barriers descended flush into the asphalt pavement to allow the convoy to pass over them. Once through, the pop-ups returned to their up position and the gate closed.

Normally the convoy would accelerate from the short portion of the driveway between the gate and the main road, but instead Jorge felt the SUV slow.

"What's going on, Raimundo?" Jorge asked, having sensed the change in routine.

"They are finishing the fiber optic line, *jefe*," Raimundo explained as he gestured out toward the front of the SUV.

Jorge leaned to his right to look between Raimundo and Tomas.

There was a small bucket excavator with a rapidly flashing amber light on its top currently working to make a three-foot-wide trench in the soil to the immediate right of the driveway. Orange cones protected the open, diagonal trench that had been made through the asphalt of the driveway, preventing traffic from stumbling into the open trench that took up the right half of the driveway, while metal plates had been placed over the open trench on the left half of the driveway to allow for passage over it.

Two men in hardhats, dirty long sleeve shirts, grungy blue jeans, and scuffed work boots stood near the excavator with shovels in hand, occasionally pulling loose dirt from the trench the excavator was working to complete. One man with a dingy reflective safety vest had a lit traffic wand in hand and was gesturing for the SUVs to drive over the plates. Two more were working a spool of fiber cable on a parked trailer down at the main road, one unspooling and feeding cable to the second, who was

11

walking along, laying it in the trench. All the men wore surgical masks that had accumulated enough grim to turn them from pale blue to dusty gray.

Jorge had a moment of suspicious unease as he took in the sight, and Tomas must have either seen his expression in his rearview mirror, or sensed it somehow, because he turned slightly in his seat and said, "*Jefe*, it's all okay – we've been monitoring them and already checked their equipment. They're laying the fiber cable to your study, the one that will enable you high speed, secure access to the crypto miners."

Ah, right...

Sitting back in his chair, Jorge gave Tomas a simple nod of acknowledgement and then reached for the bottle of Maker's Mark on the sideboard, giving the matter no more thought.

Chapter 2

The Rainbow Oasis

"We're here, *jefe.*"

Looking past Tomas, Jorge saw that the convoy had pulled up to the curb and then arrayed themselves into tactical formation: the lead Suburban turning 45-degrees, nose pointed toward the opposite lane of traffic while the rearmost did the same. The second SUV disgorged its crew of six bodyguards which formed a security cordon between Jorge's vehicle and the front door to the club.

The multicolored neon of the club's façade played over Jorge's face as he exited and buttoned his sports coat, glancing around casually to take in the surroundings – and looking for any threats. He saw nothing untoward, just the line of young men and women behind the crimson ropes waiting for their chance to get into the *El Oasis del Arcoiris* – the Rainbow Oasis.

The most exclusive club on this side of the Rio Grande.

As far as the public was concerned, their generous *patrón,* Señor Jorge Manuel de Corazón, was a man who sincerely cared about the community.

He made certain that every child in the city of Ciudad Juárez, whose family could not afford to do so, received a wrapped gift at Christmas; that every family had a bountiful meal at Eastertide; and that the Catholic Church parish had everything it needed to support the spiritual wellbeing of the masses.

He routinely sponsored festivals for the public on notable holidays. These were grandiose affairs where free food and drink were plentiful, music was provided by live bands, games and carnival rides were available for the children, and a tremendous fireworks display was lit off as night fell.

Twice a year, the patron held an open-air audience at the central park, where a lucky few, drawn by lottery, could meet with him and ask for a favor to be granted.

Did you have a grandmother who needed an operation to remove a tumor, but you were too poor to afford the medical expenses? Did you have a failing business that needed a cash infusion? Have a special-needs daughter who needed round-the-clock care? If you were lucky enough to be chosen to approach the *patrón* and ask for a favor, you could have almost any problem solved by the wonderful, caring Señor Jorge Manuel de Corazón.

Indeed, if you asked the common man on the street what they thought of Señor Jorge Manuel de Corazón, you would receive nothing but praises for the *patrón,* for his charity, kindness, and making sure that they all lived in a safe, secure place.

Indeed, gang violence, such as occurred elsewhere in Mexico, was almost unheard of under the benevolent umbrella of their *patrón* of the Presagio cartel.

Increasing the *patrón's* standing among the masses was a rumor that claimed, when the *patrón* heard that some gay teenagers had been beaten and left for dead in an alley near a dance club, he stepped in personally to work with the state police to identify, round up, and assure the swift prosecution of the miscreants who had been responsible.

Afterward, the *patrón* had gone one step further.

Recognizing that, if the gay teens who'd been beaten had their own place to safely congregate and have fun, their beating probably would never have occurred, the *patrón* decided that such a safe space was needed.

Therefore, he personally saw to the building of the Rainbow Oasis, a combination dance club, restaurant, lounge and arcade where the LBGTQ+ community could go to safely party, dance, eat, recreate, and have fun in a magical place that they could call their own.

Thus the Rainbow Oasis came to be.

It was a club that became so popular, that at any given time you could find just as many heterosexuals inside as you could find gays, queers, or transgenders. All were welcomed into its safe, fun and amazing space regardless of orientation, ethnicity, social status, or age, as long as you followed the simple rules of kindness to all, nonviolence and inclusivity.

Thus the Rainbow Oasis became "the in place" to be on any given night.

It was also a club that, if you had enough money, power or prestige, you found even more and better delights in the elite, members-only VIP section of the club on the second floor.

However, for Jorge, the Rainbow Oasis was much more than simply a place to give the LGBTQ+ community a place to call their own—

It allowed him to enjoy the full range of his deviant pleasures and served a critical role in one aspect of the cartel's diverse businesses.

While in the building above ground the Rainbow Oasis was a bright place for dancing, drinking and some (mostly harmless) debauchery, the basement levels of the club held darker deeds in its fulfillment of one aspect of the cartel's business.

The Rainbow Oasis was the final waystation in the cartel's lucrative human trafficking operation.

From entry portals in various, nearby warehouses owned by the cartel through cut-out and sham corporations, individuals who had been kidnapped or purchased by the cartel were led into the sub-basement under the Rainbow Oasis.

These individuals – boys and girls from age 5 to 17 as well as young men and women up to around age 25 – represented every Central and South American country on the map, with an equal number having been imported from places as far away as South Africa, Syria, Libya, Afghanistan, some of the former Soviet Union's states, as well as from many Southeast Asian locales and even countries within the European Union.

Traveling for weeks on end by boat, train, or truck, often with 30 or 40 of them housed in sealed 40-foot shipping containers that held the barest of food, water and necessities, they went from one waystation to another. Finally, at the end of this modern-day parody of the Underground Railroad, they arrived in a wide, plain concrete room under the Rainbow Oasis.

Here they were sorted by age, gender, and country of origin. This was easily done because every one of them had been implanted with an RFID chip that not only could be used to geolocate them, but when scanned by a special device, listed all their specifications – birthdate, blood type, any vaccinations received, any medication needs, as well as the aforementioned criteria.

One by one, like cattle, each new arrival was washed, given a medical examination, photographed front and back while naked, then given a fresh set of clothing to wear and photographed again, clothed.

After this evaluation, the new arrivals would be lined up for Jorge to evaluate personally.

It was one of his favorite responsibilities.

As he walked slowly along the row of new arrivals, he would pause from time to time, finding a most exquisite specimen, and instruct his men to separate that individual from the rest. Sometimes – rarely – it was a girl, but most of the time it was a pre-teen or teenage boy, and these *ejemplares más exquisitos* – most exquisite specimens – would then be brought up to the VIP level.

Once there, they were carefully drugged and indoctrinated for their role as "escorts" for the VIPs at the Rainbow Oasis, and housed in separate, slightly more luxurious cells on that floor.

Meanwhile, those who didn't make the "most exquisite specimen" cut were assigned a cell in one of three sub-basement levels, often placed with several others, while they awaited their fate.

This fate was determined these days via the cartel's Dark Web forum, on which each captive individual's photos and specifications were posted. Auctions for each posting were opened, bids received, bids accepted, and cryptocurrency payments made. Once payment was received, the individual who had been purchased would be sent onward, delivered to the purchaser.

While the human trafficking was an important and lucrative part of the Presagio cartel's overall business, it also served Jorge's needs.

Specifically, the Rainbow Oasis was a place where Jorge could relax, have a drink, and, if the whim took him, choose one of the "most exquisite specimen" boys he'd sent up from the sub-basement for service in the VIP lounge.

When such a whim took hold of Jorge, he'd take his chosen boy to his luxurious, private chamber in the lowest sub-basement. Here the one whom he'd chosen would fulfill Jorge's sexual needs, until at some point Jorge's desires and needs turned to more devious and diabolical things... deviant things that he needed to do to satisfy his deepest, darkest desires—

And Jorge fulfilled these needs until the boy simply had nothing more to give.

The dead, ruined remains of what had once been a boy would then be carted away by one of Jorge's henchmen, to be disposed of in the club's dedicated crematory, while Jorge cleaned his various utensils, ordered the room cleaned, and then went to his private, adjacent bathroom to shower and change into fresh clothes before returning to the VIP lounge for another round of pleasure.

Tonight, as Jorge walked to the club's entry, those in the waiting line realized who he was, and a roar of appreciation went up from them. Jorge paused briefly, turned, smiled and waved, just long enough to acknowledge their adoration of him as their *patrón*, and then turned aside, taking the few steps up to the entry doors which were being held open by his bodyguards.

Tomas preceded him inside, scanning quickly to be sure that there was nothing unexpected there, then stood aside to let Jorge enter and pass him.

Jorge quickly crossed to the gold rope that was strung between two gold pylons, blocking off the VIP entrance, with Tomas following at a respective distance.

Just inside of the alcove that the gold rope blocked, Umberto saw his boss approaching and quickly removed the rope from one pylon so Jorge could enter.

As Jorge passed, Umberto bowed his head slightly, and said, "Good evening, *jefe*."

"Good evening, Umberto," Jorge replied automatically and then thought no more of the man.

The pounding of electronica assaulted Jorge's ears as he reached the top of the stairs and pushed through the door to the VIP lounge on the second floor. Multicolored laser lights strobed around the large, darkened space, momentarily disorienting Jorge after the bright neon of the outside and lobby, but it quickly passed.

Pausing by the maître d' station, he eyed the environs before him, seeing that there were quite a few VIP patrons already here. Jorge then turned to the maître d' and took the folder the man offered. Opening it, he scanned the contents, running a finger down the neatly printed typeface of the two columns on the single sheet of ivory-colored bond paper within.

It was a list of the current VIP guests in attendance. There were the usual local, C-suite businessmen, a few politicians, and, he noted with a grin, two Americans, one a state judge from Texas and the other a Congressional representative from California.

"Have they all chosen an escort yet?" Jorge asked just loud enough to be heard over the music, as he gestured toward the names on the printed page.

The maître d' inclined his head several time rapidly before saying, "Yes, *jefe*, all are comfortably seated with at least one."

"Very well," Jorge said as he closed the folder and handed it back but didn't give the man any further consideration because he was already strolling toward his booth at the front of the lounge, taking his time so he could evaluate each of the eye-candy that were currently dancing in time to the music.

Eight 5-by-5 cubes were placed strategically around the lounge, and atop each, under a spotlight that slowly ran through the colors of the rainbow, was a dancing escort. Normally these escorts, as they were called by the club's management, were split evenly between male and female, and in a range of age. However, knowing that Jorge was coming, thanks to a head's up call from Tomas, after the VIPs already seated had chosen their escorts, the maître d' had placed eight of the younger, teenage boys from the VIP stable on these cubes – boys which Jorge had specifically chosen as "most exquisite specimens" from the last few groups of new arrivals.

They were all exactly the type that Jorge liked, the maître d' knew: shorter than Jorge, between 4-foot-10 and 5-foot-6, all fey and lithely built, and each only lightly kissed by puberty.

While the maître d' knew that the *patrón* liked a sex partner that was small, boyish and submissive, he also knew that Jorge wasn't into little kids, although the Oasis had such available here in the VIP level for those clients who preferred that type.

No, these were perfect choices, the maître d' thought, and was pleased that he'd chosen well, as he watched Jorge stroll up to stand beside the closest of the cubes. Here, without taking his gaze from the boy dancing on it, Jorge walked slowly around the cube's perimeter to see every aspect of the boy – which wasn't difficult, since he wore only a tight-fitting, white thong and a mesh, sleeveless crop-top shirt.

The boy danced in time to the music of the VIP lounge, languid moves that were enhanced by the drugs they were given to keep them from being aggressive or resistive.

Jorge then went to the next cube and repeated his examining process, then to the next, and the next, until he'd surveyed all eight. That accomplished, Jorge went to his booth and sat, finding that Tomas had already made sure that there was a good selection of appetizers and beverages arrayed.

Among the beverage options was a new bottle of Maker's Mark, Jorge pulled it to him, broke the wax seal, and poured a generous three fingers of the amber liquid over an ice cube held in a crystal tumbler. He lifted the glass to his lips and sipped while his eyes scanned the dancers on their lit cubes, considering, evaluating.

"That one," Jorge said finally without turning to Tomas, gesturing with a small wave.

"Number Three, *jefe*?" Tomas asked in way of confirmation, sitting a bit higher to see the number on the cube's side.

"Yes."

Tomas nodded silently, shuffled out of the booth's bench, and walked over to the teenager on cube labeled with a large "3".

Jorge watched over the rim of his tumbler, eyes narrowed, wanting to see the dancer's reaction, anticipating it, enticed by it. He watched as the boy knelt so he could hear Tomas above the din of the throbbing music, saw the boy's head twist slightly, clearly glancing in his direction, but Jorge was unable to see the boy's eyes with the light directly above him—

And then the boy was padding down the built-in steps, and Jorge felt his heartrate bump as he focused on the dancer's legs, soaking up the beauty of his baseball-sized calf muscles... Jorge's eyes then rose to linger on the boy's firm, dimpled ass... then drifted higher to examine his lithe torso with its six-pack abs... then the boy's toned, slim, smooth arms... and finally Jorge's gaze lingering on the boy's wonderful face, with a dusting of freckles over high cheekbones and small nose... and green, large, cat-like eyes below slender, angled, light brown eyebrows... eyes that were framed by the parted curtain of his straight, thick golden-blond hair... hair that the sun had kissed to perfection, imbuing his silky strands with highlights of varying tones.

Tomas stopped the dancer at the opposite edge of the booth's table, then stepped back a pace and clasped his hands, waiting to see if his boss needed anything more.

Standing there, Number Three kept his eyes downcast as he'd been trained.

"What's your name?" Jorge asked in English, just loud enough to be heard over the background music.

Without looking up, the dancer answered in a hesitant, soft tenor voice. "Kody." Then as an afterthought added, "Kody... with a 'K'."

Jorge nodded contemplatively. The boy's words were halting, an effect of the drug cocktail all the children were fed nightly with dinner, to keep them docile. The drug also had the benefit of making them horny, a feature Jorge relished.

Smiling, Jorge asked, "And how old are you?"

"Fourteen," Kody replied sluggishly, barely audible this time.

From our South African supplier, judging by his accent, fair skin and look. Delicious.

"Come – have a seat," Jorge said with a mischievous smile as he patted the leather beside him. "Let's get to know each other, hmm?"

Chapter 3

Nothing Ever Again

The convoy turned into the driveway a few minutes before eleven, Jorge having decided to leave the Rainbow Oasis to enjoy his new acquisition at home, rather than in his small suite in the sub-basement of the club.

For whatever reason, Jorge found himself tonight in the mood for intimacy, not torture and mutilation. Something in Kody had stirred within Jorge a need to show the boy the finery of his home and lifestyle, as well as the wealth and awe that he commanded as a *patrón* of his community, and in doing so, cajole the boy into having some sort of adoration for him.

For whatever reason, tonight Jorge wanted his chosen boy to want him as much as he wanted the boy.

So Jorge had left the club with Kody in tow, leaving the club earlier rather than later in the evening, which was his usual *modus operandi*.

But that "earlier" appeared to be moving toward "later" anyway because, as they approached the estate's gates, the excavator was parked in the middle of the driveway, its bucket arm extended to and stuck in the trench alongside the asphalt, so it completely blocked the way forward. The men in hardhats were standing around, looking into the open panel on the side of the machine, scratching their heads as one of them had his head inside, peering around with a flashlight.

The lead driver would have simply driven around it, since the SUVs all had four-wheel drive, but with the open trench running to either side, this wasn't an option. Instead, the SUVs pulled up to the excavator and came to a halt in a close line; the bodyguards jumped out, searching for threats as they formed a perimeter and Tomas went up to find out what was going on.

Meanwhile Jorge, seated in the back with Kody, put his arm around and pulled Kody closer, figuring that he might as well start the festivities while they waited.

"What's going on here!?" Tomas demanded as he stomped up to the men standing around the excavator. As one they turned to face him, looking at him curiously but not answering.

"You've got to move this!" Tomas shouted, gesturing toward the machine. "We need to get inside the grounds!"

It was then that the worker with the flashlight removed his head from the opening in the machine, turned, and complained, "It's the controller line; it's come unplugged, but I can't reach it – my arm's too thick."

"Show me!" Tomas ordered, moving up next to the man.

He shined the light inside and played it over a multi-colored bundle of wires that ended in a square plastic connecting plug that was separated from its female counterpart.

"It needs to go back into the plug?" Tomas asked.

"*Sí, señor*," the man nodded.

Exhaling angrily, Tomas tried pushing his arm into the innards of the machine, but found his arm was too thick.

"*Mierda*!" Tomas cursed, and spun around, trying to think what to do. He didn't like having the convoy stopped in a line, close together, even if it was within the coverage of the estate's security bunkers.

One of the men to Tomas's left pointed toward the SUV in which Jorge was seated with the dancer. The two were illuminated clearly in the dome light which was lit because he'd left the front door of the Suburban open. "Maybe... that boy can reach it?"

Tomas followed his finger back to the SUV where Jorge sat and bit his lip, considering it. Would *jefe* mind? It would only take a moment, and the *jefe* knew it was dangerous to remain static in an unsecure location...

So he dashed back to the SUV and opened the rear door. "*Jefe*, the machine, it's broken because of a plug that came loose. No one can reach it, our arms are too thick, but I thought maybe the boy could..." Tomas nudged his chin toward Kody.

Unbelievable!

"What insanity is this?" Jorge demanded angrily.

"*Jefe*, it will take but a moment – your security isn't good here, sitting on the road..."

"Very well!" Jorge huffed, then turned to Kody. "Go with him!" Then turning back to Tomas, ordered, "Don't damage the goods!"

"Yes, *jefe*, certainly," Tomas agreed, nodding vigorously.

Tomas took Kody's arm and pulled him gently out to stand, then together they went up to the excavator and after some back and forth, Kody peered into the machine as the worker with the flashlight shined it inside and gestured toward it.

Jorge watched for a few seconds, found the sight uninteresting, and turned to find the bottle of Maker's Mark—

At the excavator, Tomas stepped back to watch as Kody reached in to reconnect the wire bundle—

While Jorge's security detail was arrayed around the stopped SUVs, focused on outward threats—

"I've got it," Kody reported in his accented English as his body wriggled slightly from his effort to seat the plug.

Smiling, Tomas turned to wave a signal of success to his boss but froze in mid-wave when he found the business end of a .45 automatic pistol's long, fat, attached suppressor in the hand of one of the workmen, pointed mere centimeters from his nose—

The pistol spat fire, and Tomas saw nothing ever again.

Chapter 4

What're We Gonna Do?

"Two, take the kid!" One ordered firmly as he turned to cover the others as they dashed behind the excavator. Two seconds was all it took for them to get to this point of safety, whereupon One mashed his thumb down on the radio detonator.

Sixteen improvised explosive devices – or IEDs as the world had come to know them after seeing thousands used against the Americans in Iraq and Afghanistan – had been crafted from Chinese copies of the venerable Russian RPG-7 warheads, then linked together and buried beneath the fresh asphalt that covered the diagonal trench in which the fiber optic cable had been laid. Angled upward at a 60-degrees, spaced a meter apart, these high explosive, anti-tank (HEAT) rounds were designed to punch through up to 500mm of steel armor plate.

Against an armored SUV, whose protection level was designed to stop machine gun and assault rifle bullets, the HEAT rounds sliced through them from bottom to top as a man might push through a bead curtain.

The four SUVs were lined up over the long diagonal trench so that at least one of the warheads was centered below each of them. In a flash of brilliant light and thunderous sound each became a fireball that jumped five meters into the air before the shattered, blazing remains crashed back to the ground. The IEDs that missed their targets streaked skyward on ballistic paths, eventually landing with thudding explosions among the nearby new homes.

Two seconds after that, Six and Seven had shouldered RPG-7 launchers and, after yelling "Clear!" to warn of the impending backblast, fired one rocket propelled grenade into each of the bunkers. They targeted the large observation windows and, despite the three inches of bullet resistant Lexan composite, able to withstand a 30mm cannon round, the HEAT rounds made just as much mincemeat out of them as they had out of the SUVs. The bunkers filled with fire, then this fire exploded back out of the shattered remains of the windows along with a shower of debris.

"Evac!" One shouted, leaning out around the excavator to make sure no one survived the IED attack.

"What about the kid?!" Two demanded.

"Leave him!" One answered without turning.

Two looked at the kid, who as standing wide-eyed and trembling, and just couldn't do it.

"Sir! We've got to take him with us! If he stays here, he'll be killed! He's clearly been trafficked!"

One spun about, his face an intense mask as he growled. "I said leave him! We're not here to be a limo service or a social worker!"

"But sir!" Two said, taking his commander by the arm. Three stepped up to join him and said, "Sir, we can't leave him! Two's right – if we do, he's good as dead."

One glared at the boy, clearly fighting a silent battle within himself over this unexpected turn of events.

"Sir!" Three implored. "You had us purposefully get him out of the SUV, so he'd not be in the blast! Now you're just gonna leave him here?! The cartel will execute him – hell, they'll execute everyone in de Corazón's orbit on the off chance that they had something to do with this hit!"

"*Shitfuck*!" One yelled, punching the side of the excavator. "Okay Two, you've got the kid! Everyone, exfil! Go, go, go!" One ordered as he switched out his pistol for a SIG MCX Rattler assault rifle that he'd hidden in the cab of the excavator and activated its IR targeting laser. He pulled Gen 5 night-vision glasses (NVGs) from his thigh pouch, donned them, and when they'd stabilized to show the world around him in shades of black and white, he jogged off at a fast pace toward their planned extraction point. It was just over a kilometer away where they'd stored two SUVs in the garage of the brand-new home at the base of the de Corazón's hilltop mansion. These rusty, battered, eight-year-old Ford Expeditions looked barely serviceable, yet in fact they were mechanically sound and armored, with dark tinted glass to keep prying eyes from prying.

The rest of his men retrieved their own rifles from the cab and then followed, making a lose diamond formation around Two and his charge as they moved off into the darkness at the base of the hill.

Adrenaline and fright fueled Kody for the first 200 meters but after this he faltered, so Two scooped him up, draped him over his shoulders, and continued forward without missing a beat.

They pushed into the garage eight minutes later, navigating solely by their NVGs, they loaded into the Explorers, hit the button for the automatic doors, and without turning on the vehicle's lights, drove down the fresh asphalt of the driveway and onto the main road. Six minutes later they turned northwest onto State Route 45D, took off their NVGs, turned on their SUV's lights, and set their cruise controls for the speed limit.

One turned from his position in the front passenger seat of the lead Explorer to look at Two, Three, and the blond kid sandwiched in between them. The boy looked shellshocked, staring without seeing anything of the world around him.

That's not good – classic signs of shock... or maybe he's drugged? Both? Hmmm...

Well, at least shock or being drugged isn't permanent – just the PTSD you can get from it.

He eyed each of them in turn and pursed his lips.

What the fuck am I supposed to do with you, kid?

Two and Three were trying not to return his gaze but couldn't help sneaking looks.

Heh... wondering just how much shit they're in for insisting on taking the kid along...

"What's your name, kid?" One asked.

When he didn't answer, One looked to Two, who then turned to the boy and repeated the question.

The kid turned lethargically just enough to meet his eyes, then whispered, "Kody... with a 'K'," before returning to stare straight ahead.

One sighed.

He knew deep down that it had been the right call, but it was going to cause problems going forward since they hadn't planned on any additional passengers for the exfil.

Always something – Murphy always throws his fuckin' monkey wrench into the works at the worst possible time, doesn't he?

Well, the die is cast – suck it up and make it work! Hell, you just saved a kid from being trafficked – or, at least from further sexual and physical abuse – so that's a positive.

Look on the bright side – maybe you hand him over to the fibbies or the top-floor bigshots at the Agency and they get some useful intel from him that will help take down the whole goddamn international trafficking industry!

"What're we gonna do?" Four asked from the driver's seat without turning.

One flopped himself back into his seat to face forward and adjusted his Rattler so he could get it up and firing without delay.

"Hell if I know," One groused, glancing back one more time at the zombie-like kid in the back seat.

"It won't make sense if we're stopped on the exfil back to the states," Four noted.

One gave him a no-shit-sherlock look.

"Just sayin'," Four retorted with a shrug, then refocused on piloting the Suburban along the ill-maintained highway.

He's got a point, though.

One turned to look out the window and let himself focus inward.

Well, we're not leavin' him now.

So, what's the solution?

They'd driven another 10 minutes, turning east onto State Route 2 and were able to see the glow of the glow of Ciudad Juárez's lights on the horizon when One figured out what they'd do.

"Three, get on your tablet and find us an out-of-the-way hotel—"

Chapter 5

The Plan For Exfil

"I need a favor."

On the other end of the encrypted satellite call, Garrett's sigh was audible. "What else is new?"

"Well, need I remind you that I pulled your sorry ass out of that burning Hummer in the 'stan?"

"Really? You're going back to that dry well for more?" Garrett answered with a snort.

"Well, I could have left you to burn to death..."

"Okay, okay, enough already," Garrett said and laughed. "Now that we've gotten the usual banter out of the way, what can I do for you?"

"I need docs for a kid I need to exfil."

"Do you now?" Garret replied lazily. "Well, that's an easy one – why didn't you call your MST?"

He pronounced the acronym "mist"; it stood for mission support team.

"It's... complicated," One said with a sigh.

"Oh?" Garret retorted. "Something not authorized, eh?"

"Something like that," One replied.

"How much 'not authorized'?" Garrett asked, his voice softer now – he had his hand cupped over the receiver to keep his words from extending past the phone.

"It's black," One answered. "Blacker than black, actually."

"Then how come you're calling me?" Garrett demanded. "One, you and I can do serious time—"

"I wouldn't have called if it wasn't something absolutely necessary," One almost growled, but then took a steadying breath as he continued. "There's a 'green' involved, and we need to take him out with us."

Garrett knew "green" meant a non-combatant friendly.

Garrett sighed. "Just so you know, they probably won't let us be in the same cell in Leavenworth…"

One chuckled with graveyard humor. "Gotcha."

After a long pause, Garret asked, "So, I do this, and you owe me one?"

One rolled his eyes and gritted his teeth, but managed, grudgingly, to agree.

"I'll need a picture against a plain background – and basic stats, DOB, name you'll want to use—"

"His first name is Kody – spelled with a 'K'," One said quietly as he glanced over at where the boy was curled up on one of the room's double beds, completely zonked out.

"Middle and last?"

"He didn't tell me his middle name."

"So, I'll add one at random. Last name?"

After a moment's pause, One said, "Use mine."

That put Garrett into a surprised silence. "What now? Wait a second… you go and adopt a kid without even bothering to ask me?!"

"It's… not like that," One growled.

"Oh? Exactly how is it?" Garrett demanded. "We talked about—"

"Listen, we're in deep in the shit here – can we talk about this later?" One retorted.

Garret huffed loudly, paused for several beats, then finally said in a hush, "Fine. Get the pix to me via the link I'll text to your sat phone – and before you ask, yes, it's encrypted, and I'll be using a one-time email address. No foreign – or internal – eyes will peek at anything we exchange."

"I wasn't going to ask that," One told him bluntly, though that's exactly what he'd planned on asking. Instead, he said, "When and how can you get it to me?"

"If you get it to me before 3:00 pm UTC, I'll have it delivered to your hotel by noon tomorrow. I'll have to use my personal contacts for this since there's no way I'm leaving any traces in an official system." Garret paused again, and One could almost hear the gears turning in the man's head. "Along with the additional tickets and pocket litter the kid will need to be part of the tour group you planned to coattail on to get back into the US, right?"

"Right," One agreed. "Thanks, G – you're the best."

"What was that? I didn't hear that last part—"

One shook his head but couldn't help but grin. "You're... the... best."

"That's what I though you said," Garrett snickered. "Ciao!"

"So what's the deal, boss?" Three asked as he walked in with four six-packs of Corona bottles slung under his arms, one more in each of his hands, with Two and Four following behind, each of their arms loaded with grocery bags.

These three of his squad were all of Latin heritage and spoke Spanish fluently, and thus were the ones that could go out for supplies and have the least chance of raising eyebrows or being memorable to those with whom they interacted. Even so, they planned to stay hidden in the hotel as much as possible until they made the move to their final exfil to limit their exposure because they knew, right now, the mid-ranks of the Presagio cartel were in chaos, trying to put together what had taken out their boss and once they had, to move to retaliate.

After that, well, either one of the mid-level capos would manage to take control through violence of action, eliminating any rivals, or one of the other cartels would swoop in to crush what remained of Presagio and merge what was left of it into their own ranks.

Though they'd been careful to use disguises and hide their faces during the entire op, Murphy always had a say in what they did. Thus the plan had been to limit any potential for linking them to the assassination of Jorge Manuel de Corazón by hiding in plain sight, so to speak, in one of the most popular tourist cities along the shared Mexico-USA border.

"Kid's zonked," Four noted as he set his bags down on the well-worn table.

"Did he say anything after we left?" Two asked.

One shook his head. "Nah, just curled up and fell asleep."

"Should I wake him for some grub?"

"Leave him for now," One said. "Make sure to leave something for him to eat."

There was a knock at the door, which put them all on alert, but then additional knocks came, signaling it was Five, Six and Seven. Four confirmed it through the peep hole, then opened the door to let them in.

With everyone assembled, they broke out the food, set aside a portion for Kody, and then ate ravenously.

"What's the plan for the exfil, now that we have a green?" Four asked.

"No change in the basic plan," One replied as he finished off the last of his Corona and slid the empty back into the cardboard carrier. "The only mod will be that Kody will be coming out with us as my son."

Three chocked on the beer he'd started, turning his head aside just in time to spray the mouthful of beer over the wall beside him instead of in One's face.

"Yes, go ahead and make all your jokes now," One said with a resigned sigh.

"Wouldn't think of it, One," Two said with a grin and took another pull on his beer. "Honestly, he looks enough like you to have that work."

Four snorted, but when One glared his way, he put up a hand and said, "Not saying a word!"

Four might not be saying a word, but he was smiling like the Cheshire cat.

And then after that, the good-natured ribbing started up in earnest.

They called it a night at nine, returning to their respective rooms.

Kody hadn't woken, and One decided that sleep was more important for the kid than waking to eat, so he let him be. Two took the other bed, leaving One to take the first watch.

Four hours later, Two and One switched out.

Kody remained lost to the world.

"What do I do if he wakes up?" Two whispered.

"See if he wants to eat," One told him. "If not, maybe he'd like to take a shower."

"I got some clothes for him," Two said, and went to the bag with the food they'd set aside for the boy, and from it withdrew a pair of black Adidas soccer shorts, a matching white soccer shirt, a pair of Adidas boxer briefs and socks, and some Adidas trainers. "I guessed at the sizes," Two offered.

One was sure that everything would fit perfectly – Two had four kids of his own and was used to such purchases.

"I'm sure he'll appreciate it."

"If he wakes up," Two said softly, glancing at him.

"He will, and he will," One assured, then yawned. "Okay, I'm hitting the hay."

One placed his suppressed .45 H&K USP automatic on the bed beside him, and still dressed in the work clothes from the hit on Jorge, he pulled the covers over himself and slept.

One came awake at the gentle touch on his shoulder.

"Status?" was the first thing out of his mouth as he picked up his USP and brought it to ready position.

"We're good," Two told him and jutted his chin toward the closed bathroom door from beyond which the sound of the shower running was audible.

"Did he eat—" One started but stopped when Two suddenly pressed a finger to the low-profile receiver in his right ear.

Two's eyes widened as he listened. Still pressing a finger to his ear, he dashed to the window, pressed against the wall to its side, and with one finger nudged the curtain aside just enough to peer out. After just a second's glance, he spun around, going into a crouch below the line of the window.

"Fuck, One! They've found us!"

Chapter 6

Exact Our Vengeance

Curiosity and luck had saved his life.

When Tomas had taken his boy-toy away to help at the stalled excavator, Jorge had poured himself a drink. By the time he'd gotten it in hand and looked back to what was going on ahead, he couldn't really see much because the two Suburbans ahead of his had tinted glass so that, parked in a line as they were, it completely blocked any view past his own SUV's windshield.

A glance outside confirmed that his men had set up a perimeter, and being just outside his mansion's security gate, on property he owned that stretched for miles in all directions, he'd felt not one iota of worry about his safety. Thus, curious about what was going on up at the excavator, he'd stepped out the left door, tumbler in hand, and started walking perpendicular to the driveway so he could get an angle of sight on what was happening.

He'd moved maybe four meters from his SUV when suddenly everything went white; Jorge felt himself lifted from the ground and tossed through the air like a rag doll thrown by a petulant child. He came down hard, directly into the cable trench in the open field to the side of the driveway, and this bit of dumb luck was what had spared from much of the shrapnel and concussive force that radiated outward from explosions enveloping all four of his convoy's SUVs—

But he hadn't been totally spared. Bleeding from several minor shrapnel wounds, stunned from the impact against the trench's bottom and with his clothing smoldering, Jorge fell into unconsciousness.

Pale green walls and dim overhead light greeted Jorge when he finally woke. His head felt like a smith's anvil, with the smith wantonly pounding upon it with merry delight. It took him a few seconds before his eyesight cleared, and when it did, he saw Vincente sitting in the shadows to his left. His third in command was dressed in body armor and sat alert, facing the door, with a Benelli automatic shotgun across his lap and a Sig Sauer pistol in a thigh drop holster.

"Vin...Vincente..."

Vincente's eyes immediately darted to him; he jumped to his feet, letting the barrel of the shotgun point downward in his right hand as he stepped to Jorge's side and put his left hand atop Jorge's.

"*Jefe!* You're finally awake!"

Jorge looked up at him lethargically. "What... happened..."

"Let me call the nurse—"

"No!" Jorge managed to coarsely growl as he pushed himself upward, but that effort stole all his energy – he collapsed back into the soft mattress and closed his eyes.

"*Jefe*, you must rest! Don't exert yourself!"

"No... nurse... tell... what..."

"Yes, *jefe*, certainly – but remain still, please, *jefe*! You've been badly hurt."

"Mmmmm..."

Vincente took a breath, getting what he wanted to say in order before speaking. "*Jefe*, everyone in the convoy except for you died..."

The only response from Jorge was uneven, rattling breathing, and for a moment, Vincente thought his boss was returning to a state of unconsciousness.

But then Jorge muttered, "Go... on..."

With relief, Vincente continued.

"There were seven men, the construction crew for the cable laying... we have security footage from the cameras showing the convoy just suddenly exploding," Vincente explained slowly. "Each of the Suburbans was destroyed in one big blast. There were some rockets too, going into the air... I think that they used IEDs, *jefe*, buried in the cable trench across the driveway."

Jorge exhaled a rattling breath of anger. "What... else..."

"As I said, there were rockets... they used RPGs on the two blockhouses, through the armored windows... we never thought that such a thing would be possible..." Vincente dropped and shook his head, feeling shame – and not a little worry – over having failed to protect his master.

Jorge turned his hand over beneath Vincente's light grip and squeezed it with surprising strength. "Never mind... that... what... else..."

"They took the boy from the club with them... running to one of the crypto mining houses, where they'd stashed two SUVs," Vincente said slowly, still not looking up. "The last footage we have is of them turning northwest onto Route 45D."

He paused, letting that sink in before continuing. "When we heard the explosions up at the house, I rallied the men we had left and drove down to the gate. It was a mess... anyway, we spread out, looking for more attackers, but there were none. Then Roberto shouted that he'd found you, alive, in the trench to the side of the driveway. We got you into a car and drove straight here, the hospital."

Jorge exhaled again, releasing Vincente's hand. "How... long..."

"Almost eight hours," Vincente said. "It's just before six in the morning."

Jorge swallowed against the dryness in his throat. Seeing this, Vincente put the shotgun down on the bed's edge and took the glass of water from the side table, holding it out to his boss so the straw in it was level with his lips. "Here, *jefe*, drink some water."

Jorge's eyes opened languidly, first looking into Vincente's gaze, then turning to the straw poised in front of his mouth. With concerted effort he got his lips around the straw and sipped slowly. When he'd had enough, he raised his hand slightly to wave it away, and then said, "They... took... the boy too?"

"*Sí, jefe.*"

A knowing grin curled the corners of Jorge's lips. "I know how we... can find them... and exact our vengeance..."

Chapter 7

Don't Worry, I've Got You

"Avalanche, avalanche, avalanche!" One called over the radio as he simultaneously hit the mic button on the radio clipped to his belt and reseated his earpiece that had fallen out as he slept. Like all the others in the squad, he'd slept in his clothes so he could bug out immediately if it turned out to be necessary.

And it looked very necessary.

Once the "avalanche" call was made, things went forward automatically. Two shouldered his backpack, went to the door with his Rattler rifle in hand, looked through the peephole, saw the hallway immediately outside the door was clear, and then burst out into the hall to scan for threats. Meanwhile farther down the hall, Three, Four and Five emerged from their rooms, checked for threats, saw Two, and then ran for the far end for the hall where the fire stairs were. Two followed them, taking up a position to cover their rear as they entered the fire stairs and disappeared.

Six and Seven came out a moment later and ran the other direction, taking up defensive positions in the vending machine alcove which was cattycorner to the elevators. From here, they could engage anyone who might emerge from the elevators or the fire stairs farther down the hall and would be rearguard for the squad when the time came.

One stuffed his pistol into his shoulder holster, picked up his Rattler, pulled the charging handle back slightly to be sure a .300 Blackout round was chambered and then felt for and confirmed the rifle was set on "safe." That done, he spun, took the four steps needed to get to the bathroom door, twisted the knob and pushed – but it was locked.

Without hesitating One threw his shoulder against the hollow-core door, punching a dent in the flimsy wood and shearing the locking mechanism right out of its seating so that the door slammed open against the bathroom's wall—

To reveal a naked Kody just stepping out of the tub as he scrubbed water from his long hair with a towel.

The two of them froze, each staring at the other, Kody's mouth a wide "O" of surprise while One's was a grim line of focused determination.

One couldn't help what his brain did next – it was rote, the result of 12 years of training for and experience as a tier one operator; his eyes did a top to bottom scan, his mind making evaluations about the kid's health and abilities—

Looks athletic if a bit malnourished—

Seems to be lucid now after zonking out last night—

"C'mon!" he ordered gruffly. "We need to bug out *now!*"

Kody blinked several times. "What's... what's happening?!"

Having no time to answer questions, One stepped into the bathroom, grabbed the clothes Two had bought for the kid from where they were piled on the sink, and thrust them at him. "Get dressed fast! We've got to get out of here *now!*"

Without waiting for a response, One pivoted to cover the open door to the room while he kept an eye on Kody in his peripheral vision. To his credit the kid only hesitated for one more second before quickly swiping the towel over himself, dropping it, and then pulling on the new clothes. Half a minute later he finished lacing the trainers and stood.

One reached out, grabbed his hand, and forced it closed around the left strap of his backpack. "You don't let go! You go where I go, and if I stop, you hide behind me. I crouch, you crouch; I run, you run. Got it?"

"Ye...yeah – yeah," Kody stammered, his eyes wide as proverbial saucers.

Without waiting another second, One brought his Rattler to his shoulder, flicked the fire selector to "burst" and focused his gaze through the red dot holographic sight on the rifle. "One, moving!" he shouted into the hallway and then stepped into it, turning and heading to the stairs at the end of the hall. He felt Kody holding on obediently, keeping pace with him, his trainers softly pounding on the thin carpet in counterpoint to his louder stomping.

"We've got 12-plus tangos coming in the lobby," Two reported. "I hear sirens too, distant, but getting louder."

"Break, break! This is Five: I've got 16-plus tangos in the parking lot at the back, covering the fire exits and pool doors," Five radioed. "Be advised, some are wearing Mexican State Police ballistic vests and have M4s!"

Shit, this isn't supposed to happen!

State Police?! Presagio calling in favors from the cops they've bought and paid for, no doubt...

And us with ROEs that won't let us kill or injure any cops...

"Five, can you get to the cars?" One radioed as he came to the open fire stairs door, swung his rifle around to check all angles, and then started down the stairs.

"I could, but I'll be in a crossfire from at least four of the tangos!"

Shit! Not good.

"One, we need to bug out before more cops arrive!" Three radioed. "You know the ROEs—"

"Got it, Three," One replied tersely as he came to the bottom of the stairs where the bulk of his squad were crouched, looking out through the slim windows set in the fire doors, one facing the lobby, the other the rear parking area. "Six and Seven, stay in place – looks like we're coming back to you."

Before they'd crashed for the night, the squad had done a walk-through of the six-story hotel, the parking lot, and of the immediate surroundings, including the four buildings adjoining the hotel. This survey noted the best options for a quick escape from the hotel and immediate area. As a result, the squad had come up with several exit strategies, including a contingency plan that was Three's idea and – as usual for Three's ideas – was a high-risk option. One included it in their exfil plan to humor Three, knowing that it was extremely unlikely that they'd ever use it.

But now with the ground floor exits all blocked and state police on scene, Three's contingency suddenly became their only option if they were to keep to their restrictive rules of engagement.

43

"All units, this is One – we're bugging out via Three's contingency!" One radioed, then pivoted and looked at Kody. "We're going to the roof – c'mon, stay close!"

"Yes!" Three gloated over the radio.

The others with One groaned. They knew Three's proclivities for, and love of anything that made a big boom...

And how sometimes things didn't go exactly as Three said they would.

One started back up the stairs, ignoring his men's cursing in response to the fact they were putting their lives into Three's hands. He glanced back to make sure Kody was keeping pace and pleased to see that he was, adrenaline fueling him for the time being, although the kid was panting from the exertion. Behind them Two, Three, Four and Five were keeping combat spacing, their rifles scanning assigned sectors. Two minutes later they were at the chained roof access door.

"Three!" One shouted.

The squad made room for Three to come to the front. He slung his rifle, pulled his backpack off and began rummaging through it; a moment later he withdrew a small breaching charge and affixed it to the door's padlock and hasp, molding the clay-like bit of C4 plastic explosive into place.

"Back down!" One ordered, and the moved down six steps, One turning to face Kody and enveloping him in a hug a second before Three shouted, "Fire in the hole!" and there was a blast that left their ears ringing.

"Six and Seven, c'mon up!" One radioed as they charged through the smoking fire door and onto the roof

Where they could immediately hear multiple sirens and the *whoop-whoop* of a helicopter.

"Chopper, five o'clock!" Five shouted.

Oh this is too much, even for you Murphy!

Not fair!

There was nothing to do but continue with the escape. One led Kody and the rest of the squad across the long, flat roof to the west side where a 20-meter cellphone tower was affixed. It had obviously been repurposed from its former life as a microwave repeater tower because, unlike modern cylindrical towers of painted steel, this one was a tall, slim obelisk-like structure made of multiple, flat steel crosspieces supporting the solid steel legs at the four corners.

"Three, get to it!" One ordered.

"On it!" Three replied and knelt beside the steel pad to which the tower was anchored into the roof. He began pulling items from his backpack.

One spun back to face toward the open roof access door, crouching on the gravel and scanning his sector for threats. Kody crouched behind him, and One felt the teen press against him, trembling. One glanced back and saw that tears were streaking down from Kody's tightly shut eyes even as Kody pressed his cheek firmly against his shoulder.

One suddenly felt a pang of empathy, the breath catching in his throat.

He's scared shitless!

You need to say something to him!

"Kody," One said as calmly as he could. "Just stick close — everything's gonna be okay."

The kid responded with a swallow and weak nod—

And hugged One, clinging to him like plastic wrap, trembling markedly.

"Chopper's state police!" Four shouted.

One twisted back to squint up into the sky.

There! About half a klick out and edging around... shit, door gunner!

"What'll we do One?" Five asked without turning from scanning his sector. "If they open up? ROE lets us defend ourselves—"

"Not against LEOs, even if they are corrupt!" One countered, pronouncing the acronym as it was spelled, which stood for Law Enforcement Officer.

Six and Seven arrived then, sliding into positions among the squad, filling out the semicircle of protection as Three worked on the base on the tower.

"How long Three?!" One shouted, resisting the urge to glance back at him.

"Zero-Four mikes!"

The sirens were loud enough now that they were echoing off the nearby buildings and causing interference patterns in their wails, making the whole thing sound like some sort of alien orchestra.

"Chopper's closing!" Four shouted.

One glanced over and saw the helicopter was coming in for a fast pass, and seconds later it was there, like a huge white and blue raptor, the barrel of the heavy machine gun mounted alongside its open side door, so close that it looked like a telephone pole—

And then the copter passed, curving to the left. The barrel of the door gun remained trained in their direction despite the steep bank of the copter.

"Next pass they'll open up for sure!" Seven noted dryly.

"Three?" One demanded.

"Working on it..."

One evaluated the situation. Where they were crouched around the tower's base there was no usable cover to speak of – to get some, they'd have to cross back to the center of the roof, near the access door to the stairs where the air conditioning units were. They could hide among them, but the copter's machine gun wouldn't care; its heavy caliber, full metal jacket rounds would punch unhindered through the thin galvanized steel of the units and then into them even if the gunner couldn't see them directly.

No, that option was an illusion of protection... it's better to stay here, so once the tower blows, we're ready to move out without having to cross an extra 10 meters...

"Fire in the hole!" Three screamed and threw himself to the gravel of the roof beside One.

"Down!" One shouted, and pulled Kody down, rolling with him so that his back was toward the tower, completely shielding Kody from the blast that came two seconds later.

Heat washed over them followed by a wave of force that kicked up a blizzard of gravel and dust from the roof and renewed the ringing in their ears. Before the squad had even begun to get up, there was a shrieking of tortured metal and a long, drawn-out screech. When they all returned to a crouch, covering their sectors, they could see the tower beginning to topple – Three's explosives had severed the two outer-most legs of the tower and all the cables attached to it, so now with the tower's weight no longer supported there, the tower fell in that direction.

"Timber!" Three called merrily.

At first the movement was glacial, but with each passing second the tower's fall increased in velocity until, with a sharp *crack-crack* like two rapid cannon shots, the other legs of the tower snapped. Its length fell across the 20 meters of intervening space between the hotel's roof and the seven-story power company building across the street, smashing resoundingly into the concrete edge of its roof and demolishing the neon sign that hung there with an explosion of glass and a shower of electrical sparks.

"Hoo-rah!" Three shouted, pumping his fist in the air.

"Copter's coming back!" Five reported.

"Let's go!" One ordered, getting to his feet, making sure Kody was up and still holding on.

Three didn't need anything more than that – he quickly climbed to the top side of the makeshift bridge and began a waddling crossing along its top, stepping carefully but swiftly from crosspiece to crosspiece.

"Want me to take the kid?" Two asked as he started past One.

"I've got him – go!" One replied.

"Everyone down!" Five screamed.

One didn't need to be told twice – he grabbed Kody and forced him down beside him as the deep *thunka-thunka-thunka* of the door gunner's machine gun sounded over the *thwop-thwop* of the copter's rotor. Huge geysers of gravel and roofing material sprouted up in a line that started back near the roof access door and staggered toward where the squad crouched.

Jesus!

Miraculously, the machine gun fire swerved aside about a meter from where One and Kody lay, angling off to overshoot, with a few dozen rounds raining down on the cops below.

Hope he hits someone, One wished. *Some friendly fire might keep this chopper at bay, at least for a while...*

"Up! Move!" Four said as he passed by.

One popped to his feet, but realized that Kody was still on the ground, curled into the fetal position and shaking violently.

Shit!

Well, asshole, what'd yah expect? He's just a kid who's gone through who-knows how much abuse, not a trained operator! Everyone eventually reaches their limit...

"C'mon boss!" Seven yelled as he passed by and jumped onto the makeshift bridge.

Fuck! No choice!

One quickly shouldered his rifle, adjusted his gear, then knelt and scooped up Kody in a fireman's carry.

Geez, the kid weighs next to nothing...

Even though he had no trouble carrying Kody, mounting and walking across the narrow tower was a challenge. It required every bit of his concentration to step only on the slim crosspieces and not the open spaces between them, while keeping his balance on the upward slope of the damn thing. Squealing of tormented metal came with each footfall. He had no time to consider the 30-plus meter drop to the ground below or the possibility of the copter coming back around for another attack run as he worked his way up along the ever-narrowing walkway that Three's explosives had formed.

Despite Kody being of little encumbrance, by the halfway point One's legs were burning from his exertions.

Keep going...

Two-thirds of the way to the other side, he risked a look up and saw Six and Seven waving him on, ready to grab hold of him when he reached the end.

It was then that he realized there were several *whizz-zips* sounding from around him.

Fuck! They're shooting at me!

Sure enough, Six and Seven had ducked down behind the remains of the building's cornice as multiple rounds impacted the concrete, throwing shards outward from the pock holes they created.

One urged his burning legs to go faster.

In the next instant, One heard and felt bullets impacting the metal around him, their deflection angle suggesting they were coming from the roof of the hotel behind him.

Oh just great...

Then he was there, and Six and Seven popped up, grabbing hold of him and yanking him over the roof's cornice where the four of them crashed into a pile—

Whereupon Six's knee punched into One's diaphragm, knocking the wind from his lungs, and then One's head hit something hard, making him see stars.

They got untangled and to their feet seconds later. One got Kody back into the fireman's carry and found himself stumbling down the fire stairs of the new building, Six ahead of him while Seven covered their rear. It was all a blur until they pushed out into the building's underground garage.

The two-tier garage was protected from unauthorized access by a rolling steel door over the two vehicle entries, one on each level and each having a keycard-operated, pedestrian door alongside it. The fire stairs dumped the squad out right beside the doors to the outside on the top level, but the group didn't turn and exit through it – instead, they began hustling to the rows of service trucks emblazoned with the green logo of the *Comisión Federal de Electricidad*.

"These won't do!" Four complained.

They halted, scanning the surrounding area for something that could haul all eight of them, but all they saw were two- and three-axle service trucks with expandable booms and loaded with rolls of wire and festooned with ladders and other gear.

"Let's try the lower level!" One ordered.

As a group they turned to hustle down the ramp to the lower level.

"You... can... put... me down..." Kody gasped from atop One's shoulders.

Shit, I'd forgotten he was there!

One came to a stop and unshouldered the teen. "You okay?"

"Just—" he tried to explain but the words wouldn't come.

"I understand," One said. "We need to move. You good to run?

"Ye-yeah."

"Okay, hold on!" One ordered.

Kody grabbed his backpack's strap and they set off after the others, lagging by about 10 meters.

49

They'd taken only a few steps when Four shouted, "Contact left!" and the *chut-chut-chut* of his suppressed Rattler in 3-round burst mode sounded multiple times.

Immediately, the concrete garage became a popcorn maker of thunderous reports as unsuppressed semi- and fully automatic fire was returned against the squad.

One slewed right, dragging Kody into cover between two of the 10-wheel service trucks. It wasn't an instant too soon, because in their wake a series of holes randomly puckered the tires, sheet metal fenders, engine cowlings and doors of the trucks around them.

Shitfuck!

One kept them moving, all the way to the back of the trucks and around so that they were in the two-meter space between the truck's rear bumper and the wall.

"Sitrep!" One radioed.

"We've got tangos on the level above, firing down the ramp and the open railing between the levels," Two reported. "Looks like 20-plus!"

How'd they get in? Even think to come down here? It takes a card key to get in...

Unless they simply blew their way through the door!

Shit!

One struggled to think. Glancing out toward the center of the rampway, he knew that there was no way he and Kody were making it across that 15 meters of open space to rejoin the others.

"Two, we're pinned between trucks across the ramp from you," One radioed.

"Want us to come over?" Two asked.

"Negative! That won't work – they've got a kill zone there—"

"Boss, we can lay down some suppressing fire—"

"Listen! Negative, negative! You take charge and get the squad out. Head for the original rendezvous and follow the exfil plan."

"What about you? The kid?" Two asked.

One was looking around desperately as more bullets – ricochets and stray rounds from the undisciplined fire of their opponents trying to hit the rest of One's squad – shredded the fronts of the trucks they were hiding behind.

"We'll meet up with you!" One radioed back. "You see transport?"

"Tons of panel vans," Two answered. "We can get out—"

"Then do it! Go! Go!" One ordered.

"But Boss—"

"Go! *That's a direct order!* Go!"

There was a pause that seemed an eon long before the resigned reply came.

"Roger – hoo-rah, boss."

Suddenly the suppressed rifle fire increased, and there were shouts of "Frag out!" as his squad tossed fragmentation grenades to cover their retreat. A moment later he saw colored smoke start rising from where his squad was, creating a screen to further block them from their attacker's view.

Now's the time to move, while they're focused on the rest of the squad!

Grabbing Kody, One got in his face and hissed, "Stay quiet unless you see immediate danger, then you can point it out. Got it?"

Kody nodded vigorously, his eyes once again as wide as saucers, but he seemed in control and, for the moment, not petrified from fear.

One turned away from him, feeling the kid grab his backpack strap again, and considered which way to go—

In the limited sight lines available at the back wall of the garage, he saw no exit signs in any direction. Trying to hotwire a truck without anyone to provide covering fire was a non-starter. So too was hunkering down and hoping the tangos wouldn't come looking for them once the rest of his squad had bugged out.

A nudge of panic pushed against his mind, and One grunted with exertion to crush it before it grew.

Think, goddammit! Think!

The bullets had stopped plunking against the trucks nearby – a good sign, meaning that Two and the rest of his squad had gone down to the lower level with the tangos pursuing.

Need to take advantage of that distraction now!

It was then that One saw the pipes in the ceiling, specifically a red one marked "Gas Natural" and "Incendio!" in bold white letters with a white arrow beside the words, indicating the direction of gas flow.

Yes!

Follow the flow backwards, and there'll be a control room...

One flipped his head to their left, saw Kody nod his understanding, and together they quickly padded behind the trucks, following the pipe above them.

They'd gone past the fifth truck when the volume of unsuppressed rifle fire from their opponents went into crescendo, echoing wildly off the concrete walls. They heard distant calls in Spanish, men directing others forward, to flank and pursue his teammates.

Well, one bright side – they must not have seen Kody and me—

For now, anyway!

One increased their pace to a run – no sense trying to keep quiet with all the guns firing and the tangos focused on his squad. He kept one eye on the pipe above, while the other and his rifle he kept focused to their right, ready to shoot anything that appeared on the long, narrow corridors formed between the parked trucks.

After passing the fifteenth truck, with the wall of the garage turning 90-degrees just a few meters away, One saw that the pipe turned 90-degrees to the left and went into the wall. Below it was a steel door with a card key lock and a warning placard at its center:

Bingo!

One didn't waste time with niceties – with the continuing cacophony of gunfire, anything he did now would be lost in it, so he pushed Kody back between the nearest trucks, leaned around just enough to sight in on the door's knob and lock plate, and dumped four bursts into it. In a well-practiced, smooth single motion he let the now-spent magazine fall free from his rifle, retrieved a new one, inserted it, slammed his palm against the magazine's bottom to assure it was seated, and then racked the charging handle. One then moved purposefully to the door, feeling Kody obediently following, and without hesitating, One threw his weight against it.

The door smashed open, pivoting until it slammed loudly against the wall, but the sound was like a single clap of applause compared to the din of the distant firefight. He led Kody inside the dimly lit room, turned and closed the door, which reduced the gunfire to a muted roar, then took a moment to survey the surroundings.

A workbench ran against the wall to the immediate right of the door. Spying a crowbar on the rack above it, One snatched it up, and slid the wedge end of it under the door, then kicked it twice with his boot to seat it firmly in place.

That'll give us a few extra seconds if they try to force the door...

Turning to scan the room, he saw that the piping ran along the ceiling in various directions, all coming to a confluence at a bank of round valve handles along the opposite wall. Control boxes with glowing red and green lights were set in the wall to the right of this long bank, and to the left was a gated area that contained tools, spare valves and piping, and wooden crates. A narrow hallway ran down alongside this gated area, and above it was the green glow of an Exit sign.

Yes!

"Stay close," One warned, and then had his rifle up as he padded into the shadowy hallway. There were coat hooks on the wall at the start of the hall, from which hung a bright orange rain slicker, a couple of well-worn, black hoodies spattered with dried paint, and a green windbreaker with the logo of the Mexican National Football team on the left breast. Just five meters past these was the end of the hall where One saw the outline of daylight around an ill-fitted steel door.

He felt his spirts rise.

"One, you copy?" Came Two's voice over the radio, static heavily muddling his words.

"Copy, two-by," One replied, pausing a few steps from the exit.

"We're out!" Two reported. "We're... to the... but... are... closing... tion..."

"Say again, Two! Repeat!"

Only static answered him.

Fuck! Too much distance, metal and concrete between us...

Their compact UHF radios required line-of-sight transmitting. They were powerful enough to work inside most buildings, but...

It was then that One realized he couldn't hear the muffled gunfire anymore.

Time's running out...

One strode to the exit door and put his ear against it, struggling to hear anything beyond but couldn't tell if there was something because of the tinnitus lingering from the various recent explosions.

Go stealthy or in-your-face?

Decisions, decisions...

He glanced back at Kody; the whites of the teen's eyes reflected the green of the exit sign, wide and shell-shocked.

One looked down at his rifle and started to chew on his lip.

The kid's dressed casual... is it better to go out and try to blend in... or stay in my tactical gear...

One spent a few seconds to inventory his gear.

If they're out there, one rifle and three mags isn't going to do much...

Stealthy it is then...

He went back to the coat rack, studied the selection for a second, then sighed. Quickly he set his Rattler and backpack against the wall. Kneeling, he pulled the last two spare magazines for his USP pistol from the bag, then took out a clean, maroon Old Navy t-shirt, worn Adidas running shoes, and a pair of cargo shorts. In 60 seconds he'd changed into them, pulling the t-shirt over his Level 3 Kevlar vest and leaving his old clothes piled on the floor. That done, he retrieved and stuffed his sat phone into the other pocket of his shorts, along with its slimline wall charger.

He then reached under the wig of straight, long black hair he'd been wearing, undid the clips securing it to his own hair, and yanked it off.

Kody inhaled with astonishment.

"You're... blond... like me," the teen noted.

Despite the gravity of their situation, the teen's words made One chuckle.

After One fluffed his thick mop of wavy blond hair to return it to fullness, he wiped his fingers on his shirt, reached up, and removed the brown contacts from his eyes, revealing gaslight-blue ones. He flicked the contacts away, then snatched up his pistol. He took another half minute to remove the suppressor from it and stow the suppressor in one of the pockets of his shorts, then pulled the webbing from his shoulder holster, converting it to an appendix-positioned, inside-the-waistband holster. After sliding his pistol into it, he secured the weapon between his boxers and shorts at the front right of his body.

This outfit, combined with his natural hair and eye color, was supposed to have been used for getting back into the US at the border crossing in Ciudad Juárez as American day tourists, but now it would be used to completely change his appearance and, hopefully, blend in with the civilians outside.

Hopefully.

One then grabbed the hoodies, helping to slide one onto Kody and then he donned the other – it was tight on him, and baggy on Kody, but they would have to do. He pulled up his hood, and then did the same for the teen.

Kody had watched him change and prepare in tense silence, hovering just an arm's length from him, focused on every move he made, like he was afraid that this transformation meant he would be left behind to fend for himself. He relaxed noticeably when One turned to him and handed him a wad of pesos and dollars.

"Is there a pocket in those shorts?" One asked him.

Kody stared at him unblinking, as if he'd just spoken in Swahili.

"Oh! Um..." Kody pulled the waistband of his soccer shorts away and looked down. "A little one in here."

"Fold the cash and stick it in," One told him. "And, in case we get separated—" One saw Kody's face drain of color, so he quickly amended, "—not that I expect that, okay? Just in case, okay?" He nodded uncertainly, and One continued, handing him a folded business card. "Here's a number to call. My, ah, my friend Garrett. His name and number are on it. Put it with the cash."

One watched as Kody tried to put the cash and card in the tiny, inner pocket, but his hands were all thumbs.

In shock and nervous...

"Here, let me," One said, quickly refolding the items into a smaller size and fitting it snuggly into the inner pocket. "There, you're all set."

"Th—thanks," Kody managed, his wide green eyes locking into One's.

"We need to move – we've already taken up too much time!"

At the exit door One turned to Kody and said, "Just try to act normal... casual... like we're walking to the store or home after a football game. Think you can do that?"

Kody glanced up with uncertain eyes, swallowed, then nodded.

"Don't worry, I've got you... I won't let anything happen to you," One assured, and before he realized that he'd done it, One reached out and took Kody's left hand.

The teen's hand was small, warm and sweaty, but that simple contact did something that words couldn't – through that link, One felt Kody release much of the fervent tension gripping him. When One turned to look at him, he found the teen looking up at him with wide, trusting eyes.

You need to move!

Taking a deep breath, One threw caution to the wind – he was leaving his rifle, backpack and everything but his money and pistol behind.

Here goes...

One pushed against the door's bar and with Kody beside him, they strode through.

Chapter 8

We'll Finish This Ourselves

Jorge and his entourage had flowed into the hotel's parking lot seconds after the cadre of state police. As the state police fanned out and began to both encircle and enter the building, Jorge instructed his men to hang back but be ready – if the cops didn't successfully complete the wet work, Vincente was ready to finish the task with the remaining dozen ex-Marines Jorge had on his payroll.

There was suddenly a flurry of radio transmissions by the cops, and then machine-gun fire as the police helicopter opened up on the roof of the hotel – their quarry had gone up instead of down, and the cops were climbing the stairs to intercept while the chopper kept them busy.

Then the unimaginable happened.

A series of flashing explosions occurred around the base of a cell phone tower atop the hotel, and then the entire structure was falling sideways—

To impact on the building across the street, forming a makeshift bridge—

And everyone on the ground watched with astonished fascination as the men they sought deftly stomped across and disappeared onto the roof of this second building, despite attempts by the cops in the parking lot to shoot them as they crossed.

More bad news came on the tail of this failure to stop them.

"*Jefe,* we've lost the signal."

Jorge glared at Alfredo seated next to him in the rear of the SUV.

"*Jefe*, it's not my fault," Alfredo tried, unsuccessfully, to keep the whinny tone from his voice. "It's the building – the concrete, all the metal, the electrical lines…"

Vincente had his men back in their SUVs and pulling up to the gated entry to the parking garage of the *Comisión Federal de Electricidad* building just under four minutes later, having to weave through the myriad of police vehicles and the early morning traffic to get there.

"*Jefe*, I have intermittent signal now that we're closer…" Alfredo said meekly.

"Well? Spit it out, man!"

"They're entering the underground garage… as best as I can tell. The signal is below grade – and, sorry *jefe*, I've lost it again. The concrete, metal, underground—"

Jorge waved him to silence. "We know they went into the garage, right?" Jorge demanded as he twisted in his seat to face the computer nerd – only to have sharp pain from his broken ribs knife into his side. He groaned and winced; the breath was suddenly flushed from his lungs.

"*Jefe!*" Vincente said worriedly from the front passenger seat. "Please, the doctor—"

"I'm… I'm alright," Jorge growled as he pushed back into his seat in the rear of the armored Suburban, panting.

Without another word, Vincente radioed for their two squads of ex-marines to deploy, ordering one squad to make entry in pursuit, while the second was to set up a perimeter around the building. Marco, the first squad's commander, used a grenade to blast open the pedestrian access door, after which they all poured through and spread out in tactical formation at Marco's direction.

A few moments later the radio came alive. "We have them, on the ramp between levels—".

Gunfire erupted, blotting out Marco's voice for a few seconds before he was able to cup his mouth over the microphone. "We are moving to encircle them! They can't escape! We've got the exit covered!"

"Understood!" Vincente radioed back.

"Still nothing?" Jorge asked Alfredo.

Alfredo worked the keyboard of his laptop, clicked his mouse a few times, and then exhaled angrily. "Sorry, *jefe*, no – the signal's blocked."

"But if they come out?"

"Oh, well... then I'm sure we'll get the signal back," Alfredo said, wiping sweat from his forehead.

Jorge growled to himself.

Alfredo turned back to his keyboard nervously.

The radio came to life again. "*Jefe!* They've moved to the lower level, we've got—"

A tremendous series of explosions sounded in the next second, followed by a scream of white noise, and then nothing.

"Marco! Come in!" Vincente radioed, but all he got in response was the sound of the carrier wave. "Marco?!"

Vincente turned back to look at his boss.

Jorge glared at him.

Excited voices suddenly sounded from their other radio, tuned to the police band. "All units, one of the – um, one of the special agents reports that the suspects are in a white *Comisión Federal de Electricidad* panel van that just turned north on Avenida Central! Units 53 and 66 are in pursuit! All the special agents are down! We need medics!"

The "special agents" were the way the state police were told to identify Jorge's ex-marines.

"This is Air Zero-Two, we have eyes on the van," came a different voice with the thrum of copter rotors in the background. "Target van has accelerated and turned onto State Route 44, heading west. In pursuit..."

"Juan-Pablo!" Jorge croaked from the rear seat, "Let's go—"

"*Jefe!*" Alfredo interrupted, looking up with bright eyes. "The signal, it's back – west side of the building!"

"They let the boy go?" Vincente wondered aloud.

Jorge's mind raced as he tried to figure out what was going on, and then it came to him. "It's a diversion – one of them, maybe two are driving the van to lead us away from the rest!" Jorge barked, then grimaced from the pain in his ribs.

"Shall I call the police back?" Vincente asked.

"No! Have them keep pursuing the van – have them take it out!" Jorge ordered.

"Shall I call for the state police to assist us?" Vincente asked.

"No!" Jorge barked, then turned to his driver. "Juan-Pablo, drive to the other side of the building!" As the SUV accelerated, Jorge said, "Radio the second marine squad to follow as soon as they can; we'll finish this ourselves."

Chapter 9

Not Ideal

The exit door opened into a concrete alcove a story below grade, piled with trash. A metal staircase was on the opposite side of the alcove, running upward, perpendicular to the doorway, to reach ground level. One led them up the stairs, slowing as his eyes came level with the top edge of the concrete. Peering over it, he saw a four-lane avenue with passing cars and beyond, acres of trees forming a public park.

That's just what the doctor ordered!

One gave Kody a quick look and saw worry and fear expressed on the teen's face.

One gave his hand a squeeze. "We're gonna walk across the street and into that park, okay? Just try to remain clam – I'm here; I'm not gonna let anything happen to you, got it?"

Kody swallowed and then nodded curtly.

"Here we go... nice and easy..."

One led them out of the alcove and onto the sidewalk, still holding Kody's hand. At the curb One gauged the traffic, waited for two cars to pass, then pulled Kody along, crossing in a jaywalking dash. They reached the sidewalk on the other side, passed in front of two joggers, and then One led them over a short stone wall, through some shrubs and into the park.

They wove around trees, the leafy detritus crunching under foot, and eventually emerged onto an asphalt walkway with painted lines denoting spaces for bicycles and pedestrians. One moved to release Kody's hand, but the teen seemed reluctant to let go, so he re-gripped it, looked at him, and gave him a reassuring smile.

For the first time since he'd been with the teen, Kody smiled back and seemed, if not relaxed, then at least no longer fearful.

One scanned the surroundings, trying to formulate a plan for continuing their exfil. This early in the morning, the only people around were a few joggers and bicyclists, and a smattering of people walking dogs.

Not ideal for trying to blend in...

He looked beyond the walkway.

There, across the open grass... more trees.

"We're going to head toward those other trees, okay?" he whispered, leaning his head closer to Kody's but not taking his gaze from surveilling the area.

"Okay."

One stood, took a breath, and led them forward.

Chapter 10

Take Him Alive

As the SUV screeched around the corner, Alfredo said, "Signal is off to the right... 50 meters!"

Hearing this, Juan-Pablo braked the SUV hard, swerving to the curb and throwing them all against their seat belts. Behind them, the SUVs with the dozen men of the second squad halted in similar fashion.

"*Jefe*?" Vincente asked, turning in his seat to look back at Jorge.

"I don't care what it takes – end them!" Jorge barked then groaned in pain.

"And the boy?" Vincente asked, wanting to be certain of the order.

"There's plenty more fish in the sea," Jorge growled, and then groaned, leaning back in his seat and holding his bandaged side.

Vincente activated the mic of his portable radio. "The target is 50 meters to our right! Deploy! I'll give updates as you close in!"

The remaining squad of ex-Mexican Navy Marines emptied from the SUVs in one fluid motion. All were dressed in unadorned black BDUs over which they wore body armor, also black, with pouches for grenades and spare rifle magazines festooned all over. These men quickly formed a skirmish line under the direction of their lieutenant, who took the middle position. All of them raised SOPMOD M4 carbines to their shoulders, their eyes aligning with the ACOG sights mounted atop them, and then they moved forward as one into the park, enlarging the space to create four meters of separation between each of them.

"Alfredo, you've got comms," Vincente said, swinging around to look at the 20-something who was bent over the keyboard of his laptop on the swing-out table tray.

"Okay," Alfredo answered nervously. He clicked the mouse a few times, scrolling through menu selections, and made choices. He linked in the ex-marines' transponders and suddenly 12 blue dots appeared on the map overlay displayed on his laptop, moving in a line toward the red dot that was about 70 meters away. He adjusted the boom mic of his headset to be in front of his mouth, then keyed the mic. "Um, units, um... target is now 70 meters, on a 348-degree radial."

"*Control, entendido,*" the lieutenant radioed back. "Understood, control."

"Let me see," Jorge ordered.

Alfredo rotated the laptop 45 degrees so Jorge could see as well.

"We're in trees; no sign of target," the lieutenant reported.

"Target is opening range, now 80 meters, now on a 340-degree radial!" Alfredo replied.

A long minute passed before the next report. "We're out of the trees and in an open, grassy area..."

"LT, Ramirez here: I have a man and a boy in black hoodies nearing the tree line across the field!"

"I see them," the lieutenant answered over the circuit. "Control, there's just two, a man and boy, no rifle, backpack... Hard to see from here, but they're on the indicated radial."

Alfredo looked to Jorge for instructions.

Jorge motioned to give him the headset, and one he had jammed it in place, radioed, "This is de Corazón – you sure there are only two? Is the boy the one from the club?"

"*Jefe,* I cannot see from here – they've got hoods up. The boy is in football kit, and the man is wearing a similar hoodie. I see no weapons or combat gear – the man is wearing cargo shorts and trainers, not the workmen's outfits and boots we saw when the crossed to the *Electricidad* building."

Jorge exhaled a growl of frustration.

Was I wrong about the van? Were they all in it?

Then what about the transmitter? Did they discover the transmitter and attach it to a dog, or a bicycle or some such, and that's what we're seeing?

No, not likely – why would they even suspect there was one, let alone find and remove it in such a short time?

So – it's got to be the boy and one of the assassins! Focus on him, taking him alive, and I'll squeeze him until he gives up the others!

"All units, the boy and the man in the hoodies are your targets, but I need the man alive! Repeat, alive! Confirm the order!"

"Yes, *jefe*, the man is to be taken alive," the lieutenant radioed back. "And the boy?"

"If you can take him alive too, all the better," Jorge told him.

Oh, the fun I'll have when you're returned to me, young Kody...

"Understood, *jefe*," the lieutenant replied, then began transmitting instructions to his squad to encircle and intercept the two.

Chapter 11

We'll Be Free And Clear

They were about 20 meters from the tree line when One made another check of their rear and saw the line of commandos emerge from the forest and onto the walkway. He quickly turned back to face the way they were walking and focused on keeping his pace even and normal.

They have no reason to suspect us of anything, One told himself. *Just a father and son walking across the grass...*

The hackles on his neck stood up then, a warning of danger that had always served him well in the past.

Shitfuck!

He risked another glance backward, and saw the men starting to jog forward, spreading out as they did so to form a semicircle the apex of which was aimed right at the two of them.

Fuckin' Murphy! What bullshit are you pulling now, you bastard?!

"Kody, we have to run!" he said firmly, and pulled the teen forward. "As fast as you can!"

The kid responded, working hard to keep pace with One as they pounded through the wilted grass. One expected the bullets to start flying the moment they made their break, but surprisingly nothing of the sort happened. In seconds they were into the trees, and after they'd gone far enough to be obscured from their pursuer's sight, One led them 45 degrees to the right, heading roughly northeast.

After 150 meters, Kody was panting and slowing, forcing One to slow his own pace, and then they were confronted with a bevy of pricker-bushes and tanglefoot that forced One to turn left and head in a more northwesterly direction, until they came to a narrow, dry stream bed set in a deep V-cut.

"Sit on your ass and slide down to the bottom," One told him in a stage whisper. Kody did so, and together they slid to the bottom, dusted themselves off, and then One was leading them west along the rocky run.

After running for another five minutes, Kody was spent, and he stumbled; only the fact that One still held his hand kept the teen from face-planting.

Without hesitation or even bothering to explain, One snatched Kody into a fireman's carry and began jogging, wanting to put as much distance as he could between them and their pursuers. Kody had no choice but to accept the indignity of being carried yet again, and for the next few minutes all One heard from the teen was him trying to catch his breath.

One estimated that they'd put at least a kilometer between them and the hotel. Just ahead he saw that the stream bed curved back northwest, and as he rounded through it, One heard the swishing of passing cars on a roadway – there was a stone viaduct over the stream about 20 meters ahead over which he saw cars zipping by. Clumps of sage bush and flowering vines bookended the viaduct, which would make it very difficult to try to climb up out of the V-cut next to the bridge, but then One spied a dirt trail that switch-backed up to the top just shy of the fauna.

He angled for it.

Get to the top, hail a cab, and we'll be free and clear...

Chapter 12

We Wait

"I've – lost the signal again," Alfredo reported meekly.

Vincente broke into the radio channel then. "Vincente here – do you see them yet?"

The squad's lieutenant replied, his words stuttered from breathing hard. "No sir!"

"Alfredo, how close are they to the last position where you had a signal?" Vincente asked. "Guide them there!"

"Yes – ah, right," Alfredo taped a few keys, zooming in on the view. "Lieutenant, you are 22 meters from where we lost signal, on a 300-degree radial..."

Jorge leaned in slightly to see the screen, and together they watched as the squad reduced its separation, folding in on the spot to which Alfredo directed them.

"There, you're on top of it now!" Alfredo radioed.

"We have no sign of them," the lieutenant radioed back, "but there's a deep V-cut here, to a dry creek bed—"

"That's it!" Alfredo exclaimed. "They went into it! Being below grade blocks the signal."

It was the one drawback of the transmitter. Normally, Jorge kept track of his live possessions via a small, subcutaneous RFID chip that he had surgically implanted in them. The chip could be tracked by a satellite, but the chip pinged its position only every 30 minutes, which didn't make it very useful for real-time tracking of a moving target. To perform real-time tracking, an omnidirectional localizer antenna, whose viable range was only about 1000 meters, had to be utilized – like the one currently mounted to the top Jorge's SUV.

Vincente clicked the mic. "Squad, they went into the V-cut! Pursue!"

"Acknowledged!" the lieutenant replied, then directed half his men to go right while he led the rest to the left. "I'm splitting forces to cover both directions!"

"Understood," Vincente confirmed, then turned to Jorge. "*Jefe*, do we stay or move? They will eventually move out of range—"

"Stay here for now," Jorge ordered, then turned to Alfredo. "Check the satellite link."

Alfredo did so. "Um, 21 minutes until the next ping."

Jorge nodded. "We wait."

Chapter 13

The Exfil Point

At the top of the V-cut, One paused and lowered Kody to the ground. The teen looked a bit wild-eyed but had regained his wind.

"You okay? Caught your breath?" One asked as he scanned their surroundings for threats.

"I'm just... not used to running, I guess," Kody said, barely audible over the highway noise nearby.

No surprise there – you look underfed, and if they drugged you there's no way you're firing on all cylinders...

"Not a problem," One replied and patted him on the shoulder. "There's a sidewalk – let's go."

They pushed past a few scrawny bushes without scrapping their legs up too badly and found themselves next to a busy avenue. Across the street were rows of apartment buildings, with cars parked curbside nose-to-tail as far as they could see. There were a lot of kids on the sidewalk in front of those apartments, a mix of some dressed in school uniforms and others more casually in street clothes, with some adults intermixed.

One looked at his watch, seeing it was just coming up 8:00am. *School time*, One thought as he surveyed the scene.

"Let's cross," he told Kody, and once again they made the jaywalking dash across the four lanes of traffic. Once there, they were in better shape to blend in, just another parent with their child walking to school.

"Take off the hoodie," One whispered to Kody, and the kid did so. One removed his as well, then took both and as they passed an alley, tossed them into an open dumpster. They then went with the flow of adults and kids as they walked southwest along the sidewalk.

Okay, what next? We need to clear the datum fully and regroup...

At the next corner the flow of kids split: the ones with the uniforms crossed the street, still heading southwest, but the others turned to the right, heading up the side street where One could see a sign that read *Escuela Primaria Fernando Hernandez* – the Ferdinand Hernandez Elementary School – with several school buses disgorging kids in front of it.

"Go right," One whispered, leaning down close to Kody's ear. "Then we'll just keep walking past the school."

"Okay," Kody whispered back.

A few people gave them second looks since they were clearly not Mexican, but then they dismissed them from further consideration because they appeared as a father and son walking to school despite both being fair-skinned, blond Caucasians. Still, the glances there way reminded One that they weren't safe, not yet, and thus needed to speed things up to achieve that goal.

They passed the school's entry, now going against the flow of kids on the sidewalk heading toward the school's entry, but that flow became next to nothing by the time they'd gone two more blocks. Here the side street intersected another main throughfare, and One was relieved to see the checkered white and green of taxis zooming by. He cupped Kody's shoulder, guiding him to stop by his side and the curb, and put his hand up to hail a cab.

A late-model Honda Accord taxi quickly crossed over and screeched to a halt in front of them. One opened the door, waved Kody in, and then got in himself.

The driver was a 20-something with an attempt at a mustache on his upper lip that looked more like a smudge of dirt than a line of hair. Still, he had a full, white smile as he said in heavily accented English, "Where we go?"

"*Dos cuatro siete ocho Avenida Francisco Villa, por favor,*" One said in his Argentinian Spanish.

"Oh!" The driver seemed surprised that a tall, blond and blue-eyed American would speak such good Spanish. "*En seguida, señor!*"

The driver turned his attention back to driving, pushing the button to start the meter and with nary a glance for any oncoming traffic pulled the Accord out and accelerated.

The car rattled and swayed over the poorly maintained roadway, but One didn't care – each second put them farther from the point of contact and closer to the exfil point.

And then he remembered.

I haven't taken a photo of the kid and sent it!

Fucking shit!

One ground his teeth. The original plan was for the team to exfil by inserting themselves into a tour group that would bus back across the border. While that's not how they'd entered the country, they would be going out that way. The squad had fake IDs, tickets and receipts showing food and entertainment purchases for their stay all stored at the exfil site. This stuff would prove that they'd been with the group and had spent all their time in the city. But with Kody along, that wasn't going to work unless he could get Kody's picture to Garrett, who would then use it to craft an ID and the rest of the supporting documentation needed... and then wait an extra day for it to be delivered to him by courier.

Another full day...

One sighed with frustration.

One had no identification on him either. You simply didn't go on a mission like they had with your real passport or driver's license in your pocket. It was the most basic of tenants in their business – field ops were done under completely sterile conditions. No wedding, academy, or school class rings; no real ID; no credit cards in your real name; basically nothing that could link to your real identity or that you were a citizen of the USA.

The problem was that there was no getting across the border successfully and without causing a stir unless you had ID.

So, I still need to get to the exfil point, if for no other reason than to hook up with the others and get my exfil package. After I'm set, I can focus on figuring out what to do for the kid.

One glanced over at Kody. The kid was staring out the window, but his expression showed that he was lost in thought.

I can't imagine what he's been through.

One shook his head, then turned enough to look out the back window of the car. He studied the traffic behind him, looking for any obvious signs of a tail, but didn't see any blacked-out SUVs nor any police vehicles. Looking to the sky he saw no sign of the state police chopper that had fired on them back at the hotel.

Which doesn't mean that they aren't tracking me with a drone or a chopper just out of sight...

Even more reason to not delay the exfil...

The cab slowed, bringing One's attention back to what was going on in the here and now. A glance out the side window showed that they were alongside the *Fabricaciones de Metal Ilimitadas* – Metal Fabrications Unlimited – a huge manufacturing complex that took up the entire block, with a three-story office building on the northeast corner of the property and the rest of the block taken up by a warehouse and various towers and machinery. All of it was ringed by hurricane fencing topped with razor wire and faded signs spaced unevenly along it, stating, *Prohibido el Paso* – No Trespassing.

The cabbie pulled to the curb, looked out the front window at the closed-down, mothballed factory and asked skeptically, "Here, sir?"

"Yes – thanks," One said as he peeled peso notes from his roll and handed them to the driver. "Keep the change."

"Thank you, sir!" the cabbie said joyously as he saw that he'd been given a 500-peso tip. "Have a great day!"

One simply nodded at him as he slid out the door and offered a hand to Kody, helping him out. One waited until the cab had turned the corner, then quickly led them back up the street from the direction that the cab had come from, whereupon he turned and led them into a narrow alleyway that ended at a steel gate over a pedestrian access door at the base of the warehouse. Though the gate, door, and the surrounding corrugated metal was streaked with rust, the combination lock on the gate was shiny and new.

One quickly rotated the cylinder to the correct sequence, pulled the lock free, opened the gate and then the door, and waved for Kody to go into the deep shadow beyond the doorway. The teen hesitated uncertainly for a long beat, then took a deep breath and stepped inside. One quickly followed, relocking the gate and closing the door, putting them into darkness.

Feeling along the wall, One found the breaker box and pushed the metal handle upward. There was a *clunk* as the switch engaged, and a few LED light bars high up in the metal support rafters illuminated, shining down on them and, about 10 meters away, a large Pelican box sitting on the floor of the first spot in a lined parking area.

Though he'd hoped that it would all work out in the end, when One saw the box on the floor, and didn't see the van they were going to use to cross the border, he knew the rest of his squad had already bugged out.

Well, I did order them to go without us...

He didn't waste time commiserating over the situation. He jogged to the box, spun the combination lock to the correct number, heard a click, and opened it. His documents, extra cash, credit cards, and the rest of the stuff he'd need was in the only thing inside, sitting on the box's bottom – a brown paper bag stapled shut with a big "1" on it in black marker. He grabbed it, tore it open, and reviewed the contents.

By then, Kody had stepped beside him, looking up at him expectantly.

After sorting out the items and storing them in a waistband pocket on the inside of his shorts, where they'd be concealed, he turned to Kody. "You doing okay?"

"Yeah, so far," Kody replied softly. "Um... are we... staying here?"

Good question.

One pondered that for a long moment. Hunkering down would reduce the chance of them being seen by someone on the cartel's payroll, and One had no doubts that by now Kody's picture was being distributed to them by now, although One was certain that whatever pictures they had of him were going to be next to useless – at the hit and during the escape from the hotel, only his eyes had been visible. Kody, on the other hand, probably had lots of photos of him somewhere in the cartel's trafficking system, to show prospective buyers what they were purchasing.

That wasn't an insurmountable problem – another hoodie or ball cap would hide his hair, and another change of clothing, maybe something baggier this time, would help.

The main problem with staying put was that they would be staying within the heart of the cartel's seat of power and did nothing to get them home.

Trying to get across the border was no better an option until Kody had an ID. To get that, he'd need to wait at least a day for Garrett to create and have them delivered, which brought them back to the problems associated with hunkering down.

"Yeah, I think we'll have to," One finally said. He closed the box, lifted it up, and carried it back with them to the small entry area at the door through which they'd entered the building. He set it down against the wall, making a bench seat for them to sit on. "Have a seat – I need to think for a minute."

Kody obeyed, sitting on the edge of the box next to him, his hands twisting nervously.

One withdrew his sat phone and brought up the internet browser. A quick search showed that there was an open-air market just four blocks west, where everything from apples to zippers was for sale.

"Kody, there's no food here and, well, we'll need to be here at least until tomorrow morning."

The teen looked at him with a blank expression.

"I can't get you across the border without an ID," One explained. "At least, not if we're to do it legally and quickly. There're other ways, of course..." He let that train of thought drift off. "So, um, anyway... I'll need to go to get us some food, and more clothing – they've already seen you and me in these outfits..."

"Oh," Kody exhaled nervously. "Makes... sense, I guess."

One put an arm around his slim shoulders, which stopped Kody from nervously twisting his fingers. "We'll be okay here – it's not a place anyone would think to look for us."

At that, Kody looked around the cavernous area that was covered in dust and debris and offered One a wan grin. "I've been in worse places."

I can only guess.

"Listen," One said, turning slightly toward Kody, "I won't be long. I'll lock the gate behind me. Now, on the super-unlikely chance someone comes in, I want you to go hide behind that big machine press," One gestured toward the gargantuan machine, covered in cobwebs and dust. "Okay?"

"Sure," Kody nodded. The grin became a line of worry on his lips.

"I won't be any longer than necessary. Okay?"

He nodded again.

"Okay then. Stay quiet. I'm gonna leave the lights on, since it's daytime outside I'm not worried about people seeing light through the cracks." One stood and after giving Kody a final, reassuring nod, went to the door, opened it, unlocked the gate, and closed them behind him.

Kody heard the lock click and sighed, looking around worriedly. But that lasted only for a fleeting moment – he was completely drained, and unable to keep his drooping eyelids open any longer, curled up atop the big Pelican case and fell asleep.

Chapter 14

We Need To Find Them

It had taken 15 minutes for the SUVs to meet back up with the marines on the other side of the vast park. The lieutenant came to the door and Jorge rolled the window down.

The officer saluted and said breathlessly, "*Jefe*, we found fresh tracks in the dirt," the man gestured toward the V-cut behind him, just visible past the small concrete bridge that allowed the avenue to span the depression, "one large and one smaller set of trainer prints – it was them, they definitely came up here, by the bridge."

"Very good, lieutenant," Jorge said. "Rejoin your men; we're moving out to pursue."

"*Sí, jefe!*"

Jorge turned away, rolling the window up as he faced Alfredo. "Report!"

"Two more minutes until the ping," Alfredo said hurriedly and swallowed.

"Hmph," Jorge snorted and closed his eyes. His broken ribs were like ice picks jamming into his side, despite the supporting wrap the doctor had applied, and his dozen or so superficial shrapnel wounds all burned and itched at the same time. It was making cogent thought difficult, but Jorge couldn't afford to take any of the pain meds the doctor had forced on him – he needed a clear head to nip this problem in the bud, lest the other cartels get wind of it and make a play against him, sensing weakness and opportunity.

I can't let that happen! We need to find them and end this!

"What about that electric company van?" Jorge asked, eyes still closed.

This time Vincente answered; he'd been coordinating with the Chihuahua state police. "It went into an underground garage at the *Centro Comercial Juarez Central, jefe*," he reported. "The Plaza Juarez Mall has too many exits, and though it's not open yet for shopping, the food court and restaurants are, with crowds of people into which they could blend. They lost them."

Jorge exhaled a frustrated snort and clenched his jaw.

It was to be expected, I suppose... these men are clearly experienced operators, not some cartel thugs...

Still, if I can get my hands on that one man who took the boy, he'll provide much needed answers and allow me to finish this whole motherfucking business...

"Tell them to refocus on the border checkpoints," Jorge commanded. "They'll want to clear out of the area as quickly as they can, before we can get organized enough to stop them – well, we'll have a surprise for them, won't we, Vincente?"

"*Sí, jefe*! I'll coordinate with the commandant—"

"And tell the commandant that, whoever captures or kills these men, I will pay a bounty of one million pesos for each of the assassins! Understood?"

"*Sí, jefe*! I will make sure he knows."

"And then get on to our various capos – tell them the same," Jorge added.

"*Sí, jefe*!"

With that done, Jorge tried to relax as best as he could against the pain of his wounds as he waited for the transmitter to ping.

Come on, you stupid satellite! Hurry up and give me what I want!

The wait seemed to take hours. Jorge kept glancing at his watch, willing the seconds to pass faster.

"Transmitter has pinged!" Alfredo reported a moment later. "Data shows... a location on *Avenida Francisco Villa*... cross-checking now... it's outside *Fabricaciones de Metal Ilimitadas*... 2488 is the address number." A few more keystrokes and Alfredo added, "The facility is closed – out of business."

Jorge pondered that for a few seconds. "A hideout?" he asked, thinking aloud, "or perhaps a rendezvous? Regardless, it's where they are now – Juan-Pablo, drive! Vincente, radio the men to prepare for a search when we arrive! Emphasize we want the man alive!"

Chapter 15

A Crazy Idea

After leaving Kody locked in the factory, One went down the short alley and then turned right, heading south on the sidewalk along the factory complex. He chose this way to examine half of the perimeter, looking for any sign of occupancy – such as from the homeless or squatters – and discovered an encampment along the fencing on the south side but none inside the complex. Satisfied that he'd scouted out most of the perimeter and found it as secure as one could expect, he resolved to take a different way back from the market to scout the northern side of the complex.

The four-block walk to the market took One only as many minutes. The *Cooperativa Mercado Juarez* – Juarez Cooperative Market – consisted of hundreds of open stalls on a closed-down street, a mix of tents, semi-permanent plywood shacks, and small trailers that were sandwiched between two rows of permanent storefronts. The morning air was filled with heady aromas of cooking meats, flour tortillas, and spices that were augmented by a dull roar of the crowd that was flowing in and among the shops like the waters of a lazy stream.

Not wanting to spend any more time here than was necessary, One started by looking for clothing and some backpacks, heading to one side of the former street where one of the permanent storefronts had a sign denoting it as a clothing store.

It turned out to be a lot more, like the Mexican equivalent of Kohl's back in the states. One quickly selected a couple of outfits for himself, and then chose some for Kody. They had backpacks, so he chose two plain black Jansport knock-offs, and in the checkout line, saw some pocket LED flashlights, so he scooped up two of those as well and a couple of extra packs of alkaline batteries for them.

After paying for his items, he used the store's small restroom to change into one of his new outfits, transferring his items from the cargo shorts he'd been wearing to the new, dark blue ones he now pulled on. A black t-shirt, navy blue zip-up hoodie, and a black Nike ballcap, into which he stuffed his long hair, made him into a new man – at least as far as his pursuers were concerned, he hoped.

He then went to the corner bodega and spent five minutes gathering up protein bars, bottles of water and juice, some cartons of Parmalat milk, two boxes of cereal, paper bowls and plastic utensils, and some fruit. He saw that the bodega had pre-paid cellphones behind the counter, and bought four of them, a Bic lighter, a pack of tea candles, and a pair of folding knives. He put what he could in one of the backpacks and slung it over his back; the rest he consolidated into the other backpack and the shopping bags from the clothing store, which he carried in his hands.

Half an hour later his hands were laden with his final purchases. Before heading back, he decided to do a modified surveillance detection run, or SDR, by abruptly reversing direction, moving back into the busy crowd at the open-air market, pausing to window shop while seeing if anyone was following or unduly interested in him through the reflection in the glass. After 15 minutes of this and seeing no sign of pursuit, he decided it was safe enough to return to the factory.

I bet Kody is nervous as hell by now – I've been gone almost an hour.

One kept a wary eye out for any signs of trouble but saw nothing of concern. It was just after nine in the morning now, and the traffic on the streets around him had picked up noticeably, as had the number of people on the street.

One crossed the street onto the sidewalk that ran along the north side of the factory, intending to complete his scouting of the factory complex's perimeter. He came to and stepped over a set of rusted railroad tracks imbedded in the concrete of the roadway and sidewalk. Glancing to his right, he saw that the imbedded tracks went under a chained and locked gate in the hurricane fencing and continued deeper into the complex. A much newer sign had been attached to the gate – "No Trespassing

– Property of Ferromex" – next to the original, faded, factory's no trespassing warning.

Just beyond the gate a white Ferromex truck sat on the rails.

What do they call those?

Ah, right – a roadrailer.

It was a ten-wheel truck that had been modified for the task, with the flanged railroad wheels set in front of the tires in the front and the back of the tires in back. These were currently in their down and locked position so the roadrailer could run on the track.

The bed of the truck had been fitted with multiple compartments along its sides, and a hydraulic crane in the center. The truck had seen better days – its white paint job was dotted with rusty blobs, the Ferromex logo on the doors was faded, the front bumper was rusted, dented in several places, and hung on an angle. The cable in the winch atop the bumper was red with oxidation, and the windshield was starred near the center, with lines radiating outward to the edges. Still, it must have been able to run because its flanged rail wheels were shiny, meaning it had been used recently.

A train's horn began sounding nearby, drawing One's attention to the slightly raised right-of-way across the street and about 500 meters distant. A freight train, led by three red and black Ferromex locomotives was crawling northward there, its train of cars stretching out of his sight beyond the corner of the factory complex.

His eyes fell to the tracks there imbedded in the sidewalk and adjacent street, following them across and through the industrial area there, rising slowly to join the right-of-way.

Then One had put it all behind him, focusing instead on the corner ahead. He continued to scan, looking for threats and as he came to *Avenida Francisco Villa*, that old sixth sense of his put the hackles up on his neck. He walked the last dozen meters to the corner at a slow pace, then stopped just short of it. Pulling his bags of items back behind him so they wouldn't swing out into sight of anyone past the corner, One leaned forward slightly to peer around—

And saw three black Suburbans idling curbside, about midway down the block. Black clad men in combat gear were spread out on the sidewalk, some peering warily through the hurricane fence into the grounds of the closed factory, M4s shouldered and at the ready, while two others, with their M4s slung, were working a bolt cutter onto the heavy padlock that secured the gated fence of the factory's main vehicle entry.

How the fuck did they find us?!

We escaped the pursuit back at the park...

The cabbie? How would he even know to be on the lookout for us?

No, not the cabbie...

The police chopper? No... it went after the squad...

Then how?

One withdrew back around the corner.

Worry about it later – the priority now is to get the kid and bug out.

One risked another peek. The men had cut through the lock on the gate, thrown them open, and now two of the SUVs were driving into the property, with the black clad shooters following in on foot and beginning to spread out, clearly to do a search. The third SUV remained curbside, idling.

Something about that remaining SUV tickled One's memory.

What? What's interesting about that one Suburban?

Then realization struck.

It's got an omnidirectional antenna on the top...

For tracking low-power transmitters...

One's brain made the connections in a flash.

The kid's been bugged! That's how they've found us at the hotel, and now here!

One was angry at himself for not considering this possibility sooner.

So what now? The minute we move, they'll be able to follow—

Wait a second. Why didn't they go directly into where Kody was?

His brain worked furiously to solve this discrepancy.

It's a low-power transmitter... needs either direct view to a satellite, or line-of-sight to the SUV's antenna. The metal of the factory is blocking the signal...

As did the metal and concrete of the natural gas room back at the electric company! Even out UHF comms had problems with it – I lost signal with Two when we went in that room.

Okay then... they can't pinpoint where Kody's at. That's something. But I can't just wrap the kid in tin foil to keep them from detecting him...

The Pelican box! It's got a copper mesh Faraday cage interior under the foam...

He's small... he'd fit, but I can hardly carry that huge case around with him inside and try to blend in...

An idea struck.

A crazy idea.

Maybe we won't need ID for Kody after all...

Chapter 16

Set Up A Perimeter

"Still nothing, *jefe*," Alfredo reported meekly.

His men had cut through the locked gate, entered the facility, and were beginning a search. The old fabrication factory was huge, taking up the entire block, with multiple buildings, machines, towers, silos and conduits. Jorge wasn't surprised that they weren't getting a signal on the antenna with all the metalwork acting as a Faraday cage. Still, he had Alfredo keep monitoring for a signal as Vincente oversaw the deployment of their squad of ex-marines.

Jorge turned to glance out the tinted window.

Just a dozen men to search this whole place...

Maybe I should have the commandant bring in his men?

No... they'll shoot to kill, and I need that man alive! I have so many questions to ask... and revenge to take...

Still... they could be useful in setting up a perimeter... making that assassin think twice about trying to escape...

And he's got the kid with him. Clearly, he's concerned for the boy's wellbeing, since he's gone to such lengths... that could be an important fact when the time comes...

"Vincente," Jorge said without turning from the window.

"Sir?"

"Let's have the commandant bring enough men to set up a perimeter around this factory... say, out to two blocks. It'll give our assassin pause if he'd contemplating a breakout and will allow our men to focus solely on finding him, not also worrying about containment."

"Yes, *jefe*," Vincente said with a smile and a nod, then took up his cellphone to make the call.

Chapter 17

They've Found Us

From the corner to the alleyway was about 20 meters, beyond which was a sidewalk devoid of any significantly large features or objects to use as cover. So the question became – would anyone in the SUV at the curb be looking back toward this corner?

The only one who would likely be doing so is the driver, through his rearview mirrors. Everyone else was probably watching the operators as they moved farther into the complex.

The SUV is over 100 meters away... what details could the driver make out if I just saunter around the corner?

Not many... and with my new clothing, carrying bags, and alone, would he even make the connection that I'm the one they pursued earlier?

Likely not.

One exhaled through pursed lips.

I don't have a choice anyway – Kody's locked inside and alone. Who knows what horrors the cartel will do to him if they get him back...

Okay then... here goes...

One backed up about four meters, pulled the brim of his cap down a bit more, lowered his chin to hide his eyes from anyone in the SUV that might look back, and started forward, making his gait be that of just a guy with groceries walking home. He turned the corner, felt his heart rate tick up as the SUV came into view farther down the street, and willed himself to be casual.

Though he'd been a tier one operator for nearly a decade, he was human, and as such he wasn't immune to fear and worry. Both started to rise within him, tugging at his mind, urging him to break into a run and reduce the amount of exposure time he had there on the sidewalk, but One tamped them down with an effort of will and a reliance on his training. He knew that people saw what they wanted to see, categorizing everything that came across their line of sight, and this was exactly what One was counting on the occupants of the SUV to do – see him as just another downtrodden citizen of Juarez walking with groceries, a completely harmless man going about his business and no threat to anyone.

To enhance this appearance, he hunched over and made his gait into something more like a random shuffle than firm strides.

The 20 meters seemed to take an eon. One turned into the alley and out of line of sight with the SUV and breathed a long sigh of relief but didn't let his guard down. He quickly put his back to the wall, slid down it to a crouch, and leaned one eye around the corner to see if there'd been any response from the SUV.

Nothing. The big vehicle sat idling at the curb without any sign that anyone inside had even seen him, let alone recognized him.

One went to the door, unlocked the gate, opened it and the door, hurried inside, and then closed and locked them. He turned and was about to speak when he saw the teen sleeping atop the Pelican case.

One stepped to him quietly, looking down. Despite the gravity of the current situation, One paused to regard the teen, sleeping peacefully, his long, golden hair flared around his head, framing it and accenting his high cheekbones, his full lips, and the long lashes of his closed eyes.

He's a gorgeous kid, One thought approvingly, then shook his head slowly. *Who's gone through God-knows how much trauma, suffering and abuse.*

Well, you'll get him out of this, won't you?

Fuck yeah, I will!

But how?!

That question brought One from his admiring reverie and back to the immediate needs of their present predicament. He reached down and gently touched Kody's shoulder to wake him—

The boy sprung up with a gasp, pushing away and backpedaling, falling onto his ass on the concrete floor as he whined, "No! NO!"

One was shocked. "Hey! It's just me, Kody! Take it easy!"

What had the cartel done to him to make him react like that?

Kody's wild response disappeared as quickly as it had come. He pushed his back against the dusty corrugated steel wall, panting and swallowing as he hugged his knees into himself.

"Take a few deep breaths," One advised, approaching slowly to sit on the Pelican case. "It's just me."

The teen nodded several times, and wiped at his eyes, finally whispering a "sorry."

"It's okay," One said, then started pulling out fresh clothes. "We can't stay here – change into these, quickly."

Kody didn't argue or hesitate. He took the clothes, put them on the case, stood, and stripped out of what he had been wearing. In a minute he was in cargo shorts, a black polo shirt, maroon hoodie with matching maroon Adidas Sambas, and an oversized, black Vans ball cap.

"Stuff your hair up into it," One directed, but when Kody was all thumbs, said, "Can I help?"

Kody nodded and dropped his arms, letting One stuff all his long hair away, out of sight.

One then re-portioned the groceries into the two backpacks he'd purchased but hesitated as he handed one to Kody to don.

Kody saw his hesitation and looked around worriedly. "Are they... coming?"

The question took One away from his thoughts. "I'm not going to lie to you – yeah, they've found us. They've got about a dozen outside, searching—"

Kody's eyes grew large, and he began to hyperventilate.

"Hey! Hey, hey!" One said, kneeling and taking him by his upper arms. "Look at me, okay? Look at me!" When Kody finally did, still panting, One told him, "Look – I'm not going to let them hurt you or take you. Understand? It's not gonna happen, okay?"

Kody licked his lips, trembling within One's grasp, but slowly nodded.

"You believe me, right?" One demanded softly.

"I... believe you," Kody finally whispered.

One gave him as reassuring a smile as he could. "Okay... I think we have some time yet – a dozen or so guys will take all day to search this place—"

It was then that the two of them heard the distant high-low whooping of police sirens.

Oh fucking shit!

Can't you just let it rest, Murphy?

Chapter 18

Now I Have You!

"Idiots!" Jorge groused as he turned from looking out his window at his marines, who were just beginning their search, to the arriving police vehicles. "I told that *puta* of a commandant not to use sirens! Didn't I, Vincente?"

"Um, yes, *jefe*, you did," Vincente replied.

Jorge exhaled frustration. "If that assassin's in there, he knows we're here for sure now."

Eight state police pickup trucks arrived then, red and blue lights flashing and sirens wailing. The first two zoomed past the parked SUV, going to the end of the street and turning their trucks sideways across all four lanes of traffic, blocking any cars from passing. The four middle trucks pulled up behind Jorge's SUV, and from their beds, a total of 24 state policemen in tactical gear emerged, carrying shotguns and M4 rifles. The last two trucks pulled across the lanes, blocking traffic at the north end of the avenue.

A moment later, two large black panel vans stenciled with the state police logo and having red and blue flashes in their grills came to a stop just ahead of Jorge's SUV. From these 40 more policemen in tactical gear emerged, and from the cab of the lead panel van the commandant himself came out. The man was dressed in pressed urban camo-pattern BDUs and wore a holstered SIG Sauer P226 pistol high on his hip, with his gold badge over his left breast, a Bakelite name tag with "GOMEZ" over the right, and the four silver stars of his rank on the starched collars of his BDUs.

The commandant strode purposefully to stand in front of the SUV's window while his men, all 48 of them milled about, weapon barrels pointed downward, fingers along trigger guards.

When the window was fully down, the commandant saluted crisply to Jorge, and said, "*Señor de Corazón*, it's a pleasure as always to work with you..."

Work with *me?* Jorge thought angrily. *You puta, you don't work* with *me, but* for *me!*

Jorge glared at the man for several beats, and the commandant eventually looked down, realizing that he'd done or said something wrong but not sure what it was.

Finally, Jorge said in a cold menace, "*Commandante*, I believe I specifically said that you were not to use sirens."

The commandant's face blanched. He began to stammer out an apology, but Jorge held up his hand.

I've no time to deal with this fool... hopefully he can handle this simple task without fucking it up...

"I want you and your men to establish a perimeter around this factory – the entire block. You are to keep bystanders away, but more importantly, make sure that no one leaves! No one gets by you!" Jorge ordered.

"Yes, yes, I understand, *señor de Corazón*, that is what your man Vincente ordered."

"Good. There can be no more mistakes, like the sirens... and like at the hotel – understand?" Jorge said flatly, continuing to glare at the commandant.

Two strikes so far, commandant. One more and I'll send you into permanent retirement. Maybe your deputy is a better man than you are... or at least more obedient...

"Of course, yes, no mistakes," the commandant agreed with a series of nods and big smile.

"You know we are looking for a man and a boy, yes?"

"Yes, *señor de Corazón*."

"If by some insane chance these two get past my men inside, you are to not kill them – I say this again, *not kill them*. Capture them, wound them, knock them out, just *do not kill them*. Understand?"

"*Sí, señor de Corazón*, I understand," the commandant said with more head bobbing.

"Do you have – what's it called?"

"Less than lethal," Vincente said when he realized his boss was struggling to recall the correct phrase.

"Yes, that; less than lethal?" Jorge said, nodding to Vincente in acknowledgement for the help.

"We do, *señor de Corazón*," the commandant said.

"I suggest you have those in hand, not guns," Jorge said with a bit of a sneer.

"I will order it so," the commandant assured.

"Very well, get on with it then," Jorge said, dismissing the man and hitting the switch to roll the window up.

The commandant saluted his own reflection in the tinted glass, spun on his heel, and began barking orders and waving his hands. His men stiffened, then began trotting off in all directions, jogging to establish the perimeter that Jorge wanted.

Now I have you!

Chapter 19

Claustrophobia

Kody picked up on the sirens just as quickly as One had and began to tremble again.

"Kody, listen to me! Listen, okay?" One implored. The teen's eyes, wide with fear, turned up to look into his. "I said I wouldn't let anyone hurt you, and I meant it, okay? I promise! So listen; I have a way for us to get outta here, but to do it, I'm gonna need you to be really, really brave. Do you think you can do that for me?"

Kody just stared at him, tears now streaking down his cheeks and trembling so much that One had to guide him to sit on the case.

"They'll beat me again..."

Jesus Christ – poor kid!

"I won't let them hurt you, I promise!"

Swallowing hard, Kody looked up at him with reddened eyes and a look that wanted to trust, wanted to believe, but just couldn't get there.

"I want you to hear me, okay? *I won't let anything happen to you; I promise.* Now, we've got limited time to escape, and I think I've found a way to do it – but it's gonna require a lot from you."

One squeezed the teen's arms gently, trying to calm and reassure him, and it worked. His tears stopped and his trembling lessened. After swallowing a few times, Kody managed to ask, "What?"

"They've got a transmitter in you somewhere," One told him. "That's how they've been able to track us – at least, that's the most logical thing I can come up with. Now, so far, we've been lucky – the building has too much metal to let the signal through, but the minute we go outside, they'll be able to track us again. So... we can stay here and try to hide among the machinery, but you just heard the sirens... cops are coming to help with finding us, and they'll have enough manpower to eventually find us no matter what we do... especially if they bring dogs."

"So... what do... will we do?" Kody stammered.

"I have to block the signal," One explained. "To do that, we need to surround you in metal. The only way I can think of doing that and still being able to travel is... having you hide in the case." One patted the case upon which they sat. "It's got a copper mesh liner, called a Faraday cage, to block radio signals and emissions."

Kody looked down at the case and then back up at One with an expression of such terror that it rent at One's heartstrings. The teen began shaking like a chihuahua and pushed out of One's grip, hugging his knees to himself and sobbing.

"Hey! Hey! I'm not locking you in forever – just until we're clear of the men chasing us!" When that did nothing to stop the teen's reaction, One sat down next to him and hugged him close, using his much larger size to encompass Kody. "I won't leave you in there, really," he said quietly while his mind raced, sending out warnings that the window of opportunity was swiftly closing.

Why's he reacting like this?!

"Kody?" One said as soothingly as he could – this type of thing was way outside his bailiwick. He'd never been a parent, though he'd entertained the thought many times, and his life experiences and career weren't exactly that which gave him much experience dealing children and teens. "Kody, it's okay..."

"They... locked me... in... for... days..." Kody stammered so softly that One had to lean in to hear him. "When I... was... bad..."

Oh, shit – it's trauma... PTSD over confined spaces.

What kind of sick fucks do that to a kid?

One shook his head mentally. *The kind that traffics and sell kids for sex, that's who!*

One looked away, trying to think.

What's the best way to do this?

Hell if I know!

But it's the only way I can see right now...

"Kody... that sounds really horrible... and, well, just so you know, I don't like small spaces either." One gave him a soft squeeze to emphasize his sincerity.

"Claustrophobia," Kody whispered.

"Yeah, that's it," One confirmed. "But, when I was on a mission, we had to climb through sewers... it was really small and dark in there, and it took a lot of willpower for me to do the mission..."

"But... you did?" Kody asked meekly.

"I did," One confirmed. "I did it with the help of my squad – my friends. They were there to tell me things were going to be alright, and I trusted them... so I trusted what they said, even though I was shaking with fear."

"You? Shaking?" Kody asked, his trembling subsiding as he focused more on what One was saying.

"Hell, yeah. I thought I'd shit my pants! Or wouldn't be able to take another step, but each time I felt the fear, or the walls closing in, I thought of my friends, knowing they were there and wouldn't leave me alone to face the small space." One paused for a moment, then added, "You know what else helped a lot? I started thinking about all the nice places I wanted to visit on vacation, seeing them in my mind, seeing me there having fun. That helped keep my mind off what was going on around me."

One gave their surroundings a quick glance. "Look, we're running out of time fast. There's no other option I can think of – for us to get outta here, we need to block your signal. The only way to do that is the case – if I had a giant roll of tin foil, I'd wrap you in that like a mummy, but I don't, so I can't." He paused and leaned in to look directly into Kody's eyes. "It's the only way; do you trust me? Trust me when I say you'll be safe, and I won't leave you in there any longer than I absolutely have to?"

Kody returned his gaze, blinking rapidly, as he evaluated One's words against his own fears and trauma.

When Kody said, "Okay," One knew that reason and the basic instinct for survival had won out against his fears, but the look in Kody's eyes and his renewed trembling demonstrated that it had been a close thing.

Still, a move in the right direction – he trusts me enough to put his safety in my hands... that'll do as a start.

"Good, that's good," One said and hugged him one more time. "Let's do it while we still have time."

He pulled Kody to his feet, opened the case, and helped the teen inside. "You'll need to scrunch up some," One advised, and watched as Kody did so hesitantly. "Don't worry, I'll be close by. You might feel a lot of bumps at some point – I'll be driving us out of here. Whatever happens, stay quiet, okay?"

Kody's eyes showed his understanding, but also the verge of panic. "I won't run out of air?" he managed to ask.

"No," One confirmed. "We'll be far away from here before you'll even be close to that." *Or so I hope.* "Anything else?"

"I... guess not," Kody said uncertainly.

"I got you a flashlight," One told him, testing it and handing it over. "You can use it inside if you want so you're not in darkness – don't worry, nothing will shine out. Also, here's a folding knife and a cellphone. You can use the knife here," he pointed to the two lock points inside the case, "to pop the locks, if necessary, but only in an emergency, okay? Once you open the case, they'll detect your signal, and we don't want to do that. The cellphone won't work inside, but the clock on it will – if I don't come get you out in 30 minutes after I close the lid, you can come out to refresh the air in the case, but I don't expect that to be necessary. You get all that? Repeat it back to me."

Hesitantly, Kody repeated the instructions accurately.

"If you come out and I'm not there – again, I don't expect that to happen, but we always plan for contingencies in my work, so us two will as well – so, if I'm there, you call Garrett on the number I gave you. You still have it and the cash, right?"

Kody nodded.

"Good! Okay, here we go—"

"Wait!" Kody pleaded.

One paused and looked at him expectantly.

"I... just wanted... to say... y'know, thank you... for rescuing me."

One smiled. "You're welcome – but thank me when we're done with this all and safe. Okay?"

"Okay," Kody said with a hint of a smile.

"Which should, God willing, be really soon," One assured, wanting to have the last thing he said be upbeat and positive. "Ready?"

Kody nodded and scrunched a little smaller inside the open half of the case.

"Okay, here goes..."

One closed the case gently and waited a few seconds to hear if Kody had gone into a panic attack, trying to force his way out or bang on the case. When all was quiet, One clicked the locks in place, slowly pulled the case by its handles to the upright position, slung their backpacks, one over his back and the other over his front, and then got the case up and onto his shoulder.

That's one really brave kid...

One went over and shut the lights off at the breaker box then pulled his flashlight out and turned it on, panning it over the distant machinery.

Now, where's the exit to the other side of the building?

Chapter 20

It Was Simply Too Large

Vincente turned in his seat to face Jorge. "*Jefe*, they're too few."

Jorge was considering just that very fact. It had only been 10 minutes since his squad of ex-marine mercenaries had gone in to begin their canvassing of the factory and during that time, Jorge had re-evaluated the size and breadth of the closed facility.

It was simply too large for the squad of 12 men to search in a reasonable timeframe.

"Who can we pull?" Jorge asked.

Vincente already had an answer to that. "We'll pull Hector's men from tunnel security – we can close and lock the door. No one's going to bother with it. That gives us 30 men."

Turning away from the window to regard Vincente with pursed lips, Jorge considered it.

It'll mean postponing the next shipment of selected kids, but only by a day, two at most.

"That's acceptable," Jorge decided. "Make the call."

Nodding, Vincente picked up the phone and pressed Hector's speed dial number. The call connected, there was a brief exchange, and then Vincente disconnected.

"He'll be here in 45 minutes," Vincente reported. "What should I tell the lieutenant?"

"Have him keep searching – we'll feed the others in and coordinate once they arrive."

Jorge turned back to look out the SUV's window, his eyes narrowing.

You're not escaping from me this time...

Chapter 21

So Much Can Go Wrong

It was taking too long.

Encumbered with the case – not because it was all that heavy but because it was bulky – and with it on his shoulder, One had to be careful not to bump into anything in a factory full of pipes, dangling chains, and piles of half-scavenged gear and equipment lest he make noise that would attract attention of those searching for them. Thus it was slow going, and his progress was further complicated by the fact that, while he knew generally where the roadrailer truck was compared to the entry point, One had never seen the floorplan for this place, and thus had to rely on trial and error.

Ironic, he mused, *I'm doing trial and error and so are my pursuers.*

One chortled to himself, but then sobered.

He's only got so much air – you're wasting that too...

One kept going, shining his flashlight into spaces, small alcoves, and around machines that stood like silent giants in a graveyard of metal relics.

Just as frustration over not finding what he sought was equalizing with his worry over the amount of air Kody had remaining, his light played over an unlit exit sign hanging from a single, thin power line. Skirting around the steel support girders, he found an open hallway beyond which lay in deep shadow.

This is it or nothing...

One moved in, his flashlight illuminating the dusty corridor, showing that it was full of the detritus of an empty homeless encampment.

Rooms off to either side of the corridor held sagging cardboard boxes that had once served as tents, and both among these boxes, and throughout the hallway, were piles of litter. The cloying stench of urine and feces hung in the air. Continuing past it all, One turned a corner and saw a bit of welcome light eking around a loose-fitting exit door.

So much for no trespassing...

One had to turn sideways to peek out the partially open exit door, maneuvering carefully to not bump the case. Through the limited field of view, he saw the backside of the railroader about 10 meters distant.

So much can go wrong...

Does the truck even work?

Is its battery still good?

Can I get enough speed to bust open the gate?

Once we're on it, what about other trains?

One took a deep breath, trying to remain focused and not having his thoughts wander into catastrophizing.

One thing at a time...

One pushed the door open slowly, receiving a screech of unoiled hinges that lasted for a long second before the door swung the rest of the way quietly. Without another moment's hesitation, One moved quickly toward the truck, swiveling as he went to scan for threats but thankfully seeing none. He reached the driver's side door, set the case down, and tried the door's handle.

He wasn't surprised to find it locked.

He pulled his folding knife out, opened the blade, and put the tip against the bottom corner of the glass; with a sharp blow on the handle's end with the flat of his palm, the safety glass shattered, raining tiny, uniform bits down on the ground and into the cab of the truck. The noise it made was minimal, especially considering the intervening buildings and the traffic noise, but One treated it as if the alarm had been sounded.

He unlocked the door and pulled it open. Working in under the steering column, he wedged his knife into the seam, and torqued it until the housing came off. Finding the wires he needed, he used the knife to slice and splice the lines, said a brief prayer, and touched the wires.

The diesel engine growled slowly, like it was angry at having been disturbed from its siesta, until it finally came to life with a throaty, chugging roar a moment later. One quickly slapped the housing back in place, brushed the safety glass off the seat, and then picked up the case.

"We're ready to go," he said firmly with his mouth to the case's seam, hoping Kody could hear, then placed it in the truck's bed, behind the bucket lift's pedestal so, if they shot at them as they fled, the metal of the lift would block any rounds from hitting the case. He used some tie-downs there to secure the case, then leapt out of the bed, got in the cab, and closed the door.

His head bumped into a beat-up, orange hardhat hanging from a post behind the seat. One turned to it, regarded it for a moment, then snatched it up. A crumpled Ferromex safety vest was stuffed into it, and in an instant of inspiration, One took it out, donned it, and then put the hardhat on over his baseball cap.

Couldn't hurt to look the part, right?

"Here goes..." he said aloud, reassuring himself, and pressed down on the accelerator.

The truck's engine responded, throwing up a cloud of black smoke from its vertical exhaust pipe and moving forward, gathering speed. One braced himself as the truck hit 20 kph and impacted into the gate, which broke apart into a spray of large pieces that caught on the rusty bumper and were dragged along with a rooster tail of sparks against the concrete.

The roadrailer continued to gain speed as it crossed the sidewalk and onto the street. One expected that his sudden emergence would cause cars to honk, swerve or jam on their brakes to avoid the roadrailer as it shot across the little used industrial track; instead, a couple of policemen, in black tactical gear, were staring at him with wide mouths, their rifles and shotguns held forgotten in their hands.

Until he was parallel with them, that is. Then they seemed to realize that they had guns and could use them.

And did.

One ducked, heard the ping of rifle bullets and a *thunk* as a shotgun blast hit the truck somewhere, but then he was into the curve of the industrial spur that continued between the warehouses and scrap yard across the street from the factory. A quick look in the side mirror showed the cops running after him, but then a second later he was out of their line of sight.

Did it!

And that explains the sirens... Jorge called on his corrupt gendarmerie to assist.

That could spell trouble going forward...

The roadrailer followed the curving track through the industrial yard, now at 35 kph and passing between two sidings with rows of parked gondolas. One kept looking back, searching for signs of pursuit, but saw none.

This might actually work!

The track straightened then, going up an incline and One saw Murphy's contribution to his escape plan—

A switch stand, with a red circle facing him. It didn't take a rocket scientist to know this mean the switch was lined for the main track, not the siding on which he was currently accelerating.

Not unexpected, I suppose, but so soon?

Like most people not in the railroad industry, One had only a general idea of how railroads worked. In this case, to get the switch set for continuing, he'd need to stop and throw the lever controlling the switch.

He took his foot off the accelerator, and then pressed on the brake, coming to a quick stop a few meters from the start of the switch. One leapt out, ran to the thing, and took a quick second to examine it—

And saw a padlock on it – and not a cheap one either, but some sort of proprietary railroad one that looked stout and even had a keyhole cover.

One pulled his pistol and, keenly aware of the cops running after him somewhere just around the bend, knelt, slid the keyhole cover aside, took aim at the open keyhole and squeezed the trigger.

Unlike in the movies, locks didn't blow apart easily from a simple pistol round – and this was no movie. So while the lock stayed intact the bullet enlarged the keyhole. One took aim again, and fired three slow, paced suppressed shots into the hole, enlarging it each time, and then on the fifth shot the lock broke open. He stuffed the pistol back into his holster, pulled the lock remnants away, and grabbed the switch lever.

It took significant torque to swing the switch's lever around, and then he stomped on it to drive it into its fully open position. Without further ado, he jumped into the truck's cab and hit the accelerator once again.

Shots sounded from behind him as the state cops finally chugged into view, but they were out of breath and out of shape, so all their shots went wide—

And then One had the truck accelerating onto a straight run, the leftmost of four parallel tracks, and heading north with increasing speed.

Okay, you've got yourself away – now what?

One sat up higher in his seat, trying to peer farther ahead through the dirty windshield. He could see a line of freight cars on the second track to his right about 500 meters ahead as well as some lit signals, two of them on tall posts between the middle tracks while there was a small one at ground level that seemed to be aimed at his track.

And that one was red.

Great!

One couldn't afford to let up on the accelerator with the cops in pursuit. It was apparent that the track he was on merged with the one to his immediate right in about 200 meters, but there was no switch stand like he'd just thrown to get him onto that track.

Is it automatic?

If that was the case, he and Kody would be dead in the water. If the switch could only be operated remotely, he had two choices: try to slowly push through it, hoping the truck didn't derail, or throw the switch he saw on the dashboard to lift the rail wheels up and try to drive the truck normally on its tires.

He had no idea if the former would work, but the latter meant trying to drive over multiple railroad tracks to eventually return to the road, where the cop cars and helicopter, and the SUVs with Jorge's thugs could follow and intercept them.

One took the middle of the road solution to his dilemma. He slowed the truck to a crawl as he reached the merge, crossing his fingers mentally as he felt the rail wheels screech against the frogs of the closed switch and, to his surprise and relief, the truck was heavy enough to push through the switch. Next thing One knew, the truck was onto the main track.

"Yes!" he yelled happily.

You're not gonna stop me this time, Murphy!

One pushed the accelerator hard once again, and the truck responded, its engine winding up to a loud growl that rattled the cab's interior.

Then One heard the resonant, urgent blaring of a train's horn.

Murphy, you fuckin' asshole!

Chapter 22

We Can Intercept

The gunshots were the first sign that the man had been finally located.

The police scanner in the SUV came alive with hurried shouts of "Shots fired!", "A Ferromex truck is on the rails, going toward the main line!" and "Officers in pursuit!"

"Idiots!" Jorge growled. Vincente was already dialing the commandant and handed the phone to Jorge.

"*I need the man alive, you idiot!*" Jorge screamed into the phone, grinding his teeth with the pain produced by the effort.

The commandant was apologetic. "I'm sorry, *señor de Corazón*! I will send out a reminder immediately!"

Jorge tossed the phone back to Vincente with a scowl. "Juan-Pablo! Get us moving toward them!" He pivoted to Alfredo. "Well?! Any signal?!"

"No, *jefe*!" Alfredo answered, looking puzzled. "I don't understand it..."

"They found the transmitter," Vincente said flatly.

Jorge clung to the overhead strap as the SUV made a sharp U-turn, and this caused yet another stab of pain to his chest. "Or he's decided to leave the boy behind," Jorge countered.

But would he really do that?

Probably not... especially if he's American or European... they'd follow their code of honor, leaving no one behind... they'd be all concerned for the boy and the abuse he'd endured, seeing themselves as knights in shining armor and that it was their duty to save him...

So if they are together, no signal meant they found and neutralized the transmitter.

113

"Get the helicopter back!" Jorge ordered, and Vincente made the call.

"Suspect vehicle is a white Ferromex roadrailer," came the breathless voice of a cop over the radio. "It's on the industrial track headed to the main lines!"

"Juan-Pablo!" Jorge called.

"*Sí, jefe!*" Juan-Pablo replied, looking at the GPS screen on the dashboard. "We can take the avenue north... we can intercept at one of the crossings! About... er... one kilometer!"

"Do it!" Jorge ordered, then to Vincente, "Have as many of the police follow as can and see if they can get units to intercept at a crossing! And Vincente, tell them again, *I want that man alive!*"

Chapter 23

So Much For A Speedy Getaway

The rapid, urgent blaring of a train horn startled One. His eyes went to the side mirror and saw the blazing headlights of a locomotive filling it.

Holy Mother of God!

In his tunnel vision, trying to figure a way to continue their escape, One had neglected to check his mirrors to see if the track he was merging onto was already occupied. He'd seen the train there earlier during his return from the market, but it hadn't been important then.

Too late now!

One floored the accelerator, but the truck barely increased in speed; the speedometer was pegged at 80 kph and not going any higher.

A governor on the engine?

Fuck! Damn you, Murphy! Stop fuckin' up my escape plans! I've had enough of you for one day!

The locomotive's horn continued its staccato blaring as the two lower lights on the locomotive's front began to flash in an alternating pattern. One kept his foot mashed down on the gas and was relieved to finally see the locomotive behind him receding in the mirror. Facing front, One saw only open track ahead, with a line of freight cars on the track to his immediate right, coming up fast.

Taking several deep breaths to settle his racing heart after the near collision with the train behind him, One took a moment to look over the truck cab's interior. There was a radio and wired microphone under the dash, a first aid kit attached to the back of the cab, and a rack that could hold road six flares, with two currently clipped in place. Aside from this, and some crumpled paper wrappers on the floor of the passenger side, the cab was unremarkable and empty.

Looking forward again, One saw that he was coming even with three locomotives at the head of the consist to his right, waiting about 50 meters away from a red-over-red signal. The signal he assumed was assigned to his track showed red-over-green, and One wondered just what that meant, but felt somewhat comfortable with the fact that at least part of it was green, which meant "go."

Didn't it?

A flash later and he was past the locomotives at the head of the train on the right, past the signal, and his keen eyes caught sight of a switch ahead, the rails of it aligned to transfer him onto the right track, ahead of the train he'd just passed. Realizing this, he let up on the accelerator and just in time – he hit the switchover at about 45 kph, and the truck shimmied violently back and forth for a few seconds, threatening to derail, but then it was on the adjacent track and running normal once again.

Then One saw the next problem looming ahead – a crossing with a street.

From his vantage, he couldn't tell whether there were any flashing lights or lowering gates to stop traffic, so he had no choice but to brake hard, slowing the truck to around 20 kph as he approached. Sure enough, the crossing was protected only by some weather-worn, wood crossbucks. Traffic passed in front of him with carefree disregard for his presence, requiring him to inch forward at 10 kph until, finally, grudgingly, the traffic stopped long enough for him to accelerate the rest of the way through the crossing and pick up speed one more.

He saw the next crossing and repeated the process, then did so for two more in quick succession.

So much for a speedy getaway...

Should I switch to driving on the roads?

No... my plan is to take this all the way to the border, where the tracks turn into an American railroad without a break... there might be border patrol, but with my ID and wearing the Ferromex vest, I shouldn't have a problem getting past... the only issue is if they want to search the truck...

Worry about escaping first! You can deal with that later!

One checked his watch – Kody had been in the box for almost 15 minutes.

Keep going!

The track curved to the left, continuing to follow a path that led between the backsides of businesses and homes, straight through the heart of Ciudad Juárez. The curve temporarily blocked One's line of sight, so he had no choice but to slow in case there was another crossing just on the other side.

There was, and it had three state police pickup trucks arrayed there, one parked on an angle over the tracks, the other two to each side of the rails, red and blue lights flashing, with six cops aiming shotguns and pistols at him from over hoods and around open doors.

Fuck!

Chapter 24

Esos Malditos Idiotas!

Morning traffic was in full swing now and was making fast progress difficult. Juan-Pablo had just turned their SUV onto the Avenue of the Saints, less than half a kilometer from the planned interception point he'd seen on the SUV's GPS, when the police radio came alive.

"This is 516! I'm with 610 and 622! We see the roadrailer approaching – crossing at Antonio Lemus Street! Preparing to engage!"

"Tell them to take him alive!" Jorge screamed, and Vincente quickly relayed that to the commandant who he'd kept on the line as they made their dash to intercept. Behind Jorge's SUV, three state police trucks, lights flashing and sirens wailing, maintained close order but despite their lights and siren, traffic was only grudgingly giving right of way.

"Shots fired! Shots fired!" the radio reported.

"Juan-Pablo!" Jorge shouted, urging him to go faster by simply calling him by name.

Juan-Pablo hunkered down, took a deep breath, and swerved out into oncoming traffic at speed, flashing his high beams. Cars swerved and honked but had no choice but to give way under the threat of head-on collision with the big, black Suburban. Juan-Pablo narrowly missed a box truck turning in front of him at the next intersection, and even so, the truck's side mirror impacted his own SUV's right one, shearing them both from their mounts in a spray of plastic bits and metal fragments.

"516 report!" It was the commandant. "516! Come in! Report! You are to take the man alive, I say! Do you hear me, you fools!? Come in!"

Jorge groaned inwardly.

After a turn that almost flipped the Suburban, Juan-Pablo struggled with the heavy, armored SUV as it fishtailed left and right, smacking into an oncoming Honda Civic's right front fender, knocking the car off onto the sidewalk where it crashed into the wall of a nail salon. He didn't bother stopping after that hit-and-run, but powered forward, back into the correct lane of traffic and toward the flashing red and blue lights of the police trucks 100 meters ahead at the railroad crossing.

Groaning from renewed pain in his broken ribs from the tossing Juan-Pablo was putting them all through, Jorge leaned around to see past Vincente and cursed as they pulled up to a screeching halt at the railroad crossing.

Esos malditos idiotas!

Those fucking idiots!

Chapter 25

Sudden Inspiration

There was only one thing he could do.

One threw himself into the passenger footwell of the cab as he held the accelerator pushed to the floor with his left hand. He didn't hear the gunshots over the roar of the diesel engine just the other side of the firewall but felt the result of the impacts as rounds punched through the safety glass of the windshield and pinged off the interior metal of the cab.

Our Father, which art in Heaven...

One barely had finished the first stanza of the prayer when a series of holes appeared in the driver's side door, spraying bits of plastic and vinyl over him, and there was a blinding shock of hot pain in his thigh as one of the 9mm pistol rounds, or perhaps a shotgun pellet fired by the cops, found its mark. Before One could fully register the pain from the bullet wound, the 10-ton roadrailer rammed the one-ton police pickup truck that was across the tracks, bouncing One around the floor of the cab while a loud crash resounded, testifying to the impact of the two vehicles. This was immediately followed by a screeching of tortured metal for several seconds...

And then the roadrailer was accelerating again.

One got back into the driver's seat, seeing only unobstructed rail ahead through the pockmarked windshield. Then the left-side mirror shattered from a shotgun blast that caused him to duck once more, but when nothing more came, he looked to the right-side mirror, seeing the carnage he'd wrought.

The pickup that had been across the track was on its side, pushed up against the corner of the building along the right side of the track at the crossing. It was on fire, likely from a rupture to its fuel tank and lit by the sparks caused when the roadrailer had ground it along the concrete pavement. In the course of being dragged, this flaming truck had impacted against the police truck to its right, knocking it aside so that this one now pointed away from the crossing, and the two cops that had been taking cover behind it were nowhere to be seen. The truck on the left that hadn't been hit was even now swerving around to pursue by driving on the tracks.

Good luck with that!

He saw that there was a lot of car traffic at the crossing ahead – and at another crossing farther on, and another just beyond that.

I can't keep slowing down...

After the encounter with the train that almost hit him, One had an idea. He found the switch for the headlights, flicked it on, then pulled on the lever to activate the truck's high beams. He then tested the horn button at the center of the steering wheel. A deep-throated air horn sounded from the cab's roof.

Well, well...

He hit the horn like he'd heard so many trains do – two long, drawn out blasts, a short one, then another long. His mind spuriously realized then that this sequence was the same as that for the letter Q in Morse code.

He kept it up and was pleasantly surprised to see that it worked – the traffic came to a stop short of the grade crossing and he barreled past with no need to decelerate. He repeated it over and over, as he came to crossing after crossing. The police pickup gave up after only half a minute, unable to keep up by driving with one side of its wheels bouncing over the ties and one side in the ballast gravel of the shoulder.

With immediate pursuit no longer a threat, One looked to his leg. Blood seeped steadily from his thigh about six inches above the knee and along the outside of his leg. He probed it with careful fingers, wincing from the pain, and finding no exit wound.

Shit, that's not good...

He pulled his belt off and affixed it above the wound, cinching it tightly to slow the bleeding, all while he kept his right foot on the accelerator and elbowed the horn to keep it blasting as he passed through more crossings.

With the makeshift tourniquet in place, One leaned back against the seat and exhaled heavily. Ahead, the track showed an incline, and soon it was on an elevated section that was leading into a large railroad yard some 300 meters distant, a yard that he was quickly closing in on at the roadrailer's maximum speed.

He glanced in the remaining side mirror and saw no sign of pursuit. One then leaned out the window of the driver's side, searching for helicopters, and thankfully saw none.

This might actually work...

Except for this fuckin' thigh wound. Murphy, can't you, just for once, take a day off?

A glance at his watch showed that Kody had been in the case now for 23 minutes.

One felt confident that, in its nook behind the crane and with all the metal tool and equipment storage bins that lined the bed of the roadrailer to protect it, he'd been unscathed from the recent gunfire, but certainly he'd been tossed around just as much as One had from that encounter. He'd need to stop soon to let the kid breathe, and now stopping became even more important – his tourniquet was only a stop-gap measure. With no exit wound, it meant that the bullet was still lodged in his thigh, likely having carried with it some of the metal, plastic and/or vinyl from penetrating the door—

That meant the potential for infection.

He looked at the truck's first aid kit, grateful it was there, but though it would have disinfectant and bandages, One suspected it would not have the antibiotics he'd need to treat an infection.

Just great...

Looking forward now, One saw that the track he was on was leading into the center of the railyard, between two long rows of freight cars. In a moment, the roadrailer would be between them, completely masked from sight – well, except for the narrow view someone might have if they stood on the tracks and looked directly down their length—

And that gave him sudden inspiration.

Chapter 26

I Want Him Alive!

Jorge watched, helpless, as the huge 10-wheel roadrailer truck barreled into the police pickup that had parked on the tracks. The crashing impact was like a thunderclap, loud even within the confines of the armored SUV, and Jorge watched with a mix of fury and dismay as the big roadrailer knocked the pickup aside like it was a Tonka toy. There were sparks, then a roar of flame as the roadrailer dragged the pickup, now on its side, into the corner of the building abutting the tracks, where it crumpled further and brought down part of the building's roof atop it.

The cops had started shooting at the roadrailer with pistols and shotguns even before it had reached the crossing, and as it zoomed passed the two cops on the left of it, still standing in cover behind their own pickup, these cops swiveled to fire shot after shot into the roadrailer's side as it careened past. Then a heartbeat later, those two asinine cops got into their pickup and tried to pursue, driving onto the tracks, fishtailing wildly, and a moment later disappeared between the buildings of the industrial area.

"Vincente! The phone!" Jorge growled.

Vincente handed it over, and Jorge barked into it. "Commandant! What part of *I want him alive* can your morons of men not grasp?! I will have you, your whole family, and all your friends killed most gruesomely if you don't start listening to what I say! Rein in your men and get this done!" Without waiting for an answer, Jorge tossed the phone back to Vincente and pushed back into his chair, holding his ribs. "Juan-Pablo, where does that track go?"

His driver pulled to the curb and then began thumbing through the screen of the GPS, enlarging, moving, zooming, and enlarging again. "The railroad yard, *jefe*. After that..." he thumbed around the screen some more, "after that, it's about a 15-kilometer run to the border and right into the US."

Jorge turned to look out the window, thinking.

The US Border Patrol has an outpost there, but they generally don't stop through trains – they're posted there to prevent people crossing on foot.

Shit! If we don't stop him before then, he'll be out of reach, and so will be the answers to the questions I have.

"Radio the commandant!" Jorge ordered. "Tell him not to bother pursuing! Instead, let's set up before the railroad crosses the bridge into the US. I want the tracks blocked so not even a tank can get past!"

"Right away, *jefe*!" Vincente said and began issuing orders on his phone. Once he had, Jorge said, "Vincente – pull all our men from the factory and redirect the men from the tunnel to the blockade as well. We'll take lead, and let the police secure the perimeter so they'll be out of the way. I only want our men to do this – the commandant and his buffoons have shown that they aren't capable."

"*Sí, jefe!*"

"Let's go, Juan-Pablo!" Jorge ordered.

Chapter 27

We'll Stay Here For Now

One let the truck glide to a halt and put the gear selector into park. Getting out of the truck's cab and onto the ballast shoulder of the track sent a stab of cold pain through his leg, and then climbing into the truck's bed repeated the process. But he was mobile, for now, and could deal with the pain thanks to his training and the adrenaline that was still coursing through him – but once that wore off, he'd be feeling it a whole lot more.

He got to the Pelican case and bent next to the seam. "Kody! I'm going to move you! Keep calm! I won't leave you!" he shouted so the teen could hear him inside.

With significant effort, One managed to raise the case, bring it to the tailgate, and set it down. He gently lowered himself to the tracks, took the case and set it on the ballast. He then went to each side of the truck, opening compartments, looking for specific tool he hoped he'd find.

Thankfully, it was there. *Ah, finally a victory against you, Murphy!* One lifted the large set of bolt cutters from their bin and turned to face the row of boxcars along the right side of where he'd parked.

To reduce theft, the boxcars' doors all had a welded, thick metal band locking their doors closed. It, along with a thinner customs seal, were not great antitheft devices, as such things went, because a pair of bolt cutters could make short work of them. But it was more cost-effective than putting a padlock on each door, and then needing to have a key for each individual lock to open them, which would have been a logistical nightmare – and besides, a bolt cutter could just as easily slice off a padlock as the finger-thick metal ring that was used.

One was unaware of these details, and for him it had no meaning anyway – all he was looking to do was get inside one of the boxcars, and now had the tool to do it.

He selected the nearest boxcar and used the cutters to shear away the locking ring and customs seal. Rotating the handle on the locking mechanism allowed him to slide the door open a half-meter and look inside.

The car was almost full, with a huge, palletized machine of some sort under shrink-wrap taking up the left-most and a second, similar one in the right-most part of the boxcar. They were both secured to the car's floor with tie-downs, but the center had just enough empty space to accommodate Kody and him.

Another strike against you, Murphy! First car I open has just what we need!

One didn't waste any time after finding the boxcar suitable. He lifted the Pelican case into the boxcar, pushing it in gently, then went to the roadrailer's cab to retrieve his backpack and the truck's first aid kit.

Next, One began searching for the other items he wanted. It took a couple of minutes, but he found them. Dumping out a small toolbox, he placed them inside and then shoved the toolbox into the boxcar along with his backpack and the first aid kit.

That done, he retrieved a second, small toolbox he'd found in his search, one that contained a bunch of hand tools, and then went around the truck to close all the compartments he'd opened.

Back at the open driver's side door, One put the toolbox on the driver's seat, then stood up on the running board. He reached over, put the truck into gear, lifted the weighty, small toolbox, and then wedged it onto the accelerator.

The diesel engine growled as it spun up. As it began to move, One jumped down onto his good leg and slammed the door, hobbling clear as the roadrailer accelerated, headed toward the US border about 10 miles – 15 kilometers – away.

One crossed to the open boxcar door, pulled himself up and inside, and then leaned out to watch the roadrailer recede into the distance. Satisfied with the diversion he'd created, he put his weight to closing the door of the boxcar so only a few inches of space remained open and then turned to let Kody out of the case.

Light showed from the seam as One pushed the lid up, and found Kody curled and staring up at him, his breath ragged, his face as white as bone—

And then the teen threw himself against One, hugging him with trembling arms and body as he began sobbing.

The pain in his leg faded into the background for One as a wave of powerful empathy for what he'd put Kody through rose within him. Awkwardly, One returned the hug, sighed, almost pushing Kody away, but then relented, allowing himself a moment to relax and just be the comfort that the teen needed.

"Hey... it's okay now... you're okay... you're okay now..." One said as soothingly as he could while Kody's emotions and fears dumped out. One continued to coo words of comfort until the teen's sobs subsided and he felt Kody gently pushing back.

One looked into his red eyes and smiled at Kody, to offer a simple expression of reassurance to augment the moment they'd just shared. "You okay now?"

Kody sniffled, wiped at his eyes and nose with the cuff of his hoodie, and managed to say, "I thought we were gonna die..."

"Nah," One said, trying to brush it off as if such had never even been a possibility. "I just, well, took a little time to get used to how to drive the truck."

That elicited a snicker from Kody, and a slight upturning of his lips.

"Oh? Find that funny?" One said facetiously, pleased to see Kody rebounding from what must have been an unimaginably frightful experience for him – having trauma-induced claustrophobia and then being locked into a small case, which was then bumped all over the place for nearly half an hour.

"A little," Kody admitted shyly, sniffling.

"Thirsty?"

"Mmmhmm," Kody replied.

One broke open his backpack and handed Kody a bottle of water and a power bar. When he did so, Kody noticed the blood on One's hands for the first time.

"You're bleeding?!" he exclaimed, eyes wide.

"Nothing to worry about," One said with bravado. "It's nothing that's not happened before."

Which is true, but when it happened, I had a team medic who took care of it right away and had access to antibiotics.

"You eat up, and I'm gonna get myself bandaged, okay?" One told him.

Kody looked uncertain and skeptical. "You need... help?"

"Nah, I've got this," One assured him.

Still, Kody watched with attentive eyes as One pulled up the leg of his cargo shorts to keep any more blood from soiling them, opened the first aid kit, and began to clean his wound. Once he did, he flicked the blade of his folding knife open, used the flame from his lighter to sterilize it, and one it had cooled sufficiently, pushed the tip into the wound slowly.

Kody stopped eating and stared worriedly at One when he tensed and growled at the painful intrusion of the blade's tip. Kody watched, horrified and fascinated, as One pushed the blade in deeper, seeking the bullet, gently twisting and probing with the blade as sweat ran down his forehead and nose and his skin went pale from the exertion and pain.

There! Thank God!

With a bit of pressure, a twist, and a flick, a slightly deformed, .32 caliber ball of double-ought buckshot popped free from the wound and clunked to the wood floor of the box bar.

So it had been a shotgun pellet... looks like they used double ought...

One let out a long, low groan and pulled the knife free from the wound. He turned to Kody, gave him a smile and nod of reassurance, and then cracked open a fresh bottle of water. Bending his leg at the knee and leaning to his left so his leg lay parallel to the floor, but not touching it, he irrigated the wound with half the bottle's contents.

After drying the area with a gauze pad, he unwrapped a fresh one, dampened it with disinfectant from the kit, forced the gauze into the wound, and using his index finger, twisted it deeper inside and around. One's hope was that this would be sufficient to prevent infection.

There was about half of the disinfectant left in the bottle at this point. One removed the pad from the wound and discarded it. He applied a generous squirt of disinfectant to a fresh gauze pad, made it into a cone, then stuffed it into the wound and left it inside. He then placed a pressure bandage from the kit over the wound and used surgical tape to secure it in place. Only after he'd done this and was satisfied with his work did he remove his makeshift tourniquet. After rethreading his belt in his shorts, he gathered up the soiled medical waste and tossed it farther into the boxcar.

"There, all better," he told Kody with a smile as he theatrically dusted his hands.

"Really?" Kody remained worriedly skeptical.

"Yeah, I've had a lot worse," One assured him. Then, purposefully changing the subject, he asked, "The power bar, okay?"

Kody nodded slowly, looking at the half-eaten bar. Hesitantly, he said, "It's good... I haven't had chocolate in, like, forever."

"I'm glad," One replied, taking up a power bar and the remainder of the water in the bottle. He tore into the pack and enjoyed the chocolatey bouquet it created as he chewed, and felt it quell some of the building hunger in his stomach after all the excitement of that morning.

"So, where's this place?" Kody eventually asked.

"We're in a boxcar in a rail yard," One told him. "This car is made of steel, so your signal will be blocked for now."

Kody looked around. "But we're not moving?"

"For now, no," One answered. "I thought the truck was the way out, but on further consideration, not one of my better ideas."

"Oh," Kody said, taking another bite of his power bar and chewing as he looked at One expectantly.

"We'll stay here for now, until things quiet down," One told him. "They'll have no idea where we went – I sent the roadrailer truck on ahead. If we're lucky, it'll get all the way to the bridge across the Rio Grande before they realize I'm not in it."

Just then the two of them heard the *thwop-thwop-thwop* of a helicopter increase in volume as it approached, heard it pass overhead, and then heard its rotor noise fade as it opened the distance between them.

"See?" One said with a smug grin.

Kody grinned back.

An awkward silence descended then as both ate and drank. One glanced over and found Kody studying him with those big green eyes of his, that somehow seemed very cat-like in the dim light streaming in through the slit in the doorway.

"Questions?" One finally asked.

Kody pushed the last of the power bar into his mouth and chewed it for a long time before swallowing. "Um... like... a million?"

One laughed and realized that was the first time he'd had a deep-down good one in several days. "Well, it looks like we have a lot of time on our hands, so go ahead and ask whatever you want. I'll try to answer, but some stuff I can't talk about. You understand?"

Kody studied him for another few seconds before nodding.

"So, ask away!" One told him as he pulled the toolbox he'd liberated from the truck to him, opened it and began pulling items out, setting them down in orderly fashion on the floor next to him.

Chapter 28

So Much Awaits

The police helicopter quickly found the roadrailer truck on the main line as it exited the railroad yard and headed north toward the US border at what appeared to be its maximum speed.

"This is Air Zero-Two; we have eyes on the suspect's truck, on the main railroad line just exiting from the rail yard. Estimated speed 80 kph," the helicopter reported over the radio.

"That gives us about eight minutes to get the roadblock set up," Vincente noted aloud.

"Make sure those idiots are working on it!" Jorge ordered as he clung to the ceiling-mounted handle above his head while Juan-Pablo put the Suburban through tortuous paces, trying to reach the intercept point before that time limit. He'd put the SUV's emergency flashers on and this, coupled with the police trucks in close line behind them with their sirens and lights strobing, and his rapid flashing of Suburban's high beams, had traffic moving aside just enough for Juan-Pablo to keep up a steady, if jolting, 60 kph.

Vincente still had the cellphone connection open to the commandant, and after a quick exchange of words, Vincente pivoted to Jorge and reported, "They have six units up on the tracks, and have found a tractor at the construction site nearby to use as well!"

Jorge grinned wickedly. "Excellent! Now we have him! But again, Vincente, make sure they know I want this *hijo de puta*, this cocksucker *alive! Alive! No wild shooting!*"

"I will, yes!" Vincente nodded aggressively and returned to talking on the phone.

"Juan-Pablo, how long?"

Jorge saw the man's face contort into a grimace in the rearview mirror. "*Jefe*, I'm trying," he said as he grunted with exertion, turning the wheel sharply right to avoid an oncoming car, then correcting aggressively, which slammed them all against their seatbelts. Jorge saw his eyes flick to the GPS, then look at him in the rearview. "It will be at least 10, maybe 15 minutes – there's no direct way there—"

"Do your best," Jorge told him flatly. Though it was an unsatisfactory answer, he knew that it wasn't Juan-Pablo's fault. The morning traffic, roads that didn't lead directly to their destination, and distance couldn't be magically changed.

Turning to Alfredo, Jorge demanded, "What of the signal?"

"Still nothing, I'm afraid, *jefe*," Alfredo said apologetically. "The system will ping again in two minutes..."

Jorge grunted and sneered at the computer nerd. *If I didn't need him for managing all the cryptocurrency work, I'd strangle him right now... When he first suggested the tracking system, he boasted it was foolproof...*

The police scanner came alive again. "This is Captain Rodriguez – the truck is in sight! It does not appear to be slowing despite the tractor and trucks on the tracks!"

The commandant's voice came over the circuit a second later. "No gunfire! I repeat, no gunfire! We need to take the driver alive! Make sure you have tasers and beanbag guns ready, all units! Captain Rodriguez, confirm my order!"

"I understand, commandant! It is as you ordered!" Rodriguez replied.

A beat later, and the captain radioed, "It refuses to stop! All units, stand clear!"

Jorge found himself with a death-grip on the Jesus-strap and the arm of his chair, his ears straining to hear the next broadcast on the police circuit.

It finally came. "All units, the suspect's truck has rammed the tractor, derailed, and is on its side, on fire! I've made the call for the fire brigade!"

Mierda! Jorge raged to himself.

134

When Jorge's SUV and the accompanying police units finally got on scene, they were directed onto the property of a concrete production facility.

Driving toward a billowing column of smoke, they found the roadrailer truck engulfed in orange flames with roiling heavy, brown-black smoke swirling around it. It had tumbled down about 10 meters from the elevated railroad track that abutted the concrete facility to land on a pile of gravel. The concrete company's front-end loader was still up on the tracks, but it had clearly been pushed back a few meters because of the impact, noticeable because the ballast alongside the tracks had piled up behind its wheels.

Two police pickup trucks were also up there, parked on the shoulders of the right-of-way about 10 meters ahead of the front-end loader, with their associated policemen looking down at the burning wreck.

As soon as the Suburban came to a halt, Jorge was pushing the door open to exit, gritting his teeth against the pain from his broken ribs. Vincente was out a moment sooner, and together with Juan-Pablo, they took up a defensive position to protect their boss, their eyes scanning for threats.

A police captain rushed up and saluted. "*Señor de Corazón*! I'm Captain—"

"Yes, yes, captain," Jorge interrupted him and gestured angrily toward the burning truck. "Did the man get out?!"

The captain looked deeply apologetic and fearful at the same time. "*Señor*, I'm... well, no, we... we didn't see anyone in the cab—"

Jorge glared at the man. "What are you saying?"

"Sir, there was no one in the cab as it approached—"

"He ducked down because you were shooting at him?" Jorge growled out the question.

"No! No! We all had non-lethal weapons," the captain quickly replied. "No one shot anything! The truck – it never slowed! It just rammed the tractor!"

Jorge's eyes flicked to the burning truck. In the distance, he heard the coaster sirens of fire trucks getting closer.

Turning back to the captain, Jorge barked, "Get those fire trucks here and put this out as fast as you can! I must know whether the man was in there or not!"

"*Sí, señor*, I will!" the captain saluted, and then dashed away, barking orders into his handheld radio.

Vincente drifted back to stand beside his boss, still in bodyguard mode but asking, "Sir, you think he jumped out somewhere? The truck's a diversion?"

Jorge didn't immediately respond, but just stared at the roiling smoke and flames. He pursed his lips, then exhaled heavily. "We'll know in a few minutes."

Vincente considered that, then asked, "Should I divert our men from the tunnel protection detail, and the police that were at the factory, to start a search? Along the rail line?"

Jorge glanced up at him, his eyes narrowing. "If he did get out somewhere, that type of effort will be wasted." Turning back to look at the burning truck, he added, "No... we'll wait to see if he's in the truck and, if not, we'll need to approach this differently..."

Vincente nodded, and after some thought, asked, "You still want him alive, sir?"

Slowly Jorge nodded. "Yes... it's more than just wanting to personally end my would-be assassin's life," he said with a slow, deliberate menace. "I want him to suffer... suffer painfully, so that in the end, he will *beg* me for death... and that boy, he'll be my first instrument of suffering for the assassin... I'll slowly dismember the boy, all the while telling that *puta* that it's *his fault* that the boy must die in such a way..." Jorge then chuckled evilly, stroking his chin. "I might even make that *puta* eat the boy's cock and balls..." He chuckled again. "Yes, so much awaits this man." Turning back to Vincente, he locked gazes with the man and asked, "You understand me?"

Vincente swallowed hard and shivered. "Yes, sir."

"Good," Jorge said softly, the turned and got back into his seat in the Suburban.

Chapter 29

The Car Was Moving

"So... um, what's all that for?"

One glanced up at Kody as he took out the last few items from the toolbox he'd taken from the roadrailer. "I'm going to make a RF detector."

Kody looked puzzled. "RF?"

"Radio frequency," One explained as he picked up the lineman's meter and used a Phillips screwdriver to remove the screws holding the back of the meter to the front part. "I'm almost one-hundred percent certain that there's some sort of RF transmitter in you somewhere."

"In me?" Kody asked incredulously.

"Yeah, that's the only thing that makes sense," One answered. "With the RF detector, I should know for sure." He looked askew at the teen. "Do you remember if anyone injected you with something? Or had a doctor look at you?"

Kody looked disconcerted and his hand holding the half-full water bottle began to shake.

One reached out to put a calming hand on his wrist. "Hey, it's okay if you don't want to think about it, or talk about it..."

Kody looked down at One's hand, took two deep breaths, and shook his head slowly. One felt the trembling stop and removed his hand. "I don't... remember anything like that."

One stopped what he was doing. "I know I said you could ask whatever you wanted... but, um, could you tell me something?"

Kody's big eyes found his, and after he stared into them unblinking for several beats, he looked away and said, "I guess."

"Just so we're clear, if you don't want to talk about it, you don't have to... and you can stop anytime... it's just that, well, I'm curious and it may, somewhere down the line after we're safely outta here, well, it might help keep other kids from having to go through what you did."

One paused, watching Kody for a few seconds, then softly asked, "How did you end up being held? Being here?"

Kody studied the water bottle, slowly rotating it between his hands, his slender fingers following the contoured ridges in the plastic, but he remained silent.

One went back to work, glancing occasionally at the teen.

Just when One thought Kody wasn't going to say anything, the teenager blurted, "I was at a football match with my friends, back in Cape Town."

One paused, looked at him and asked, "South Africa?"

"Yeah," Kody nodded.

"Okay – go on."

Kody sighed. "I went to the toilet to pee, and was washing my hands when a guy came outta a stall and stood next to me to wash his hands... he asked me if I was alone, which... I thought was weird. I finished and went to dry my hands... and felt a sharp stab. I think I shouted, and then the room spun, and the next thing I know I'm in a dark room with wood walls, handcuffed to a bed... and a man... he was... was..."

He began to sniffle them, tears forming and running down his cheeks.

Shit, probably now wasn't the best time to ask about this stuff!

One put down the things he'd been working on and shuffled over to sit up against Kody; the moment he did, the boy hugged him like he was a drowning man, and One was the sole, lifesaving piece of floating flotsam available. "I'm sorry... you don't have to say anything more..."

Kody buried his face against One's shoulder and sobbed so deeply that One felt sympathetic tears forming in his own eyes.

Eventually Kody wound down, and after a few more sporadic sniffles, he sighed and relaxed his hug, just leaning against One, as if savoring the security the contact offered.

"You okay now?" One asked softly. When Kody didn't immediately answer, he added, "I didn't mean to... bring up bad stuff for you."

Kody sighed, a long, drawn-out exhale. "I... it's..." He sighed again. "I'm just all... mixed up."

"Understandable," One replied and gave him a short squeeze. "We can talk about it later – I mean, our immediate predicament is more pressing. I should be focusing on that, not asking questions."

Kody shifted away and gave him a wan grin. "It's... okay."

One went back to working with the stuff he'd taken from the truck. "So, I did say you could ask me anything..."

Kody considered that in silence for a long moment, then said, "Did you come for me?"

That froze One mid-move. "Um... no, sorry..."

"Oh..."

One gave him a smile as he resumed his work. "I think it's obvious we were there for—"

"Killing that man... the one who..." Kody looked down and sniffled.

"Something like that, yeah," One admitted soberly. "Does that... bother you?"

Kody thought about it with pursed lips. "Not really," he finally said. "I mean... some of the other kids... they said that man... well, sometimes he'd take kids and... they'd never come back."

One looked up from his work. "Did they say why?" One asked but was sure he knew the answer.

"No, the kids didn't know... but we... we guessed..."

"Right," One said.

"They kept us drugged most of the time," Kody went on. "A couple of the kids tried, you know, to fight it... but they'd get punched and drugged up anyway."

One didn't know what to say to that, so he just grunted and shook his head.

"Mmm," Kody agreed noncommittally. He inhaled and exhaled in one quick motion, then changed the subject. "So... are you with the army?"

"Umm..." One said as he started tightly rolling some 20-guage wire around a steel bolt. "I can't tell you everything – it's just not something I'm allowed to do, nothing against you – but, I can say I've had military training."

139

Kody brightened a bit at that. "I thought so... you just seem a lot like in the movies."

"Oh?"

"Yeah, with the guns, body armor all black, and, well... you never, like, lost your cool. I kinda remember the hotel, but I think the drugs were still messing with me... but I remember you carrying me over that bridge thing that one of your guys blew up."

One chuckled, recalling that he'd been too pumped up to be frightened by it all – had he not, he'd never have attempted that crossing. "That's not something we normally do."

"And you were so... um, intense, when everyone was shooting at us... but you still were, like, all focused."

"That's me, yup," One nodded.

Kody pondered that. "So... what are we going to do now?"

"First, we find that transmitter in you and remove it," One said matter-of-factly. "Then, well, we need to get some new transportation because I sent our truck off on a diversion. By now they've probably discovered we're not in it... and will be wondering where we got off. It's about 10 miles to the border from here, so it's a big area to search. I'm betting they won't look here in the rail yard because it's all open space – they would see us running across the tracks from the helicopter that went over earlier if we had."

One worked the tightly coiled wire off the bolt and stripped the insulation from the straight pieces on each end of it. He was just about to say something, when suddenly the boxcar jolted, making both lose their balance and topple over.

"What the?!" One muttered.

It jolted again, a little less aggressively this time and then everything was quiet.

One put the items in hand on the boxcar's floor and went to the open door, peeking out. He didn't see anything, but as he turned away from the door, he heard a hissing noise. Pausing, he tried to locate it but couldn't.

"What's that?" Kody asked, looking slightly alarmed as he stood and looked around for the source of the noise.

Another jolt then had them staggering for balance, and then the car was moving—

South, away from the border.

"Shit!" One growled, spinning around and going to the crack in the door. He saw that the freight cars across the way were slowly passing by. Turning back to Kody, he said the obvious. "We're moving."

Kody took a few steps closer, as if he was going to look out the door himself, but then stopped. "That's good, right? Make it harder to find us?"

"That's true," One agreed. He went to the door and slid it all the way closed. "But we're heading away from the border... not exactly what I would have done..."

Or would I?

Moving away from our goal might be the last thing they'd expect... and thus, maybe actually a good idea...

Hmmm...

Well, it's out of our control for the moment. Until we get Kody's transmitter neutralized, we can't move anywhere anyway...

"It'll be okay," One said reassuringly, to address his own concerns as well as Kody's. "You're right – it's probably a good thing."

"For real?"

"Yeah, I think so," One said as he returned to his work. "Go ahead and have a seat. First things first – we'll get the transmitter problem taken care of and then we'll start thinking on what to do next."

The train continued moving, rocking slightly and *clicky-clacking* over the segmented rail. One guessed they were moving at about 50 kph, which meant that every six minutes they were five kilometers farther from those pursuing them.

"Any more questions?" One asked. "We've apparently got the time."

"We going to the US?"

"That's the goal, yeah," One replied.

Kody absorbed that in silence for a few beats before asking, "What's gonna happen to me?"

One paused, looking at him. "I'm gonna make sure you get home," he said with intense surety.

Kody blinked at him rapidly, and One saw tears form again in his eyes. "Really?" Kody asked weakly.

"Absolutely," One replied firmly, and it didn't take a psychologist to see that Kody needed comforting. "Come here," One said softly, opening his arms and Kody came to him, collapsing against him and sobbing on his shoulder.

One had the oddest thought then:

Parenting by the seat of your pants...

"You're one brave kid," One said softly, not sure what else to say to comfort Kody further.

After a short stretch of silence, Kody asked, "Um... you never told me your name."

One grinned slightly. "You can call me 'One'."

He mulled that over, his brow furrowing. "One?" Kody whispered against his shoulder once his sobbing had wound down.

"Hmm?"

"You won't... let them... take me again, right?"

One held him a bit tighter. "Of course not – not gonna happen."

"Okay..." For a long while Kody was quiet, the only sign of life was his breathing which One could feel through their embrace. Eventually, hesitantly, Kody asked, "You think... will my mom and dad... will they even... want me back?"

That struck One was an odd thing to say. "Of course! Of course they'll be happy to have you back!"

Kody sniffled. "Even... after so long... after what... what I've done?"

One gently pushed Kody away so he could look meet his gaze. "I don't understand – what you've done?"

Kody was unable to meet his eyes. "The... stuff I've done... you know, letting them... drug me... have, y'know... sex with me... make me do things with... the other boys..."

Oh Jesus...

One took a deep breath and exhaled it sharply. "Kody, let me ask you this – did you want what happened to you to happen?"

He slowly shook his head, tears falling from his cheeks to splash on One's hands.

"So, you haven't *done* anything," One continued gently. "You were in a bad situation. Could you control what happened? Did you have a gun or were you stronger than they were?"

Again, a slow shaking of his head.

You're no shrink, but you've been through enough after-action counseling to know how to help here...

So help!

"Kody, if you couldn't control it, and didn't want it... why do you say, 'what you've done'?" One took him back into a hug, and just held him for a long moment, feeling Kody softly crying. "Kody, you've done nothing wrong – you're a *victim* here, not a bad person... and even though you're probably thinking you are, or maybe that you're somehow dirty because of what you were forced to do, or maybe you're convinced that it's your fault this all happened to you... well, I'm telling you that it's a lie... it's completely false." One let that sink in before he added, "I think you're a really brave kid, who has survived a lot of bad shit, but you did what you had to do – it's all you *could* do, to simply go along with it all because you didn't have the power to stop or change it... do you hear what I'm saying?"

Kody sniffled a few times, then nodded.

"Good," One said and ruffled his hair as he pushed them apart. "So you've probably got a lot going on in your mind about this all right now but do your best to just set it aside. We've got more immediate problems, and I need you to help me get through them. Think you can do that?"

Kody finally met his gaze and offered a bit of a smile. "I... yeah, I can."

"Great... but listen. If you feel bad, or have thoughts like what's happened is your fault, you can talk to me about it, okay? Sometimes voicing the bad or worrying stuff we're thinking about, or what we're feeling, is a good way to just... get it out of our system. Put it out there, in the light of day, and see that it really doesn't have any power over us. Will you promise me that you'll do that, talk to me and let me know what's wrong if you ever feel it's just overwhelming, or you feel really sad?"

Kody's smile got a little bigger, and he nodded.

"Perfect... okay then, now first things first... let's find that transmitter."

143

Chapter 30

Send A Clear Message

There was no charred body in the roadrailer as expected.

Jorge stood looking at the blackened remains of the truck as the firemen pried the cab door open to show only an empty, fire-gutted interior.

Turning away and slowly walking back toward the Suburban, Vincente following on his right at a respectful pace behind, Jorge said, "He thinks himself clever, does he? Dropping out somewhere between the rail yard and here..."

"He could be anywhere now," Vincente noted.

"Yes... true," Jorge agreed. "But at least we know it's somewhere between here and the railyard, based on what the helicopter and police reported, yes?"

"*Sí, jefe.*"

Jorge climbed into his seat in the rear of the SUV and turned to Alfredo. "Who do we currently have with us?"

Alfredo looked at his laptop's screen nervously. "The security force from the tunnel, 30 men, plus the squad of marines, and whatever resources you want to pull from the commandant."

Jorge nodded thoughtfully. Leaning forward to catch Vincente's eye as his lieutenant returned to his place in the front passenger seat, Jorge said, "I think I'm done with the commandant for now – he's more trouble than he's worth. Order the tunnel security force to the north end of the rail yard. They're to form a blocking line there, letting no one past without scrutiny. We'll have the squad of marines start from here and work their way back to the railyard, canvassing the immediate area to either side of the tracks.

Get a picture of the boy to their phones but emphasize that the man and the boy may not be traveling together, so don't have any preconceived ideas when they stop people or search places."

"Yes, sir," Vincente acknowledged. "What about the man? No one's seen his face and we have no photos of him."

"What do we have from the police and our men?"

Vincente consulted his tablet. "He's tall, about 180 to 190 cm, around 85 kg, muscular and Caucasian. That's from the observations at the hotel – before that, he appeared Latino, from the surveillance footage at the estate."

"A disguise..." Jorge thought aloud. "Not much to go on, 185 cm, muscular and white. Hopefully he's doing what we expect of an American, making sure to keep the boy with him, to protect him. That will be his downfall."

"Do we know he's American for certain, *jefe*?"

Jorge pursed his lips as he considered that. "It's a best guess," Jorge admitted. "I suppose he and his men could be a hired team of mercenaries, South African, Belarusian, Ukrainian or the like... sent by one of the other cartels... a desperate bid to remove us from the apex," Jorge chuckled at the absurdity of that comment. "But no... it just feels like something the Americans would do. We've successfully brought billions of dollars of fentanyl, cocaine and heroin into their country, not to mention all the boys and girls we've supplied to their decadent elite... this would be just the way their new, tough-on-crime president would want things handled – 'cut off the head of the snake' so he can 'send a clear message'."

"In any case, we'll have all the answers when we capture this man." Jorge glanced at Alfredo. "Any word on the rest of his squad?"

"No, *jefe*, I'm sorry," Alfredo said with a quaver in his voice. "They... well, after the police helicopter lost them at the mall... we've had no more word."

"They've already made it over the border?" Vincente asked.

"Most likely," Jorge agreed, his mouth twisting as if he'd tasted something bitter. "So, we must find this man and quickly. There's much I want to ask of and do to him... so, the marines will start here and work their way back along the tracks. They are to question everyone living alongside – homes, businesses, schools, whatever – because I am certain that somebody, somewhere saw something and once we get that information, we will act. Understood?"

"Yes!" Alfredo and Vincente chimed.

"Then it will be my turn 'to send a clear message' back to that *puta* American president!" Jorge chortled.

Turning back to the computer nerd, Jorge told him, "You will build a grid search using maps and satellite views. I want you to keep track of all areas we investigate, and to suggest places based on your maps as needed."

"Yes, *jefe*!"

When Alfredo didn't move, but just sat there, looking much like a shivering chihuahua, Jorge slapped him – not hard enough to leave a mark, but enough to bring the man from out of his reverie and back to the matter at hand. "Get started!" Jorge ordered, and finally Alfredo moved to start working on his laptop.

Turning to address Juan-Pablo, Jorge demanded, "Where's a restaurant or coffee shop near here? I need something to eat! Find one and we'll set up our headquarters there!"

Chapter 31

Whatever Opportunity Presents Itself

"That's gonna find the transmitter?"

One looked up from what he was doing to see a very skeptical look on Kody's face. Ever since the teen had confessed his worries and One had reassured him, he'd become more vocal and animated.

"It's a simple thing, actually," One replied. "And it's done."

He held out the makeshift device for Kody to see. The coil of copper wire he'd rolled over the steel bolt was at the top, attached to the innards of the lineman's meter.

"So what now?" Kody asked.

"Stand up, legs apart, arms out straight," One said and got up with him. One re-inserted the batteries into the space on the meter for them and saw the LED readout light up, the readout bouncing around lethargically between 000.6 and 003.1 as he stood there. "Here goes..."

Slowly, starting at Kody's ankles, he held the copper coil about an inch from his leg as he moved his hand up along the outer side of his left thigh, then down around the inner thigh back to the ankle, and repeated this for Kody's right leg. While the meter's readout bounced around, One didn't see a noticeable tick up in the reading.

He repeated the process along the backside of the teen's thighs, then around his abdomen, crotch and buttocks. Finding nothing still, he went to the arms, and then started in on Kody's upper chest and upper back, coming over the left shoulder—

The meter jumped to 289.4 as he passed over the fleshy area just in front of the shoulder.

"Can you take off your shirt?" One asked.

Kody complied, and One started scanning the area at a crawling pace, zeroing in on a small section of skin just below the collarbone on his left.

One set the meter down on the Pelican case and took up his flashlight. Shining its beam on an oblique angle, he got his eye to within a few inches and carefully examined the teen's skin.

"There's a thin line here, barely visible," One said as he moved slightly back and forth, eyeballing the area. "A slight scar." He stepped back and clicked the flashlight off. "You injure yourself there?"

Kody frowned, thinking. "Not that I remember."

One nodded. "Well, we'll see. Have a seat – leave your shirt off."

Kody complied. One retrieved the first aid kit, got out his knife and lighter, and sat next to him, so Kody's left shoulder was angled toward where he sat. "I'm sorry, but this is gonna hurt a little," he said. "There's no lidocaine or cold spray in the kit. I'm gonna cut the skin to get it out..."

"Just do it quick," Kody said and clamped his eyes shut, his lips forming a tight line in anticipation of the pain.

"I'll try," One agreed. He used the lighter's flame to sterilize the knife, then dampened a gauze pad with some of the remaining disinfectant and cleaned the area on Kody's shoulder where he intended to cut. Taking hold of the teen's shoulder near the neck with his left hand to keep him from jerking when the cutting began, One repositioned himself closer and took a moment to plan on how to make the incision, and then used the knife's tip to slice a thin line.

Blood welled immediately and Kody's body became a tense ball of tightness as he hissed out a strained breath.

"Almost done," One told him as he went back to the start of the cut and pushed the blade's tip in a bit deeper, re-tracing over the incision to make it slightly deeper.

Kody began panting through clenched teeth against the pain.

"You're doing really good... being really brave," One assured as he worked, trying to be as careful and quick as he could.

One hadn't found anything yet, so had no choice but to cut even deeper. The adage, "third time pays for all" became applicably true on that third try; One encountered noticeable resistance and heard a slight *click* noise. Turning the blade, he wiggled the tip, feeling it slide under something, and with a flick, popped a small cylinder from the open wound. It was about 25mm long and 5mm in diameter, being clear plastic with noticeable, tiny electronics inside.

"It's out!" One announced and quickly placed the gauze pad with disinfectant over the slit, applying pressure to staunch the bleeding.

Kody let out another hiss, but then his breathing pace returned to normal, and One felt his tense muscles relax under his touch.

"Not too bad?" One asked.

Kody exhaled. "I guess..."

One squirted some of the disinfectant into the slit, pressed a fresh gauze pad over it, and held it there. "There's no sutures in the kit, but it's got some butterfly bandages – that should do to keep the wound closed until it can heal."

Kody twisted to eyeball the wound as One removed the bloody gauze pad and used the last fresh one from the kit to dab at it. Once it was clean and barely oozing blood, he pinched the small slit together – making Kody hiss again – and quickly applied two of the butterfly bandages. Once he'd done that the bleeding stopped, and the incision he'd made didn't look all that bad.

"Just try not to move around too much or too fast for the rest of the day," One advised.

"I hope we won't have to."

One noted how he'd said "we" and not "I".

Retrieving the small cylinder, One washed the blood from it with a bit of water from one of the bottles he'd packed. Holding it up under the flashlight's beam, he saw a clear plastic cylinder with silver metal tips. While no authority on eavesdropping or monitoring devices, he could see a thin line of circuit inside, and suspected how it worked, having used similar devices in the past on terrorists turned into not-very-trustworthy informants.

"Probably has a thermocouple, to keep itself charged with from your body heat," One said, turning the small device from side to side between finger and thumb. "And with one of the silver ends touching your collarbone, it used your skeleton as an antenna... calcium in the bones is pretty good at doing that."

Kody inched closer, his cheek almost against One's as he examined it with curious eyes. "It's so little."

"Doesn't need to be more," One remarked, looking sideways at him. "Probably uses a commercial security service's satellite monitoring system to track it. If that's the case, those companies usually only have a few satellites in orbit because of the expense, so they can only look for a signal periodically... anywhere from a half hour to a few hours, while the satellite is zooming overhead and is within range. Once it's over the horizon, it can't detect the signal."

"You said metal blocks the signal?"

"Yeah, and we're in a big metal boxcar, so I think we're good for now," One said.

One pocketed the small device and rinsed his hands with some of the bottled water, then kicked the soiled medical supplies against the wall to join the other stuff from his bullet wound treatment.

The boxcar continued to rock and bump as the train made steady progress along the rails. Every now and then they could hear the muffled moan of its horn as it sounded a warning at grade crossings.

"Let's take a peek, shall we?" One asked and moved to the boxcar's door. Pushing hard, he managed to grind it open a few inches, and saw buildings passing by, their walls mere meters from the open door. "We're still in the city."

Kody leaned around to look out. "Not going too fast."

"Around 50 kilometers per hour," One agreed. "Once they get out of the city, I would think they will go faster."

"So what now?" Kody asked, stepping up and leaning against One.

"Good question. Let's see what we have..."

One retrieved his sat phone and activated it, pointing its thick antenna out the slit in the door. Once it connected with the network, he brought up Google Maps. He found the fabrication factory, then scrolled north to find the rail yard, then scrolled south, seeing where the railroad tracks would take them.

"Looks like it angles south by southwest after leaving the city... paralleling State Route 45." One sighed. "That's taking us farther away from the border."

They felt the train rock and heard the squeal of the steel wheels torquing against the rail. A moment later, they heard the sound from the wheels of the freight cars close ahead change to a *clack-clackity-clack-clack*, and then felt their car move to the left. Looking outside, they saw that there was a parallel, second track, and then a third came into sight as their train crossed over to the left-most track of the three. Shortly after that, they heard the hiss of air brakes and felt their train deaccelerating.

A couple of short horn blasts echoed in the distance, then two more, and their train came to a stop. The growling of diesels sounded faintly from their left, getting louder with each passing moment. One took a risk to lean out just enough so, with one eye, he could look down the tracks.

"It's a northbound train," he said, coming back into the boxcar.

An idea blossomed in his mind.

Quickly, one went to the toolbox. He pulled out three screwdrivers, and using the first aid kit's surgical tape, bound the three screwdrivers together to form a caltrop-like shape. He then taped the transmitter he'd cut from Kody's shoulder to the center of the contraption and went to the door.

"What's that for?" Kody asked, watching him the whole time.

"More diversion," one answered, "to let us put even more space between us and them."

Back at the narrow opening in the door, One waited, watching. When the first red and black Ferromex locomotive ground into sight, One put his left shoulder against the backside of the boxcar's door, with his right hand and arm in alignment with the opening.

Now it was a waiting game. First to pass were two locomotives, followed by several boxcars, then a long line of automotive racks. One began to worry that what he was waiting for wouldn't be part of the train, but as the last of the cars came into view, he saw what he had been hoping to find – a line of open, empty gondolas, from the same company he'd passed during his roadrailer run in the industrial spur track.

With an underhand throw, One tossed his caltrop with the transmitter into the third open gondola, seeing it disappear over the side.

"Now, whenever it transmits again, they'll see us still in the city, at least for a while," One said as he closed the boxcar's door.

"For how long?" Kody asked.

"If we're lucky, for at least a couple hours... the key factor is that the transmitter is out of you, so you can move around without having to be incased in metal."

One studied the Google Maps of the area to the south of the city that was displayed on his phone.

If we could get off at the recreation area near Salamayuca... looks like it's a popular tourist area.... We could rent a car maybe, and drive farther south, out of Presagio controlled country... hole up in Chihuahua until I can get ID for Kody, then fly out...

No, not Chihuahua... Presagio still has significant presence there, even if the Vamos Chicos cartel claims it as home turf... farther south then?

Not ideal, though it's kinda a Catch-22: the farther we go from Presagio controlled areas the better, but it also means farther from safety in the US...

Instead if we get off near Salamayuca, maybe take State Route 16 east and plan on crossing the border at Ojinaga. We'll find a hotel, I'll check in alone and get Kody into the room quietly, wait for Garrett to do his thing, and then just blend in with the other day tourists crossing over into the US. It's still technically Presagio controlled, but with their focus on Juarez, it should be safe enough...

It all depends on this train... if it stops along the way to do switching service for business and factories, we can get off... but if it's running straight through... we'll have to wait.

So, it's a matter of keeping our options open and looking for opportunities...

Story of my life.

After closing the boxcar's door, One re-lit his flashlight and set it on the floor to provide some ambient light as he sat down, exhausted and his leg throbbing. He reached for the bottle of water that was still half full after washing his hands and downed its contents in four quick gulps, then tossed the empty aside.

"Still hungry?" He asked Kody as he fished out a couple of snack packs and power bars for himself.

"Yeah."

One handed him what he'd chosen and took out more for himself. "Might as well eat and get comfortable. It'll get hot in here soon when the sun comes up, and we can't afford to leave the door open in case someone sees... but if all goes well, we'll be off this train in about an hour."

Kody's eyebrows rose. "If not?"

"Then we'll just have to take whatever opportunity presents itself."

Chapter 32

More Eyes See Clearly

"*Jefe! Jefe!* I have a signal!"

Jorge swiveled in his chair to look at the laptop's screen.

"Its position is near the railroad tracks at *Del Ebanista Madereros* and *Pino Verde Beta*," Alfredo pointed to the screen and used his mouse to zoom in. A red pushpin marker was throbbing, indicating the position of the transmitter when the signal had finally pinged the satellite.

"What's near there?"

Alfredo clicked the mouse several more times. "A few office buildings... the *Juzgado Quinto Civil* is a block away, but otherwise nothing remarkable..."

"Lots of buildings, though?" Jorge asked.

"Yes, many... and parking lots."

Jorge considered that for a moment. "They'll be looking for transportation! To steal a car, get on a bus, something!" He spun to Vincente. "Let's go!"

"Just us, *jefe*?" Vincente asked worriedly.

"It'll take 30 minutes or more to regroup with all the men. Have a couple of the tunnel security team break off and join us as quickly as they can!"

Juan-Pablo had the GPS programmed with their new destination when Jorge, Vincente and Alfredo got in the SUV. In the past 20 minutes, while the search was underway, at Jorge's request the commandant had supplied Juan-Pablo with a magnetic mount, mini-light bar and siren unit that attached to the roof of the SUV, and a red and blue flasher unit that slid over the passenger-side sun visor. With these in place, the siren wailing and the strobes flashing, the SUV made much better time through the traffic than they had earlier when they'd tried to intercept the roadrailer.

"Just be sure to shut off the siren when we're half a kilometer away," Jorge reminded. "We don't want to spook our quarry!"

"Yes, *jefe!*" Juan-Pablo replied.

Even with the lights and siren, it took them 15 minutes to travel the six kilometers to the area from which the transmitter had pinged. As they pulled onto *Del Ebanista Madereros* and slowed, scanning for any hint of a man and boy, or either traveling alone. Vincente got a call then and informed those in the SUV that eight of the tunnel security team were just behind them, ETA five minutes.

When they reached the T-intersection with *Del Ebanista Madereros* and *Pino Verde Beta*, Juan-Pablo pulled the Suburban to the curb and looked back at Jorge. "*Jefe*, which way?"

Jorge looked left and right, pondering that question. "Pull over there, to the other side of the street on that gravel, pointing back up *Del Ebanista Madereros*," he told him. "We'll be the anchor. Vincente, have the tunnel security men stop at the other end of *Del Ebanista Madereros* and work their way toward us on foot."

"Understood," Vincente said, and gave the order over the open phone line. Turning back to his boss, he asked, "Sir, it's been over 15 minutes – wouldn't they be long gone by now?"

Jorge nodded thoughtfully. "It's quite possible – likely even. But we got a ping on the boy's transmitter. Perhaps I gave him too much credit... for not realizing that the transmitter existed. Since it can only be pinged every 30 minutes, they've just been lucky in being in the right places and the right times."

"Perhaps," Vincente acknowledged uncertainly.

"You think otherwise?" Jorge asked with a raised eyebrow.

"I hesitate—"

"Vincente, you've been in my service for how long?"

Vincente swallowed then said, "Eight years, *jefe*."

"And with Tomas gone, and so many others in the cowardly attack against me, I made you my right hand, yes?"

"*Sí, jefe.*"

"So, please, do not coddle me; I don't need anymore 'yes men' than I already have. Just tell me what you think; as my second in command I must trust you to speak plainly, to help me see things objectively – even if I don't like it and even if I may, well, yell and curse about it."

That made Vincente grin despite himself. "Very well then... I must say that this man, and those that were with him, and all very professional, very... courageous, despite how they attacked you, *jefe*."

"Go on," Jorge said neutrally.

"They have been several steps ahead of us this entire time," Vincente noted. "I think it is safe to say that this man, the assassin you seek, he's found the transmitter, removed it, and sent it somewhere as a diversion."

Jorge considered that for a long, silent moment. In truth, it had been exactly what he'd been worried about, but had convinced himself that the likelihood of the assassin thinking that the boy had a tracker imbedded in him was remote at best.

Perhaps I need to reconsider that possibility as more probable than not...

"If so, what is next?" Jorge asked finally.

Vincente waved toward the outside of the SUV. "We are wasting time here. He's long gone, or gone to ground somewhere secure, and it will take more manpower than we have available to root him out."

Jorge frowned. "So I do nothing? Let this *puta* go? Get away with almost killing me? For killing our brothers?" Jorge growled.

"No... no *jefe*, of course not," Vincente said quickly. "But we need to stop focusing on doing this ourselves. Instead, we need to get the word out to every policeman, every government official, and all our men in the network, from the lowliest corner lookout to the most important capo, to watch for this man and boy. '*Más ojos ven claramente*' – more eyes see clearly."

If I do that, then everyone will know that I was attacked at my home, my stronghold, my brand-new community for the elite... that's a lot of lost standing... loss of control. Can I afford it? Can I accept it?

It will make me look weak for certain... and give my competition ideas...

"I cannot," Jorge said firmly. "It will make me look weak—"

"If I may, *jefe*?" Vincente interrupted.

Jorge huffed, but then waved for him to say what he wanted to say.

"There's no need to say anything about the attack," Vincente said. "We didn't tell the commandant about it, only that you wanted this man and boy captured. I went so far as to imply that they'd stolen from you, American smugglers who had betrayed your trust – not one word was mentioned about an assassination attempt."

Jorge glared at him for several beats before slowly nodding. "So the word we put out is this man betrayed me, and thus he and his boy are wanted... to be captured and returned to me for questioning and vengeance?"

"Exactly, *jefe*."

"I like this," Jorge said with a wicked smile. "Not only does it get the job done, but if anyone has been thinking about betraying me, now they will see the extent to which I will go to take my revenge! It's brilliant – kills two birds with a single stone." Jorge smiled and nodded. "Yes, let us proceed on this Vincente. Make the calls." Turning to Juan-Pablo, he said, "Back to the mansion, Juan-Pablo."

"Right away," the driver replied, and put the armored SUV into gear, turning back onto *Del Ebanista Madereros*.

"And Vincente, send the men that came down here back up to help with the search along the tracks. I don't want to assume anything; I will not make that mistake again! The assassin and the boy may still be hiding out in that area, and if so, someone was certain to have seen them at some point."

"Certainly, *jefe*; it shall be as you order."

"Good... so now we wait. In the meantime, once we're back at the estate, I need to survey the damage and see what must be done to rebuild and strengthen our defenses," Jorge said.

He looked wistfully off into space, his eyes becoming unfocused as he added, "I need to erase any sign of the attack, so if anyone does question that it happened, we can demonstrate that it didn't." Jorge gritted his teeth, his eyes re-focusing now directly meeting Vincente's gaze. "And now we need to find out just how much of a setback there is with the cryptocurrency servers. Yes, there is much to do..."

Chapter 33

One Step Ahead

The train picked up speed.

So much for planning to get off the train anytime soon.

A quick peek out the door showed that the freight train was making a steady 60 or 70 kph over track that must have been welded, not jointed: there were seldom any *clickity-clack* sounds, such as those they'd heard constantly before when the train was passing through the city.

It was also quickly becoming hot in the boxcar. Uncomfortably hot, which wasn't surprising since the boxcar was of all steel construction, and they couldn't leave the door open even a bit, lest someone detect the fact that the boxcar's door had been breached. This, coupled with the steady humming of the train as it traveled, his leg wound, his body having been stressed to the limit because of their daring escape and firefight first thing that morning, their mad dash through the park, and the energy he'd exerted for the roadrailer escape, all conspired to make One's eyes droop.

Kody was spent as well. The stress of the trauma he'd already suffered, compounded by that of their escape, and the drugs still lingering in his system made the teen sleepy. Without a word Kody used his backpack as a pillow and curled up alongside One, nuzzling up against him and falling immediately into deep slumber.

Resolved to stay on watch, even if the likelihood of someone coming through the boxcar's door while the train was at speed was nil, One managed to do so only for a few minutes before he too fell asleep.

One dreamt that he lay on his back atop a salt-encrusted raft that bobbed lazily in a shallow lagoon of a sunny, tropical island. The heat and humidity had him perspiring, but this discomfort was offset by the fact that Garrett was there with him, his bony, freckled, seldom-gets-out-from-behind-his-laptop body reddened despite the layer of SPF 75 he'd applied. Garrett was nuzzled against him, his head resting in the crook of One's arm, his left leg thrown over both of One's, and his hand snaking down and into One's boardshorts...

Something was wrong.

One woke with a start, but unlike how he normally came out of sleep – alert and ready for action – he felt sluggish and disoriented. Thus it took him a few seconds to realize what had awakened him—

Kody had his head in the crook of his arm, his left leg bent at the knee, so it draped over One's thighs, and Kody was slowly pushing his hand into One's boxer briefs.

"Hey!" One exclaimed, reactively jerking aside and taking Kody's hand by the wrist, yanking it away from any further progress. "What are you doing?!"

Kody came off his shoulder, pushing himself up on one arm and looked genuinely confused. Blinking rapidly, Kody's eyes went to One's big hand around his wrist, then to One's open pants, then back to One's gaze.

"I... I wanted you to... to feel good," Kody said, almost whining. "You... you saved me... been so nice to me... and I wanted to thank you..."

One was dumbfounded. "Thank me?" One mumbled, both confused and astonished.

"Yeah," Kody said, squirming back to nuzzle against One's side, smiling. "I mean, I'm really good at it – all the men tell me I am... and they all tell me I'm pretty, and like it when I suck on them—"

"You mean the men that have sex with you?" One clarified sternly. "That kidnapped you and drugged you?"

That made Kody pause, his face scrunching up into deeper confusion. "I... I just... wanted you to feel good... to... to really like me..."

How fucked up is this? They've brainwashed and traumatized him to a point where the only way he can express thanks, or care for someone is to sexually pleasure that person? Or to offer his body up?

Despite the lethargy that One felt, he gently pushed away from Kody and sat up, still holding Kody's wrist. For a long moment he stared at the teen, trying to push through the haziness that seemed to have veiled his brain.

Eventually cogent thought became possible.

As gently as he could, he took Kody's hands in his and looked him in the eye. "Kody, you don't have to ever thank me, or anyone, with sex, or do something sexual to make them like you or help you." One paused, not just to let that hopefully sink in for the teen, but because he was at a loss as to what more to say.

"You don't think I'm pretty?" Kody asked in a small voice as he seemed to fold in on himself, tears welling at the corners of his eyes.

"That's not what I'm saying," One said, and it took an effort not to punctuate this with an exasperated sigh. "Listen – you've been through some horrible crap, and I won't even start to guess just how bad it's been for you... what you've had to do to survive... or what they've forced you to do with drugs, abuse and whatnot... What I'm saying now is – and I want you to hear me clearly, okay? – I'm saying that you're your own person. You don't ever, *ever* have to do anything you don't want to do from here on out. You're a person, not a possession! And I hope you'll trust me when I say that I'm going to do everything I can to get you back home to your parents. Do you understand?"

Kody stared at him for the longest time, silent tears streaking his cheeks, his green eyes wide like glimmering pools. Finally, in a tiny voice that was something One would have expected from a 4-year-old, not a 14-year-old teenager, Kody said, "I... understand... but I really... really like you."

Jesus, Mary and Joseph!

The cloudiness in his head wasn't making this any easier for One, so it took him time before he could form a response. "Kody, I'm really flattered... really, I am. And yes, you're a good-looking kid, despite what's happened to you, so don't think that you aren't – but what you are is a victim. Are you following me so far?"

Kody nodded slowly, hesitantly, his eyes never leaving One's.

"There's a natural tendency for people – especially young adults and kids – to develop feelings for their rescuer, or someone they look up to. It happens a lot in hospitals... patients fall in love with their nurse or doctor, because they misinterpret the care that the doctor or nurse gives for something deeper... but it's a false love, a one-sided love... the nurse or doctor doesn't feel the same way. This also happens in situations like... like between you and me... you were in trouble, kidnapped, abused, held against your will and forced to do things, and then me and my squad came along and freed you from it. Since then, it's been just you and me – and I've had to put my trust in you just as you have had to put it into me, for us to escape and keep one step ahead of the cartel."

One suddenly felt woozy; he put a hand to the floor to steady himself, then wiped at his brow and eyes, which felt hot – hotter than even the temperature in the boxcar.

Oh shit... a fever. That means infection... but so soon? Normally it takes 12 to 24 hours... well, you are in Mexico, and haven't had a shower since before the assassination... who knows what I picked up on my hands or clothes?

Hmm, I guess I didn't clean out the bullet wound as well as I thought. Fuck!

Okay, one thing at a time... finish with Kody...

"So, it's natural that you would find a me to be your savior, and be attracted to everything that this represents," One continued. He squeezed Kody's hands in his, a gesture of sincerity, then added, "You just think you like me – it's just feeling because of the 'savior complex', nothing real."

Tears reformed on Kody's cheeks. "So... you don't like me?"

I'm not getting through...

"I like you just fine," One assured. "And again, yes, you're a very attractive boy... but I see you as a friend and as someone I need to protect, not anything more than that... can you understand?"

The expressions that crossed Kody's face in the next moment were hard for One to read. But when Kody forced his hands free from between One's and scooted away from him to increase the distance between them, One realized his attempt to let the teen down gently through clear, honest communication hadn't worked. Instead, Kody was taking his explanation as a personal affront. With quick, angry motions, Kody knuckled away his tears, snatched his backpack, and lay back down, turning his back to One and curling up into a fetal ball.

Great... the cold shoulder times ten...

Well, I was honest and clear at least... I tried my best to be understanding and compassionate... obviously I need to work on this some more...

One glanced at his watch; he'd been asleep for almost three hours, and the train was still moving.

Well, at least we're putting distance between the cartel and us. The question is, when will this train stop, and where will it leave us?

With a sigh of frustration, One let the situation between Kody and him, and the unknown aspect of the train's destination, go for the moment, turning instead to examine his wound.

One pulled up the leg of his shorts and looked at his bandage covering his upper thigh. There was no sign of blood, so the pressure bandage was doing its job. However, when he unbandaged the wound and withdrew the gauze he'd stuffed into the hole, blood started to ooze anew and there was noticeable tenderness and reddening around the site, more so from simple bullet damage – indicative of the beginnings of an infection.

Not good... and no antibiotics, or any likelihood of getting some anytime soon...

The first aid kit had only an assortment of Band-aids left and the ounce or so left in the disinfectant bottle.

Not ideal by any means...

One grabbed another bottle of water from their limited supply of water and used half its contents to re-wash the wound. He then took a new t-shirt, one of the items he'd purchased at the clothing store and tore it into strips with the aid of his knife. He cut one of these strips into shorter rectangles, rolled one into a cone, dampened it with disinfectant, and stuffed it into the wound as he'd done before. The pain this time wasn't as bad, but it remained afterward as a dull, persistent, annoying throb.

Wish I'd thought to buy some Advil... or something stronger...

Using strips from the t-shirt and more surgical tape, One put a fresh cover over the wound site.

Kody studiously ignored him the entire time. One glanced at him, and saw his ribs slowly expanding and contracting, indicative of sleep.

Sorry, Kody... I've just not had a lot of experience dealing with kids... I thought honesty would be the best way to approach you...

Damn... poor kid. They've fucked him up pretty good, so that he equates providing sex with being needed or wanted... I hope once he does get back home, he can get some professional help and overcome it all.

One drank the remainder of the water from the bottle he'd opened and tossed the bottle away to join the other empties. He leaned back against the Pelican case and closed his eyes, knowing that the only medicine he had for his wound was conservation of his energy and rest.

He was soon asleep.

Chapter 34

What Would You Do?

"*Jefe*, it's Samuel – they've found the transmitter."

Jorge was sitting in a chaise lounge, shaded under a white, 15x15 foot pop-up tent that had been set up alongside the driveway by the ruins of the two guard stations, a cold, half-full bottle of *Dos Equis* in hand.

"Where?" he asked without turning from gazing at the crew currently using a front-end loader to dump the charred remains of the armored Suburbans into a waiting semi-trailer dump truck. The twisted, burned-out metal would be taken to one of the scrap yards the cartel owned and disposed of as if they'd never existed.

"In a gondola car of a northbound freight train," Vincente answered. "It stopped in the rail yard and stayed there for two consecutive pings."

Jorge nodded sagely. "So, they found it," he mused to himself.

"Yes, *jefe*," Vincente agreed, thinking he was being addressed. "It had been taped to some screwdrivers."

"So, they are in the wind," Jorge said airily, taking a long draw of his beer and finally turning his head to regard Vincente.

"It would appear so, *jefe*." Vincente nodded.

"The status of our... mobilization?"

"Fully underway. Texts have gone out with a photo of the boy, but we have no photo of the man, as you know, so all I could do was provide a general description."

"Have you tried the hotel's security cameras?" Jorge asked, returning his attention to the work being done on the driveway.

"*Sí, jefe.* The men were professional – baseball caps, face masks – so many still wear them from the pandemic – sunglasses, and uncanny knowledge of where the cameras were. No clear facial shots at all."

"Nothing at the electric company?"

"They have none internally, just around the outside of the building," Vincente said with a shaking head.

Jorge finished off the beer and dropped the bottle to the ground beside him, then placed a fist to his lips and looked pensive. "If you were this man, Vincente, what would you do?"

The question caught Vincente completely off-guard. "Well..."

"No rush – give it some thought," Jorge told him as he returned his attention to the ongoing clean up.

After several minutes Vincente said, "*Jefe?*"

"Go ahead."

"Well, if I put myself in his predicament..."

"Yes?"

"I'm separated unexpectantly from my unit and have a noncombatant in tow who has no value in the escape, nothing but being dead weight, and who is likely still under the effect of the drugs we give to keep the boys docile... I'm in Presagio territory, with no allies... worse, I can't be certain that any person with whom I interact isn't on the Presagio payroll or won't report me to the cartel for the bounty we've offered. Every time I show my face, walk on a street, talk to a vendor, or get a room at a motel, I have a chance of being detected."

"Logical," Jorge agreed.

"In addition, I'm stuck in the middle of a city that the cartel controls, people are searching for me, and I have limited weapons and limited support – maybe none. Daytime travel is a serious risk; therefore, I need to remain in hiding until nightfall, and then either try to cross at the border, or do what we wouldn't expect, and go deeper into the country to get out of our territory... once outside of our territory, I'd take a plane out of the country or cross at some other border crossing."

"And the boy? He'll have no identification – how does he cross the border or get on a plane?"

Vincente couldn't help but laugh, which he quickly stifled because, well, it wasn't wise to laugh at the boss. "Um, sorry, *jefe*..."

Jorge waved it away. "Go on."

"Papers are easy to get with enough money."

"Ah... yes, right." Jorge sucked in a sharp, quick breath and exhaled it in a huff. "For this gringo though, it will not be too easy. It's not likely that he has a list of such freelancers, ready and waiting to do passports for him."

"If he has a phone and calls to his controller, he could easily be provided with that list," Vincente countered.

"Hmmm... indeed." Jorge agreed. "But, as for the border and the airports, bus stations and the like... we have people at all these locations, do we not?"

"Not necessarily our people, no," Vincente replied. "But though they are not 'ours,' they are the type of people who are more than eager to earn some significant cash for simply making a phone call."

"Then let us make certain they do call," Jorge said, waving a hand in the air. Vincente went to the cooler behind the chaise lounge, took another bottle of beer from the ice, popped the cap, and offered it to Jorge. After he'd taken a long pull, Jorge said, "Let us increase the bounty for making such a call to two million pesos, and apprehension and *returning them alive and undamaged* – well, mostly undamaged – to me, ten million."

"I shall see to it right away," Vincente said with a slight bow and stepped away to start making calls.

"Oh, and Vincente?"

"*Sí, jefe?*"

"Also let them know that, if they are not in talking, alive, viable condition when they are delivered to me, I will kill whoever failed to do so, and all their immediate family, by crucifixion. Clear?"

"*Sí, jefe!*"

Chapter 35

Hotel Mexico

The side-to-side motion of the boxcar accompanied by noticeable deacceleration, and the squealing of air brakes being applied woke One with a start. The boxcar was unbearably hot, but despite this One felt cold and shivered as he sat up – and felt a wave of nausea nearly overcome him. He leaned back against the Pelican case and panted, trying to keep from hurling. The nausea soon passed, but it was replaced by a slowly encroaching dizziness that had the interior of the boxcar looking like a carousel to his sight.

This isn't good...

He groped for his backpack, managed to find it and pull out a bottle of water. Snapping the cap off, he slowly drank, the hot liquid moistening his parched throat and calming both the nausea and vertigo. When it was empty, he tossed the bottle aside with a flick of his wrist and ran a hand over his face.

It came back dripping.

One looked down at his shirt, seeing it clinging to his torso. Glancing over at Kody, he found the teen had pulled off his shirt, laid it flat out beneath him, and lay atop it, facing the ceiling. He snored softly, still asleep.

The train continued to slow; One looked at his watch, seeing it was 4:45pm local time.

Better get ready to see if this is where you and Kody can get off this damn train...

Getting to his feet was another battle with nausea and vertigo, but after he stood it passed quickly, for which One was grateful. He moved to the boxcar's door and pushed it open a few inches. Putting his eye to the narrow opening, he saw buildings running within a few dozen meters of three railroad tracks, with his train on the outermost, so two tracks were between his boxcar and the buildings. Peering right as far as he could, One saw that the track farthest away had a siding that curved away into an alley of sorts between the buildings, and he could just make out the tops of a few hopper cars parked there.

Immediately in front of the opening, garbage, dead leaves, empty plastic grocery store bags, and scraps of paper fluttered around the area on a dry, hot breeze, some of them catching on the short, browned weeds that grew around the tracks.

To the left, the tracks extended as far as his limited range of vision permitted. There was no sign of anyone standing or walking nearby, but in the next instant he saw a hopper car come into view with a railroad employee, dressed in hardhat and dirty yellow safety vest, hanging off the end of the car as it rolled in on the far track. One quickly shut the door down to a bare slit, and watched as the hopper car went past, followed by four more, and then the three locomotives that One assumed had been pulling his train.

They've stopped to switch out cars...

Time to go!

One spun, but that was a mistake – dizziness gripped him, and he stumbled, going to one knee, his hands pressed against the floor to steady himself. After a few slow, deep breaths, he regained his balance and stood, more slowly and carefully this time, then crossed to where Kody lay.

"Kody?" One said in a soft voice, and gently shook his shoulder. "Kody?"

The teen groaned, rolled onto his back and knuckled his eyes. "What?" he asked sleepily.

"We need to get off the train," One told him. "Get up and get your stuff together."

Kody grumbled something noncommittal but sat up, got his shirt from where he'd laid it out under him, shook it out several times, then donned it.

Meanwhile One grabbed his own backpack. He pulled out a fresh shirt to swap out with the sweat-soaked one he wore, then took what was left of their food and water, the remnants of the first aid kit, and his other items, and quickly and economically packed them inside. Each motion felt sluggish, and he ached all over, but he managed to push through the pain and the wooziness thanks to a combination of his training and sheer willpower.

"Where are we?" Kody whispered.

Well, he's talking to me again, I guess that's a good sign...

"Don't know yet," One said. "I want to get off the train while the crew is busy switching cars. Once we get some cover away from the train, I'll look."

Kody absorbed that for a moment. "Shouldn't we stay on the train?"

"I think we've been on it long enough," One said with a shake of his head. "They've probably found your transmitter by now and could easily assume we'd been in the railyard when we got rid of it. A simple look at the freight train schedule would lead them to this train. We must assume that's what they've done and are only minutes away."

"Oh?" Kody blurted, now clearly worried.

"Not that they actually are minutes away," One quickly added. "It's just that, well, I've been trained to always consider the worst-case scenario."

"Scenario?"

"Yeah... 'scenario' is another word for a, um, sequence of events."

"Mmmm," Kody murmured his understanding.

"C'mon, let's go," One said, standing carefully and walking slowly to the door.

"Does your leg hurt?" Kody asked.

"Only a little; why?"

"You're limping," Kody told him.

Am I? Shit, I hadn't noticed... the infection and fever must be worse than I thought...

"I'll be okay," One assured him. "Let's be very quiet now – keep looking around, and if you see anyone, whether they're coming closer or not, just tug on my arm and point."

"Okay."

173

They shouldered their backpacks, went to the door, and before opening it enough to pass through, One paused to look out the sliver of open space he'd left. Seeing nothing close by, he pushed the door open, sat on the boxcar's floor, and gently lowered himself to the ballast shoulder alongside the boxcar.

A stab of fire in his left leg welcomed him as he fell the meter of distance, then went into a crouch. He could see the locomotive's nose from the siding across the way, but at the distance One was at from it, he couldn't make out if there was an engineer in the driver's seat. It didn't matter – what mattered was getting out of here quickly, so as to keep being seen to an absolute minimum.

Kody followed what he'd done, sitting on the floor and pushing off so he landed on the ballast with a crinkle of scattering stones. One stood, grabbed the door handle, and slid the boxcar's door closed, locking the handle in place. That done, he whispered, "Follow me!", took Kody's hand, and in a crouch, led them to the space between cars, where they crossed to the other side of the train and out of sight of the switching operation on the other side.

Here they found themselves standing in front of a steep embankment, dotted with scrub growth and weeds, which ran upward to a height of about four meters. Past its top, they saw the green and brown leaves of several trees waving in the breeze.

To their right and left, the freight cars of their train extended well past their ability to see the ends. The embankment appeared to run this entire length as well, but it was difficult to tell based on their position.

One paused and evaluated.

Go up, left, or right? Left or right means a lot of walking, with no guarantee of finding a way up and out any less difficult than right here... and more chance of a train crew member walking the train and spotting us...

But going up this sheer, earthen embankment will kick up a cloud of dust...

Up presents less exposure time, and if it turns out to be unsuitable, we can always try left or right...

So up it is.

One turned to Kody. "We're climbing up."

Kody's eyes went from his gaze to the sheer rise and frowned.

"Don't worry; just go where I go," One told him.

"Um... okay," Kody was clearly skeptical.

"You're able to climb, right?" One asked, realizing that the teen's skeptical look might have been due to him feeling ill, weak, or perhaps having some sort of phobia about climbing.

"Um... yeah..."

"Okay. If you feel yourself slipping, just push your chest right to the wall and let yourself slide until you can stop. It's not a long distance, so even if you slide to the bottom, you're not going to get hurt."

With that said, One steeled himself for the inevitable pain of the climb – he knew the moment he put weight on and tried to push with his wounded leg, it would scream its protestations at him quite loudly. He tested some handholds on chunks of protruding dirt and roots, found them secure, and started up.

The pain came just as he expected, and after just a few meters he was sweating, his skin felt cold and clammy, and he was panting more heavily than he would have liked. Nevertheless, he pushed through it all and halfway up glanced back at Kody, seeing that the teen following faithfully, not looking up at him but rather focused on griping and climbing.

One reached the top, turned, knelt, and helped Kody the rest of the way up. One then led them into a stand of pine trees, going to cover behind one of the larger ones, and from here, One surveyed their surroundings.

There wasn't much to see, just a forest of pine trees of a sort that had a familiar look but were nothing One could classify. It didn't matter; they were numerous enough to make sight lines farther than a hundred meters impossible. Then One focused on what he was hearing – road noises from their two o'clock radial.

Ah ha!

"Follow me – like before, grab my backpack and stay close behind, okay?"

After a sigh, Kody said, "Okay."

One led them off, and he realized he could feel his imbalance now; he was favoring his left leg which made his gait more like ambling than walking. Still, he pushed through the discomfort and after maybe 200 meters came within sight of a street. He went to one knee, glancing back to make sure

Kody had as well, and then studied the street from the cover of the tree line.

Cars and trucks zoomed by at irregular intervals. One observed the street and its traffic for 15 minutes before deciding that there was no one trolling the roadway in hopes of finding them.

He pulled out his sat phone, booted it up, and checked the GPS.

Delicias... Still in the state of Chihuahua... But over 400 kilometers from where we started. They can't possibly be looking for us this far south.

Hold on a moment – what did you tell Kody? Worst-case scenario is what you said... so don't assume that the cartel won't be looking for you here. You're still in Chihuahua, a state that the Presagio cartel basically controls. Every person here could be an informant, on their payroll, or one of their thugs.

Maybe Kody was right, and we should have stayed on the train?

One huffed out a short, soft breath in frustration.

No, it was a good decision to get off. Who knows if the train was even going any farther? You saw the locomotives switching out cars. What if it was heading back north afterward? And getting rid of the transmitter was a good move, but finding it in a gondola means they'll guess where I dumped it from, and maybe even when, which would put them on our trail sooner rather than later...

And I'm not going to be of much use to either of us unless I can get some antibiotics and treat my wound better than I have. So, that needs to be the first consideration...

Which means going to ground. But where?

One brought up Google Maps and a pin appeared at their current location among the trees. The street in front of them was *Avenue Ferrocarril Ote*, a service road that paralleled State Route 45D. Just 600 meters or so north of them was the *Hotel Mexico*, a privately owned establishment that overlooked the small rail yard that One assumed was the same one in which their train now sat. It got decent ratings on Google, and One saw that of those who rated it, many were railroad workers who used it for a crew rest stop. This meant that it had a high turnover of unfamiliar faces passing through it, a perfect venue for yet another unfamiliar face to be lost in the mix – his unfamiliar face.

One also liked it because it wasn't part of a chain. Chain hotels were more likely to be owned by the cartel to launder cash, and as such were more likely to have employees willing to make a call when someone unusual, or someone they were specifically told to look out for, came in.

Finally, the hotel overlooked the railyard, so if any of Presagio's thugs came looking, One had a decent chance of seeing them before they even knew he'd seen them. The other three directions from the hotel overlooked open, flat space, with an empty, garbage-strewn lot to the north, the hotel's parking lot to the west, and undeveloped land to the south.

It's a good thing I saved that hardhat and safety vest, One thought with satisfaction. *I can walk in and no one will notice me as anything unusual... Kody, on the other hand...*

We'll have to wait until dark. I'll get a room and figure out a way to smuggle him in unseen. The cartel will be looking for a man and a boy traveling together, not a railroad worker alone coming to a hotel that frequently hosts railroad workers.

Satisfied with that aspect, One turned his thoughts to treating his fever and infection. Turning back to the map on the phone, he saw that the Valia Trading Corp mall was less than 200 meters north of the hotel and after a quick check on Google, saw it had a pharmacy. All the mall's stores were open until 9:00pm, which would give One enough time to do what he needed to do.

"Okay, I've got a plan," he said, and outlined it all for Kody.

They started out by going to the mall. One stowed the hardhat and safety vest in his backpack and returned to his casual, nondescript look with baseball cap hiding his blond hair and the brim pulled down as low as it would go to help hide his eyes.

Originally One had planned on leaving Kody here in the relative safety and anonymity of the small, wooded area while he did his shopping and surveillance of the hotel and its immediate area, but when One had suggested it, the teen immediately began trembling and looked very distraught. So, One nixed that in favor of risking them going together, as father and son should anyone bother to ask. It was clear to One that, despite the awkward encounter in the boxcar, and subsequent cold shoulder Kody gave him, the teen still trusted One to some degree and realized his safety was increased only when they were together.

Which suited One, at least for the moment. Trauma of the type that Kody had gone through wasn't something easily erased or countered by one, brief heart-to-heart talk. But if they were to survive, One couldn't afford to alienate Kody nor have him lose trust in him, so One resolved to back-burner any further discussion about Kody's immediate past and what he'd had to endure under the cartel's control.

No one gave them any notice as they walked, heads down, along the dusty street. It was close to six o'clock now, but the sun was still high enough in the sky to make walking under it a sweaty process. The buff-colored concrete of the street and the wheaten color of the dirt alongside reflected the waning sun's brilliance almost like mirrors, and the accompanying heat penetrated both clothing and skin so that the short trek to the mall seemed like they were walking inside of a furnace.

Now I know what Shadrack, Meshack and Abednego felt like, One mused sardonically.

The mall wasn't like those you'd see in the United States – it was a lop-sided affair that apparently had started out as a strip mall, then had a three-story addition tacked on to the rear, northeastern corner in a style completely different than the original structure, and then sometime later, a two-story car park had been added to the northwestern corner of the property. But it was busy, with cars and pickup trucks moving in, out and around it, and when One led them through the glass entry doors on the three-story part of the building, the air conditioning that enveloped them was a welcome shock to their overheated bodies.

But the intense heat and the short, half kilometer walk hadn't helped One's leg any; his limp was pronounced now, despite his conscious efforts to walk normally, and it was sending staccato pings of sharp agony up his leg and into his buttocks with each step. One could feel himself sweating despite being in the air conditioning, and when he brushed the back of his hand over his forehead, found his brow radiating more heat than he expected.

"Over there," he whispered to Kody, who was walking beside him with his head lowered, as he'd been instructed to do.

One led them into the indicated pharmacy, got a shopping basket, and beelined for the aisle with pain reliever where he grabbed a bottle of 200mg ibuprofen tablets. One then swung into another aisle, getting toothbrushes, toothpaste, and a bottle of shampoo, and next moved to the aisle with first aid supplies, snatching up gauze pads, pressure bandages, two bottles of disinfectant, some surgical glue, and a digital thermometer. He then led Kody back to where the pharmacist was stationed.

"*Hola*," One greeted.

"*Hola*," the pharmacist replied with a slight upturning of his mouth. "How may I help you, sir?"

"I'd like a 14-day supply of amoxicillin – 42 caplets at 500 milligrams," One told him.

"We have that in stock, yes, sir," the pharmacist said as he turned and moved toward the rows of shelves behind the counter. "It'll be just a minute. May I ask what's this for?"

One was ready with a viable explanation. "Tooth abscess... haven't had time to see the dentist yet."

"Ah," the pharmacist said sagely. "Well, don't let it go too long... antibiotics are only a temporary fix for that sort of thing."

"I understand," One agreed.

"I'd also suggest an oral rinse, one with cetylpyridinium chloride – aisle four."

After the pharmacist handed him a small bag with the amoxicillin bottle inside, One went dutifully to grab a bottle of the oral rinse so it would reinforce what he'd said was the reason for the antibiotics. After paying for the items and stowing them in their backpacks, One led them to the first clothing store they came to and went inside and quickly purchased two more nondescript outfits for the two of them. That done, they hit the grocery store in the strip mall part to get some more power bars and snacks.

With their backpacks now full to the brim, One led Kody to the Starbucks at the corner of the mall. They ordered iced tea and sandwiches and settled in to eat in the back corner of the open seating area. One consumed his rapidly, and then got up, giving Kody a reassuring squeeze on the shoulder, and whispered, "You've got your phone?"

Kody held up the pre-paid phone One had given to him, then slipped it back into his hoodie's kangaroo pocket and gave One a nervous smile.

One squeezed his shoulder a second time. "You'll be fine, just keep to yourself and don't drink everything so you've got a reason to still be sitting."

"Okay," Kody answered softly.

One took out the Ferromex safety vest and hard hat, donned them, and shouldered his backpack. He then did his best to walk without limping across the street and into the Hotel Mexico.

The lobby was what he expected: drab, dated and with a lingering scent of cigarettes and Pine-sol. A handful of railroad workers in safety vests like his were waiting in line at the desk where one tired, middle-aged woman was registering guests. Each of the workers carried either a small duffel, a backpack, or both that were dusted with the local dirt, and weren't very talkative among themselves, something that One was grateful for because he wasn't really a railroad employee and if any of them queried him, he'd have difficulty responding meaningfully.

One tried his best to listen carefully as each worker dealt with the hotel's representative, so when it came to his turn, he could be prepared.

But the aching wound and fever had muddled his brain so much that he didn't catch the fact that the woman was asking each worker for their employee number.

So when it came time for him to get a room, he was panicking, trying to figure out a fake number that would make sense, but he hadn't been paying that much attention to what the other workers were saying for their employee numbers, so he had no idea where to start—

"Ah, Mr. Velez," the woman said, squinting slightly over her half-frame readers at his chest.

Huh?

"How many nights?" she asked.

"Um..." One struggled to process what was happening – why had she called him "Mr. Velez"? Then he thought to look down at the front of his safety vest, where she had peered—

Where faded block letters were stenciled, "VELEZ," under which was a number, "109883."

Oh thank God! Finally! Murphy, go fuck yourself! Ha!

"Three nights," One told her, then once his addled brain finally reminded him, added, "Oh... a top floor room, if possible."

"Certainly," she said, typing on a worn keyboard. "Employee number..." she peered at his chest, typing on the numeric pad without looking down, as she read it out aloud slowly. "One-zero-nine-eight-eight-three... got it." She returned to looking at her screen, and after a few more keystrokes, she announced, "You're all set, Mr. Velez. Room 324." She processed two key cards and handed them to him, then produced a printed paper and had him sign. "Coffee service is in the lobby all day, with breakfast between six and nine." She jutted her chin toward the eating area adjacent to the lobby.

"Thanks," One said, taking up the card keys and heading toward the elevators.

The room was at the end of the hall, a corner room on the northeast corner of the building, affording a clear overwatch of the railyard, the mall across the street, and part of the parking lot for the hotel.

One left the vest and hardhat in the room, reshouldered his backpack, and went down the fire stairs to the base, where there was a door to enter the hall for the first-floor rooms on one side, or the exit to the outside opposite it. The exit door had a push bar, which kept it locked, but there was no attached alarm. One pushed it open slightly and paused, listening for any alarm and thankful that there was none. He spent a moment jamming some of the strips of t-shirt he'd made in the boxcar into the hole for the push bar's locking mechanism. That done, he exited from the stairwell and made his way back to the coffee shop, taking a casual look back at the exterior of the hotel, searching for any surveillance cameras and seeing none.

Another victory against Murphy! I'm on a roll...

Careful, don't jinx yourself...

181

Kody was waiting dutifully where One had left him, the empty plate and soup bowl sitting on the table, and only a few sips of his iced tea left in the cup.

The look of utter relief that Kody gave him when he returned tugged at One's heartstrings, and One knew in that moment of locked gazes that any of the earlier problems that the teen had with him were history.

"Ready?" One asked.

"Yeah," Kody said, getting up quickly and clearing his dishes to the wash station and joining One as he led them out the side door.

The crossed the busy street at a run, then One slowed them to a casual pace, heads down, like a father and son minding their own business as they were going home—

Except that they turned into the hotel parking lot, moved between the Ferromex roadrailer trucks and mix of more common cars parked there, and slipped quickly and quietly into the hotel via the fire stairs door that One had jammed open. As they entered, One removed the cloth from the hole in the jam and checked to be sure the fire door locked behind them. One led Kody up the stairs, each step an ice pick of pain that shot up from his thigh and through his back to stab at the base of his skull.

I can't keep going on like this...

Even though he was in agony, feverish, and running on empty, One's training wouldn't let him ignore protocol – he paused at the door to the third-floor hallway and listened at it for a full minute before cracking it open, peeking out, and seeing no one in the hall, crossed quickly to his room's door and entered the room with Kody on his heels. After a final glance down the hall toward the elevators, One closed and bolted the door and only then did he allow his level of anxiety and situational awareness to wane.

One crossed to the window, drew the curtains closed, and turned the air conditioner to high, hoping to quickly cool the stuffy room.

"One, you okay?" Kody asked as One sat down heavily on the edge of the bed.

Not by a long shot, kid... But I'm not going to tell you that.

"Just sore and tired," One told him with a wan grin. "Getting shot takes a lot outta you."

Kody looked both concerned and skeptical.

"How about you? Holding up okay? Anyone at the Starbucks look at you sideways?"

"Nah, no one even looked at me," Kody answered.

"That's good," One said as he wiggled out of his shorts while he remained seated. The nausea and dizziness that he'd managed to hold at bay was now circling his conscious like an eager shark.

Out of his shorts, he looked at his wound. The makeshift bandage was dark with coagulated blood and was now clearly inflamed and bloated. Getting the bandage off wasn't a problem, but when he withdrew the cloth that he'd soaked in disinfectant and stuffed into the wound, he though his brain would explode. He must have made some sort of sound because Kody was there next to him, looking at him with serious worry on his face.

Kody's eyes scanned the wound, and his worried look became a frown. "That looks really bad – you sure that you're okay?"

"Yeah, no worries," One said. "I'm gonna take a shower and then redress it. You gonna be okay out here?"

Kody met his eyes, still frowning, but then his lips became a line of acceptance. "Sure." He looked around the room, his eyes falling on the TV. "I'll watch TV."

"Okay, good. Just don't answer the door if anyone knocks and stay away from the window. Got it?"

"Yeah, okay."

"Cool. I got some new clothes and sneakers for you to wear after you take your turn in the shower."

Kody nodded and used the remote to turn the TV on.

One took the items he'd purchased at the pharmacy into the bathroom, set them on the sink, removed his pistol and set it atop the clothes, and then turned the shower's hot water full on. The showerhead spat brownish water spasmodically for the first few seconds before it streamed a constant, clear spray. It took a minute for it to steam, and when it had, One stripped and got in carefully, working himself slowly under the cascade because, once the water hit his wounded thigh, the agony level went exponential.

The dizziness would no longer be put off; One found himself collapsing into the stained tub, flailing for any grip that would prevent him from crashing, found nothing, and landed heavily. His sight became a kaleidoscope of brilliant starbursts, the wind was knocked from his lungs, and it took One a good five minutes before he caught his breath, and as he did, things came back into focus.

It's worse than I thought...

Slowly, with great effort that left him panting, One got to his feet and rinsed himself from head to toe, then grabbed the small hotel soap bar, unwrapped it, and lathered up. He waited until the end of that process to clean the area around the wound, wincing each time the soap traveled closer to the puckered hole left by the bullet. He used the shampoo he'd purchased, washing his hair twice to get all the sweat and grim out of it. One then turned the water to full-on cold, groaning as the iciness enveloped him, but it served its purpose – he was reinvigorated, if temporarily, and ready to work on his wound.

He stepped out of the shower, toweled off, and sat on the toilet seat. With the bandages and disinfectant, he was able to finally give his wound the attention it needed, but based on his fever, and the heat radiating from and the bright redness circling the wound, One knew it was a good thing that he'd gotten antibiotics – the damn thing was heavily infected.

One managed to get into the new clothes he'd bought, moved the holster to the inside of his new trousers, and then slid his pistol into it. He retrieved a bottle of water from his backpack, uncapped it, then popped an amoxicillin and six ibuprofens and washed them down with the entire contents of the water bottle.

Feeling somewhat human again, he emerged from the bathroom to find Kody hugging his knees, sitting against the headboard of the bed, eyes looking at the TV but not really seeing what it displayed.

"You're up," One told him as he pulled out the clothes he'd bought for Kody, piling the sneakers atop the stack and holding them out.

Kody unwound from his position and took the pile for One, then headed lethargically into the bathroom without saying anything.

One sat on the edge of the bed, staring after the teen.

He seems different somehow...

Coming down off the drugs they've forced on him?

One vowed to keep an eye on him, turning next to pulling out a bottle of juice. He needed to stay hydrated to fight the fever and infection, as well as lots of rest.

I'm not likely to get much of the latter, he mused sourly.

One finished the juice, dumped the bottle in the trash can, and went to the door. After checking the hall via the peep hole, he took the "No Molestar – Do Not Disturb" sign from where it hung, unlocked the door, and hung it on the door handle facing the hallway. After one more scan of the empty hall, One closed and locked the door, throwing the security bolt and then took one of the room's chairs and wedged it in under the doorknob for added security.

That won't stop a dedicated breaching effort, but it'll give me a few extra seconds if worst comes to worst.

One lay on the bed, and only then did it occur to him that there was just one bed in the room. Sure, it was king-sized, but with everything going on to that point exacerbated by his fever and pain, he'd never thought to ask the receptionist what type of rooms were available. Now One confronted the idea that sleeping arrangements might not just be awkward for Kody but cause an adverse reaction of some sort for him based on the traumatic abuse he'd endured.

Well, shit... guess I can take the floor...

One stood, wincing with the agony and stiffness that made his body feel like he was a rusted tin man. He began to gather up the bedspread and a pillow for him to sleep on the floor beside the bed, when Kody emerged from the bathroom dressed in the gray cargo shorts and black t-shirt One had bought for him. He carried the low-rise pair of socks in one hand and the sneakers in the other and had a bath towel draped around his head like a nun's veil.

Kody stopped, his head tilting as he stared at the partially pulled bedspread and pillow in One's hands.

"I'm going to sleep on the floor," One told him.

Kody looked confused, his mouth parting slightly, and his eyes scrunching. "Why?"

To his surprise, One felt a blush come to his cheeks. "Um... well, it just wouldn't... well, wouldn't be right for us to sleep together." When he

185

saw Kody's eyebrows raise and his lips curl inward, One quickly added, "I mean, we're not related... it'd be different if, y'know, I was your dad or brother or—"

"Oh," was all Kody said as he looked down at the sneakers he held. "Do I need to wear these to bed, like you do?"

"No, just leave them close by, that's fine."

Nodding, Kody set them on the nightstand and sat on the side of the bed opposite where One stood, his back to him as he leaned forward to rest his elbows on his thighs.

One finished gathering up the bedspread, dropping it and the pillow on the floor near the a/c unit. Peering at him, One asked, "You okay, Kody?"

"I'm fine."

Doesn't sound fine... now he's pissed at me again?

What the hell?

Then the thing he'd been forced to put off because of the earlier attack on them at the hotel, and everything since, came to the forefront of his fevered brain.

"Listen, um, I need to get a photo of you, okay?"

Without turning, Kody asked, "Why?"

"To get a passport for you, so we can cross the border without any problems."

That seemed to liven Kody up out of his mood. "Oh? So we're really... really leaving?"

"Of course!" One replied, getting the sat phone out and powering it up. "You didn't believe me when I said I'll do everything I can to get you out of here safely and back to your parents?"

There was a long pause, and when Kody finally answered it was just above a whisper. "No... I believe you... just... well...." He sighed. "Never mind." He twisted around just enough to see One. "The picture?"

"I don't want you wearing the shirt you'll be wearing in the photo when we leave," One told him as Kody slowly stood and came to the end of the bed. "So after I take the picture, you can wear the shirt for now, but when we leave, you'll need to change."

"Fine, whatever."

One directed Kody to stand in front of the faded yellow wall near the entry door. He turned on the alcove's overhead light and took the shade off the nightstand lamp so there would be adequate and flat lighting for the shot. He then told Kody to look straight ahead, not a smile, just a relaxed face, which Kody did, and One snapped four shots in quick succession.

"That's all, thanks," One told him.

Nodding, Kody shuffled back to the bed, and sat on it, hugging his knees once again to himself as he rested his back against the headboard.

One went to the window, aimed the sat phone antenna outside, and waited for the unit to connect to a satellite. Once it had, he emailed the photos to Garrett, and then called him.

"Where the hell have you been?!" was the first thing One heard when the call connected.

One winced, pulling the receiver away from his ear for a moment, then answered. "It's been a helluva day – sorry I didn't call sooner."

The was a pregnant pause before Garret said, "It better have been – I've been worried."

"No need," One assured him in his best everything-is-A-okay tone. "Listen, I just sent the photos of the kid over—"

"Where are you?" Garrett demanded, and One heard the clicking of keyboard keys.

"Holed up at Hotel Mexico in Delicias, Chihuahua," One told him. "Top floor, room 324."

"I see it," Garrett said a few seconds later. "And got the pix – wow, good lookin' kid!" More computer keystrokes sounded. "Hmmm... it's almost eight your time, too late to get anything off to you today. I wish you'd called sooner—"

"Garrett, we've been on the run all day from the cartel."

Silence descended on the line. "So you weren't making a joke about it being a helluva day?"

"Fuck, no!" One exclaimed, a little louder than he'd planned. He cleared his throat, and then gave Garrett the Cliff Notes version of what had happened.

"Well, I suppose in light of all that, I can forgive you for not checking in sooner," Garrett said sardonically. Then he got serious, his tone one of sincere concern. "You alright? The GSW going to slow you down? Did it hit anywhere serious?"

One debated whether to tell Garrett just how bad the gunshot wound was and decided to downplay it for now – no sense worrying him needlessly if they'd have Kody's passport in 48 hours and be out of country. "Yeah, it's good – I'm good. Remember, I'm no slouch when it comes to battlefield medicine."

The skepticism came through clearly when Garret answered. "Really? What about that little adventure we had in the Congo?"

"Again with the past history," One growled, but Garrett was making a point. One of his squad's men had received a very similar wound during that mission, and One had treated it as he'd treated his own, current gun shot wound.

The problem was that his man had lost his leg to infection.

Not gonna happen to me – and no wrenches in the works from you, Murphy!

"I'm fine, really," One assured.

"Well, not much I can do from here anyway – at least for that," Garrett admitted. "Is it safe to stay there for the next two days?"

"I think so," One said. "There's only a thin thread attaching us to the train, and even so, we're over 400 klicks from where it all went down. It'd take a miracle to find us here now, especially if we stay holed up and if I only go out for supplies. They never got a good look at me, so it's unlikely that my photo's anywhere – the kid, well, I'm sure there's tons of photos of him, but I've limited his exposure."

"Sounds like you've got it all covered," Garrett agreed. "Okay, I'll early-AM this out to you for delivery before 8:30 am on Thursday, about 40 hours from now. Just hold on that long and you're golden."

"Well, I won't be golden, but getting there," One countered. "We still need to get to a border crossing."

"What are you thinking?"

"Whatever I choose, it's a long trip," One replied. "Initially, I thought my best bet was rent a car and drive to the border crossing at Ojinaga, but that's still in Presagio controlled Chihuahua state... the pros associated with that are that it there's no Mexican checkpoint to stop at, just the

American one. The cons are that it's a long-ass drive, meaning there's always a chance for someone to see us traveling together and questions to be raised."

"You said 'initially'?"

"The other option I thought of is, why not just stay in Mexico longer, leaving them to focus on the border. I could drive down to Monterrey and the two of us get on a flight to somewhere other than the US – I mean, they've got to assume by now that it was Uncle Sam that made the hit, so they'd be looking especially close at any flight back to the states."

"I suppose that's one way to look at it," Garrett said. "But here's something you may want to think about – I've checked, and there's absolutely zero, zilch, nada about Jorge de Corazón having been killed, or even attacked. You'd think that, if he had, the cartel would be tearing itself apart from within as his lieutenants and capos all sought to take over the reins – but there's been nothing."

That sent a ball of arctic ice into One's stomach. "Garrett, I need you to—"

"I know, I know," he interrupted. "Check it out, see if he's still alive 'n' kickin'?"

"Please."

"And you can't call your people on this either because?"

One exhaled sharply. "It's an NCM."

NCM, or no contact mission, meant that they were on their own for it. There could be absolutely nothing allowed that would even have a hint at incriminating the US government for the assassination in lieu of the delicate political environment currently existing between the USA and Mexico. By asking Garrett for help, One wasn't technically in violation of the NCM tasking, since he wasn't officially calling on any government agency for support, but that nuance wouldn't mean jack-shit in a court martial.

"Right," Garret said with noticeable exasperation. "You're going to owe me two big favors now, y'know."

"That works for me," One said and couldn't help himself from grinning. Then his expression sobered. "Find out about de Corazón as quick as you can – but Garrett?"

"Yeah?"

"Something tells me you're gonna confirm that he's still alive," One said angrily. "It's the only thing that makes sense about why I'm being pursued."

"Not because of the kid?" Garrett countered.

"Nah, he's one of a thousand, ten thousand," One said shaking his head. "That sick pederast de Corazón doesn't give a rat's ass about Kody – he's just a thing to him, something to be used and when he's tired of it, discarded. He's got thousands more waiting for him to choose from. No, this is about either revenge, or getting info, or maybe both."

"Then you need to be even more careful," Garrett warned.

"Yeah... yeah," One agreed. He took a deep breath and exhaled it. "Listen, I'm dead on my feet – thanks for everything, but I've got to get some sleep."

"Okay, I'll have the passport to you by Thursday in the AM, and I'll do my best to see what's what with de Corazón. Leave the sat phone on in case I find something sooner rather than later."

"They can't trace it—"

"For the hundredth time, no!" Garrett said with exasperation, but then realized he was letting his emotions get the better of him, and added more calmly, "They can't. No worries there. Just get some rest and stay frosty, okay?"

"Will do, and always am," One answered and disconnected the call. He pulled the charger for the phone out and plugged it into the phone, and the other end into the wall socket, leaving the phone atop the a/c unit by the window.

Turning back, he found that Kody was already under the covers and asleep.

Stress and exhaustion will do that...

One folded the huge bedspread in half, creating an unzipped sleeping bag of sorts, slid inside and lay down, his feet pointing toward the room's entry door while his head was near room's window a/c unit. If anyone tried to bust in, his USP pistol was beside him, out of the holster, cocked and ready for instant use, and if Garrett called, he was within easy reach of the sat phone.

Satisfied that he'd done all he could to secure the room and prepare for a potential attack, and with the stress of the day, the pain of his wound, and the fever it induced all conspiring against him, One began to drift off...

His last thought before sleep took him was what he'd told Garrett—

It'd take a miracle to find us...

Taunting Murphy like that was never a good idea.

Chapter 36

We Have Our Miracle!

"It'll take a miracle to find them!" Vincente bemoaned as he disconnected from the call and shook his head disdainfully.

Jorge had finally returned to the mansion, leaving the final clearing of the debris from the morning's assassination attempt to his underlings. He sat now at the dining room table, the carcass of a Cornish game hen and a few stray, untouched string beans being the only thing left on his plate. Vincente sat to Jorge's left; his meal only half-eaten because he'd been fielding calls throughout their dinner.

"Patience," Jorge urged with a sardonic smile. "Someone, somewhere saw something and when that bit of information finally comes to us, we will act."

"*Jefe*, how can you be so confident?"

Jorge topped off his wine glass with the final dregs of the fine Chenin Blanc his chef had paired with his meal and walked with it slowly toward the study. "It's the nature of the world," he said over his shoulder. "Money motivates and buys anything."

Vincente nodded but if he was going to make a response, the trill of his phone drew him away from making one.

Jorge left him to it. His body still ached from the aftereffects of the SUV's explosion and the tossing around he'd received in the futile attempt to catch up with and capture the team that had attacked him. But the fine meal and wine was helping, marginally, to cope with it all, and he knew what would make his coping even better – a fine Cohiba Behike cigar savored on the terrace.

Entering his study, he went to his desk, opened the humidor, selected one of the $500 cigars, used a platinum cutter to remove the end, and then flicked on a torch lighter to ignite it. He inhaled with slow, short intakes until the end glowed orange on its own and he tasted the beginning wafts of the cigar's rich flavor. With wine glass again in hand and cigar between his lips, Jorge wandered through the billowing curtains and onto the terrace.

The night was clear, breezy and cooling down quickly. Jorge leaned on the stone balustrade, looking out over his baby, *El Cielo Escondido*, the enclave for the elite he'd spent so much time planning and building, the one which hid his cryptocurrency enterprise.

A minor setback... lost a handful of the hired help, and now I'll have to hire another company to finish the fiber optic installation, but this time I'll have one man for every one of theirs, looking over their shoulders every step of the way...

Losing Tomas was unfortunate, but as Vincente has shown, right hand men are plentiful for the right price, so no real loss there...

Mierda! I still have no answers about the attack – was it the Americans? The Venezuelans? The Vamos Chicos? The Manos Rojas, the Red Hands? So many enemies, and thus so many possibilities....

And now to try to find out, I've had to halt the latest shipment across the border, taking the men from it to help in the search...

And on top of it all, my evening has been ruined... that boy, so delectable... what a disappointment... I had such interesting things planned for him...

Oh well, there's plenty more waiting for me at the club...

"*Jefe!*"

Vincente's shout startled him. Jorge turned in time to see his lieutenant rushing into the study, phone in hand and an anxious expression on his face.

"What?" Jorge asked as he turned and came back into the room.

"We have our miracle!" Vincente exclaimed. "Well, at least part of one, *jefe*."

Jorge gently placed himself in one of the leather easy chairs beside the cold fireplace. "Explain!"

Vincente came to stand in front of his boss. "I received a call from the chief of police in Camargo; he had a call from one of his men. It seems that this officer of his has a friend who is a Ferromex police officer, and this Ferromex man mentioned to him that he was investigating a strange break-in at the railyard."

"Where is this leading, Vincente?" Jorge asked impatiently.

"*Jefe*, I'm almost finished." Vincente paused to gather his thoughts, then continued. "The railroad, as you know, is under our protection and no one who lives in Chihuahua would ever consider breaking into a rail car..."

"Yes, yes, so?" Jorge urged with a get-on-with-it motion.

"When he came across the broken seal on a box car, he investigated, and found that someone had been inside – and that there were empty water bottles, protein bar wrappers, and the remnants of bloody medical supplies, indicating that—"

"Whoever was in there was injured," Jorge interrupted, sitting up straighter. "The assassin? One of the cops must have wounded him in that roadrailer!"

"There was also a Pelican case in the boxcar, which wasn't on the manifest," Vincente added. "He sent photos of the interior – it was empty, but interestingly had a copper mesh liner. Do you know what this means?"

"It blocks cellphone and radio signals," Jorge said with a grin. "*Bastardo inteligente!* That clever bastard! That's how he smuggled the boy out and we didn't detect him by the transmitter!"

"Exactly, *jefe*! Or, well, it at least fits the evidence."

"I'm sure of it," Jorge said, getting to his feet, puffing on his cigar eagerly as he began to pace the room. "So, where was this all? Camargo? That's what, 500 kilometers from Juarez?"

"About 520, yes," Vincente said.

"So he managed to fool us at some point when he took the railroader into the railyard," Jorge surmised, "and used something to keep the truck moving. That's why there was no body in the truck!"

"Well, we always assumed he'd jumped out somewhere along the way and was holed up somewhere in Juarez," Vincente added. "We were close – he did get out, but not to go into hiding in the city – instead he got onto a southbound train!"

"So, what's this mean for our search?" Jorge asked.

"Well, *jefe*, there's more—"

195

"What?!"

"The train stopped at two points to switch cars into industries between here and Camargo: a stop in Chihuahua and another in Delicias. I've contacted our people in these other cities, as well as the police chiefs there, to start investigating. They'll start at the railyards and work their way outward, and the forces in Camargo will be doing the same, of course."

"This is excellent news, Vincente!" Jorge praised. "Good work!"

"Shall I pass that on to the police chief in Camargo?"

"Absolutely," Jorge agreed. "Let's give him a 'thank you' of, say, 200,000 pesos... he didn't see anything himself, but it's important to encourage true cooperation... and remind him of the actual bounties. And let's give 50,000 to the railroad cop – find out who he was and see to it."

"Right away, *jefe!*"

I will have you soon!

Chapter 37

Hole Up Here

One startled awake.

It took him a moment to remember where he was, and when he did, he realized that his shirt and pants were clinging to him, soaked with sweat.

Getting to his elbows was a monumental task, a fight against dizziness and protesting muscles that made One feel like he was a septuagenarian not a trained tier one operator in his prime. Despite the cool air in the room, he felt hot, but then as he managed to get to his knees, felt a wave of icy chillness sweep through him, making him shudder.

Fever's still with me...

The light from the parking lot fixtures was peeking into the room around the edges of the curtains, making twilight illumination that was just barely adequate for One to navigate to the bathroom. Once he'd closed the door, he turned the light on and winced against its sharp brightness. His hands found the edges of the sink, he locked his arms at the elbows to steady himself there, and just took slow, steady, deep breaths for the next minute to still the aches and vertigo. When it had passed, he fumbled for the medicine bottles he'd left on the sink, popping another amoxicillin and six more ibuprofen, swallowing them dry.

By the time he'd finished, his damp clothes were chilling him, so he peeled them off, ran the hot water in the shower, did a quick rinse, then stepped out and toweled himself dry. He hung the damp clothes over the shower's curtain rod to dry, flicked the bathroom's light off, and then padded quietly back into the bedroom where he dug out a fresh set of clothes.

He'd just donned them when a sharp whimper sounded from behind him, then a long groan.

One turned, seeing that Kody had kicked aside the covers in his sleep, and was now balled up on the bed, rocking back and forth on his side and moaning.

What's wrong?!

His own pain and fever momentarily forgotten, One went to the bedside and sat down gently. He reached out, intending to check Kody's forehead for fever, but hesitated.

Is it going to startle him? Bring back some trauma event if I touch him while he's asleep?

The decision became moot when Kody suddenly cried out, an agonizing groan of pain, and rolled over toward One, his eyes tightly shut. He hugged himself and continued to rock back and forth.

"Kody?! Kody?!" One stage whispered urgently. "What's wrong?!"

Through trembling lips and clenched teeth, Kody murmured, "It hurts... hurts so bad..."

With everything that had happened, and in his current poor state of health, One had set aside some vital information—

That the cartel drugged their human sex slaves to keep them compliant, a fact that Kody himself had mentioned earlier to One—

Now Kody was obviously going through some sort of withdrawal aftereffect.

What a great pair we make, One thought ruefully. *I'm wounded, infected and feverish, and you're sick with withdrawal...*

Murphy strikes again... and just when I thought he'd given me a break...

Kody groaned again, a long, drawn-out exhale of suffering that tugged at One's heartstrings.

One stared at the teen for a long moment, then got up, retrieved his pillow and the bedspread, sat on the bedside opposite Kody. One then slithered over next to the teen as gently as he could and threw the bedspread over them both. After fluffing his pillow behind him so he could sit comfortably – or as comfortably as his many aches and pains allowed him – he reached down, took Kody by the shoulders, and tucked him in against his chest.

The teen gave no resistance whatsoever to the move, continuing to shake, moan and groan within the grip of withdrawal.

One let his cheek gently rest atop Kody's head, and gently rubbed his arm, letting him know through these simple contacts that someone was there to watch over him.

"It'll be alright," One said softly. "You just gotta work through it... it just takes time... don't worry, I'm here... I'll be here...."

A sliver of sunlight from the imperfectly closed curtains shined into One's closed, left eye, and the suddenness of its radiance woke him instantly. Still, the lingering fever and fiery heat of his wound interfered with his mental functions for the first few seconds until, after running a hand over his face a few times to banish the last dregs of sleepiness, everything came back into focus.

He was lying on his back in the middle of the king-sized bed, his pillow tucked beneath his head where it belonged. Kody curled up along his left side in a position identical to the one he'd been in back in the boxcar when they'd fallen asleep, but this time Kody wasn't doing anything more than sleeping soundly.

Regarding Kody in profile and seeing the shaft of sunlight had moved to fall in a long line down the side of the teen's face, making the golden strands of his hair glow in sympathy. One had an unexpected pang of something that he struggled to quantify...

Pride?

Astonishment?

Affection?

Some combination of the three?

One sighed.

He's been through a lot – in some ways, as much as you have over your career, just different types of stress and trauma...

Glancing at the clock on the nightstand, One saw it was 6:44am. Deciding that there was no sense in waking Kody, especially after his rough night of withdrawal and the fact that he was finally sleeping soundly, One extricated himself as slowly and carefully as he could so as not to wake him. It took extra effort, since overnight his ravaged muscles had tightened, and were sending shockwaves of pain as way of protest to being forced into action.

In the bathroom, he stripped and showered, washing away the stink of his fever-generated sweat from the night before, then toweled dry, popped more amoxicillin and ibuprofen, and then removed the digital thermometer from its blister pack. He switched it on and stuck it in his mouth, sliding the probe tip gently under his tongue, and looked at his watch. A minute later the hit the hold button on it, withdrew it and studied the readout.

Hmm, 99.6°... still fighting the infection...

But I don't feel nearly as hot or sick as I did yesterday, so that's some progress...

He gathered up the medical items and put them into the outside pocket of his backpack.

There, ready to go in case we need to bug out fast.

Unlike most hotels he'd stayed at, this one didn't have a coffee machine in the room. He recalled the receptionist mentioning breakfast and coffee in the room adjoining the lobby and wondered if it was worth the risk of exposure to go down to partake of it. One wrestled with himself over the pros and cons of it for several minutes, then decided that the pros outweighed the cons – it would give him a chance to get a feel for who was staying at the hotel, identify the workers who were on the day shift, and it would allow Kody and him to stretch their food supplies by taking advantage of the free meal.

With that decided, One donned his baseball cap and pulled it down low, reinserted his pistol into his appendix carry position inside his trousers, and left the room. He took the fire stairs at the opposite end of the hall to recon it for possible use, and found it was basically a mirror image of the one he'd used the day before to bring Kody into the building, except that instead of a landing with doors leading to the outside and into the first-floor interior hallway, there was also a short set of steps led downward to a basement access door marked "Electrical Room – Hotel Staff Only."

One quietly padded down to this basement door, tried the handle, and found it locked. Bending down – and feeling his knees creak in protest – he saw it had a standard Swage lock, something he could either pick – if he had his tools, which he didn't – or bust in with a solid kick or two. But without knowing if there was a second exit from the room, its utility as a hiding place or escape route was nil, so One gave it no further consideration.

Entering the first-floor hallway, One sauntered down to the lobby, picking up the rich aroma of brewed coffee the moment he entered it. In the lobby there were a dozen men, all in safety vests with the Ferromex logo on them, holding to-go cups in one hand, and napkin-wrapped donuts in the other, chatting in small groups. One skirted along the edge of the lobby so as not to make eye contact or run the risk of conversation, and once he was into the breakfast area, saw that there was at least another dozen Ferromex men there, some seated around small, round tables or standing and chatting.

One wasted no time in setting up two to-go cups of coffee, light and sweet – none of this "I'm a real man so I take my coffee black" bullshit for him – and then scooped up eight donuts from the half-full serving trays, piling them onto a layered four-stack of paper plates for a sturdy carry. He was balancing it all in hand when he spied several small bottles of juice in an ice bowl, so he detoured, set everything down, and stuffed the pockets of his cargo pants with four bottles before taking everything back in hand and retracing his route out of the room and into the first-floor hall.

He was grateful that no one attempted to speak to him – indeed, he saw nothing but a few passing glances as he went through the lobby. At the door to his room, One had to set everything down to work the keycard and handle, but then a moment later he was inside and setting everything down on the room's small, round table.

Kody was still asleep, dead to the world, and hadn't moved an inch since One had left him some 20 minutes ago. That gave One worried pause – he stopped, stared at the teen's chest, and when he saw it slowly rising and falling, One realized he'd been holding his own breath.

One exhaled, feeling a brief second of thankful relief.

What, you thought he'd died during the night?

Get your head on straight... someone might think you've fallen for the kid...

That sudden thought startled One.

Have I?

Nah, that can't be... you're just feeling sorry for him, that's all... empathy, or sympathy or whatnot...

One shook his head, dismissing the notion. He pulled out one of the worn chairs, sat, and popped the top on his coffee to let it cool some before he tried to sip it. By this point, One's nose was desensitized to this, but Kody's clearly wasn't – a few seconds after he'd popped the top, Kody stirred, stretched, rolled onto his back and knuckled at his eyes.

After he finished that ritual, he rolled over onto his side and gazed over toward One. "Coffee?"

"Yeah," One said, taking the cup in hand and sipping experimentally. "Want some? I brought a second cup – or there's juice."

"Mmmmmm," Kody murmured, arching his back and stretching out his limbs like a house cat, before he sat up and swung his feet to the floor. He let his head fall into his hands and groaned.

"You feeling any better?" One asked.

"I'm... all achy..."

One set his coffee down, grabbed a bottle of juice, and crossed the room to sit beside him. "Drink this – you need to hydrate," One advised. When Kody had unscrewed the top and taken a gulp of juice, One asked, "You, um, remember anything? From, um, last night, I mean..."

Kody's head swiveled, his large green eyes finding One's blue ones, and a small grin turned up the corners of Kody's lips. "Yeah... I, uh... I'm sorry that—"

One held up a hand as he shook his head. "No need for apologies – I understand what you went through... and frankly, you've probably got at least another few days before it works its way totally out of your system."

"But I was fine yesterday..."

"Until you crashed," One interrupted. "I'm guessing they gave you a dose or something, or pill every day, sometime in the afternoon?"

Kody pondered that for a moment. "Yeah, every day we had to drink juice before dinner... they made sure we took it."

"Probably something like valordin or ketamorizine was in it... it's popular with human traffickers. These types of drugs suppress the decision-making areas of the brain, making you compliant without making you drowsy or inattentive. A positive side effect of the drug – well, at least as far as the traffickers and pimps go – is that it often makes the recipient really horny." One shook his head and frowned. "The problem is, if you stop taking it regularly, the withdrawal from it will hit you like a mule's kick after 24 to 36 hours... then after that, well, you feel like shit for a few more days, but you're functional. I bet one of those, or something like it, was what they had you on."

Kody stared at him. "You really know a lot."

One chuckled. "I know a little about lot of stuff – mostly, just enough to get myself in trouble."

Kody gave a short chuckle in reply.

"You drink coffee?" One asked.

"No, not really," Kody said, his grin fading. "My parents did, though."

"Well, there's three more juices for you, and four donuts," One said, patting the teen's knee. "Eat and then shower – I'm sure you were like me, sweating through a fever last night."

"I do feel icky," Kody admitted, sniffing at his own armpits and wrinkling his nose as what he detected from them.

One laughed again. "No worries. I got you several outfits." One reached into his backpack's outer pouch, found the ibuprofen, and shook out three. He told Kody to hold out his hand, poured the tablets into his palm, and told him to swallow them.

Kody did, chasing them down with the last of the juice in the bottle One had given him.

"C'mon, let's eat."

Seated together at the table, they ate the donuts and drank their respective drinks. "So, what do we do now?" Kody finally asked. "Is it really safe to be here?"

One popped the top on the second coffee. "We need to hole up here so my, ah, friend can send us documents for you. That'll be early tomorrow morning. Once we have those, I can get you out of Mexico without any hassle."

Kody digested that. "But is it safe here? Didn't you want to keep moving, like on the train yesterday?"

"It can't be helped," One admitted, and couldn't completely keep the worry out of his voice. "We need to be here for the delivery." One sipped coffee, then added, "I think we're good enough for at least until tomorrow. The chances of anyone from the cartel tracking us to this place is basically zero..."

But if Garrett's right, and de Corazón survived the assassination, can you really make that assumption? He's probably pulling out all the stops, calling in every favor, and posting bounties on your head that are in the millions.

But what choice do you have? You need a valid passport for the kid, and there's no way you're crossing at any border point within Presagio controlled Chihuahua... so, trust the plan, trust your training, and trust your instincts!

One fell silent as he considered his thoughts.

Okay, we'll do it your way... but remember, Murphy has a say too...

Finished with their breakfast, Kody hit the shower and changed into another new set of clothes. While he was showering, one took out his pistol, broke it down, checked it for defects, found none, and reassembled it.

One spare magazine and one in the pistol, 25 rounds, not a lot with which to defend if they come for us...

But I've worked with less in more trying circumstances... you'll be okay...

When Kody came out of the shower, One gathered all their dirty clothes, dumped them in the tub, turned on the hot water, and filled the tub halfway, adding a generous dollop of shampoo from the bottle he'd purchased at the pharmacy to the water. One then agitated the clothing in the soapy water, squeezing the suds through each item, and then leaving them to soak. After drying his hands on a towel and taking the towel along with him, he went back to the table where Kody remained finishing off the last juice bottle.

"Let's take a look at your shoulder," One told him.

Kody shuffled his chair forward and pulled off his shirt. One looked at the crude incision he'd made in the teen's shoulder the day before, and saw it was a bit red but not hot to the touch nor puffy. "No infection," One decided, "but this might sting a bit..."

Kody winced but didn't make a sound as One pulled the butterfly bandages off and a bit of blood oozed from the slit in the skin, the wound opening slightly without the tension of the bandages to keep it closed.

One withdrew the med supplied from his pack. Using a hand towel held beneath the wound, One poured a steady, small stream of disinfectant over it. Being a water based, quaternary ammonium salt, it didn't have the sting of alcohol, so Kody made no move as he poured. He did, however, wince again when One patted the wound dry after waiting a minute for the disinfectant to work and let out a long hiss when One laid a line of surgical glue into the slit and pressed it closed with his fingers.

"Sorry," One said apologetically. "It'll just take a minute to set."

"What are you doing," Kody said through clenched teeth.

"Surgical glue – basically crazy glue, but for wounds," One explained. "It'll close it so it can heal properly – hopefully without a scar."

Kody just nodded.

"There, all done," One announced.

Kody turned to look down at the wound, that now had a nice, square adhesive bandage over it, and then up at One. "Thanks."

"You're welcome," One said, and then added, "and sorry again for having to do that."

Kody's head bobbed a few times. "Had to get done, right?"

"Right," One confirmed.

One stowed the supplies and sat down. "I've been thinking... I'd like you to be able to defend yourself in case of emergency."

"Me?" Kody tilted his head at him. "Like how?"

One withdrew the USP pistol from its holster. He hit the magazine release, dropping the magazine into his ready hand, and after setting it on the table, racked the slide to pop out the chambered round, catching it deftly in midair as it arched downward. He set the bullet on the table and pulled back on the slide to release it from its locked-open position and de-cocked the hammer.

Kody's eyes were wide as he watched the process.

"I want you to be able to use this," One said, turning the pistol in profile, his right finger and thumb holding the end of the pistol by the barrel's opening, while his left finger and thumb supported the pistol from the bottom of its grip.

"This is the Heckler and Koch USP Compact Tactical pistol, Variant 9, in .45 caliber," One explained. "It is double action/single action, with a safety lever but no de-cocking lever. It uses a 12-round, detachable box magazine," one gestured toward the magazine sitting on the table, "which is fed into the underside of the pistol's grip." One then held the pistol by its grip in his right hand, picked up the magazine with his left, and demonstrated how it was inserted. "Always give it a firm hit with the heel of your palm to be sure the magazine is seated," One did so, "and then you must pull back on the slide – use the slotted grips on it for a good hold – to chamber a round." One demonstrated. "It is now ready to fire."

Kody didn't say anything, just stared at the gun in One's hands.

One cleared the round and dropped the magazine as before, but this time he re-inserted the round he'd cleared so the magazine was full again.

Holding the pistol in front of himself once more, One said, "It has a set of dovetail sights on the rear of the slide, and a post sight on the front," he touched each in turn with his left index finger to point them out, "and they are filled with tritium gas, so they glow green in the dark. This allows you to shoot even in low-light conditions."

One went on then to describe sight pictures, proper lining up of the sights, demonstrated proper grip and stood up to show proper shooting stances, and after he'd finished, told Kody to stand.

"We'll dry fire – that's pulling the trigger with no bullets in the gun – so you can get a feel for how heavy it is, how much tension is needed to pull the trigger, and proper sighting... if you're okay with that?"

Kody looked skeptical and a bit worried. "Um... do I really have to?" he asked in a small voice.

One was a bit surprised by his question. "Well, no, you don't have to," One said, looked at the pistol in his hands, and then set it down on the table between them. "But listen Kody, I'd like you to at least try it... it's only the two of us now, and well, honestly... even though you may think I'm some sort of superman, I'm not. I've already been shot once, and thank God it wasn't too serious, and I got some antibiotics to deal with the infection it caused, but—"

The sat phone decided to interrupt with its urgent trilling.

"Um, hold that thought," One said and answered the phone. "Yeah?"

"Busy?" Garrett asked rhetorically.

One answered anyway. "Just showing the kid how to shoot – in case, well... as a contingency."

Garrett went silent for a few seconds, then said, "Probably can't hurt to have him at least know how, but with your big ol' USP? I'm surprised he can get his hands around it."

"It's a bit of a challenge, but he's managing."

"Hmm, okay... anyway, what do you want first, the good news or the bad news," Garrett asked.

One couldn't help but roll his eyes. "Bad, I guess."

"Jorge Manuel de Corazón is alive," Garrett said with distaste. "Looks like his nickname of the 'Presagio Tiger' is true – he's got a cat's nine lives."

"Fuck!" One growled. "I had a feeling... but, *goddammit*! How's that even possible? I saw his SUV blown into flaming scrap!"

"I don't know," Garrett said flatly, "but he's alive. Based on intercepts – and I called in a bunch of favors, I'll have you know, to get this intel – he's orchestrated a hunt for you and the kid. He's posted a 10-million-peso reward for bringing you to him alive, and two million for information on your whereabouts. You'll have every cop, government lackey, informant, cartel member – hell, probably even the grandma on the corner in her rockin' chair keeping an eye out for you so they can cash in."

One grumbled out a long exhale of curses.

"But the good news is, I've got the passport for the kid coming to you via FedEx out of a cut-out in Costa Rica – it'll be there by 8:30am tomorrow... and I've got a few extra, 'special somethings' coming to you from one of my sources in Mexico City. He'll be hand-delivering it there by 6:00pm today, so expect a call from the reception desk to come down and get it – and before you ask, yes, its return address and payment code are for Ferromex, keeping in line with your cover."

One mulled over everything. "You think we're still okay to be staying here?"

"As far as the intel goes, there's nothing to suggest that they have any leads on you except for the fact that you were last seen in the roadrailer, which crashed into a barricade on the rail line short of the border and caught fire. There was no body inside, so they started a house-to-house search for you back along the rail line, but so far, they've come up empty. My sources agreed to feed me any pertinent updates as they got them. Unfortunately, it's not going to be in real time – they can't just drop what they're doing to focus on my request, but they've set up keyword algorithms to manage it. If something kicks out, I should get an email within a few hours of a hit."

"That's not ideal, but a lot better than nothing," One noted.

"You should be glad that I got even this much! I had to cash in a bunch of favors—"

"I get it," One interrupted. "So, we'll hunker down here, keep the sat phone on in case you come up with something more, and then once the FedEx package arrives, bug out."

"Basically, yeah," Garrett answered. "You still thinking of Monterrey?"

"Now that de Corazón is alive, there's no way I'm staying any longer in Presagio controlled territory than I have to. Getting down to Monterrey puts us in the gray zone among the warring factions – the Presagios, the Vamos Chicos and the Manos Rojas. The latter two aren't gonna do shit about something that de Corazón wants."

"Most likely true," Garrett opined. "So, when you're close, call me and I'll give you the flight information. For now, I've booked a bunch of tickets for you and the kid over the next four days – one morning, one afternoon, and one evening flight each day. They're all initially going to locations in Central America or the Caribbean where you can change planes for the trip back to the States."

"What's that gonna cost me?" One asked.

"Nothing until you're actually on a plane," Garrett said. "The tickets are of the all full-fare, first-class, refundable, no questions asked type. I'll just cancel and get refunds for the ones you don't use, but I thought it smart to have multiple options ready for you, since who knows what will happen between then and now."

"Yeah, Murphy," One complained.

"Exactly," Garrett agreed. "But I've planned as much as I could to avoid his interfering with your exfil."

"I appreciate it, Garrett," One said sincerely.

"No worries. Once you are on a plane, we can settle at that time," Garrett told him with a chuckle. "I'm thinking a steak dinner, nice bottle of wine, and fancy dessert at some posh, rooftop restaurant..."

"Whatever you want, you can have," One assured him, chuckling as well.

"Okay then, brother, stay frosty. If I get any intel, I'll call, so stay close to the phone and be sure it's charged up."

"Yes, mom," One said sarcastically.

"You only wish that your mom had taken as good care of you as I do," Garrett rebutted, and hung up.

One set the phone on the windowsill and turned back to face Kody, finding the teen running an exploratory finger over the slide of the USP, which he snatched back as soon as One turned but wasn't fast enough to prevent One from having seen what he'd been doing.

"So, where were we? Oh, yeah, not wanting to shoot..." One picked up his pistol and held it in the palms of his hands closer to Kody. "As I was saying, we've only got each other to rely on – what happens if I get knocked out? Or I get shot again? Or if we need to cover opposite directions? It'd be really great if you not only could shoot but be confident that you could, to defend us both." One paused, waiting until Kody glanced up to meet his gaze. "I'd really like to be able to rely on you, Kody."

That simple statement created a transformation that One clear saw in the teen's eyes and expression, changing from uncertainty and trepidation to resolve and a something akin to pride. "Okay, I'll... I'll learn."

"Great," One said with a smile and stood, indicating for Kody to stand as well.

For the next two hours, with breaks in between, One guided Kody through dry firing, using the small rate card on the back of the room's hallway door as a target, practicing stance, how to squeeze and not jerk the trigger, how to rack the slide, and how to keep your finger straight alongside the trigger guard until you were ready to shoot. Once One was confident that Kody had the fundamentals down, he allowed him to practice loading the magazine into the pistol, chambering a round, and then clearing the pistol, and then went to techniques for holding the weapon at various at-ready positions, showing him how to bring the pistol up, sight and fire in one smooth motion. Kody practiced this as well.

"You did really good," One complimented as they sat down at the room's small table.

"My arms and hands are sore," Kody commented, but not in a complaining manner, just stating the fact.

"It'll take time to build the muscles needed," One said. "But now you have the basics. We'll try some more later this afternoon."

"Okay."

"Just so you're prepared – when you shoot, it's really loud, and can startle you if you've never shot a gun before, so expect that."

Kody nodded.

"Also, there's nothing that says you have to wait to line up the perfect shot, especially close-in," One continued. "In fact, if someone is right next to you, the best way not to miss and still do damage is to jam the barrel into them," One made a gun shape with his finger and thumb, and pushed his finger into Kody's chest firmly, "and just keep pulling the trigger until they go down."

Kody blanched at that. He looked down at One's finger pressed against him, swallowed, and then looked back up. "Um, okay."

One tried to reduce the scary factor of what he was telling Kody to do by smiling as he pulled his hand back. "Just something to keep in mind – again, I don't expect it will ever come to that point, but if it does, I want you to be prepared."

One then broke out food they'd bought the day before at the bodega, making a lunch out of shelf-stable staples. After that, with nothing to do but wait, Kody turned on the TV and sat on the bed to watch while One reviewed the planned route to Monterrey he'd decided upon the day before. He used Google Maps to get not just routes planned, but what the terrain features were like along the way, and what alternatives he could take in case this new plan fell apart.

Kody fell asleep about an hour into watching TV, and One felt himself becoming drowsy as well. He popped his next dose of amoxicillin and six ibuprofens then put his pistol on the nightstand, ready to fire, and slid onto bed next to Kody.

Just a few minutes of shut eye...

The room phone jingled, waking One abruptly. It took him a few seconds to orient himself before he picked up the receiver.

"*Sí?*"

"Sir, there are two packages for you at the front desk," a young man's voice told him.

Two? "I'll be right down," One said.

One looked over at Kody, who was stirring because of the phone's ringing.

"I'm hungry," he said.

One shook his head. *Teenagers.* "I've got to go down to the desk to get a package. Stay here – I'll go across the street and get us something."

"Okay."

One got out of bed while Kody languidly stretched to bring himself fully awake. He holstered his pistol, shouldered his backpack, and left the room.

At the desk in the lobby, the clerk handed one large and one small package to One with a smile. Because of the large package's size, One couldn't bring it with him across the street to the mall, so he returned to the room to drop both off.

"What's in those?" Kody asked from the bed where he was once again watching TV.

"We'll see when I get back," One told him.

As far as he could tell, no one was interested in him at all as he purchased a dozen beef soft tacos, four burritos, four bottles of Coke, and some churros from the shop at the mall, and as far as he could tell no one followed him back to the hotel. The parking lot was once again filled with Ferromex service trucks and the lobby with Ferromex workers signing in for a room.

To One's astonishment, Kody ate his half of the carryout food without hesitation. Clearly the withdrawal and stress of the escape had drained him of calories which his body urged him to replace – and though the teen wasn't exactly skin-and-bones, he was close to that, and though One was no authority on kids, even he could see that Kody was undersized for his age.

"Good?" One asked.

211

"Mmm-hmmm," Kody murmured as he downed the final morsel of his allotment. "Thanks, I was really hungry."

"I can see that," One noted with a smirk.

After clearing away and trashing the remnants of dinner, One first opened the large box.

"Well, shit," One said in amazement as he pulled out items. "I'm gonna owe Garrett more than just one nice dinner."

Kody stepped next to him and peered down. "What's that?"

One withdrew a black, Shark Skin Tactical Armor shirt. "Body armor, the latest tech. It's form-fitting, lightweight, flexible and can stop pretty much any pistol round, even some rifle rounds if they are fired from distance." One realized that was another one beneath it, and when he pulled it from the box, saw it was too small for him—

But a perfect size for Kody.

"Well, well," One commented, turning and holding the armor shirt up against Kody's torso. "Looks like this one's yours."

Kody's eyes got big, and he took hold of the shirt when One pushed it against him. "For me?"

"Garret's outdone himself this time," One said as he saw more items in the box and pulled them all out, setting them on the table—

Four loaded, spare magazines for his USP pistol, plus two boxes of ammunition – .45 ACP Guard Dog hollow-points—

An extra battery for his sat phone—

A pistol cleaning kit—

And a bundle of 10,000 in pesos, and 5,000 each in euros and dollars.

"Excellent!" One murmured to himself.

"Who's Garrett?" Kody asked while his eyes scanned the array of items One had just laid out.

"He's a... co-worker and, um, a close friend," One answered.

Kody looked up at him then, catching One's eye. With a smirk Kody intuited, "He's your boyfriend?"

One felt his face blushing. He cleared his throat awkwardly and said, "Why would you think that?"

Kody smirked, nodding his head slowly. "Not answering the question... means I'm right. Right?"

One sighed. "Let's see what's in the other box."

What, suddenly this kid's omniscient?

Kody chuckled softly at the diversion, but let it drop.

Opening the small box showed it was full of packing peanuts, with a printed note card atop the material. One lifted it, unfolded it and read:

> **Thought the kid would be better off with his own, something he could handle instead of the cannon you use.**
>
> **--G**

Eyebrows raised, One dug through the peanuts and pulled out a black plastic carry case, stenciled with the SIG Sauer logo. The sticker on its edge, to the side of the carry handle, stated it was a P365-380.

Shaking his head with surprise and appreciation both, one undid the case's latches and opened it. A pristine, new P365 in .380 caliber sat in the retaining foam of the interior, with two, 10 round magazines imbedded beside it.

"Another gun?" Kody asked.

One pivoted and held the open case out to Kody. "Seems like Garrett thought you should have your own."

Kody's eyes flicked back and forth between One's gaze and the open case for several repetitions, his mouth opening with surprise. "Um... really?"

"Yeah," One said, setting the case on the table and handing Kody the note.

While Kody read with amazement, One felt around in the box for what he assumed he'd find, and sure enough, he found a 50-round box of Guard Dog hollow-points in .380 caliber and an appendix holster sized for the pistol.

Garrett thinks of everything...

"Here," One said, handing the heavy box of rounds to Kody. "Let's see if you remember from this morning how to load magazines."

"Uh, um, sure," Kody said hesitantly, sitting down and pulling one of the P365's magazines from its insert.

One watched, approvingly, as Kody loaded the magazine slowly but successfully. He did the second one at One's prompting, then stood when One told him to do so. One showed him how the holster fit inside the waistband of his cargo shorts, and how the pistol slid in and was retained there, then withdrew them and had Kody do it himself. Once he had, One had him withdraw only the pistol, take the magazine out, rack the slide to assure no round was in the chamber, and started in on more dry firing drills with the new weapon.

Kody had a much easier time with the P365, since it was half the size of One's USP and thus fit his better into his smaller hands. Like One's pistol it had tritium sights, so Kody found the only difference between the USP and the P365 was the weight and size. One told him that the bullets were smaller than the USP's, as would be the recoil, and because of the smaller caliber Kody needed to know that it might take more than one hit to stop someone with the P365 as opposed to the larger caliber USP.

Once One was satisfied Kody had a feel for it, he allowed him to chamber a round, top off the magazine with a round from the box – giving the pistol a 10+1 capacity – and holster it with the manual safety engaged so Kody could get used to the bulkiness at the front of his pants.

"Again, I don't expect you'll need to use it," One told Kody softly. "It's a... well, it's always difficult to take a life, Kody... I want you to understand that..."

Kody turned his green eyes to One. "I don't know..."

One put a reassuring hand on his shoulder. "You're a brave kid, to have survived despite everything you've been through... and only you know what they've done to you... if that's not enough, not enough to deal the justice that they deserve, then don't focus on that – focus on the ultimate binary choice... you know what binary is?"

Kody looked sheepish as he shook his head.

One couldn't help but chuckle. "It's a yes or no, on or off, a choice between only two options."

"Oh."

"So, for you it's an ultimate choice – either they die, or you will. Which would you prefer?"

Kody smiled grimly. "I'd, um, rather they died, not me."

214

One nodded. "If you need to use the pistol, it will likely be just that." One held Kody's gaze. "Just remember that, okay? I don't want to sound fatalistic – sound down about it, but it will be you or them if it comes to it. Just, ah, something I want you to think about – but not too much. Just to be ready should the time come."

"Um, okay."

One then left Kody to go to the bathroom to rinse the clothes that had been soaking and hung them up over the shower curtain rod and on the backs of the room's chairs to dry. By then it was close to nine o'clock and both were exhausted. One fed Kody some more ibuprofen to help with his aches and fever lingering from his withdrawal and downed more himself, as well as his next dose of amoxicillin. Each of them got into bed still in their clothes, put their pistols on their respective nightstands, and got under the covers.

Kody shifted himself to come up against One's side, draping an arm over One's stomach and resting his forehead against One's shoulder. "Goodnight."

"Goodnight," One whispered and reached over to turn out the lights.

Only after he lay there for a few minutes in the darkness did One realize that he'd given absolutely no thought to any concerns he'd had the previous night about sleeping in the same bed with Kody.

He'd separated himself from Kody the night before out of a sense of security – he wanted to be facing the door from a low, ready position in case it was breeched – but in fact One had to admit to himself that he'd been hesitant about being in close quarters with the teen after Kody had tried to thank him with unsolicited sexual favors in the boxcar. Even if Kody hadn't made such an advance, One was hesitant too because, well, in One's mind it just wasn't seemly for an unrelated man and a boy to share the same bed.

However, after finding Kody moaning in painful withdrawal, he'd given in, gotten into bed beside the teen, and comforted him. When One had awakened the next morning to find the teen spooned with him, he really hadn't been put off by it. One realized that there had been nothing sexual or untoward about it, but rather it was something done out of mutual support for one another – and for Kody, perhaps it had even been some sort of need for a parent-figure's warm embrace, something that provided tactile safety. If it made Kody secure and helped even a little bit to comfort him against his past trauma, One could put aside his concerns and be there for him.

With Kody beside him already in a deep sleep, One soon drifted off to join him.

Chapter 38

Closing In

Unlike One and Kody, there was no drifting off for restful sleep for Vincente and his men.

Vincente commandeered the mansion's dining room for the coordination of the search, which, ironically, was beginning to take on the character of something the US Marshal Service or FBI had done when trying to hunt down infamous personages such as Manuel Noriega and Pablo Escobar. They had their phones plugged into chargers fed by two power strips at the dining room table's center, and a white board on a stand, on which they had three columns printed – Camargo, Chihuahua and Delicias – under which they had lists of sightings and their approximate times. To the left of it stood a corkboard, with paper maps pinned to it, and push pins punched on it to show where the sightings had been.

As a sighting was discovered to be dead end, or proven unconfirmed, the pins were removed, and the sighting erased from the whiteboard.

After disconnecting the latest call, Vincente sat back and rubbed his temples. With a deep exhale, he looked at the whiteboard and maps pinned on the corkboard. It was becoming clear that no one had truly seen the assassin and the boy in either Camargo or Chihuahua. All the pins had been pulled from both these cities on the map, and every lead had been erased from under the columns on the whiteboard.

Delicias, on the other hand, had a handful of leads still listed, and a scattering of pins on the map. The last sighting that was still under investigation was from the day before, at a small mall's coffee shop in the late afternoon. As Vincente stared at it, Hector stood, phone to his ear, and used his sleeve to erase one of the lines under the column, then stepped over and pulled the pin. A second later Julio was at the board, erasing two more of the potential sightings and pulling two more pins, leaving just three.

Vincente glanced at his phone, seeing it was already 3:55am.

His phone trilled and he stretched out to grab it and put it to his ear. "Vincente here."

"Sir! I've confirmed that the boy was here!"

Vincente was up and moving to the boards. "Tell me!"

"He was with a *gringo*, like they were tourists," Geraldo said excitedly. "I had to track the barista down at his home, and that took longer than I thought – these *maldita sea*, these goddamn streets here aren't labeled, and none of the buildings have numbers—"

"Yes, yes, Geraldo, get to the point!"

"Sorry, sir! Anyway, yes, I showed him a picture of the boy and he said he was there, wearing a baseball cap. He didn't have long hair, but..."

"It could have been tucked under, yes, I see," Vincente interrupted.

"I assume so, yes. He was not able to describe the man well, just that he had fair skin, had a baseball cap on that shadowed his eyes, but the man, he was very fit – like a boxer, the barista said."

"So, the café is confirmed?"

"Yes sir!"

Vincente gently put his finger on the pin, pushed into the small block labeled "Valia Trading Corp." He spun to grab his tablet, put the phone on speaker and, started swiping through pages until he got to Google Maps for the location. He zoomed in and studied it for a moment.

There!

"Geraldo! Do you know the Hotel Mexico?"

"Uh, yes sir – it's over on the *Avenue Ferrocarril Ote*, maybe two blocks from the mall. Why?"

Why? Why do you think?!

"Listen to me very, very carefully Geraldo. You listening?"

"Of course, sir!"

"Good. You have what, five other men in your team?"

"Yes..."

"I want you to stake out this Hotel Mexico. Now this is critical – *you must not be seen!* Can you get hold of some vans with dark windows?"

"That should be easy enough, yes."

"Do it. Park across the street, or some place that would make sense to be there, or in the hotel's parking lot if you must – but do not allow yourself to be seen! Also, you must be able to see all four sides of the building between the two vans. I want you to keep a look out for the man and the boy and the minute you see them, report to me by phone. *Do not, I repeat this, do not attempt to intercept them, or contact them in any manner!* Do you understand?"

"Of course, it shall be as you say, sir."

"I want you to watch for them and that is all. If they leave, you are to follow at a distance, and keep reporting to me. Clear?"

"Yes, sir!"

"Good! Then get to it and report back to me the instant you're in position."

Vincente disconnected before Geraldo could answer and turned to the others in the room. "I need all the men recalled. We'll meet here at the mansion and be ready to move out the instant we're all assembled. Go!"

While they made the calls, Vincente rushed up to Jorge's room and, after knocking perfunctorily on the door, pushed through, turned on the overhead light, and went to Jorge's bedside.

The light and noise had already awakened him, and he sat upright with pistol in hand even before Vincente had gone halfway.

"What is it?" Jorge demanded, returning the pistol to under his pillow.

"We have a solid lead, sir! In Delicias."

Jorge was out of bed and moving into the master bathroom after the words "solid lead."

"How far?" Jorge asked over the sound of water flowing from the taps, followed by some splashing noises.

"Roughly 540 kilometers. By car, a straight shot down State Highway 45D, which means about four hours travel time—"

"What about by helicopter?" Jorge called.

"About half that, sir," Vincente answered. "But the Jet Ranger can only hold six."

Jorge came out of the bathroom wearing only his boxer briefs. "We need the men, so that won't do."

"I had the same thought," Vincente nodded. "I've asked the tunnel security team and the marine squad to assemble here. We'll have plenty of vehicles, men, weapons—"

Jorge spun about, and jabbed a finger at Vincente as he growled, "I want them alive, you remember that!" He then went into his closet and began to dress.

"Of... of course, *jefe*, that goes without saying!"

A moment later Jorge came out dressed in cargo pants, a tan cotton shirt with plain epaulets, and lace-up hiking boots. "Just so I am absolutely clear," he said matter-of-factly. "Come, let's get some breakfast in us before it's time to leave."

The staff was already clearing the dining room table and the smells of cooking sausage and eggs wafted from the open door to the kitchen. He sat, gestured for Vincente to sit to his left, and soon place settings were before them with freshly made burritos, orange juice, coffee and a fresh fruit cup. As they ate, SUVs arrived periodically with the security force and the hired squad of ex-marines, and with a wave, Jorge gestured for them to go and be fed in the kitchen.

By six o'clock their convoy of ten SUVs – all black, all with heavily tinted windows and heavily armored – were accelerating to 150 kph, with Jorge's Suburban, it's red and blue flasher lights and siren activated, leading the way to clear traffic.

Vincente got the call shortly after they merged onto State Highway 45D, and relayed the information to Jorge, seated next to him. "They've established a perimeter – the four men under Geraldo Vasquez, our capo for Delicias."

"Excellent! Anything yet?"

"No, sir, nothing, but the sun has just risen there."

Jorge mulled that over. *Do I have one of them go in and ask the receptionist if this man and the boy are there? Chances are he has not – it'd be more likely that the night clerk would have interacted with them. Is it worth the risk? What if the assassin has some high-tech way to monitor the lobby, the parking lot, the hallways?*

220

No, it's better to be patient and careful... once I'm there, we can proceed with direct control.

"Remind them to make no moves, to observe and call only," Jorge ordered.

"Yes, *jefe*."

After Vincente had done so, and disconnected the call, Jorge asked, "How long until we're there?"

Vincente looked at his phone's time display. "Three hours and 40 minutes or so, *jefe*."

Jorge smiled wickedly. "Good. I suggest we get some sleep." Tapping the driver on the shoulder, he told him, "Wake me when we get close."

With that, Jorge reclined his seat, took a night mask from the compartment beside his seat, donned it, and reclined his chair. Minutes later he was asleep. Vincente waited until his boss was snoring softly and then reclined his own chair to grab some much-needed sleep himself.

Chapter 39

You're On Borrowed Time!

Both had slept like the dead, their bodies needing the rest and recuperative refreshing that only sleep could provide.

Uncharacteristically for One, he didn't automatically wake at six o'clock like he always did – it was a sure sign that the stress of the last few days coupled with his infection had brought his body to the very precipice of its endurance. When the alarm went off, One couldn't immediately understand what the sound was, so infrequently had he heard it, but then he dragged himself upward from the depths of REM sleep and to wakefulness, punching the off button on his phone to silence the alarm.

Next to him, Kody grumbled in his sleep, his arm tightening reflexively across One's chest as he felt One move beside him.

With slow care, One lifted Kody's arm from his chest, slid out of bed, and let the arm gently down into the warm depression in the mattress that he'd just left. He then went to the bathroom to clean up, take his meds, and check his temperature. He found it to be close to normal, and when examining his wound, saw that while it was still red and sensitive, it was no longer radiating the heat that it had – it simply ached, which was a good sign that the amoxicillin was doing its work well.

Showered and rebandaged, One donned the Shark Skin body armor then tugged on some of the clothing he'd laundered the day before. That done, he left the room and went to the hotel's lobby where, like he had the day before, piled a bunch of donuts on paper plates, made two coffees for himself, and scooped up four juice bottles for Kody. As he did so, he kept a surreptitious eye out for anyone that looked like they were giving him more than passing interest, and seeing that no one was, padded down the hall to take the stairs back up to the room.

Kody was awake and just sitting up in bed when he returned. "Breakfast," One told him, setting out the food and beverages.

Yawning and stretching cat-like, Kody shuffled to the edge of the bed, wobbled from it, and plopped down in one of the two chairs.

"Feeling better?" One asked.

"Yeah, a lot, thanks," Kody said with a genuine grin.

"Me too," One told him. "The infection is finally under control."

"Good," Kody replied, biting into a donut while simultaneously trying to open a juice bottle.

"Here, let me," One said, and took the bottle from his hand, twisting the top off and handing it back.

"Tanks," Kody replied around a mouthful of donut.

The food and drink were quickly consumed, and Kody went off to shower and change. One checked on Kody's wound – which looked in great shape – and helped him into his own suit of Shark Skin body armor, over which he donned the laundered clothing from the previous day. By the time this was all done it was 7:30am, and One had them both packed and ready to go.

"Once the delivery comes, we're leaving," One told him as he slid the Ferromex safety vest over his shirt and donned the hardhat.

"Okay," Kody answered and turned on the TV.

Antsy, One went to the window and peeked outside around the curtain. The parking lot had emptied of the Ferromex service trucks, leaving just a few well-worn cars and a rather new looking dark blue van.

One felt the hackles on his neck rise when he looked at the van.

Was that there yesterday when I went down to get food?

Don't know... I didn't recon the parking lot – like I should have!

Just then his sat phone trilled. One snatched it up and pressed the button to connect the call.

Without preamble Garrett said, "I just got intel – from the chatter picked up, looks like de Corazón knows you're in Delicias, and has been canvassing the area around the railroad yard for you."

"You're just telling me this now?!" One nearly screamed.

"I just got it! The intel's fresh – six hours or so – but there's no mention that they've any sort of lead on where you are!"

One gritted his teeth and exhaled angrily. "Shit, Garrett, *six hours*? I could parachute in, blow an ammo dump, exfil out and be home enjoying a beer in six hours!"

"Hey, don't yell at the messenger!" Garrett replied firmly. "I can only give you what I'm given! If you want better, you should call your own—"

"It's an NCM, like I told you—"

"Don't get snippy! I know you're under a lot of pressure but yelling and screaming at me isn't going to help!"

He's right! Bring it down a few notches!

"Sorry – I'm sorry," One said, calming. "It's just, well fuck, after I got rid of the transmitter, I thought we'd be golden. I've done everything right—"

"Right, wrong, here, there, it doesn't matter," Garrett interrupted. "You're on borrowed time!"

"I'm waiting on the passport," One reminded.

"I just checked; it'll be there in 15 minutes, according to the real-time tracking. I suggest you go to the lobby and wait on it there instead of expecting a call."

One eyed Kody. "And the kid?"

"Is there somewhere on the first floor you could stash him for an immediate exfil?"

One thought about that, and remembered the basement electrical room, which wasn't really in a basement, more like partly below grade. "Yeah, I think so."

"Then get to it," Garrett said. "I've called an Uber for you; it'll be at the front in 25 minutes under the name 'Sanchez' – I just forwarded the confirmation to your phone."

One felt the phone vibrate with the incoming data. "Great, thanks Garrett – and again, I'm sorry—"

"Just get home to me safe," Garrett said softly. Left unsaid between them was the additional risk Garrett was taking to help One on a black mission that was specifically compartmentalized outside of the agency where Garrett worked.

"I will," One replied, softening his tone as well. After a quick glance at Kody to see if he was listening, and finding him engrossed in the TV, One turned away from him and whispered, "I'm sure the kid will appreciate it, after what he's been through..."

"I understand," Garrett replied softly.

One took a breath, glanced around to be sure Kody couldn't hear, and whispered, "I love you."

There was a long pause before Garrett responded. "I love you too – be safe."

One disconnected the sat phone from the wall charger, stowed the charger in is backpack, put the phone is his cargo pants thigh pocket, and donned the backpack.

Kody saw this. "We're leaving?" he asked hopefully.

"Yeah! Let's hit the bathroom one more time, and then we're outta here."

They did so, and after checking to see if there was anyone in the hall and finding no one, One led them to the fire stairs, down the staircase, and to the electrical room's door. Turning away from it, One back kicked with his new high-top sneaker, crashing into the door just below the knob, and the door swung inward. One paused them, listening for any signs that someone was coming to investigate, but hearing none, turned and peered into the room.

It was as he expected. Wire cages guarded electrical panels and conduit that One was sure wouldn't meet code back in the USA, and the room had that peculiar odor associated with electrical rooms – ozone, burnt metal, and plastic. It wasn't large, maybe three meters square, but it was enough for Kody to hide in until he came for him.

"I want you to hide in here," One said. "I'm going to the lobby to get the delivery and once I get it, I'm coming right back for you, okay?"

Kody looked uncertain and afraid.

Seeing this, One crouched to bring himself to eye level with the teen and said softly, "I'm not gonna leave you, don't worry, okay?"

Kody bobbed his head once, hesitantly.

"You have the pistol?"

He nodded again.

"Take it out," One ordered.

Kody lifted his hoodie, grasped the P365, and withdrew it, fumbling slightly to get a good grip on it, but then holding it in both hands at a chest-high, against-the-body ready position One had instructed him to use.

Kid's a fast learner...

"Okay, I will knock like this," One tapped the door twice, paused, then three times. "If you don't hear that before the door opens, be ready to fire, okay?"

Kody stared at him wild-eyed.

"Hey, hey – it's just a precaution, okay? I'm not expecting anything to happen, but better safe than sorry, right?"

Kody gulped and nodded again.

"Okay, I want you to go stand over there, behind that workbench and crouch down – you'll still have a clear shot at the doorway, but you'll be in cover from anyone coming in."

Kody looked behind him, then back at One. "You're... you're not gonna leave, right?"

"Not without you, no matter what," One assured, and put his hand on Kody's shoulder, squeezing it gently to reassure him.

Kody let out a deep breath, then took the position One had instructed. Seeing that he was in place, One smiled, waved, and closed the door behind him.

As he climbed the stairs to the first floor, his sat phone vibrated with another message. A quick look showed it was from Garrett, with just two words. "It's arrived."

One made his way to the lobby which, close to nine o'clock now, was empty save for the desk clerk, who one saw was facing the counter behind the desk, his back to the hotel's entry from the outside. A uniformed delivery man was just pushing through the double doors to return to his truck parked just outside.

"Sir, is that for me? Velez, Room 324?"

The man turned, looked down at the address label on the flat, carboard mailer, and then back up at him. "It is, sir." One saw the clerk's eyes dart to the stenciled "Velez" on his safety vest, then back to meet his gaze. With a smile he handed the envelope to One.

"Thank you," One said, and then headed back down the hall.

In the stairwell, he stood listening for a full minute, then checked the first-floor hallway, but heard and saw nothing. Returning to the electrical room door, One knocked as proscribed, pushed the door open a bit to let Kody see it was truly him, then pushed the door the rest of the way open.

Kody came out from behind the bench, gun still at chest level. "Is it... okay now?"

"Yeah, you can holster," One said as he took off the hardhat and vest, leaving both on the workbench. One then tore open the envelope and found two plastic bags. The first contained two dark green passport books, two around-the-neck passport holders and a folded piece of paper. The second was filled with a bundle of pesos.

One opened the first bag, took out and unfolded the paper, and read:

> **Here you go – since the kid is from South Africa, I've made you father and son from that country. Discard any other papers you have.**
>
> **--G**
>
> **P.S. I've also enclosed another 20,000 pesos – maybe buy me a souvenir?**

One couldn't help but chuckle softly to himself.

Up to my armpits in shit, and he wants me to find a souvenir?

One opened each of the passports in turn. They had been cleverly prepared to look used but not dog-eared. Inside the first was a picture of Kody, his information, and a few immigration stamps on the subsequent pages, one for Costa Rica, one for Argentina, and one for Mexico. The other passport was for One, with his stats and showed identical immigration stamps.

"Here, put this around your neck and under your shirt, on top of the Shark Skin," One said, sliding Kody's new passport into the neck holder, zipping it closed, and handing it to him. As Kody donned it, One did the same with his, then stowed the extra pesos in one of his thigh pockets. One then removed his previous passport and other documents, took out his lighter, and burned it, letting the flaming debris fall to the concrete floor of the room.

"Ready?" One asked after the flames had consumed the passport.

Kody nodded hesitantly.

One's phone pinged then, showing that the Uber ride was there at the front of the hotel.

"Let's go," One said, and led them back upstairs and into the first-floor hall. As they walked, One said, "We're taking an Uber ride downtown. Try not to talk unless it's something important. I want the driver to remember as little about us as possible."

As he crossed the lobby, One glanced at the desk clerk, who had his back to them, sorting through papers and stacking them in piles. Through the glass front doors, One saw a dusty, late-model Lexus with a man sitting in the driver's seat.

"We're taking that car," One whispered to Kody as he pushed on the glass door.

Outside for the first time in over a day, the heat hit them like a slap in the face, but then One was pulling the back door open and motioning for Kody to enter as he scanned the parking lot for threats.

The blue van was still parked where it had been, but something was off.

Were there men in the front? Did they just duck down?

There was no time to check. One dumped himself into the back seat, closed the door, and then brought up his sat phone to show the driver his confirmation code.

"We're going to the Hertz downtown?" the man asked.

"Yes," One replied.

One tried to watch the blue van out of his peripheral vision, but the Lexus they were in turned around the corner before One could see whether there were indeed men in the front seats or not. Coming around the hotel, One saw that there was a second van, this one black, parked in an almost mirror-image location to the blue one in front, and this time One did see two men in the front seats briefly before they ducked below the dashboard—

And one of them had a cellphone to his ear.

Fuck!

Chapter 40

Have Them Follow!

The convoy was passing through downtown Delicias, just 15 minutes or so away from Hotel Mexico, when Vincente's phone rang.

"What?" Vincente asked eagerly. "One moment!" He turned to Jorge. "*Jefe*, the man and the boy just left in a black Lexus! Geraldo thinks it's an Uber. What do you want them to do?"

Jorge's eyes lit with excited fire. "Have them follow! Do they have their radios?"

Vincente relayed the instructions, "Yes, *jefe*, they have them on channel 33."

Jorge leaned forward to address Juan-Pablo. "Channel 33, Juan-Pablo!" Turning back to Vincente, he said, "we'll use the radios now – have them give us a running commentary so we can join on them!"

Moments later the car's GMRS radio sounded with Geraldo's voice, announcing that they were about 200 meters behind the Lexus, and heading downtown.

Jorge demanded the microphone, and Juan-Pablo handed it over obediently. "This is the Tiger," he said, using his moniker of infamy instead of his name, since the GMRS radio wasn't encrypted. "Don't get too close so he sees you!"

"We will not, uh, Tiger..." Geraldo replied, but then hesitated. "Shit, they've turned, and we have a red light!"

Have them go through? No, the man will see.
Meirda!

"Do the best you can," Jorge told them, "but don't let them see you break laws – at least for now."

"*Sí*, Tiger."

Of all the cursed luck!

"How close now, Juan-Pablo?" Jorge asked.

"We should see them in the next few minutes," the driver replied, yanking on the wheel to avoid a truck then swerving around a line of cars waiting at a red light. The SUV's emergency lights and siren weren't doing very much at punching through the downtown traffic, and Jorge could see Juan-Pablo was getting frustrated – and a bit reckless as a result.

"Don't crash us," Jorge warned. "I'd rather lose them temporarily than wreck and be out of the chase."

Juan-Pablo darted a glance back at Jorge in the rearview mirror, then nodded. The SUV slowed some, but not by much.

A few minutes later, Juan-Pablo swung them onto a main boulevard and leaned forward, peering into the traffic ahead. "There, *jefe*, just past the next intersection!"

Jorge leaned forward as well, peering, and caught sight of Geraldo's black van. He tried to see the Lexus, but there was too much intervening traffic.

"Turn off the lights and siren!" Jorge commanded, and Juan-Pablo did so.

"We've lost them," Geraldo radioed as traffic began moving again.

Jorge didn't say anything in response, but simply threw himself back into his seat and narrowed his eyes.

Why go downtown? There's no train here... no airport... a taxi? No, they'd be at the mercy of the driver, who'd want to be talkative with two foreigners in his cab... and they wouldn't likely take a bus, too slow, too many chances for people to see them and maybe call for the reward...

"Quickly, Alfredo, are their rental car outlets near?"

It took the IT henchman a few moments to search. Meanwhile, Juan-Pablo struggled to get the SUV through the snarled traffic.

"Three of them within a kilometer, sir," Alfredo announced in his timid voice. "Hertz is about 500 meters straight ahead, there's an Avis to the left, about a kilometer west of us, and Mexicali Auto Rental ahead on the right, about 800 meters to the east."

Jorge turned to Vincente. "Have two cars go to the Avis, two to Mexicali, and the others stay with us," he ordered. "Tell Geraldo to join us once we catch up!"

Chapter 41

He's Here

"Pull over here!"

The black van that had followed them out of the hotel's parking lot had fallen far enough behind that the intervening traffic was, for the moment, blocking sightlines between it and the Uber ride they were in.

One didn't know how they'd been discovered, but it didn't matter – Garrett's info had been correct, and the chase was on again. The question was, if they knew Kody and he were at the Hotel Mexico, why hadn't they just gone in, made the desk clerk tell them where they were, and storm their room?

Because they didn't have a photo of me, there was no way to ask the desk clerk if he'd seen me, and though they no doubt had one of Kody, they knew I'd be smart enough not to have him seen, that's why.

That made some sense – they'd *suspected* he was there, and had to wait for the two of them to show themselves...

Which One had done, although there really hadn't been an option available to the contrary.

The driver twisted around enough to look back at them. "*Aquí señor?*"

"*Sí Sí! Uh... allí, junto al camión!*" One confirmed. "Yes, yes! Uh... by that truck!" One pointed toward a refrigerated 10-wheel box truck that was unloading crates of milk from a ramp extended to the street.

The driver complied, mumbling something under his breath.

"Stay close," One whispered to Kody as the car came to a stop. One quickly completed the Uber transaction, gave the driver a generous tip for the shortened ride, and exited, pulling Kody by his hand. On the street,

One slammed the car door, stepped onto the trash-covered sidewalk, and looked for the black van. He soon found it, about three blocks away, roughly 300 meters, trying to pass through cars that seemed to want to go every way except forward.

"C'mon!" One said, leading Kody away from the van at a fast pace up the street, his eyes scanning for likely targets.

At the corner One had them go right, out of sight of the boulevard. Luck was with them – there was a car park to the left, across the side street, about one-third full. One led them quickly across, dodging a few speeding cars that seemed to have no interest in stopping for pedestrians, and into the car park. He walked them swiftly along the first row, and not finding something suitable, started down the next, seeing a dusty and slightly dented dark blue Ford F150.

"That one," One told Kody and led them to the driver's side door which, to One's delight, he found unlocked. "Get in and stay low."

Kody scrambled in and hunkered down into the passenger side's footwell. The cab of the pickup smelled of lingering pine from the hanging air freshener on the rearview mirror, and there was also a small painted statuette of the Virgin Mary glued to the center of the dashboard, looking a bit faded and unhappy.

Once more using the skills taught to him, One used his knife to pop the steering column and worked wires he pulled from within it for several seconds until the engine turned over with a throaty growl. He slapped the column back into place as best he could, and then strapped on the seat belt, motioning for Kody to sit and do the same. As the teen got himself situated, One leaned forward to look out the driver's window toward the boulevard and saw the black van, finally free from the traffic snarl, zoom past. One was confident that they wouldn't see him here in the pickup because they would be focused on catching up to the Lexus, not having seen Kody and him exit from it.

One had just exhaled with relief and was turning to focus on driving when he saw six black Suburbans with heavily tinted windows zoom through the intersection in rapid succession.

What the fuck?!

THE COST OF ONE'S DECISION

One stared at the small convoy as it raced northward and out of sight and felt a chill flow through his bones.

It's got to be de Corazón!

Shitfuck! We're in worse trouble than I thought...

Kody sensed his increased worry. "What's wrong?" he asked softly, his eyes widening with fearful expectation.

One exhaled sharply again. "It's de Corazón – I think he's here."

At that pronouncement, Kody began trembling and withdrew into himself. One quickly put a hand to his shoulder and squeezed, the action making Kody look at him.

"Don't worry, they can't catch us now," One assured. "We broke the trail they had on us."

"You... sure?" Kody asked in a small voice.

"Yeah, and by this time tomorrow, we'll be in the United States and this all will just have been one long, bad dream that we've put behind us. Okay?"

Kody nodded and his trembling subsided.

"Good – now let's get the fuck outta Dodge!"

One wedged his sat phone on the dash next to the Virgin Mary and brought up the GPS and mapping function. He input his destination – Monterrey's international airport – and watched as the hourglass icon swirled. A moment later, the route was displayed with an estimated travel time of 8 hours 15 minutes to traverse the 750 km.

He glanced at the fuel gauge, seeing it at just below half.

"First thing we need to do is put some distance between us and the bad guys," he told Kody as he put the truck in gear and pulled out of the lot. "Then we'll stop for gas and something to eat – you hungry?"

"A little," Kody said distractedly, still hugging himself.

"Don't worry, everything's going according to plan – I just didn't expect them to have found us this quickly... but it doesn't matter. We're a step ahead."

Kody tried to smile in response, but it came out more like a not-really-believing grin of acknowledgement.

One followed the phone's prompts, and within 15 minutes was on State Highway 45D heading southeast out of the city. The truck's air conditioning worked, which was a godsend since it was already 95°F under the cloudless day's sun. One kept the truck at the speed limit and worked his mirrors to search for any sign of the black van, the Suburbans, or that anyone was taking undue notice of them in their stolen truck. By the time they passed through the town of Saucillo, One was confident that they'd given de Corazón and his thugs the slip.

When the signs for Ciudad Jiménez appeared about two hours later, One was feeling confident that his exfil plan for Kody and him was going to work. As the state highway had them going through the middle of the city, One looked for signs for a gas station, since the Ford's gas tank needle was hovering just above the "E" and the little yellow light warning of low fuel had been on now for the past half-hour. Seconds later, he saw the Pemex sign, and signaled to pull off the highway. Coasting down to the access roadway, One turned their truck into the lot and pulled up to one of the open pumps.

Before he'd shut down the truck, two young boys were already to either side of the cab, putting down well-worn white 5-gallon buckets to stand on so they could reach the windshield. As One opened the doors, the boys were already sloshing soapy water onto the bug-encrusted windshield and scrubbing at the bugs with squeegees wrapped in rags.

One exited and closed the door, staring at the boy closest. The boy noticed him staring, turned, and gave him a huge smile that showed white teeth with one incisor missing. "We clean it good for you, sir!"

One chuckled and nodded. "You do that."

Satisfied with One's response, the boy turned back to furiously scrub the glass.

One came around and found the attendant had already opened the gas cap and was about to start pumping in Premium into the pickup's tank.

"Excuse me, sir, just Magna, please," One told him. "Fill it."

The man nodded rapidly, apologizing and switched nozzles to the 87 octane Magna. Out of habit, One glanced over to be sure the pump was zeroed, saw that it was, and stood there watching both the attendant and the boys. When the pump clicked off, indicating the pickup's tank was full, One glanced again at the pump, and saw the truck had taken just over 21 gallons. One knew that the F150 base model had a 23-gallon tank, so that made sense, and it also meant that he'd let the tank go down to just a gallon or so before he'd stopped to refuel – not a wise move, and one to avoid in the future.

He paid the attendant and gave him a 100-peso tip, then went to the two boys who stood expectantly staring up at him with their wide smiles. One looked over the job they'd done – it was very good, the windshield now sparkling in the sunlight in stark contrast to the rest of the truck's dusty exterior – and handed each boy 100 pesos, which earned him excited pronouncements of thanks.

Back in the truck, One re-started it and turned to Kody. "Hungry?"

It was nearly one o'clock by then. Kody looked out his window to the 7-Eleven there at the station. "Yeah – can we go in and get something?"

"Better if I go in alone," he said, pulling the truck over to the parking area, nose pointed outward for a fast escape if needed. "I don't want them to catch you on any cameras."

Kody sighed and pouted for a moment, then said, "Fine."

"What do you want? I'm sure they have burritos, tacos, hot dogs..."

"Anything's fine – I'm used to Mexican food."

"Fair enough," One told him and opened his door. "Lock up after I go – I'm leaving the engine running for the a/c."

He watched Kody lock the door, then after pulling his baseball cap low on his brow, marched into the convenience store. To the immediate right of the entry was a stack of white Styrofoam coolers, which gave him inspiration. He took one, and then moving up and down the aisles, loaded the cooler with a few bags of snacks, chips, four Cokes, six bottles of water, and four energy drinks. He grabbed a bag of ice from the freezer, and at the hot food bar, he bagged eight burritos and four hot dogs, took packets of mustard and ketchup, and brought it all to the checkout where he paid cash and had the clerk bag everything into two plastic shopping bags, except the bag of ice, which he put into the cooler.

Back in the truck, they feasted on what he'd bought, and during it One saw that Kody had final, fully relaxed. They gorged on the burritos and hot dogs, and feeling sated, One tossed their trash in the receptacle by the parking area, and then iced the extra drinks in the cooler, stashing it behind their seats for cold refreshments later.

Back on the road by 2:00pm, One was himself finally feeling that he could relax his guard at least a little bit. After checking his mirrors for 10 minutes and seeing no signs of a tail, he settled into the driver's seat, and sighed.

Things are going my way for once...

Chapter 42

Without Delay

"Tiger, we've lost them!"

Those were the last words Jorge wanted to hear.

"Continue to the Hertz!" Jorge ordered, and Vincente relayed the command to the others via the radio while Juan-Pablo weaved past two more trucks and a series of cars.

They pulled into the Hertz location two minutes later. It was a small facility, with a two-bay garage and attached combination office and waiting room, with a fenced lot adjoining it that contained a dozen vehicles. Cameras and floodlights mounted on poles were stationed around the lot, covering all angels to deter theft both day and night, and signs along the fence every 10 meters warned of armed security.

The six Suburbans pulled into the entry driveway and halted in a line. A quick scan from their seats showed no Lexus, and no man and boy in the waiting area, just a woman behind the reception counter and an armed, uniformed guard standing at the end of it.

"Go see if they took a car!" Jorge ordered, and Vincente shot from the passenger seat, dashing into the office and up to the woman. Jorge watched them exchange a brief series of words, saw the armed guard watch Vincente like a hawk prepared to scoop up its prey, but then Vincente dashed back and into the SUV.

"They have not come here," Vincente relayed.

"Would she lie for them? If they paid her?"

"I gave her 2,000 pesos to be sure, which she took – and I saw nothing in her eyes or expression to suggest that she was lying when she said no such two people had come today."

"So we've lost them somewhere between here and when Geraldo lost track of them," Jorge concluded.

Just then Geraldo's van pulled in and screeched to a halt. The slim, mustached capo sprung out of the passenger's seat and dashed around to Jorge's window.

Jorge rolled it down with the control. "Find them?"

"No, sir – I am deeply sorry... very sorry sir... but we've, ah, lost them," Geraldo apologized, clearly frightened at having to report the failure.

As well he should have been, because de Corazón's temper and lack of accepting failure was well known within the cartel—

And this was not the first failure of his men regarding the assassination attempt against him, and the subsequent failures to capture the damned *gringo* assassin.

It was the straw that broke the proverbial camel's back. With pursed lips and a nod, as if he was considering the matter settled and Geraldo's apology accepted, Jorge twisted slightly toward Geraldo, feeling the pain in his bruised ribs stab at him as he did so. Then, in one smooth motion, Jorge withdrew his gold-plated Berretta Model 92 FS Inox pistol and fired once, point-blank, into Geraldo's chest.

The 9mm hollow-point blew a softball-sized hole out of the man's back with a spray of crimson. Like a ragdoll dropped from the arms of a child, the man collapsed to the ground, a pool of blood expanding from his corpse.

The shot made everyone's ears ring, and Alfredo, not accustomed to such raw violence, was sniffling and trembling, pushed up against the door with his hands over his ears and eyes closed.

Jorge de-cocked his pistol and holstered it. The coppery smell of blood mixed with cordite wafted into the SUV's cabin. "Have his men dispose of the body," Jorge told Vincente, who immediately left the SUV to see to it.

When Vincente had returned and was re-seated in front, Jorge turned to the still-trembling Alfredo. With a quick slap, Jorge smacked the computer nerd on the back of the head and growled, "Get ahold of yourself you good-for-nothing *puta*!" When that didn't get the expected response, Jorge smacked him a second, and then a third time.

Finally, eyes tearing, Alfredo turned but couldn't look Jorge in the eye. *It was enough... for now, anyway,* Jorge mused.

"Get on that computer! There's got to be cameras in this city. Find them and where they went!"

For a long moment Alfredo's eyes were downcast, his hands shaking, and his body unresponsive. Just when Jorge thought he'd need to deliver some more physical incentive, Alfredo swallowed, and eked out a halting, "Yeeeesss, *jefe.*"

"Good," was all Jorge said. Addressing Juan-Pablo, he then said, "Get us back toward the city center while Alfredo tries to find some clue."

With a nod, Juan-Pablo did as instructed, turning the big, armored SUV back onto the boulevard and toward where they'd lost track of the Uber Lexus.

"Where do you think they are going?" Jorge asked aloud after a few minutes of silent driving.

"I was just wondering the same thing, *jefe,*" Vincente admitted.

"Go on," Jorge prompted.

Vincente exhaled sharply through his nose. "Why here in Delicias? It has no airport, no passenger train, and buses are not tenable. A rental car was their goal, obviously, but we thwarted that. So what's left?"

"An Uber?" Jorge hypothesized.

"Unlikely, just as a taxi would be," Vincente said. "Few drivers will undertake a fare that goes far afield from their home base, and even if they did, this assassin risks having to engage in too much conversation with the driver – who are well known for being chatty and inquisitive."

"So, back on a freight train?" Jorge suggested.

"Not likely either," Vincente countered. "The schedules are not published, and it's too hit-or-miss to hope a freight train leaves soon and goes both the direction they want to go and for the entire duration of their planned trip."

"So?"

"Steal a car," Vincente said. "For a man such as this assassin it would be easy, and certainly part of his training. Just look at how many cars are stolen in the US – there is even a YouTube video on how several models of Kia vehicles have a flaw that allows them to be turned on and driven with only a cellphone app and USB cable."

"That makes much sense," Jorge said with a sage nod of his head. "Where would they go then?"

"There are only two major roads leading out of the city: State Route 45D and Route 22, *jefe*," Vincente answered. "I doubt they would take 45D back toward Ciudad Juárez, so that leaves going west on Route 22, or southeast on Route 45D."

"Farther into Mexico?" Jorge considered the idea aloud.

"Route 22 ends at a north-south highway, Route 24, and once again, they won't go north back toward where they just came from. That leaves the southern direction on Route 24, but it just puts them deeper within Mexico. The nearest major cities of Sinaloa and Durango are half-a-day's travel."

"That makes sense," Jorge agreed. "So, turn for the border?"

"That makes the most sense, yes," Vincente replied. "Or... well, the other option I can think of is an airport... one in a state or city where we have limited or no presence."

Jorge mulled on that for a long while. "Which do you think?"

Vincente retrieved his tablet, and after going to Google Maps, did some swiping and tapping, brought up a map with some proposed routes to three of the closest airports with international connections.

"No matter what they do, if they are headed for an airport with international flights, they have only a few choices within reasonable range: Culliacán or Mazatlán in Sinaloa or Monterrey in Nuevo León. Its 12 hours, 10 hours, and nine hours respectively to them from here."

"This assassin won't want to stay in Mexico any longer than he has to, especially if he's totting around the boy," Jorge conjectured. "Who do we have in Monterrey?"

Vincente had to go to his tablet again to find that answer, and it wasn't encouraging. "Only low-level intermediates for supply and enforcement, *jefe*." Vincente saw that this information was a slight shock for his boss, so before the man flew off the handle, he said, "We could call in some favors from the locals..."

"What sort of favors and from whom?"

"We worked to fix a problem for one of our associates on the other side of the border, Hugo Ledder," Vincente said, as he read from his notes in the database Alfredo maintained. "He's an ex-pat Slovakian who took over from Rafael Encino when the federales took him down a few years ago. He had the connections to Eastern Europe that funneled Afghan heroin and has since expanded. According to the database, he has men working out of a export company warehouse at the *Aeropuerto Internacional de Monterrey*. I could have them watch for and apprehend the assassin and boy."

Jorge considered that.

On the one hand, I cede control of this whole affair to some people I don't know, don't trust, and whose capabilities are undefined...

On the other, they will know the airport, have contacts and informants, and if the assassin and the boy do plan to escape by air, there are a limited number of security points and flights that will be available to them, creating pre-made choke points that can be monitored...

"What will it cost, do you think?" Jorge finally asked.

"It should cost us nothing," Vincente replied. "But in my opinion, *jefe*, if we want to optimize the percentages to achieve your goal, we should let them know of the rewards that you made available and pay them if they are successful... in addition to cancelling the debt that they owe to you."

"How much do they owe?" Jorge asked, eyes narrowing.

Vincente looked to Alfredo, who nervously licked his lips.

"Um... *jefe*... a little over 800 thousand pesos," Alfredo stammered out.

"It's not much, in the scheme of things, *jefe*," Vincente said with a nervous shrug. "You're offering a reward much more than that..."

Jorge liked that. "Very well, make it so. I will cancel their debt."

"And the reward?" Vincente asked, looking for clarification.

"They can have that too, as long as I get what I want!" Jorge declared.

Vincente nodded.

Turning to Alfredo, Jorge asked, "Anything?"

The man flinched when he was addressed. "Um, no, *jefe*... not, um yet... but I am trying!"

"Keep at it," Jorge ordered. "But regardless, we will go with what we've postulated. Juan-Pablo! Let's get onto this Route 45D, heading south. Recall the other men and have them fall in with us."

"Yes, *jefe*," the driver replied, and then after a pause, said, "*Jefe*? We will need to stop for fuel again soon."

"Very well, at the next place you see that isn't a dump," Jorge agreed. Then feeling his stomach rumble, added, "We should also find a suitable place to stop to get food – but only a short break. I want to pursue this assassin without delay."

Vincente then spoke. "*Jefe*, are we to leave the other airports from consideration?"

"Yes," Jorge answered immediately. "This snake of a man, he's slippery, but he knows we're on to him now – and perhaps that's not a bad thing. It will be Monterrey – you see, he'll want to leave as quickly as possible, and that will make him rush, which in turn will put pressure on him... pressure I hope will cause him to make a mistake... and once he does, we'll have him!"

Vincente digested that for a long moment, then hesitantly asked, "*Jefe*, is it wise for you to... to leave everything behind? If I may respectfully remind—"

Jorge turned to eye him. "That the shipment is still waiting to cross through the tunnel? That I risk attack against myself, or my various interests, by no longer staying in Chihuahua?"

"Well, *jefe*..."

"I understand your concern," Jorge said coolly. He sat in contemplation then for a few minutes before he looked back up and said, "Do we need all the men for this, do you think?"

Vincente looked relieved. "No, *jefe* – we can certainly make do with just the marine squad that's left. We'll be relying mostly on Hugo's men to find and apprehend the assassin and the boy. If the two of them are indeed headed to Monterrey's airport, we are at least an hour behind them, probably more like two."

Jorge considered that, nodded, and said, "Very well. Radio the tunnel security force to return after we stop to refuel. Coordinate with Alfredo here to set a new delivery date and make all the necessary arrangements for the shipment." He nodded again and offered a rare, sincere smile to Vincente. "I'm glad that you're here with me, to remind me of my commitments and to see to them for me."

"Certainly, *jefe*," Vincente replied, clearly pleased with the praise. "I'll make the arrangements right away."

Minutes later, the convoy pulled off the highway and into a Pemex station. After each filled their tanks, the men redistributed, with the marine squad taking the two vans that Geraldo's men had been using, and all but Jorge's Suburban heading back to Ciudad Juarez to resume the effort to get the next shipment of trafficked children across the border.

They were back on the road for only 15 minutes before Juan-Pablo saw a restaurant and guided the now-smaller convoy into its parking lot.

"Make sure to get enough food for us and see if they have a decent pinot – I'm thirsty," Jorge told Vincente. "No more than 15 minutes, then we get back on the road!"

"*Sí, jefe!*"

Twenty-two minutes later, the three-car convoy was back on State Highway 45D, heading southeast. Jorge ordered the emergency lights turned on, and with them to aid in passing traffic along the long, straight stretches of highway, Juan-Pablo did his best to keep his speed around 160 kph to make up for some of the distance between them and those they pursued.

Just after they merged onto from State Highway 45D to State Highway 49D about 35 km southeast of Ciudad Jiménez, Alfredo barked, "I found them!"

Jorge turned immediately to him. "What? Where?"

Alfredo swallowed nervously. "I'm sorry, *jefe*, that it took so long... but I can only get satellite internet in the car, and it's so slow—"

"Yes, yes, I understand – what have you found? Tell me!"

Alfredo spun the laptop on the fold-out desk to face Jorge. "This is a camera showing the parking lot for the *Edificio Municipal Delicias* –

across the street are the municipal offices for the city and region, with the courts—"

"Alfredo, the man?" Jorge demanded.

"Oh, um, yes, *jefe*, here…" Alfredo moved his finger over the track pad and a decent video image came up, showing a bird's eye view of a parking lot. "See here, a man and boy coming into view from across the street… and this…" Alfredo switched to a different camera, which showed the two closer up, "is where they went up one row of cars, then down the next, stopping here…" Alfredo worked the track pad a third time, then pointed. "They got into this pickup truck!"

The camera views weren't of sufficient resolution to show details of the man's face, and even if they had been, the man wore a baseball cap low over his forehead, masking everything on his face but part of his chin.

Jorge watched as the two of them got in the truck, backed it from its space, and left the parking lot, turning left and driving out of sight.

"It hasn't been reported stolen as yet?" Jorge asked.

"No, *jefe*. I was able to work on the best video capture images and managed to resolve the plate number – ZMB 62F. I checked on the state police database – it hasn't. Chances are it belongs to a municipal worker, and he hasn't left work yet and discovered it gone."

Jorge looked at his Breitling watch and saw it was only just after two o'clock.

Jorge turned to Vincente. "Call the commandant and have him make sure to squash any bulletins about this stolen truck," Jorge ordered. "I don't want some backwoods policeman to stop it and ruin our chances of capturing the assassin! Clear?"

"Yes, sir, I'll call now."

"How much time until we get to Monterrey?" Jorge then asked.

Juan-Pablo looked at the GPS for a moment. "A little over five hours, if I can keep this speed, *jefe*."

"Good – do your best," Jorge replied, then turned back to Alfredo. "Any unusual features on this truck they stole?"

Alfredo bit his lip and began working his laptop. After a few minutes, he turned it back to Jorge and pointed to an enlarged, pixelated image of the back of the truck. "There's a big dent in the rear bumper on the left side."

Jorge peered at it. "Good. Send that picture, along with the video and license plate information to Vincente's tablet – Vincente, make sure Hugo and his men have this latest information."

Both men acknowledged.

So, finally, some solid leads to identify these two...

Now, if only he doesn't switch out vehicles along the way...

Chapter 43

Bad News

I wonder if it would be smart to switch out vehicles...

It was just after three o'clock and One's thigh wound was throbbing. He'd been seated in pretty much the same position for the last five hours, with only a couple of hasty stops to piss and to refill the Ford's tank once more. They'd passed through the city of Torreón and were now on State Highways 40/40D, headed almost due east toward Monterrey, which was four hours away according to the GPS on his phone.

Kody had already succumbed to the mind-numbingness of the drive and was now sleeping quietly in his reclined passenger seat. One was beginning to feel sleepy himself and tried all the tricks he knew to resist it – he drank another Coke (despite knowing he'd have to stop to piss it out again), turned on the radio and listened to up-tempo music, and did some simple stretches there in his seat. So far it was working.

Nah, no sense trying to steal something new... it'd just be one more chance to get caught in the act and involve the police. Even if this truck was reported stolen, it'll take time for that information to trickle down through the system, and the Mexicans aren't well known for their interstate cooperation...

Besides, it's just four more hours and then we're outta here!

That reminded One of what he needed to do next. He worked the sat phone and placed a call to Garrett, who answered on the second ring.

"Hey there, everything okay?"

"Peachy," One said with a smirk. "Turns out that they had the hotel under surveillance."

"What?" Garrett nearly shouted.

"We're okay, no worries," One assured him quickly. "They must have arrived early this morning because I didn't see them the night before when I went out. Still, it was a close thing – they followed us in our Uber and if it hadn't been for morning traffic downtown, we would have been hard pressed to keep ahead of them."

"So what happened?" Garrett demanded.

One filled him in, and added they were now just four hours from the airport.

"Okay, hold on..." Garrett said, and One could hear the tapping of computer keys. "There's an Aero México flight, number 964, departing for Santo Domingo, Dominican Republic at 2038 hours, arriving at 2315. Think you can make that?"

One checked his watch. "That gives us roughly 90 minutes to check in, get through security, and to the gate... it's doable, yeah."

One heard more keys being tapped with machine gun rapidity. "Okay, I've booked you and the kid on it, first class, as adults so if, by some reach, they can access the airline's database, they won't see an adult and child listed. The DR doesn't require a visa for tourism of ten days or less, so you're golden in that regard... now let's see... I've got you on American flight 2310 departing at 0755 tomorrow from Santo Domingo to Dulles International. Flight time just under four hours."

"Great, that'll work – thanks, Garrett!"

"My pleasure," Garrett answered smoothly. "How's the kid holding up?"

"Good... he's sleeping."

"You on speaker?"

"Yeah," One replied.

"Go private," Garrett requested.

When One had cancelled the speaker function and put the receiver to his ear, Garrett said, "I've got some bad news... I did research on the kid. He's listed as missing by both the local Cape Town and the national, South African Police Service since October of last year. He was at a football match, and according to the reports the last his friends saw of him was when he went to the toilet just after the second half of the game started."

"That's what Kody told me, essentially," One said. "I don't see how that's 'bad news'."

"The bad news is, his parents are dead," Garrett said. "They were two of the 134 that were killed in the bombing and subsequent shootings by ICOA at Cape Town's Yokico Blue Route Mall."

One sighed, then shook his head. ICOA stood for Islamic Caliphate of Africa, radicals whose convoluted logic had them trying to bring the entire continent of Africa into the bosom of Islam through terror and murder. "Well, that sucks."

"It does," Garrett agreed soberly.

"Any other relatives?" One asked.

"I knew you'd ask – no, none that aren't second or third cousins removed a bunch of times," Garrett replied. "I'm guessing they'd be unlikely to take him in, but I could get the ball rolling for him, if you wanted me to, just to see if there were any takers..."

"Nah, not yet," One said. "Let's get home first, then we can worry about that stuff."

There was silence on the line then.

"You there?" One asked.

"I'm here," Garrett answered. "You sure you want to keep this intel from Kody? He's got a right to know..."

"Yeah, he does, I know that," One said in a whisper, cupping his hand over the receiver in case Kody wasn't actually sleeping. "But now's not the time – the kid's pretty fragile right now, and I don't want to lay anything more on him."

"Yeah, you're right – that was stupid of me," Garrett said. "So, back to the matter at hand; I don't have any more intercepts or intel. Looks like de Corazón has gone dark."

"Well, I know they were on our tail in Delicias," One replied. "And at this point I'm not assuming our escape from there was perfect, and I'm not letting my guard down... Not until we're on the ground at Dulles and in the jetway – and maybe not even then."

"Wise," Garrett agreed. "Okay, I sent your boarding passes to your phone, you have your passports, and I assume you'll be taking all reasonable precautions?"

"Of course," One said with a chuckle. "No need to mother-hen me."

"I'd never think of it!" Garrett told him with a chuckle of his own, but One could sense that he was thinking exactly that. After a pause, Garrett got serious, saying, "Stay frosty."

"I will," One said, disconnected the call, and brought the GPS back up.

After setting the phone back next to the Virgin Mary icon, he glanced over at Kody.

Poor kid... kidnapped, used for a sex toy, drugged, and now this... no parents to go home to...

Lord, can't we please have something good happen for a change?

Chapter 44

Keep Looking

"*Jefe*? Sir?"

Jorge opened his eyes reluctantly, feeling sleep still wanting to maintain its grip on him.

"We're an hour away, *jefe.*"

Jorge nodded to Vincente, sat up straight, and stretched his sore body – but not too much, for past a certain point his bruised ribs stabbed at him with fiery pain, reminding him that he'd survived the assassination attempt the previous day by sheer fortune.

"Any word from Hugo?" Jorge asked as he opened the Suburban's refrigerator and selected a bottle of sparkling water.

"Yes – he's gone all-out for you, *jefe*," Vincente reported, taking up his tablet and swiping on it a few times. "He's got some men set up at the airport's roadway entrances, and at the ticket counters."

"Unobtrusive, I hope?"

"Of course," Vincente replied. "He's been very adamant that he's doing everything discretely and with expectation of success."

Jorge snorted. "We'll see about that." He uncapped the bottle and took a long drink. "Are the marines ready in case we need them?"

"Yes. I alerted them to the one-hour mark before I woke you."

"Good... good... so, any sightings?" He turned to Alfredo.

The little computer nerd looked wrung out, and Jorge got a whiff of the man's sour body odor.

Disgusting...

"Um, no, *jefe*," Alfredo answered. "There aren't any cameras along the highway, just some at gas stations and the like, and though they are easy to access, I've found no sign of the truck or the man and boy."

I guess that's to be expected...

"Very well, keep looking," Jorge ordered and returned to silent contemplation as he finished his bottle of water.

Chapter 45

A Waiting Game

"So what are we doing to make this happen?"

Hugo Ledder couldn't believe his good fortune. Two hours ago, Vincente, Jorge Manuel de Corazón's current aide-de-camp, had called with an offer to not only clear the debt that he owed to the Presagio cartel, but there was the promise of 10 million pesos to find and capture a man and a boy who were of interest to the cartel.

Ten million pesos... let's see, that's about...

Half-a-million dollars! These two must really have pissed off the cartel!

Even if there hadn't been a monetary reward, Hugo still would have done the favor just to clear the debt he owed, but with so much cash thrown out there, who was he to say no?

"Sir, I managed to convince Lieutenant Calderón to reassign the three men we have on payroll to do screening duty at the entrance," Boris answered. "Calderón is instituting random car inspections for contraband, so he's set up checkpoints to do inspections on incoming vehicles."

Hugo frowned. "Won't that alert the guy we're looking for?"

"No sir," Boris replied. "He's doing random spot checks, so it shouldn't cause any worry. There will be signage stating this along the roadside. It's quite a common occurrence, as I understand it... they do these a couple of times a month. He's been told that, if he sees the truck in question, he's to simply wave it through and then have one of his men tail it on a motorbike."

Hugo nodded his satisfaction. "Good. What else?"

"I've placed 12 men in the terminal, seated near the ticket counters and at the security screening checkpoints. We obviously want to try to take them before they pass through security, because after that, well, it becomes more difficult to snatch them without a fuss."

"They've been told to take them alive, right?" Hugo asked.

"Yessir, and all have tasers, autoinjectors with ketamine, zip ties, and radios," Boris confirmed. "None of our men inside have any guns – it's too dangerous with the state police on patrol."

"Too bad we haven't recruited more to the cause," Hugo noted dourly.

"We continue to try, of course, but what we have now is all we can muster for this work," Boris said.

"So once we get them, then what?"

"We take them to our warehouse there on property and hold them until de Corazón arrives. No one is going to say or see anything if they know what's good for them."

Hugo smiled at that. "So, now it's a waiting game, eh?"

"Yessir."

"And we still have nothing more on these two that what de Corazón's lackey told us?" Hugo asked.

"Right – a man, Caucasian, possibly an American, around 85 kg and somewhere around 180 cm in height, broad shoulders and athletic build, like a boxer. The boy is easier – we have several photos of him that are clear and high resolution, which I've already sent to everyone's phones."

Hugo nodded again. "Good. All bases covered then." He stood, stretched, and turned to Boris. "Let's take a ride out to the warehouse. I want to be there when we catch these two."

Chapter 46

We've Made It!

It was 6:48pm when One pulled off the highway and onto the service road leading to the airport.

As they got closer and closer to their destination, it had taken all One's patience and willpower to not go over the speed limit to dash to the finish line. Saving a few minutes wasn't worth the risk of being pulled over by a local cop, who might call in the truck's plate and discover it had been stolen. If he didn't discover it was stolen, the traffic stop would delay them enough to miss their flight or worse – to allow de Corazón to catch up with them.

One was convinced now that de Corazón was indeed hot on his trail. He had no substantive proof, just a tingling feeling at the nape of his neck and a predator's sense that he was becoming the prey.

"Hey, Kody, wake up," One said softly, reaching over to gently squeeze the teen's shoulder.

Kody came awake slowly and stretched. "Where are we?"

"Almost to the airport," One answered.

"Okay," Kody said and began looking out the windows at their surroundings, which were cloaked in pre-dusk glow.

A jet airliner roared nearby, and a moment later could be seen rising into the sky in the near distance, its anti-collision lights flashing brightly.

That perked Kody up. "We're really going to leave?" he asked, turning to One.

"That's the plan," One said with a smile, but still felt uneasy – the gnawing feeling of pursuers closing in tempering his optimism.

Turning into the airport's two-lane roadway, One immediately saw flashing red and blue lights in the distance with a portable light tower shining brightly onto the roadway. Two yellow, fold-out diamond signs stood on either side of the road, one in English stating "INSPECTION AHEAD" while the other announced the same message in Spanish, "INSPECCIÓN POR DELANTE."

Aw, fuck you, Murphy! Why now of all times?!

One sighed heavily and rolled his lips to form a pensive line.

Not much we can do about it... chances are it's just an inspection for bombs and other terrorist related activity... which we don't have any of...

Unless you consider the two guns, which in Mexico is a felony...

Nah, don't get your panties in a bunch! The signs are obviously not something they whipped up by hand, but are reusable... and after 9-11, airports in the US do this too...

Okay, so we're all calm now, right? Just be cool and it won't be a problem...

"What are they inspecting?" Kody asked as they passed the signs, and then immediately pointed, "there's cop cars up there!"

"Relax, okay?" One reassured him. "It's just a routine inspection... they do this at airports all over the US and the world. It's standard... but if they stop us, let me do the talking. If you are asked a direct question, answer it as simply as you can and be respectful. The more you say, the more they can trip you up..."

Kody's eyes got wide, and he licked his lips.

"Now, now, nothing to worry about... chances are we won't even be stopped. These things are random usually." One glanced at him, seeing that Kody was still nervous. "You remember the stuff on your passport?"

"Yeah," Kody said after a pause. "Only my last and middle names are different, and I can... um, I can remember them fine."

"Okay then, nothing to worry about," One said.

As they closed to within 100 meters, they saw two Nuevo Leon State Police pickup trucks parked to either side of the road, their noses facing traffic on an angle, so that the roadway was reduced to one lane that ran between them, down the center's painted, dashed line. They had their roof light bars on, strobing the oncoming traffic in red and blue, with the light tower parked on the dry, brown grass to the left side, its four halogen lamps making the area in and around the police trucks daylight bright.

One queued their pickup truck behind the line of merging cars, and leaned sideways, trying to see the nature of the checkpoint. After watching for a minute, he was pleased to see that an officer with a traffic wand was waving cars through without stopping them for inspection, then he suddenly stopped one. Two officers then walked around the car with inspection mirrors – concave mirrors on wheels and a long handle, so one could remain standing while scanning the underside of a vehicle – followed by a quick popping of the hood and trunk to see if anything unusual was within. As far as One could tell, no one was asked to step out of the car, and personal belongings within the car weren't being searched.

That gave him some semblance of relief, but the nagging itch that his pursuers were even closer now wouldn't abate.

When One got to within a few car lengths of the checkpoint, he saw two more large signs on portable stands, red and white octagons that stated in English – "STOP – SECURITY CHECK POINT" – and in Spanish – "ALTO – PUNTO DE SEGURIDAD."

Just as I thought...

Traffic started moving again, and One forced himself not to death-grip the wheel, to relax, that everything would be just fine...

The cop was waving through the cars ahead of him... one... two... three... four... and then it was his turn—

And the cop held up his wand and hand to stop him.

Great...

One slowed and was almost stopped when one of the cops with a mirror yelled something to the one with the traffic wand. The cop with the wand looked at One, meeting his eyes, then looked over the front and side of the truck in a quick scan—

And waved it to proceed.

Well, well Murphy... decided to finally give me a break, huh?

One didn't wait around to question his good fortune. He gently accelerated the truck through the gap between the pickups and then merged into the right lane, keeping to the 40 kph speed limit.

Once they were past, Kody noticeably relaxed as well. "I'm glad we didn't have to stop."

"Me too, honestly, though I'm sure it would have been fine if we had to," One said, and exhaled a long, satisfied breath.

We've made it! Now, just to get onto the plane...

One followed the signs to the parking areas and stopped at the booth to get a ticket. Once the arm on the parking lot gate rose, he piloted the truck into the lot and found a space, backing into it so that, if for some reason things didn't work out as planned, he wouldn't have to spend precious moments backing the truck out of the space.

"We're here," One declared with not a little sense of relief. He reached up, took the sat phone in hand, and typed out a quick text to Garrett, announcing their arrival. He then tucked the phone into his thigh pocket.

"When's our plane leave?" Kody asked.

"At about 8:40," One answered. Looking at his watch, he added, "gives us about 90 minutes to get through security and to the gate."

A thought suddenly occurred to One. "Have you flown before?"

Kody nodded. "Yeah, a bunch of times on trips with my mom and dad."

The mention of his parents brought the bad news Garrett had relayed earlier to the forefront of One's thoughts.

Now's not the time to say anything....

"Okay, good, so you know what to expect," One said, more of a statement than a question.

"Yeah, sure."

One eyed the terminal, lit up brightly in the waning day's light. Sunset had already occurred, but there was still a colorful glow of mauve, pink and mango mixing above the horizon.

The nagging sensation of danger was still there, strong and annoying.

"Listen, I'm going inside to take a look around," One told him. "Then I'll come back for you. You still have your cell phone?"

"Yeah," Kody said, fishing it from the pocket of his cargo shorts and showing him.

"Is it on?"

Kody chuckled, "Yeah."

"Okay, if there's a problem, I'll call you. If for some reason I'm not back in 20 minutes, I want you to call Garrett and tell him. He'll direct you what to do next."

Kody's eyes got big, and he leaned forward, putting a hand on One's thigh. "Are they here? Is that why you're telling me this?"

One put a reassuring hand atop the teen's. "No, no, it's not that... it's just... well, I can't help but be careful, y'know? It's how I'm built." One shrugged. "So I'm going to scout things out first, and then I'll be right back. I'll leave the engine running so you'll have the a/c."

Kody looked at him skeptically, biting on his lower lip, but then took his hand back and tried to smile. "Okay... I trust you."

Unaccountably, those last three words pulled at One's heartstrings. He suddenly felt out of breath and tears welling in his eyes.

What all this about?

"Um... well, thanks... I, um, appreciate that," One said haltingly, knuckling at his eyes before the tears could come fully out. He cleared his throat and smiled. "I trust you too... so stay here, okay? Keep out of sight, down below the windows."

Kody nodded and squirmed down into the footwell on the passenger side.

"And remember, if something happens, and you need to, use the pistol, okay?"

Kody's hand went reflexively to the handle of the P365 under his hoodie. "Okay," he said hesitantly.

"It's just in case," One confirmed. "Okay, I'll be right back."

Chapter 47

A High-Pitched Scream

"They've been spotted!"

Despite the pain that flared in his ribs, Jorge leaned forward to pat Vincente and Juan-Pablo on their shoulders. "Well done!"

"We're about an hour away," Juan-Pablo said.

"Hugo wants us to meet him at the air cargo warehouse he owns," Vincente said as he listened to the phone call with Boris, Hugo's right-hand man. "I've got the location." Vincente told Juan-Pablo, who programmed it into the GPS.

"Radio the marines and tell them to be ready – if Hugo's men screw this up, I want to be ready to handle things ourselves."

"Right away, *jefe*!"

One entered the terminal building focused on being casual and relaxed, even though inside he was anything but.

He went into full Tier One Operator Mode, his eyes scanning even as he walked nonchalantly toward the information display hanging from the ceiling supports. He quickly found AM Flight 964 and saw the flight was on time at 8:38pm, out of gate B6 in the Southern Concourse.

One turned to walk down the terminal, examining the security checkpoint and its immediate area as he strolled past—

And he saw two men taking an interest in him.

They were pretty good at surveillance.

The first was reading a magazine while wearing a ball cap low over his brow, shadowing his eyes and making it difficult for someone nearby to see exactly where he was gazing.

The other was sitting on a roller suitcase to the side of the security area, headphones over his ears, eating from an open bag of crisps, and looking in no particular direction – a traveler waiting for his flight, but not yet ready to go through security.

But at counter-surveillance, One was better.

He noticed the micro-expressions on their faces when he came within their view, and the slight change in their postures – indications that were clear to him, but to those making them, they were unaware.

I knew it was too good to be true!

Damn you, Murphy!

One continued strolling by, checking in the tall, glass windows to see if the men were following.

They were.

Shitfuck!

It all came crashing down for One. His mind raced, trying to think of a way out of the trap that had developed.

This is what you get for letting your guard down – for going soft, taking the kid along with you when you should have exfiltrated with your men!

One growled to himself.

That's just anger talking – you know you'd never leave an innocent behind, so don't even go there!

Besides, Kody's become more than just that... you like him, don't you?

You know you do... and you promised him... to protect him...

You're wasting time – you've got to clear the datum!

Easy to say, but I've blocked us in! Fuck! How could I have been so stupid?!

Even though you thought you were on top of things, truth is, you got complacent in your rush to exfil...

Now you're in it deep. There's only one exit road from the airport, and by now it'll be watched, if not ready to be blocked off.

Fuckin' shit!

One calmly exited the terminal, the broad sliding glass doors automatically opening for him and letting in a waft of dry heat from the outside. One continued onto the sidewalk, knifing past arriving travelers, dashing quickly through taxis and traffic to cross to the parking lot. He glanced into car windows and outside mirrors as he walked through the lot, seeing the two men exiting the terminal behind him, and then splitting up, one going right the other left.

Well, the pickup truck can go off-road... if needed, I can get past a roadblock...

Maybe we forget the truck, double-back and lose the tail in the concourse, then take a taxi into downtown Monterrey...

So focused was One on his predicament, trying to think through options and keep an eye on those following him, that he neglected to notice what was coming in from his left. It wasn't his fault – so much was going on, and after being wounded and infected, his body and mind weren't functioning at 100 percent. But when the screeching of tires shrieked directly in front of him, One's attention swung to it immediately—

A van pulled up, screeching to a halt, its sliding door flying open, and from it three masked men in balaclavas rushed out and aimed tasers—

One instinctively dodged, jinking right and rolling onto his shoulder, trying to get to cover behind the nearest parked car even as he went for his pistol. The taser barbs of the first two men's shots missed, clattering against the pavement, but the third got One in the back of the neck, just above the line of his body armor, its gas-propelled darts piercing into flesh—

One's world became a dazzle of kaleidoscopic agony, every fiber aflame, and then for him there was no thinking, no moving, just immobilizing pain.

"Get the zip ties on him!"

Through the numbness, One felt himself being rolled over, his arms yanked behind him, and zip ties cutting into the flesh of his wrists. Dimly, he realized he was being sat upright, and then what little sense of sight he had was taken as a black cloth bag was tugged over his head.

"Find the kid!"

"I don't see him!"

"Idiot! Look for the truck they came in! It's gotta be parked around here somewhere, if this big fuckin' gringo was heading into the lot!"

"Okay, okay!"

"I see it! There – there's the truck!"

Suddenly, One was hauled to his feet and began to get a little bit of his awareness back as he was propelled forward crashing down against a hard, metal floor.

A van? One thought.

The numbness was fading quickly, and One managed to get himself into a seated position, feeling his right shoulder glide against the interior of the van's side. Just as he managed this, he heard the shattering of glass nearby, the *pfft* of a taser shooting, the *tick-tick-tick* of a taser discharging its voltage, and then a high-pitched scream.

Kody!

That was the last thing that flashed through One's mind – he felt rough hands grab him and before he could start to resist, there was the sting of an autoinjector in his neck...

Seconds later everything went black.

Chapter 48

They Have A Thing...

"Sir, he's coming out of it."

Hugo turned from the television – the football team, in which he was a silent investor, was winning by one goal – and asked, "When's de Corazón due?"

Boris glanced at his watch. "Another 40 minutes or so."

"Let's take a look," Hugo said as he pushed himself out of his chair and walked toward the storage room behind the warehouse's spacious office.

One was zip-tied to a metal folding chair, his hands behind his back and additional zip-ties held his arms and calves so they were immobilized. The chair itself zip-tied in multiple places to a steel support beam that ran up to the ceiling's support lattice, preventing One from toppling it over or moving it. One's head was lolling slowly, drool dripping from the corner of his mouth as the effects of the small dose of ketamine he'd been given worked its way out of his system.

Kody had his hands zip-tied in front of him and another set of zip-ties around his ankles. He lay on the storage room's ratty couch, a strip of silver duct tape over his mouth. He was awake, and his eyes immediately flicked to Hugo and Boris as they entered.

Hugo strolled over to One, lifted his chin, and regarded the stupefied look on the man's face. "Dumbass, getting on the wrong side of the Presagios!" Hugo let the man's head fall back onto his chest and turned to Boris. "You searched him?"

"Yes, sir," Boris replied and motioned over toward the workbench. Hugo glanced that way and saw a H&K USP pistol in a clip holster, two extra magazines for it, a single .45 caliber hollow-point round sitting nose up, a suppressor for the USP, a wallet, a sat phone, a cheap, pay-as-you-go cell phone, a South African passport, and a folding knife.

"Right," Hugo nodded as he stepped over and took up the pistol.

Boris had removed the magazine and locked the slide open with the slide lever. Hugo tilted the pistol so he could look down into the interior magazine well to confirm it empty, snorted a "Hmph," and then set the heavy pistol back down.

"What do you think will happen to them?" Hugo mused aloud as he turned and leaned his backside against the edge of the workbench, stroking his chin thoughtfully as he stared at One.

Boris grinned, joining his boss at the bench. "I'm guessing he'll make the father watch as he rapes the boy, then carves off selected pieces, keeping the kid alive as long as he can by cauterizing the wounds."

Kody's eyes widened.

Hugo nodded sagely. "That sounds about right. The Tiger does like to smash his toys after he plays with them – or *while* he's playing with them." Hugo snickered and eyed Kody, making sure the teen met his gaze.

"That's what I hear," Boris agreed. "And these Mexicans, they have a thing about cutting off your dick and balls and making you eat them."

Kody's eyes got even wider as he listened.

Hugo laughed evilly. "You think he'll cut off the boy's and make the kid eat his own, or make the father eat the kid's?"

Boris shrugged. "Who knows?"

Hugo glanced at him sideways. "Bet?"

After a moment's consideration, Boris said, "Sure – what're you thinking?"

"Let's say... 20 thousand pesos?"

Boris nodded. "I'll take that... I'm going with de Corazón makes the father eat the kid's junk."

"Fine – I'll take that he makes the kid eat his own dick and balls."

"What if he makes the boy eat his dad's junk?" Boris asked.

"Same bet, but with the father?" Hugo asked.

"Okay, I'll take that bet too," Boris answered.

"Done!" They bumped fists.

Kody felt bile rise in his throat and started to hyperventilate.

The two men noticed. "Shit, kids panicking. Take the tape off!" Hugo ordered.

Boris stepped over quickly and pulled the tape away. The sharp pain of that startled Kody into stopping his hyperventilating long enough that he gained his breath back, although he continued to pant weakly.

And then Kody rolled his head just off the couch's edge and vomited.

"*Mierda!*" Boris exclaimed and jumped back. Some of the foul-smelling semisolid splattered over his expensive alligator cowboy boots.

Hugo broke out in riotous laughter. "Maybe we shouldn't have talked about this in front of the kid!"

Boris glared up at his boss, but wisely didn't spit out the retort that had formed on his lips.

"Get him up and move him to the other end," Hugo said, stepping carefully around the pool of puke to help Boris lift Kody by his arms and thighs, seating him at the other end of the threadbare couch. "Go get someone with a bucket of Fabuloso and mop – it won't do to have it stink in here and puke on the floor when de Corazón arrives."

Boris got up and went to call one of the workers. Before he got to the doorway, Hugo added, "And some air freshener or some shit like that!"

Boris nodded and left on his assigned errand.

After a glance at the kid, who was clearly still woozy, he went to the office's refrigerator and pulled out a bottle of water. Twisting the cap off, he returned and sat on the couch's arm. "Here, drink some," Hugo told Kody and put the bottle to the teen's lips.

Kody eyed him suspiciously but drank nonetheless. After a few swallows, Hugo removed the bottle and asked, "More?"

Kody nodded, and Hugo helped him finish the bottle off in a series of slow feedings. That done, Hugo tossed the bottle into a trash can at the far end of the room, then stepped back to the workbench where a roll of duct tape was sitting. He pulled off a piece and came back toward Kody with it.

"Sorry, but I have to gag you up again," Hugo said in a tone that suggested anything but sorrow. "Your tormentor will be here soon, so don't worry... in the meantime, I'm going back to see the end of my football game."

Kody managed a half-angry glare but said nothing as the man reapplied the tape over his mouth and then pushed him back into the couch.

"Stay put and you might live a little longer," Hugo advised with a chuckle.

Kody trembled and couldn't help sniffling, feeling tears streaming down his cheeks, but he remained where he was, bound hands in his lap.

When the man named Hugo turned away and left the room for the office beyond, Kody wiped his eyes on his upper arms, first right, then left, and turned his attention to One. His protector was mumbling, his head still lolling to the side in the upright position he'd been forced into by all the zip-ties attached to him. Thick drool formed a long tendril that hung from the corner of his mouth and an instant later, it separated to splat on the concrete next to One's chair.

Kody closed his eyes and tried to both control his breathing and still his racing heart, but what the two men had said had instilled a deep fear in him, and at that moment, the fear was running rampant and uncontrollable.

Boris came back a few minutes later accompanied by a worker dressed in stained coveralls. The man scooped up most of the vomit with a rusty metal dustpan and hand brush, dumping it into a small pail, and then left the room with it all. A moment later he was back, pushing a well-worn yellow roller bucket with attached squeegee with the handle of a mop that was immersed into the bucket. Kody smelled the familiar, pleasant odor of Fabuloso, and watched as the worker methodically wrung out the mop, mopped the area of vomit, and repeated until the was only a damp, clean, fresh-smelling spot on the floor. He then left without saying a word, and never once meeting Kody's gaze.

Hugo peeked back in a short time later, leaning around the doorframe to check on his prisoners. He sniffed the air experimentally, and pleased with what he smelled, nodded, smiled widely at Kody when their gazes met, and then disappeared back into the office.

Kody glanced over at One again and was both pleased and surprised to find him sitting upright. He was licking his lips to clear the drool, hawked up a wad of phlegm and spat it out onto the floor, and then began to gently rotate his head from side to side, trying to work out kinks. Kody watched with eager anticipation, trying to get One's attention by raising his bound hands and shouting through the tape, but his voice was so muffled it came out as a soft though urgent growl of incomprehensible syllables. Nevertheless, a few moments later One's head must have cleared enough because he turned to Kody and focused on him.

"You okay?" One whispered, his words somewhat slurred.

Kody nodded, then his eyes darted to the open doorway between the storeroom and the office. He raised his bound hands, kept his left hand closed in a fist, and put up two fingers on his right, then pointed toward the open doorway.

"Two men here with us?" One asked softly, his voice a bit clearer.

Kody nodded, then, after glancing that way again to be sure no one was watching, reached down and awkwardly lifted the bottom edge of his hoodie, showing One the handle of his P365 still in its appendix holster.

Oh thank God!

"My stuff?" One asked *sotto voce*.

Kody gestured toward the workbench, and because his line of sight was only slightly lower than the workbench's level, One was just able to make out the items that had been taken from him sitting there.

Fuck, need that knife!

Wait a second...

"You still have the knife too?" One asked.

Kody nodded, then held up his bound hands to remind One that he had limited mobility too.

"Where is it?" One said.

Kody patted the right thigh pocket of his cargo shorts.

Okay, I can work with this...

Stupid bastards... assuming Kody's younger than he actually is because of his size, and made the assumption – a very dumb, wrong assumption – that because he was so young that he didn't need to be tied down to something like I am.

That's a mistake that will cost them!

A sudden wave of dizziness flowed through One and he groaned.

Damn, what did they shoot me up with? Everything feels like its wrapped in cotton and tingly at the same time...

Focus, dammit! You've got one chance at this, and time's not on your side!

"Is de Corazón coming?" One asked quietly.

Kody nodded and held up one finger.

"One minute?" One despaired.

Kody shook his head aggressively, trying to whisper through the tape, but then gave up. Again, he raised one finger and jutted it at One for emphasis.

"One hour?"

Kody nodded happily, but then squinted, thinking, and then shook his head. He held up three fingers on his right hand, then made an open circle with his left, and held them together.

"Thirty minutes or so?" One asked.

Kody nodded.

Abruptly, there was loud shouting and happy exclamations from the open doorway to the office. Someone yelled, "Ggggoooooooaaaalllllll!" and applauded.

They're watching a soccer game?

One closed his eyes and strained to listen. There was a lot of noise in the open floor-plan warehouse – beeping of forklifts, slamming of boxes and crates, the hubbub of distant conversations and the occasional, muffled roar of a jet taking off – but One was still able to barely discern the sounds of a televised soccer match.

Well, it's go for broke time!

"Can you get the knife out? Open it and come over here – cut through the ties on my arms first then hands?"

Kody looked worriedly toward the open doorway.

"Don't think about it," One advised quietly. "We need to take the risk – it's our only shot. If we fail, well..." He left the rest unsaid, but Kody clearly understood.

One watched as the teen gathered his willpower.

Will he be able to do it? Despite the fear and all the trauma he's endured that has him trained to be docile and obedient?

Kody shuffled to the edge of the couch then, and with continuing glances toward the open doorway, managed to deftly get to his feet. The zip-ties around his ankles had a tiny bit of give, so Kody shuffled forward, his new sneakers making rapid *scuff-scuff-scuff* sounds.

That's it, Kody! Be brave and don't think about anything else than getting over to me...

Within a minute he'd crossed to One's side, and with his bound hands, fumbled to get the knife out of his pocket—

A pocket that was Velcroed closed. As Kody started to pull up on the pocket's flap, the *sccrrrech* of releasing Velcro sounded inordinately loud and Kody stopped pulling, looking at the doorway with terrified eyes.

"It's okay!" One whispered a reassurance. "Just pull it up in one quick motion."

Kody looked back at him, swallowed, took a breath, and pulled. The flap came loose, but Kody froze then, his head turning to the open doorway in expectation of the two men coming to get them.

"Relax!" One said, "Just focus on the job."

Kody met his gaze, and One could see he was trembling, his pupils fully dilated, and he'd begun panting.

Oh shit, not now!

"C'mon Kody," One urged softly, "you can do this... c'mon, stay calm, stay focused on the task..."

One continued to mutter words of encouragement and calmness to Kody, and within a few moments, the effort worked. The teen's breathing returned to something close to normal, he trembled only slightly now, but One could see perspiration standing out on his nose and forehead. Nevertheless, Kody managed to get the knife in his hands and flicked the blade open.

"Excellent! Now cut that tie first," One encouraged, jutting his chin at the ties over his right biceps. "Don't worry about cutting or stabbing me – it's okay. We need to get free fast..."

Kody didn't acknowledge One's advice, but did push the knife's tip under the tie, edge of the blade up toward the ceiling, and started sawing. The tie came away within seconds, and Kody went to work on the one around One's right wrist, managing to get that one cut in about the same amount of time, but causing a shallow cut on the side of One's wrist in the process.

"Don't worry about it," One said hastily as he grabbed the knife from Kody in his now-freed right hand. He ignored the tingling of blood returning to the hand and worked the knife under the tie on his left wrist, then his left bicep, and then his ankles.

Kody's eyes followed the process interspersed with frantic glances to the open doorway.

One freed himself fully and stood, only to be overcome with vertigo that toppled him to the floor with a loud *thump*.

The world spun, twisted, and stretched sideways all at the same time for One as he felt the rough concrete of the floor impact on his cheek and forearm, abrading them.

Kody whined his distress from behind the tape.

Get up, fool! You have only seconds!

One pushed himself up and had just got to his hands and knees when the nausea came with surprising rapidity and force. He vomited explosively, his guts feeling like they'd been ripped from his abdomen, and that convulsing, involuntary effort drained him completely. It was all he could do to roll to his right, away from the stinking puddle he'd created, to lie on his back, chest heaving.

Get up! Get up! You don't have time for this nonsense! You're stronger than this!

Though his brain screamed at him to move, the lingering effects of the ketamine on his body were not to be so easily overcome by simple willpower.

A second series of excited shouts came from beyond the open doorway, and another shouted "Gggggooooaaalllll!"

Kody shuffled closer to One and looked down at him, seeing that One's eyes were shut tight, his mouth pressed into a thin line, and that he was shaking all over. Kody tried to speak, to urge him up, to ask what was wrong, but was frustrated by the tape—

And then Kody realized – and cursed himself for his stupidity – that his hands were not immobilized, and if he wanted, he could simply pull the tape off himself.

It wasn't really his fault. Since his kidnapping, he'd been conditioned carefully through abuse, drugs, and violence to be docile and subservient like a trained animal. But after having been with One the past few days, and no longer under the effects of the daily drugs forced on him by the cartel, he'd begun to, ever so slightly, regain some free will and think for himself once more.

This regaining, coupled with the urgency of the moment, enabled Kody to pull the tape from his mouth, stifle the scream of pain as he did so, and looked down at One again.

"One?! Get up! They're gonna come back for us soon! You've got to get up and get us out of here!" Kody urged in a rapid-fire stage whisper.

One wanted to obey, but he just couldn't get his body to do it. His head felt like it was an old-fashioned child's top, spinning at a million miles an hour, making his stomach queasy despite having thrown up all its contents.

Kody didn't know what to do. He looked wildly around the room and tried to think—

Do I cut myself loose first? Where's the knife... over there, One dropped it by the chair...

Do I get the gun off the workbench first? Make sure One has it when he's able to stand...

Do I call Garrett? I still have my cellphone...

Through all his panicked thoughts, Kody's brain recognized that he could no longer hear the TV.

They're done watching the TV! They're coming!

Kody decided – he shuffled as quickly as he could toward the bench, reaching it and grabbing one of the pistol magazines. With it in hand, he pulled the pistol to the edge of the bench and struggled to insert the magazine with his hands bound the way they were, but finally got it inserted. He lifted the heavy pistol, held it perpendicular to the tabletop, and bumped the magazine's bottom to seat it, then took several seconds to finally depress the slide lock so that the slide clicked forward, chambering the first round.

He glanced worriedly toward the open doorway, then toward One, who lay on the floor groaning and shaking. Seeing One in that condition and knowing that the men could return at any second made Kody start to shake too, but despite it, he shuffled forward as fast as he could toward One. It seemed like centuries for him to close the distance, but Kody did and then had to struggle to get to his knees beside One without crashing to the floor and making even more noise.

One was groaning, one hand over his eyes, the other holding the back of his neck.

"One! One! You've got to get us out of here!" Kody pleaded. "I've got your gun! Here!"

Kody poked One in the chest with the barrel – in hindsight, probably not a wise action, but at this point Kody panicked and had no thought for gun safety. One continued to groan, but when he felt the jabbing of the hard, steel barrel, it was enough to restore some of his awareness.

"Wha?" One moaned, and took his hand from his eyes, cracking them open and seeing Kody there kneeling beside him.

"Here! Your gun! They're coming!" Kody hissed urgently.

God, why won't the world stop spinning?! One complained silently.

Idiot! Take the gun! You've only got seconds now! answered his inner voice.

The warning was enough – barely – for One to suck it up and just deal with the suffering.

Kody watched worriedly as One moaned again, then slowly, ever so slowly roll onto his side. Once he was there, breathing heavily from that simple exertion, One lamely swatted around with his right hand. Kody realized he was trying to feel the gun, so Kody quickly took it by the barrel and pushed the grip against One's searching hand.

There, take it! One's inner voice demanded.

One felt the cool rubberized grip pushed against his bent fingers and managed to take hold of it.

"It's loaded and ready!" Kody told him.

One sighed his response. "Ohh...kayyy..." then began swallowing, fighting against another rising tide of nausea.

C'mon you fuckin' asshole! Shake it off! You've had much worse happen and came out fighting!

One gritted his teeth, subvocalizing a deep, long growl, and then he was pushing to his hands and knees again, the USP pistol in his right hand, flat against the concrete. He took several long, deep breaths, holding each for a four count, before exhaling with another four-count.

It was enough. The vertigo and nausea abated, and One sighed with relief.

"*Que carajo*?!" Hugo exclaimed from the doorway. "What the fuck?!"

Kody's head rocketed up to meet Hugo's gaze. One's head was slower, lifting like a herd cow's, slow and uninterested—

"Boris!" Hugo shouted and dashed forward—

The flight instinct took hold of Kody; he tried to get up and run but fell onto his ass instead, forgetting his ankles were tied—

Hugo had closed half the distance, withdrawing a Taser from his belt—

Boris arrived in the doorway and froze, his face lit with surprise—

One pushed up to kneel, sitting back on his heels, slowly, too slowly, raising the pistol—

Hugo had the taser up and its red aiming dot danced over One's chest as the man skidded to a stop a meter away, his finger closing on the Taser's trigger—

Though the pistol was only at hip level, One pulled the trigger. A .45 caliber hollow-point exploded out of the pistol, its report a deafening blare, and the bullet struck Hugo a few centimeters below the knee, shattering his left shinbone and spinning the man left—

It was just enough to cause the Taser dart to miss, its trajectory taking it above and past One's left shoulder. Though it missed One, it did find a mark—

In Kody's left forearm, discharging its debilitating voltage into the teen—

But it had been only a one second burst, if that, because the Taser fell from Hugo's grasp, his finger coming off the trigger as his left leg failed and he toppled to the floor with his back to One.

Through the haziness, One brought the pistol around and without sighting, discharged another round at the range of half-a-meter. The hollow-point punched into Hugo's back, a centimeter to the right of his spine, tearing through bone and lung.

Hugo collapsed and lay still.

Boris had recovered from his surprise and had pulled his Taser. He shot at One from five meters, a long way to make a Taser shot, and not unexpectedly, the dart missed by nearly half-a-meter. Shakily, One brought up the USP and tried to sight it, but his vision was still blurred and his brain fuzzy; nevertheless, he fired once, twice, and a third time, moving the gun

ZAYNE KULDER

slightly right and left after the first shot, hoping at least one round would find its mark.

Boris flinched reflexively as the first round smashed the doorframe in a spray of wood shards just above his left shoulder, then leaned farther away as a second round went wider to the left, hitting a stack of file boxes on a shelf. But One's third round hit, although not cleanly; Boris grunted as the bullet tore a line across his lower left side, slicing away a thick gouge of flesh and muscle.

Boris crashed into the doorframe with his right shoulder, and stumbled into the room, trying to keep his balance as the shock of the bullet hit began coursing through him. He raised the Taser to fire its second cartridge, found his hand shaking violently, and used his other hand to grab the Taser to steady it. In the second it took him to do so, One had taken a shaky breath, held it, and then let loose with two more rounds from his pistol.

These struck true, although had he been shooting at a range, the rangemaster would have chastised him for the poorness of his grouping.

The first hit the man low, through the top of his left thigh, where it was stopped by fracturing the man's thigh bone; the second was slightly more to the left, penetrating the man's abdomen a few millimeters from Boris's bellybutton. As designed, this bullet flattened out and tumbled after making entry, shredding Boris's intestines.

The henchman collapsed to the floor with a gurgle of bloody, expelled air.

The smell of cordite and the ear-piercing reports of the pistol worked magic on One – the smells and sounds of battle were the tonic he needed to finally push aside the pain, disorientation and nausea, at least enough where he felt coherent and was able to stand.

Check the kid!

One turned and scrambled next to where Kody lay convulsing. For someone as small and underweight as the teen was, even a one second burst from a Taser would wreck him, and it had.

"Hang on, Kody, hang on!" One said soothingly. "It'll pass in a minute... just try to relax..."

Get your stuff!

One obeyed the inner voice. He stumbled to the workbench, and in the next 30 seconds he scooped up the spare magazine, pocketed his knife, took the single bullet and, after popping out the magazine currently in his pistol, seated the extra round in the magazine. Rather than work with with half the magazine's rounds already gone, One took the necessary six seconds to swap out the half-full magazine with the fully loaded spare. That done, he press checked to assure a round was in the chamber, and then scooped up the rest of his items, stuffing the items into his cargo pants pockets.

One looked at his pistol and frowned.

Fired seven rounds – that leaves 12 in my fresh mag, and only six in the other...

Eighteen rounds isn't enough for shooting our way outta here... so hopefully it won't come to that...

One went to the open door. Beyond it he saw a plush office, with a desk and filing cabinets at the far end of the roughly 8x15 meter rectangular space, and closer by, there was a couch and a couple of worn easy chairs arrayed before a 100-inch flatscreen TV that was currently dark. The wall of the room to One's left, and the one opposite him, had large windows but these were all covered with closed blinds, as was the window in the single door set in the middle of the wall to his left. Unlike the storeroom in which they'd been held, the office had a drop ceiling about three meters high.

Seeing no one else in the office, One took 30 seconds to search the bodies of the two men. Each had a wallet stuffed with pesos, a cell phone, a set of keys, packs of opened cigarettes, nice Zippo lighters, and of course their Tasers, only one of which still had a usable cartridge. One took it all except for the bulky Taser and the smokes, stuffing his booty into the empty pockets of his shorts.

Then he stood and realized—

We've got to move before de Corazón gets here!

One turned back to Kody and was grateful to see the teen sitting up – then One realized the kid was still bound. One crossed to him, scooping up the teen's knife from where it lay on the floor, and quickly cut away the zip-ties around Kody's ankles and wrists.

Tears streaked Kody's cheeks, and he was very pale and wobbly as One helped him to stand.

"You alright?" One asked, and then immediately chastised himself for asking such a stupid thing.

Of course he's not alright! He just got tased!

But it doesn't matter – what does matter is getting the hell outta Dodge!

"Can you walk?" One demanded urgently.

"Uh... uh, yeah," Kody whispered, his voice tremulous.

"We need to go – you said de Corazón will be here in 30 minutes?"

Kody rubbed at his sore wrists, trying to restore circulation more quickly. He nodded. "Probably a lot less now," he conjectured.

Even more reason to go!

One handed the knife back to Kody, who reflexively folded it and dropped it back in his pocket. Then, despite the urgent demands of his inner voice, One took time to do his breathing exercise once more. It helped to banish the last of the ketamine's aftereffects.

A minute later, he was pulling Kody along into the office and toward the office's door. As he passed the couch, he saw an open bottle of Coke that was still mostly full and beaded with condensation. He snatched it up, and drank the icy cola greedily, emptying the bottle and tossing it onto the couch.

I needed that!

He then led Kody to the door, belching twice along the way, and after coming to a stop, he lifted a slat in the blinds just a fraction to peer beyond.

What he saw froze him to the core.

Chapter 49

Exportaciones y Logística Internacional

"We're here, *jefe!*"

Jorge brought his attention from wistful thoughts – on how he was going to extract information slowly, painfully from the assassin – back to the here and now. "Excellent."

Juan-Pablo brought the Suburban to a halt alongside several lined parking spaces against the north wall of the warehouse as dusk fell. A black Mercedes G-Wagon, its windows tinted to opaqueness, sat nose-out next to a black Lexus GX with similarly tinted glass. Small signs, light blue lettering on white, were fastened to the building's corrugated steel sides with the simple word "Reservada." Around the corner on the east side were four unused truck docking ports with faded, black rubber hoods, and beyond those, a raised concrete platform to access six open garage bays. Forklifts moved in and out, loading or unloading trucks that were backed up to the platform.

To the left of the parked luxury vehicles was a glass door inset with chicken wire under a faded maroon awning. A sign in the upper portion of the glass door stated "*Exportaciones y Logística Internacional*" – Exports and Logistics International. A single white LED lamp shined a pool of light down on the door's threshold from under the awning.

Vincente jumped out and opened the rear door for Jorge while the two vans pulled to the left and right of the door, their noses pointed outward and parked to form a defensive "V". As Jorge stepped out, the side doors of both vans swung open smoothly, and the 12 ex-marines stepped out deftly, six of them setting up a perimeter while the other six formed up in a stack to the right of the door.

Jorge turned back to Juan-Pablo. "Stay here so Alfredo has some company," he said, then eyed Alfredo to let him know to stay seated.

Alfredo met his gaze for only a second, then turned back to his computer.

At the door, Jorge paused to let the marines open it and flow in to secure the space beyond. Vincente stepped up to join him and together they waited patiently for the all-clear—

Which came just two minutes later. The squad's lieutenant came to the door and leaned out. "Secure, *jefe.*"

Jorge turned slightly to glance at Vincente and give him a slight nod, then stepped through the door held open by the officer, Vincente following one step behind and to his right.

The air was stifling and still. The sounds of cargo being moved and stacked echoed from deeper into the building, mixed with the hum of dozens of distant conversations, shouted orders, and the *beep beep beep* of backing forklifts. This section of the warehouse was for custom-secure items, having hurricane fencing running floor to ceiling blocking off 10x10 meter sections of the open floorspace with tall, wide gates in each section that were secured by a heavy, round padlock. The sections were arranged in rows, creating aisleways broad enough for a forklift, and overhead LED strips lit the cavernous space.

The aisleway directly in front of them led to an interior office about 50 meters distant, a small building within a building, with a sign over the door declaring "Oficina." The ivory blinds on the door and the windows of this office were all drawn, with a little bit of flickering light coming from the blinds over the right-hand windows. An air-conditioning unit on the roof of the little building whirred softly.

Jorge strode toward the office's door, his lips curling into a smile of anticipation, while Vincente followed at the one-pace distance as the six marines formed an escorting line of three to either side of them, combat-spaced, their SOPMOD M4 rifles held across their chests in an at-ready position, their helmeted heads swiveling slowly, looking for any threats as they padded along.

As they approached the door, the lieutenant, in the lead on the left, held up a closed fist and the marines stopped. "*Jefe?*"

Jorge nodded.

The lieutenant turned, came to within a half-meter of the door, knocked perfunctorily, the turned the knob, pulling the door outward so the lead marine on the right could enter. Once he had, the lieutenant flowed in and took the other side of the doorway just inside the room, then seeing it was clear, nodded to Jorge.

Jorge stepped into the room and looked around, expecting to find Hugo Ledder. Instead, he saw a dimly lit, rectangular room with a drop ceiling, roughly 8x15 meters. The only light came from a desk at the end to his left, on which a modern-style LED desk lamp shined down onto its surface, and a large flatscreen TV mounted to the wall which was currently displaying an advertisement for hemorrhoid medication. The TV's light was so bright that it obscured everything beyond at the far-right end of the room, while the distance between there and the desk lamp kept the middle part of the room in shadow.

Jorge turned to Vincente as the man entered and looked around. "I thought you said he was here, waiting for us?"

"Ah, yes, *jefe*, that was my understanding." Vincente replied.

The lieutenant cleared his throat. Jorge glanced at him, saw that the man's frown and expression of concern.

"What is it—" Jorge started to ask—

Suddenly the TV went dark, leaving purple spots before their eyes—

And then Jorge was splashed with something hot and sticky, and the marine to his right collapsed to the ground.

Chapter 50

As Ready As He Could Be

"Back into the storeroom!"

When Kody didn't move One turned to him and saw a look of fear and confusion. "Quick, go back and get behind the couch in there, flat on the floor! Do it – do it now!"

The urgency in One's voice finally pushed through the inaction that had paralyzed Kody. He turned and ran for the room.

One turned his attention back to the view through the slat. He saw a group of six black-clad men with SOPMOD M4 rifles flow into the warehouse from the door at the far end, then spread out and conduct a search up and down aisleways that were formed by fenced sections.

Murphy kicks us in the nuts again! One groused silently.

He let the slat down slowly and then turned to examine the room with an eye for defense, and quickly saw that the only thing that could possibly be called a defensive position was the desk, but it was a poor choice. One continued to scan the room, his mind trying to consider myriads of possibilities despite the lingering drugs still in his system.

Finally an idea came. He dashed to the desk, turned the desk lamp on to its lowest setting, dashed back to the door, turned off the overhead lights with the switch there then used the butt of his pistol to smash off the switch's toggle, making it inoperative. The room fell into almost total darkness save for the desk lamp's weak output. One then went to the couch, found the TV remote, and clicked it on. Bright light came from it a second later, showing some sort of drama series – One clicked the brightness control to its maximum. That done, One took the controller with him, went into the storeroom, and closed the door so it was only open a few centimeters.

He stuffed the TV controller in his pocket, took out his suppressor, and attached it to the barrel of his USP. He settled himself in the store room's open doorway, partly concealed behind the doorframe and spreading his feet to get a good, solid shooter's stance. Holding the base of the pistol's grip in his left hand, he brought the USP up to eye level, leaned into the doorframe, and put his left wrist against it to steady his aim. He then used his right hand to retrieve the TV controller, holding against the pistol and pointing toward the TV.

Looking down the Triton sights on his pistol, One was troubled by the fact that, despite resting against the doorframe, the sights were bouncing around a lot more than he would have liked.

Damn drug's still fuckin' with me...

He glanced back to the storeroom's couch, and saw Kody on his knees, peeking around the corner of its backside. "Listen whatever happens, stay flat on the ground. Can you get behind those boxes too?"

Kody looked to his right, where several boxes were stacked. "Um, I think so," Kody replied, his voice trembling with encroaching fear.

"Move them around if you have to but do it fast!" One ordered. "I want you to be shielded from any bullets!"

Kody struggled to do as he was told, pulling and shuffling boxes around, making what One thought was a ton of noise. But Kody finished quickly and then disappeared from sight.

"Stay there until I tell you it's safe to come out," One warned.

"Okay," came the muffled answer.

One flicked the light switch on the wall, putting the storeroom and him into darkness. Turning his attention back to the office, One focused on steadying his breathing and clearing his vision by slowly closing and reopening his eyes as he brought the sights to bear on the office's door.

Chances are two of the operators will come in first to check the room... then wave de Corazón in, taking up intimidating, guard positions to either side of the door...

288

The bright TV should hide me here... too much contrast for the eye to see past... that will give me the chance to take out de Corazón before any of them realize I'm here...

Then it's the two operators... got to be face-shots, because they're wearing body armor and helmets... fuck, I wish they weren't in helmets, 'cause the way I'm feeling right now, I'm not sure I'm up to two rapid, precision shots like that...

Buck up, compadre! You've been in worse shitholes with worse weapons with worse circumstances before and came out fine... you just gotta want it badly enough!

The office door opened, and as expected, two of the black-clad operators came in, weapons in an at-ready position over their chests, fingers straight out along their rifles' trigger guards. They scanned the room, and seeing no threats, the one farthest from One turned back to face outside and nodded—

And then de Corazón stepped into the room, the bright light from the TV bathing one side of him in whitish blue radiance, making him look two dimensional.

One pushed the off button on the remote, saw the TV flick off, and dropped the controller. Quickly with his now-freed right hand, he added it to his left, forming a proper shooting grip on his USP.

In the split second it took One to do this, the men who had just come into the room blinked rapidly, their vision thrown into blue and yellow aftereffect by the sudden loss of the bright TV's light. Without any hesitation, One sighted along the USP's tritium sights, exhaled half a breath, and squeezed the trigger.

They were backlit enough from the desk lamp's light to give One a great silhouetted target picture—

The USP burped—

The operator on Jorge's right suddenly had his lower jaw blown away by One's shot, the heavy, .45 caliber hollow-point making bloody debris out of flesh and bone—

The problem was, One had been aiming at Jorge's head, just above the man's ear.

Fuck!

As the operator with the missing jaw was in the process of collapsing to the floor, One shifted his aim, saw de Corazón's ear come back into his sights, and squeezed the trigger—

But the operator to de Corazón's left had grabbed the collar of de Corazón's shirt and yanked him backward, crashing de Corazón into the slightly taller man who was just now crossing the threshold to enter the office. This second man was startled and unprepared as his boss was flung into him, and together with de Corazón, they both fell backwards through the doorway and out of One's sight—

But One's bullet still was in flight. It impacted just below and to the right of the operator's nose, plowing into the man's cheek, flattening and expanding, then tumbled upward, carrying fragments of bone with it as it carved a path of bloody destruction into the man's brain—

The man collapsed to the floor just as the first one had.

Double fuck!

Without taking de Corazón out on the first shot, things became much iffier. One had gambled that, by taking out the boss and thus the man who paid their salaries, the henchmen might, just might, be willing to listen to an offer of letting Kody and him go if paid a huge bundle of money. Or, seeing just how quickly things had gone to shit, they would opt for self-preservation and withdraw and take up a wait-and-see, defensive position outside the warehouse. One would have gladly taken either of those options because it gave him something to work with for Kody's and his escape. But these plans, however marginal they were, went out the window when de Corazón was thrown clear.

One felt the creep of hopelessness step up to the edge of his thoughts.

Stop it! You're dead anyway if you let yourselves be caught, so keep going! You've got nothing to lose!

One closed the storeroom's door quickly, flicked on the lights, and went to the workbench. He quickly moved it perpendicular to the doorway, using every muscle in his abused body to do it because the damn thing was heavy wood and metal. This would be his defensive position, thick wood and metal between him and the doorway.

That done, he looked around wildly for something, anything else he could use or do—

And saw cardboard boxes of *El Jimador Blanco* tequila on the shelf behind him.

One pulled a box down to the floor, pulled the top open, and grabbed four bottles. He dashed to the door and set the bottles on the open wood framework over the door, then went back and smashed four more bottles of the high-proof liquor on the concrete floor just past the doorway.

He turned out the lights, went back behind the bench, and crouched down with his pistol leveled and ready. He pulled out one of the Zippo lighters and set it nearby.

"Kody," he hissed.

"Yeah?" came the small voice from behind the couch.

"They might have flashbangs – open your mouth wide, close your eyes tight, and cover your ears with the flat of your palms. It'll be loud and bright, but it'll be okay... Just stay like that until I tell you otherwise!"

One settled in, as ready as he could be.

Chapter 51

Chaos and Confusion

"Cover Tiger! Get him out! Get him out and to cover!"

Chaos and confusion reigned for Jorge – the suddenness of being pulled and tossed backward into Vincente, the sprays of hot blood splashing him in the face, and Vincente and him falling backward to the floor where the wind was knocked out of them—

All within the space of a single heartbeat.

Jorge felt someone take a handful of his suit coat, and then he was being dragged unceremoniously and rapidly backward, out into the warehouse proper. He had a vague sense that two of the marines were charging forward, rifles up, their attached laser sights beaming green while a third had pulled something from his vest and a second later tossed it through the open doorway.

A sharp, echoing *BOOM BOOM BOOM* accompanied by a blinding series of flashes silhouetted the marines in the doorway to the office, and then Jorge lost sight of them as they pounded into the room.

"Let go of me!" Jorge shouted angrily.

The marine pulling at him didn't obey – he continued to drag Jorge the length of the warehouse until he reached the doorway to the outside, whereupon two more marines from the perimeter detail charged in to lift him by the armpits and half-carry, half-drag him toward the Suburban.

"Let me go!" Jorge ordered, but it was like trying to convince a stone wall to listen.

The marines literally stuffed Jorge into his SUV and slammed the door closed, then four of them took up cardinal points around the Suburban, their rifles pointed outward to scan their assigned protection sectors, while two marines, plus the one who'd pulled Jorge from the office, charged back into the warehouse.

"Are you alright, sir?!" Juan-Pablo asked, twisting in his seat and looking at Jorge with sincere worry since his boss's face and torso were splattered with blood. Having seen this, Alfredo was ashen and trembling, trying to press himself into his seat as if doing so would make him invisible.

Jorge goggled at his driver, panting and trying to regain his wits.

The SUV's radio came to life with sharp, professional orders as the marines inside coordinated their efforts.

"Office is clear! There's a door to another room!"

"Cover! Cover!"

"Get ready to breach!"

"Jose, you and Julio cover from the couch; Umberto, ready a flashbang! I'll hit the door and when it opens, toss! On my mark!"

"Three, two, one, mark!"

A series of dull pops sounded over the circuit, and someone urged, "Go-go-go!"

A scream of inordinate agony came over the radio then, followed by someone shouting, "Pull him back! Back!" and then another series of screams.

A second later, a different voice shouted, "On the right! Contact right!" and a series of suppressed rifle shots could be heard.

At that, Jorge finally came to his senses. He lunged over the divider between the front and rear seats, grabbed the radio mic, and shouted into it, "Take him alive! Alive! Take him alive!!"

"Roger!" came a panting, hurried response with several additional suppressed shots sounding.

What are these idiots doing shooting?!

"This is Tiger! I need the man alive!!"

There was no response.

"Come in! Come in someone! Anyone!" Jorge ordered.

A panting voice finally answered. "We have the man in custody – shot through the arm, and a head wound, but neither are life threatening!"

Jorge felt himself relax. "The boy?" he asked.

"We found him; he's in custody too."

Jorge smiled. "I'm coming in!" he radioed.

"We found him; he's in custody too."

Jorge smiled. "I'm coming in!" he radioed.

Chapter 52

The World Closing In

Things developed pretty much how One expected.

When the door suddenly flew open, One dropped below the lip of the workbench, squeezed his eyes shut, covered his ears as best he could, and opened his mouth. Despite that, the multiple *BOOMs* punched against his chest and the flashbang's strobing staccatos seared his eyes even with them tightly closed.

But One had gone through training to deal with flashbangs and had been exposed to them in real life scenarios before, so the attempt to disorient and stun him was mostly ineffective. An instant after the incendiary device had finished its explosive work, One was up, flicking the Zippo's flame to life in his left hand, while aiming his pistol at the bottles above the door with his right. Backlit dimly by the desk lamp at the far end of the office, when One saw the motion of the first man swinging into the storage room, he shot twice, smashing the bottles over the door, then tossed the lighter.

The operator coming into the room walked into a rainfall of tequila, saw the small orange flame of the Zippo arching toward him, swung his rifle toward it, but could do nothing else as the Zippo hit him in the chest and he became a blue-flamed bonfire—

Then the lighter hit the floor, where there was nearly a gallon of alcohol pooled—

And suddenly flames were engulfing the man's legs as well as his head and torso—

The man shrieked with blood-curdling agony, dropping his rifle so it fell against his body, and stumbled backward, frantically and ineffectually swatting at the flames consuming him.

The man in the stack behind him – Umberto – grabbed his burning compatriot by the handle on the back of his plate carrier and yanked him back into the room, tossing him to the floor while Julio and Jose looked at him with horrid surprise. The man on fire started to roll, trying to put out the flames but too much damage had been done too quickly: the man stopped moving, and a moment later stopped breathing as well.

Meanwhile, Umberto turned back to the open doorway and started firing rapid 3-round bursts through the open doorway.

One ducked and heard rounds impact into the workbench, some ricocheting off with loud twangs, while other rounds smacked into carboard boxes on the shelves behind him. When the rile fire stopped, One popped up, ready to fire but all he saw was the faint, flickering blue of the tequila fire that licked around the doorway.

This might actually work—

One spoke too soon. The three remaining operators tossed in two more flashbangs, forcing One to duck and cover – but the operators hadn't pulled the pins on the grenades. It was an old trick, a trick that One had used himself before, but hadn't expected these men to use it. When nothing happened after a second and a half, One popped back up, swinging his pistol to sight on the doorway, but the men were already into the room, one of them painting One with the green beam of his M4's laser sight—

One fired a controlled two-round burst from his pistol, but with the rifle blocking most of the man's exposed face, One aimed for the man's left arm gripping the side of the rifle, hoping that, once he hit, the man would spin away and give One a second shot chance at the part of his face not covered by his helmet. He got his wish; the first .45 round hit the barrel of the rifle, sparking and tumbling off over the man's shoulder but the second his squarely into the man's forearm, causing him to spin and stumble, and then One took his anticipated shot, putting a single round into the man's face—

THE COST OF ONE'S DECISION

The man spun and collapsed forward, carried by his momentum, which then exposed the second and third men, who had come into the room in proper tactical formation—

One would have continued shooting, but in the same instant that the man he shot in the face went down, the man's rifle discharged a 3-round burst as his finger yanked convulsively on the M4's trigger. The first bullet created a long furrow in the bench's top; the second hit One his exposed shoulder, flattening against his body armor; and the third creased the top of his head, making a bloody furrow—

The shoulder hit was like getting kicked by a mule, but it was the grazing headshot that did One in. The impact, while it didn't punch through the bone, did fracture his skull and sent a resulting concussive shock into One's brain that caused him to drop his pistol and collapse.

In the next vague moments, One felt his hands being zip-tied behind him once more, his body searched, and all his items removed. Ungentle hands then hauled him to his feet, and One swooned, feeling wild vertigo take hold even as blood cascaded down over his forehead. They dragged him from the storeroom and tossed him unceremoniously onto the office couch, where one of the men jammed the barrel of his M4 into One's groin, and growled, "You move, *gringo*, and you have no more *cojones*!"

One couldn't have moved at that moment even if he wanted to do so.

He'd never felt so sick, dizzy and helpless.

He heard some shuffling and managed enough coherence to look up, through the one eye not obscured with blood, to see Kody being hustled out of the storeroom, zip-tied hands behind him. They pushed Kody roughly into one of the easy chairs where the teen lolled, dazed. The barbs and trailing silver wires of a Taser were still stuck in the teen's forearm.

One wanted to say something, to offer some sort of assurance, but he couldn't; his voice wouldn't work, and he felt the world closing in on him…

And then everything went black.

Chapter 53

Good of You To Rejoin Us

A shock of cold forced One to return to consciousness.

Opening his eyes – which was a task all unto itself – One's surroundings came into focus. He was secured to a folding chair, likely the same one he'd been in before in the storeroom, but this time the chair was set in the middle of Hugo's office, facing the now-deceased man's desk.

One felt a steady, dull thudding in his head, and smelled the telltale, astringent odor of blood mixed with the faint remnants of cordite, burned flesh, and charred wood. He took a few shaky breaths, coughed, and coughed several times more until he managed to expel a wad of blackened phlegm.

He felt like death warmed over.

"Ah, good of you to rejoin us," a voice said from behind him.

Jorge Manuel de Corazón's voice.

One tried to turn his head, but found it immobilized somehow.

"Don't bother trying to turn around on my account," Jorge advised dryly.

"Where's—" One started, but then a coughing fit interrupted him, and he spat out two more wads of phlegm before he croaked, "Where's Kody?"

"The boy?" Jorge asked facetiously. "Hmmm... he's safe and sound – well, for the moment anyway."

"I... I want to... to see him!" One wheezed.

"Tsk tsk tsk... you're in no position to make any sort of demands, *mi querido amigo*," Jorge scolded, then stepped around and into One's view, coming to the desk and leaning his buttocks against its edge, a Cheshire smile on his slim face and his dark eyes glowing with eager malevolence. One saw that his open-collar white dress shirt was splattered with dried blood. "I will be making all of the demands from here on, you see... and if I get unsatisfactory responses, well, let's just say that the pretty little boy that you've so painstakingly dragged along with you on your little odyssey will suffer the consequences..."

Fiery rage pushed through the grip that disorientation, pain and exhaustion had on One. With a growl of focused intensity, he said, "You hurt him and you'll wish for a quick death instead of what I'll be doing to you!"

Jorge laughed. "Ooooo! So scary!" he teased sarcastically. "I'm not going to do a single thing to the boy – rather, it's all in *your* hands, Mr. Assassin. What you do, or don't do, will decide the boy's fate."

Jorge waved and a slender man in a sports coat came into view, carrying a silver Halliburton case. He set it on the desk, flicked the locks open, and lifted the lid. One saw the glimmer of stainless-steel tools inset into the foam of the case's top and bottom halves. Jorge turned to the case, took it by the edges, and rotated it 90 degrees so the case's long side was parallel with the desk's edge. He then stood there, looking down at the case's contents, tapping a finger to the side of his chin as he murmured, "Hmmmmm...."

The man who had brought the case stepped back, turned, and walked out of sight behind One. One tried again to turn his head, but it was held firmly by something.

Jorge apparently saw his attempt this time. "Don't bother trying to move your head – I had one of my men secure it."

One tried again anyway but was just as unsuccessful as before. Some sort of brace encircled his neck, keeping his head immobilized. One then tried to look down, and managed to see the tops of his wide-spread thighs—

Which were bare. The pressure bandage over his thigh wound was gone, showing the scabbed, reddened pucker of his bullet wound.

They've stripped me...

Jorge finally decided on a choice, reached into the case, and came up with a small micro-torch, like one would use for hobby crafting. "Yes, I think that we'll start with this," he said, rocking the little torch back and forth in front of One's face, as if taunting him with it. "After all, it's only fair – you burned one of my marines to death, so I think he'd like to see an eye for and eye – that is, if he was still alive. Since he's not, well, I'll just have to do it for him, hmmmm?"

This is like some sort of James Bond movie... except that I don't have any gadgets or convenient script writing to get me out of it!

Jorge lit the torch and twisted the adjustment knob until there was a small, sharp blue flame growling from the micro-torch's tip. "So, let's see... where do we go? Hmmmm...."

With a satisfied grin on his lips, Jorge brought the torch down and touched the jet of flame to the top of One's right thigh, a mirror image placement to the bullet wound on his left one. The crackling of cooking flesh and its sickly, sweet odor came immediately, and One gritted his teeth against the agony of the 2,000°F pinpoint flame. But as Jorge continued to hold the flame there, burning into the muscle below the skin, One couldn't contain himself any longer—

He howled in misery.

Laughing, Jorge removed the torch and slowly, dramatically stepped back, bring the torch up to hold it like a gun alongside his face, and again One had a wild vision of a classic villain's pose straight out of the James Bond movie that he had just mused about.

One struggled to breathe, gulping at air, his body convulsing from the abuse just inflicted upon it.

Jorge let One go on like that for several moments before he smirked and said, "Just a tiny, tiny taste of what's in store, and a strong man like you howls like an infant! Tsk, tsk, tsk... I thought you American Special Forces soldiers were heartier than that..."

He's fishing... don't you say a damn thing!

When it was clear that One wasn't going to response, Jorge tsked again, and brought the flame down, this time aiming right between One's legs. "I wonder how much of this your manhood can take?" One felt Jorge take hold of his penis in his left hand and fondle it. "Such a shame... such a nice one too, and large... how long is it hard? Eighteen centimeters? Twenty?" Jorge chuckled amusedly. "Perhaps more? And girthy, I should think... too bad...."

303

One tensed, his whole body becoming a taut steel wire as he felt the approaching, searing heat of the torch increase. Jorge was purposefully moving the flame close by tiny increments, all the while fondling him, letting the anticipation of pain and loss build while he carried on a monologue, all of it designed to create maximum psychological impact.

"Such a shame really... I bet the boy had a chance to enjoy it though, no?" When One refused to answer or look at him, Jorge pulled the torch back slightly and looked surprised. "Don't tell me you didn't fuck his smooth, tight little ass while you two were at the hotel for those few days?" One still didn't answer, and Jorge's eyebrows rasied. "I can't believe you didn't... he's so beautiful, slim and perfect, wouldn't you agree? How could a man not take advantage of such a treat, especially when the boy is so willing... and wants it so badly..."

Don't listen to him! He's just trying to inch his way through your defenses, to get under your skin and make you react! Remember your SERE training!

Like all his squad, One had gone through SERE training – Survival, Evasion, Resistance and Escape – back when he'd joined the Special Forces and had refreshers for it every few years. It was as close to the real thing as the military could get without causing any lasting physical damage. It was designed to provide the skills necessary for each of the steps in its acronym.

But the SERE instructors had been crystal clear about one thing: if you were caught and interrogated, eventually, as sure as the sun rose in the east and set in the west, you were going to break and tell all, or do something to stay alive. No man was an island, and no man could simply turn his pain receptors off and withdraw into himself. The key was to last as long as you could without divulging anything, or giving in, to make the interrogator and your jailers work for every iota of information or cooperation.

That was a fine and dandy philosophy if it was you yourself undergoing torture or imprisonment. You got to decide if and when you said anything, and just how much pain, loss of flesh or appendages, and suffering you would endure.

But when someone else was at risk, someone you cared for, or loved, or was innocent, the equation dramatically changed.

And Jorge seemed to realize this. "You know," he said slowly, letting One's penis fall from his grip and then reaching up to turn the micro-torch off. "I think I can get all the answers I need much more quickly by another means."

Jorge turned back to the desk, turned off and stowed the micro-torch in the inset for it in the Halliburton case, closed the case, and then set it down alongside the desk. Then with one arm, he quickly swept all the desk's contents aside, sending them flying off the end and onto the floor with a crash of glass and metal. Turning back to face One, he smiled and said, "Bring the boy!"

Two of the black clad marines dragged Kody into view. Kody was still dressed in his hoodie, shorts and sneakers, with the hood pulled back, and his hands were zip-tied behind him. The teenager's face was slack and his eyes unfocused.

Jorge gestured dramatically to the desk, and the marines pushed Kody against it, forcing him to bend at the waist so his chest was pressed down into the desktop and his crotch against the edge. The marines cut away the zip-ties, then each took one of Kody's wrists and, while holding on, walked to the sides of the desk. By doing so they forced Kody to remain face down onto the desktop and held him there, his arms spread out 90 degrees from his body.

Jorge came directly behind Kody then and used his foot to violently spread Kody's legs widely apart.

"A very nice ass, as I said," Jorge commented with a smirk and a wave toward Kody's backside. "Don't you think?"

One glared infernos of hate at Jorge.

Jorge turned to face Kody and put his arm up, palm open toward the ceiling. The marine to Jorge's right reached down and took out a combat knife, its slim blade as black as the knife's handle, then reversed the knife and laid the handle of it into Jorge's open palm.

With an evil grin Jorge closed his fingers around it, nodded thanks to the man, then took a step back, tilting his head and once again placing a contemplative finger alongside his jaw.

"Hmmmm... how to do this?" he mused aloud, then turned to One. "What do you think?"

One's teeth clenched. "Don't you—"

"Oh ho! So, now we're getting somewhere!" Jorge declared with a dramatic twirl of the knife. "Tell me, what unit are you with? Who contracted you to kill me? What's the access code on your sat phone?"

One just glared back at him.

"I see... well, it's too bad the innocent must suffer for your 'code of honor'," Jorge made air quotes while still holding the knife, "but honestly, all that's happened over these last few days, the anticipation of capturing you and the boy, well, it's created strong needs within me, needs that I'm more than happy to release – and you get the honor of watching! Not many can say they've ever received such an honor from me!"

Jorge turned back to Kody. He slowly slid the flat of the knife between the bottom cuff of his cargo shorts and the skin of his right leg, sliding the knife up until the entire blade was flat against the teen's skin.

One watched in quiet rage, seething, and hating himself for being unable to do a damn thing to stop what was happening.

Think! Think! There's got to be something you can do!

But there wasn't. Jorge turned the blade, raising it slightly to tent the fabric of the cargo short's leg, and then in one swift motion, yanked the blade upward. Its razor-sharp edge sliced through the fabric with barely a sound.

One could see that Kody was trembling, but nevertheless the teenager hadn't made a move to resist...

And One understood why.

Despite being weaned off the drugs they'd given to Kody to keep him docile and subserviant, it was the mesmerizing, psychological conditioning the teenager had been put through that was now in control.

A control that was total and complete, the reins of which were held by Jorge.

Jorge twisted to look back at One. "See, that was easy... and how tantalizing, eh?"

Jorge didn't wait for a response. He turned back and used the knife to but farther up the shorts, all the way to Kody's crotch, revealing the white boxer briefs the teenager wore beneath the shorts. But he wasn't finished. Methodically and slowly, so One could see each move, Jorge cut and pulled away the right seat of the shorts, folding the fabric to the side where it hung limply, then repeated the process on the left side of the shorts.

"Much better," Jorge commented with a wave of the knife toward the small, firm buttocks that were gripped in tight, white cotton, "but not quite good enough, I think... let's see..."

Jorge slid the flat of the knife between the cotton and Kody's thigh, repeating the process that he'd used to cut away the cargo short's backside. Soon Kody's buttocks and the backside of his scrotum were laid bare, framed by the remnants of his shorts and briefs.

Kody was visibly shaking now, panting but otherwise silent, controlled by Jorge's conditioning.

One seethed. The suffering that Kody was enduring was breaking One's heart... and One felt hot hatred and burning bile rise in his throat in response to both their helpless states.

What can I do?! I've got to do something!

One struggled against his bindings then, a furious assault that he threw every bit of his strength into, but it got him nowhere.

It did, however, attract Jorge's attention. "Oh, the warrior, once strong and virile, now tied and impotent," Jorge teased. "But me? I'm by no means impotent..."

Jorge turned to face One then, kicked off his shoes, undid his belt, and shucked out of his trousers. Jorge wore a pair of tiger-striped, bikini briefs which clearly showed his erection laid to one side, straining to get past the confines of its tight polyester.

Jorge gently stroked the length of his erection with two fingers while he smirked evilly at One. "So, are you going to tell me what I want to know, without any reservations? The truth and nothing but the truth, eh?" He tilted his head toward One, raising an eyebrow to emphasis his inquiry. "Or do I start in on this lovely boy here?"

One could see Kody shaking with fear and anticipation of the abuse to come and could hear him sobbing, accented by a soft, plaintive whining like a wounded animal.

Jorge paused then, studying One for a long moment, enjoying the panoply of conflicting emotions twisting and crossing One's face. "So, what's it going to be?" he asked with a snicker.

The mission is sacrosanct!

But Kody, he's already been through so much – you can't let this happen!

But the mission is sacrosanct! You took an oath!

But you promised to keep him safe...

Remember your training! You must hold out!

When is enough, enough? Your SERE training instructor told you flat out – eventually all men break! Why hold out now? What good will it do? All you're doing is making an abused kid suffer even more abuse!

Tell them nothing! They're going to kill you anyway – so what if the kid gets abused some more? Both of you are already dead – you need to treat yourselves as if you are already dead! If you and he had to suffer before the end, what difference does it make? The bottom line is you must stay true to your mission and your oath! You can't divulge anything about your mission!

You must stop this!

You musn't stop this!

You must!

You musn't!

Tears streamed down One's face. If he could have dropped his head in shame, he would have, but since it was held in place, the best he could do was close his eyes and steel himself to say what he said next.

"You win... What do you want to know?"

Chapter 54

Just Like One Had Instructed

"What is your nationality?"

One took a reluctant breath and went to speak, but he couldn't. He wanted to answer, but it was as if a hand had come up from his bowels to snatch the words back down into his lungs before he could utter them.

Jorge was no longer willing to be patient. Without a word he turned to Kody and stepped up to the teen and aggressively rubbed the front of his briefs – and the erection they barely withheld – against Kody's ass while making loud, dramatic moaning sounds as he smiled wickedly at One.

Kody shuddered but otherwise stayed silent.

"I'm American, damn you!" One shouted.

Jorge rubbed himself a few more times against Kody's bare ass for good measure, letting One know that he was more than ready to have his way with the teen if One didn't divulge answers more quickly in the future. "It's tough to stop once you get going," Jorge told One matter-of-factly as he stepped away from Kody. "It's like potato chips, no? Can't just have one?" Jorge laughed out loud.

Now Kody made a sound, a faint, short whine – it was a pathetic sound that crushed One's soul.

Jorge leaned back against the desktop to Kody's right side, purposefully sliding his hip up against the teen's and then letting his open hand rest atop the teens' right butt cheek, which he then gently caressed in a manner that was more hungry than romantic.

"So, who actually sent you, Mr. American Assassin?"

One gritted his teeth again. "I'll tell you but let Kody go first."

Jorge was already shaking his head as One spoke. He raised a finger and wagged it at One. "No, no, no, that's not how this works," he lectured, and let his finger push into the crack of Kody's ass. One saw the teenager begin to tremble again but still Kody made no sound.

One knew he had nothing to bargain with, but still he tried. "C'mon de Corazón... you got me. I'm not going anywhere, and I told you I'd tell you whatever you wanted. The kid's got absolutely nothing to do with what's between us... just let him go."

Jorge withdrew his hand from Kody, then folded both in his lap as he tilted his head upward, assuming a contemplative pose. "Hmmm... an interesting proposition... but, no, I think not – not yet. Maybe, just maybe... if I get some valuable information from you, then I will consider it."

You can't divulge anything! It will cause the cartels to strike back if they know who was sent against them!

What does it matter? You know you're already dead. Those people will just have to take care of themselves. Besides, when you don't come back, they'll know you're compromised and likely spilled your guts before you went, so they'll take precautions – maybe even re-strike against de Corazón immediately...

One exhaled dejectedly. "I honestly don't know who sent my squad... we never know. We just get orders through a secure server after notification texts are sent to our encrypted cellphones."

Jorge snorted disdainfully. "Come now, you really expect me to take that convoluted uninformative nonsense as a final answer? Who... sent... you?"

"I don't know—"

Jorge turned to Kody, reached down and grabbed hold of the teen's scrotum and yanked it backward, forcing Kody to go up onto his tiptoes and howl in agony. With a smirk gracing his face, Jorge extended his hand, and the marine to his right slapped his combat knife back into Jorge's hand—

"NO!" One raged, straining and wriggling against his bindings—

Jorge let the blade slide around his hand, the tip of the razor-sharp blade resting atop the flesh of Kody's scrotum, just below where it was connected to his body.

"Answer the question," Jorge said flatly, his eyes boring into One's

One raged for another few, ineffectual seconds, and then deflated, falling back against the chair's back.

"Answer!" Jorge demanded again, and let the blade move forward a fraction of an inch, drawing blood.

Kody howled and was shaking so violently that the marines had to use both their hands to keep him prone against the table.

"I can only guess!" One screamed back.

"Then guess!" Jorge countered.

It took an effort that was more than One expected before he was able to blurt out, "The President!"

Jorge let Kody's scrotum fall from his hand and stepped away, idly swinging the knife around his fingers. "Really? The *comandante en jefe* himself? I'm actually flattered that someone like him, the 'leader of the free world'," Jorge made air quotes, "is so keenly interested in my wellbeing... so, now we're getting somewhere... this is so much more fun than I expected!"

With a move that was cobra fast, Jorge flipped the knife into the air, grabbed it by its handle, and then slashed One's right and left pectorals, creating long cuts a few millimeters deep.

At first there was no pain; the knife's blade was so sharp, that the ruined sections of skin and muscle didn't transmit any warnings to his brain –

Until they did, and One growled with the sudden, fiery agony from the damage.

"So, back to my original questions," Jorge said nonchalantly as he leaned back against the desk, toying with the knife in on hand while replacing his open hand on Kody's right buttocks and letting two of his fingers slide into the cleft. "What unit are you with? What's the access code on your sat phone?"

Panting, One glared up at de Corazón and growled out, "We only have a designation..."

"And?" Jorge prompted, giving Kody's ass cheek a squeeze which caused the teen to mew again in fear.

"Zulu Delta," One said angrily.

"And that's part of what agency? CIA? DIA? Some other stupid acronyms?"

One swallowed, fighting against the new pain. "CIA."

Jorge smiled, and looked first at the marine on his right, then the one on his left. "See, we're making progress!" Turning back to One, Jorge tapped One's shoulder three times with the flat of the knife's blade. "The sat phone access code?"

One subvocalized an angry growl. "8-5-5-2-4-4-3."

One knew that, even by giving them the access code, it would be nigh impossible to get anything useful from the phone's memory. It self-erased 30 minutes after being used. Yes, it could still connect to the satellite network, but again, that would be of little use to them because it needed a PIN number to make a call. Furthermore, if they didn't enter the correct PIN number, the phone would set off a pyrotechnic charge in its innards, melting itself into a blob of smoking, useless plastic and metal composites.

One saw Jorge's eyes look to someone behind him, out of One's sight. "Tell Alfredo – take the phone and see what he can do with it."

"Right away, *jefe*," the man said from behind One, and One heard him walk out of the room.

Turning back to One, Jorge said, "See? That wasn't that difficult now, was it?"

One glared at him in silent response.

"Well, I think my work is done here, for the moment at any rate," Jorge said, standing and handing the knife back to the marine. "As for fun... well, that's just begun."

One's eyes widened. "No! I told you want you wanted to know! No! You can't—"

"Gag him!" One ordered.

The marine that was holding Kody's right arm down moved to stand on the side of the desk across from Jorge and took Kody's other wrist from the marine on the left, bringing both of Kody's arms straight out, above Kody's head and over the far side of the desk. This freed the other marine to grab a roll of duct tape, tear a piece off, and press it over One's mouth.

One tried to move his head to resist, but it was futile.

Jorge cackled gleefully as he watched One's efforts to avoid the tape.

Turning to Kody, Jorge reached out and used two fingers to trace the line of Kody's jaw, then swirled them along his skin, down to caress his neck.

"Now my dear boy, I'm going to have him let go of your wrists – but you are to stay exactly where you are, understood?" When Kody did nothing more than tremble, Jorge reiterated patiently. "I said, they are letting you go now, but you are not to move – you are to stay exactly where you are, understood? I want to hear you say it."

In a tiny, dull voice, Kody said, "Yes."

"Yes what?" Jorge demanded softly.

"Yes... I won't... move."

"Won't move, what?" Jorge demanded softly.

"Won't move... master," Kody said lifelessly.

It was the most heart-wrenching three words One had ever heard from anyone.

"Excellent!" Jorge said, smiling broadly. Turning to One, he made a "ta da!" gesture with the knife and free hand. "See how easily they obey? It's the conditioning, you see. I have a specialist, a former Russian KGB man who has made the process a refined art..."

One glowered back at him.

Smirking evilly back at him, Jorge tsked. "Well, the results speak for themselves, no?" He waved a hand at Kody, who hadn't moved an inch since the marines had let go of his arms.

Jorge then signaled for the marines to leave the room. They nodded, each eying One warily as they filed out of the room. A moment later, One heard the office door close.

Kody lay face down on the table, still making no effort to move, even though no one was now holding him in place.

"So... now it's just us!" Jorge clapped his hands with a Cheshire grin on his face.

One tried another time to free himself, but it was to no avail. He then tried to blow outward against the duct tape and suck it back in several times quickly, hoping to get his teeth into the backside adhesive and perhaps chew through it, but it had a firm grip on his lips and kept them tightly shut.

Jorge smiled at his futile efforts. "So, now you get to watch!" Jorge said with a dramatic flourish. "I bet you like the thought of that, eh? Getting to watch? I heard all you American men like to watch, yes?"

One struggled and shouted muffled curses from behind his duct taped lips. Veins stood out on his forehead and his face became crimson with rage and exertion.

Jorge simply laughed, then turned slightly toward Kody but kept a sideways gaze locked onto One's eyes as he slowly, dramatically slipped out of his tiger-striped briefs, freeing his erection to stand at full attention. Jorge twirled his underwear on one finger for several revolutions, relishing the look of rage and terror on One's face, and then flung them so they landed atop One's head.

Breathing as hard and fast as he was, One caught Jorge's stink from them immediately, a mix of sweat and pheromones, the odor of which enraged One even more—

But he was completely impotent—

There was nothing One could do—

He'd broken his promise to Kody.

One decided in that moment that he was going to watch every disgusting, vile moment what came next. One did so because he wanted to have the frustration, the rage, and the feelings of violation and helplessness there with him, fresh in his mind, when it came time to destroy Jorge Manuel de Corazón.

Yes, I'm not just going to kill de Corazón, but I'm going to make him suffer for days and days, to force him to endure the suffering he's imposed on Kody, and all the others, in one long, agonizing, terrifying event...

At the beginning, Kody let out only a weak bark of pain, then went silent again, although One could see him trembling beneath Jorge.

Laughing, Jorge suddenly bit Kody's neck and shoulders, leaving bloody teeth marks behind; Kody violently shook, let out a long, low moan—

And then Kody went completely still and silent.

He's gone into shock! Goddamn you de Corazón!

For One, seeing this was worse than watching a fellow operator get his head blow away by a sniper's bullet; worse than having your legs torn away by the blast of an IED; worse than being slowly beheaded by a jihadist—

It was an indescribable agony, made exponentially worse by the fact that One, despite all his years of military training, and everything that he'd been subjected to during those years and managed to survive, was powerless to do anything to stop or even influence what was happening.

Jorge stood and withdrew himself from Kody with a long, overly dramatic sigh of pleasure.

Meanwhile, Kody remained completely immobile and silent with blood streaming from his anus and the small cut on his scrotum.

The cartel leader then reached over into the Halliburton case and pulled out a pair of bright, stainless-steel pliers.

One raged anew, tried to break free, but the only thing that happened was that the zip-ties bit deeper into his flesh, abrading the skin so it bled freely. Nevertheless, One continued raging, ignoring the pain and blood, hoping that Kody, by hearing his struggles, would still know that One was still there, and that Kody wasn't alone.

What a stupid reason! He trusted you! You promised to keep him safe! Look at him! Look!

One realized what was happening and all the rage suddenly drained away from him like a bathtub whose plug had been pulled. One whined, a sorrowful, pathetic response to his state of complete helplessness as he saw Jorge look back at him, grin wickedly, take Kody's scrotum in hand, put the pliers to one of his testicles and clamp down on it hard and fast, smashing it into uselessness.

The only response from Kody was a visible shuddering of his entire body and single, long, shrieking squeal.

"Well, one down," Jorge said with a Cheshire grin, straightening and leaning to his side to look at Kody's face in profile. "Shall we go for two? No? Then, how about this..."

Jorge took the pliers, spread them, put them down against the nape of Kody's neck, clamped them tight and pulled—

Yanking a chunk of skin from the teen's neck—

This time there was no silence from the abuse. Instead, Kody wailed, a heart-wrenching sound that brought tears of furious anger to One's eyes.

Jorge set the pliers down, stroked himself a few times and then thrust back into Kody, working himself into an ecstatic frenzy. As he did, Jorge bit Kody's neck again, drawing blood each time which he happily lapped up, then reached up with one hand to gather and then enclose around both of Kody's wrists, keeping him down as he reached climax and let out a wild series of pleasured groans, which he made purposefully more dramatic to incite higher levels of rage in One.

But by now, One was an unmoving bundle of simmering fury, biding his time and husbanding his remaining strength for when the time came – and he was positive, in his heart of hearts, that that time would indeed come – for payback.

"Oh my, my, my!" Jorge said with a long sigh of satisfaction. "That ass was sooooo tight!" Jorge frowned then, making a tsking sound. "Although, it would have been a lot better with some lube…"

Jorge's face then turned into a smile as he raised an eyebrow and said to One, "Really, Mr. Assassin, you should have taken your shot at this nice, tight, smooth boy-ass when you had your chance back in the hotel."

One simply stared at him, glowering.

Laughing, Jorge stretched languidly, his erection still full. He stepped up to One, standing in front of him and blocking his view of Kody. Jorge ran two fingers over One's shoulder, to the bump of collarbone there, then across his Adam's apple to the other shoulder's collarbone bump.

"You know, you're not a bad specimen, Mr. CIA Assassin…"

He reached down and took One's manhood in hand.

"I might just do you as well, though you're not really my type." Jorge snorted his amusement. "Did you at least have some fun sex in your life? Some bimbo high school girls that you fumbled around with under the bleachers or in the back of your father's car? Some recruit during basic training out behind the mess hall in the woods? Some one-night stands in the far-flung locations to which the CIA sent you?"

Jorge now purposefully waggled his hips back and forth, making his erection swing side to side slowly, like a cobra anticipating striking.

"I hope you did, because after today, well, you won't be on the market anymore – even if you could escape, when I'm done with you, this down here," he gave One's equipment a tug that made One see stars and punched the breath from his lungs, "will be too ruined to use… That is, if I allow you to keep any of it at all. Hmmm… we'll have to see about that, won't we?"

Jorge snorted again with amusement at his own clever repartee before continuing. "I supposed it does not matter because, well, you see, your destiny is to die when I've had my fill of you. Besides, I know that without my own manhood, I wouldn't want to live, so I'll do you the courtesy of making sure that happens for you when all is said and done, eh?" Jorge chuckled evilly. "But no quick deaths for you, Mr. CIA Assassin, no... no quick death for you."

With one hand on One's manhood, Jorge pivoted to find the pliers—

Unmasking One's view of where Kody lay across the desk—

Except that Kody wasn't face down on the desk anymore, but was standing there, facing Jorge, the P365 pistol in both hands, and a look on his face that One would never forget until the day he died.

Out of the corner of his eye, One saw Jorge's expression freeze, then watched the cartel leader's eyes go wide even as he let go of One's manhood and lunged to grab Kody's pistol—

But the distance was too short, and Jorge too late. Kody stepped forward against Jorge, pushing the pistol into the man's stomach, and pulled the trigger—

And pulled, and pulled, and pulled, and pulled—

Just like One had instructed him.

Chapter 55

Wait and Pray

The pistol's reports were barely louder than a sick man's coughs, both because of the small caliber bullets it fired and the fact that the muzzle was pressed into Jorge's flesh – without any distance for the expanding gases from the pistol's firing to travel, the sound of firing was as if the teen's gun had a suppressor attached.

One was stunned, then he realized that, though they'd searched him and stripped him naked, Jorge's men must not have bothered to search Kody. They had simply assumed that Hugo and his men had already done the task, and unlike him, who had been stripped naked by Jorge's men, these same men – likely at Jorge's direction – had left the teen clothed. This had clearly been done to allow Jorge to demonstrate his control over them both, and to build fear and anxiety in Kody by cutting away Kody's clothing as he'd done.

The way Jorge had cut away Kody's clothing, with Kody stomach-down on the desk, had left the pistol attached to the front of Kody's cargo shorts in its appendix holster where it had remained hidden from view. Jorge had been confident that his conditioning of Kody was complete, and Kody had demonstrated that this conditioning was indeed in force by his passivity and compliance to all the abuse Jorge had inflicted upon him up until—

Until somehow that conditioning was superseded by something deeper within Kody.

What a brave kid...

Jorge Manuel de Corazón collapsed with a final look of shock and astonishment on his face, frothy blood spewing from his quivering lips, and then he lay still, blood oozing from the scorched bullet holes in his abdomen.

Everything went silent then.

Kody stood frozen and blood-splattered, with the smoking pistol still in his hands, his eyes downcast to stare unblinking at de Corazón.

It took One several beats before his brain registered what had just happened, but when it did and he saw Kody's state, One began screaming from behind the tape to get the teen's attention focused away from de Corazón and to him.

C'mon Kody! Don't let yourself slide deeper into that mental abyss! Look over here at me! At me!

One had to assume that the marines from Jorge's security force had heard the muffled shots but was also betting that Jorge had instructed them that, no matter what mayhem they heard from the other side of the office's door, they were not to enter until he called them. That would fit Jorge's personae, which demanded absolute control and obedience from his subordinates. But while that was most likely the case, One wasn't going to rely on that any more than he absolutely had to.

C'mon Kody! Snap out of it! Help me!

As if he read One's mental plea, Kody's head slowly lifted, turned, and his eyes regarded One—

One shuddered when their gazes met – Kody's eyes were dull and lifeless, something he'd seen many times in fellow soldiers who had been through and seen too much, and the fact that it had taken so long for Kody to respond to One's thrashing about, made it likely that the teen was suffering from some sort of partial catatonia or conversion disorder.

After what just happened, it's not surprising...

But you've got to push past it, Kody!

One screamed again from behind the tape, and again, and again, moving himself around as much as the tight bindings would allow.

Moments later, One's efforts finally pushed past whatever it was that had vapor locked Kody. The teen's eyes blinked, then blinked again, and then the pistol fell from his hands, thunking dully as it bounced off de Corazón's bloody stomach and onto the floor. Kody followed the pistol to the floor, collapsing lethargically and panting, then curling into a fetal ball as he sobbed.

Not good! Not good!

C'mon Kody, you must free me!

One continued all he could do to get the teen's attention, but One quickly saw that his efforts were hopeless. Jorge's violation and abuse had pushed Kody over the edge of sanity, and at this point, only time would tell – either Kody would fall into a catatonic state or, if he was strong enough, he'd recover enough of his wits to function.

Please, God, let Kody recover – if you do, I can get us out of here and, well, at least fulfill half my promise to him...

One tried to relax, closing his eyes and trying to conserve his energy so that, if Kody did manage to come out of his fugue, One would be ready.

All he could do now was wait and pray.

Chapter 56

World Imploded

The coppery, astringent odor of blood mixed with the foul stench of released bowels and exposed intestines wafted around them.

Sometime later, Kody's sobbing finally stopped. One opened his eyes and looked down.

Kody sat hugging his knees with his forehead resting atop his hands. He still sniffled occasionally but seemed to be coherent. Then One heard Kody whisper, talking to himself.

"You obeyed him... let... let him fuck you... you did nothing...to stop..."

Oh God no! C'mon Kody, you can work through it! I know how strong and brave you are and can be!

Kody began to rock back and forth slightly, whispering words One couldn't quite hear.

Free me already! We can still get out of this if you untie me!

One noticed that there was a clock. It had been on the desk facing away from him, but when Jorge had swept everything from it earlier, it had fallen, upside down, facing him.

It read 9:24pm.

Shit, we missed the flight...

Not important right now, dummy! Get out of this, and then worry about how to get out of the country!

One struggled against his bonds anew, screaming from behind the duct tape.

Kody finally looked up, his eyes very red and swollen, but he seemed to grasp the reality of One's situation because his mouth formed an "O" of

323

surprise. After several long seconds, during which One wondered if the teen had registered their still-dire circumstances, Kody pushed himself up and looked around the desk and floor.

One tried to use his eyes to point to the open Halliburton case, assuming that there was something sharp in it that could cut his bindings, but Kody didn't notice. One was beginning to finally give in to panic when he saw Kody reach into his pocket and pull out the folding knife, the same one he'd used in the storeroom to free One earlier. He unfolded the blade and came to One's side like a zombie, and seemed to take forever to figure out how to use the knife...

But then was cutting, and a moment later, One had his left arm and hand free. Pinpricks of returning circulation made the appendage flame, and for the first half a minute, it remained numb and useless while Kody went to work silently on the other arm.

When circulation returned, One reached up and tore the tape from his mouth. "Great job, Kody!" he whispered. The teenager didn't acknowledge him, just kept sawing at the binding with the knife.

One gently took his hand, stopping him. "Here, let me," he said and gently took the knife from the teen's hand.

Kody let him do so without a word, shuffling aside. One went to work on his other bindings, freeing his head, then bending down to cut the bindings across his thighs and ankles—

When he was fully free and felt circulation once again returning to his limbs, he sat up to find Kody with the P365 pistol in hand, the barrel pressed against the side of his head.

An arctic hand gripped One's heart, paralyzing him with shock and horror.

As calmly as he could muster given the exhaustion and pain that lingered, One said, "Kody... give me the gun."

Kody's glazy stare pivoted slightly to focus on One. "I... I'm... I'm disgusting... I... I let him..."

One swallowed, trying to moisten a mouth suddenly gone desert dry. "Listen to me! *Listen!* You *are not* disgusting! You are a good, kind boy! *You're a good person!* Don't let what happened drive a bad decision, please

Kody, please!" One made a move to step closer, but Kody jumped back, lowering the pistol.

Trying again, One implored, "Kody, listen! You've been so brave! You overcame letting me lock you in that case; you've never once doubted me! That's so brave of you – don't let fear in now! Stay brave!"

Tears streamed from Kody's eyes, mixing with the splatter of blood on his cheeks to form pink rivulets that dribbled to the floor. "Who would want me now? I'm... I'm disgusting!" The last word was shouted with rage and disgust so intense that One felt it like a physical blow. "*I let him do it! I let him... let me do it all to me!*"

Kody was yelling now, and thrusting the pistol angrily at One, a deadly extension of his accusatory finger.

"*I let him do it! I let him do it all to me!*" Kody was almost maniacal now, half crying and half screaming. Specks of foam had formed at the corners of his mouth as he continued to thrust the gun toward One with every emphasized, enraged syllable. "*I let him do it! I let him do it all to me!*"

With all this noise, One threw a worried glance to the office door, wondering why in all that was holy that the marines hadn't already burst into the office to see what all the yelling was about—

Then he remembered; Jorge would have told them to stay out until he specifically called for them, and what Kody was ranting about now in the throes of psychosis would be exactly the type of cruel, sadistic thing Jorge would make Kody scream for his sadistic pleasure.

Still, I can't let this go on – for Kody's mental sake and both of our lives!

Suddenly Kody's ravings stopped. Zombielike, he stepped back, farther out of One's reach, and met One's gaze.

"You... you promised! *You promised me!* ... Promised no one would... hurt me..."

One felt his heart fall to the floor. "Kody, *listen to me* – I meant that, *every word*, but things..."

Kody shook his head slowly, as his eyes dropped back down to the pistol in his hands even as he stepped farther away, talking more to himself now than to One. "You lied... they all lie... 'you'll like it'... 'it will feel good, you'll see'... 'I'll protect you, I promise'... But it's just... just no use... just all lies..."

325

"Kody, listen – everything's going to be alright, you'll see! Just take a breath – just a few breaths and calm down! We can figure—" One implored but stopped when he saw the change in the teen's demeanor—

Kody's body tensed, the teen coming fully erect with a look of cold determination in his eyes.

"I'm not worth anything!" Kody screamed—

He raised the pistol to his head again—

"I'm not worth... anything," Kody said in a whisper as his eyes took on a far-reaching look—

One could clearly see the end unfolding and so he made his move, but his limbs were slow, the effects of reduced circulation still lingering, the distance between them too great—

The pistol fired—

Kody collapsed, a mist of expanding pink hanging in the air where his head had been.

"*NO!*" One raged as an encompassing despair so strong that it physically pushed One backward, causing him to stumble into the chair to which he'd been bound. Together they crashed to the floor—

And One's world imploded.

Chapter 57

I Could Have Done More

"Why?!"

One gasped for breath between wracking sobs.

"Why?" he demanded of the world. "*Why?!*"

What's done is done... a voice inside said softly.

I could have done more!

What more could you have done? Really?

One sniffled, his sobs slowing.

I could... could... have said I loved him... because I did... in that short time, I found myself loving him as my own son... I could have told him his parents were gone, but Garrett and I would take him in... be his family... and together we'd make everything alright...

I could have... have done more...

I could have... said what I felt... how I felt...

The voice inside didn't say anything more.

It didn't have to.

The monster, Jorge Manuel de Corazón, a being thoroughly and truly evil, had caused a wonderful, beautiful boy to kill himself out of guilt and horror, shame and complete loss of self-worth from all the physical and psychological abuse rained upon him. Despite the trust that One had begun to build with Kody, in the end it hadn't been strong enough to break de Corazón's hold—

And now Kody was dead.

How many more children were destined to have the same fate as Kody's, or worse, due to the Presagio cartel's trafficking?

Even without de Corazón, the cartel would continue under someone equally horrible and heinous. As long as trafficking was profitable and there was a demand, it would continue.

What will you do about it? the voice asked.

I'll show you! One answered.

The steely resolve that gripped One was like an infusion of fuel into a jet engine's afterburner: it revived him, energized him, and gave him penultimate purpose.

One knuckled away his tears, got to his feet, and scanned the room. He saw his clothes and items dropped atop one of the armchairs, and went there, getting dressed and equipped despite the bleeding of the two knife slashes on his chest.

The wounds didn't matter – One no longer felt them. He no longer felt anything except for an inferno of focused, intense purpose.

He went to Kody's body, taking a moment to regard the teen. A halo of red encircled his head, coloring his splayed blond hair in various tints of crimson. If there hadn't been a puckered hole at the teen's temple and the pool of blood, anyone happening upon Kody might have assumed he was merely sleeping, exhausted from a long day of activities.

One knelt and allowed himself one final, slow caress of Kody's hair, then took up the pistol Kody had used and stuffed it in the waistband of his shorts.

At the door, One carefully lifted the slat in the blinds and took in what lay outside the office.

Jorge's men were in guard positions at the far end of the warehouse, by the entry door, sitting on some crates talking and smoking. They clearly thought that their boss would be spending hours inside the office having fun with the two captives. With those captives having finally been caught, there was no longer a need to be on high alert, and so they were doing what all soldiers do under these circumstances—

They were relaxing.

One press-checked his USP pistol to make certain a round was chambered and ready to fire. Seeing that it was, he brought it up to a ready position with his right hand, and with his left, he pushed the office door open. The sounds of the warehouse came to him then, the beeps of backing forklifts, the roar of truck engines, and sounds of hoists, and the murmur of conversations, the closest being from the four marines at the end of the aisle.

One strode forward, purposeful and unhurried, bringing the sights of his pistol to bear as he went forth, centering them on the face of the closest marine.

It wasn't until One was halfway to them that the first of the marines noticed him.

One saw the man's eyes go wide, his mouth open and his body begin to turn toward where he'd leaned his M4 against a crate—

But One's single, suppressed .45 caliber round hit him just above his left ear and made mincemeat out of his brain.

It was an amazing shot, made from 25 meters – about 82 feet – with a suppressor attached. Even in the hands of an experienced shooter, pistol work farther out than 15 meters was challenging, but One was now in rage-induced top form, so the shot struck precisely where One had placed it.

The other three marines froze with incomprehension when their compatriot collapsed and a spray of blood and bone splattered them, but they were trained operators and that moment quickly passed.

All three went for their rifles.

They never had a chance.

Stepping steadily forward, One squeezed off three, paced shots, taking the first of the three marines in his exposed neck, blasting away the man's trachea and Adam's apple and severing the carotid arteries; the next took a .45 slug to the head, just forward of his right ear, blasting his brains out the other side of his now-ruined skull; and the final marine went down gurgling as arterial blood sprayed out from his ruined jaw and neck.

Three shots in just as many seconds, and without a sound from any of the marines.

One crossed to their bodies and took up an M4, examining it and finding it well-maintained. It had an ACOG sight, currently flipped down in favor of a laser reticle, which would be used in conjunction with a green aiming laser attached to the Picatinny rail below the barrel of the rifle. There was also a suppressor on the end of the barrel, a MagTech variant that One knew was a top performer.

Perfect...

One scooped up a few extra magazines of ammunition from the plate carriers the dead marines wore, stuffing them into the pockets of his cargo shorts. That done, he ejected the magazine in the rifle, checked to be sure it was full – it wasn't – and so swapped it out for a fresh one taken from a dead marine's carrier vest. Now properly armed for the next phase of retribution, One went to the glass door that led to the outside and peeked around its edge to get a feel for the battlespace.

He saw the two vans parked in an inverted V, and at the open end of that V, an idling black Suburban with heavily tinted windows, a magnetic-mount light bar/siren combination, and an omnidirectional antenna, one he'd seen before.

It was Jorge's Suburban.

He won't be needing it anymore, the voice noted.

One ignored the voice, instead focusing on the four marines he could see that were standing around the Suburban, their rifles pointed barrel-down and fingers alongside trigger guards. It was night outside, but the light over the door and the tower lights around the warehouse were giving off plenty of overhead illumination for One to mark each of them in their respective positions around the SUV. He saw that these guards were scanning for threats, but lackadaisically; One could see that they were talking among themselves, shouting to be heard as they turned briefly to talk back over their shoulders, and then facing back to their sectors of coverage.

One glanced back at the dead marines, his eyes alighting on flashbang grenades attached to their carriers, and an idea formed in his mind.

Those will be handy...

"How long is this gonna take, do you think?" Rafael called over his shoulder.

"Who the hell knows with the Tiger?" Victor replied from the front of the idling SUV. "All I know is that even with the sun gone down, it's still fuckin' hot out here with all this gear. Think the LT will let us go inside? I mean, hell, what threats are there gonna be here at an airport with the police on Ledder's payroll?"

"Don't even bother," Pedro interjected. "The LT's a hard ass – you'll get no sympathy from him! You should know that by now – you've been with us, what, four months?"

"Five and a half," Victor answered.

"Whatever," Pedro said dismissively, then seeing the glass entry door to the warehouse begin to open, twisted to shout back over his shoulder. "Looks like the LT's coming—"

That's when Pedro heard the metallic skidding of a grenade on the asphalt. He turned just in time to face the flashbang as it went off, its thunderous *BOOM-BOOM-BOOM* and brilliant firecrackering of half a million candlepower magnesium charges deafening and blinding him into senselessness. Pedro had only a second to howl in pain from the point-blank discharge before a 5.56mm rifle round punched through his nose and obliterated his gray matter.

The grenade had less of an impact on Carlos, who was on the other side of the SUV, but for Rafael and Victor, the effects were almost as bad as they'd been for Pedro. With the vans acting as a channel for the grenade's sound and light energies, both these marines were stunned and fell to the ground—

Whereupon One stepped up and placed a three-round burst into the heads of each in turn, silencing their screams of agony with a hand-off to the grim reaper, courtesy of the US government.

Carlos reflexively turned to the threat and saw a man silhouetted by the light over the entry to the warehouse approaching. For the first second he thought that it was the LT, but when the man came forward enough for the tower lights to illuminate him, he saw that the man had an M4 rifle against his shoulder, its green laser finger visible through the smoke cause by the grenade—

Dancing in a tight circle on his right cheek.

Before he could dodge, before he could bring his own M4 up to fire, One's rifle spat a three-round burst that shredded the man's face and destroyed the lower half of his brain. Carlos dropped to the ground, dead before he even heard the shots that killed him.

Without pause, One glided quickly to the open side door of the nearest van and saw two marines inside struggling to find their rifles. They'd been napping on rotation, and for once, One was pleased to find that Murphy was working against the enemy.

Two, three-round bursts to their heads put the last of Jorge's mercenaries down.

Continuing past the van, One came swiftly to the rear door of the SUV and yanked it open, thrusting his rifle's barrel into the vehicle's interior and scanning for occupants.

The driver was facing him, holding a Beretta 92M in a trembling hand as he brought it to bear on One. The driver fired the pistol, its muzzle blast illuminating the cabin of the SUV like a camera's strobe and sounding tremendously loud in the confined space.

One felt the bullet whiz past his left ear, its passage a high-pitched whine, and in the brief second of the pistol's flash, he saw there were three occupants in the SUV: the driver, a young man of perhaps 24 or 25 years of age; the well-dressed man who had brought the Halliburton case to Jorge back in the office; and another young man who was making every effort to open the rear, left-side door but couldn't seem to get his hands to do what he wanted them to do. A half-open laptop had fallen from a fold-out desk at this third man's seat, and that desk seemed to be what was impeding the man from getting the door to open.

One squeezed the trigger, sending another three-round burst into the driver's chest and was satisfied when the man was pushed back by the impact, bouncing off the steering wheel and slumping against the door with a nice, tight grouping of holes from which blood blossomed. A fraction of a second later he put a second, three-round burst into the face of the passenger, splattering the interior of the windshield with blood, bone fragments and brains.

One then swung the rifle to the young man, who upon seeing this, froze and began babbling rapid, loud nonsense Spanish, his hands raised and shaking violently.

"STOP!" One ordered. "SHUT THE FUCK UP!"

Whether it was the force of One's shout, or the deadly end of the rifle pointed at his face, or both, the man immediately complied.

"Who are you?!" One demanded.

More babbling and stammering came from the man's trembling mouth.

One exhaled angrily, but decided that this guy wasn't a threat, so he let the barrel of the rifle drop away slightly. With practiced ease, One ejected the rifle's magazine, inserted a fresh one, slapped its bottom to assure it was seated properly, and pulled the charging handle to make it ready to fire.

He then more calmly asked, "Calm down – I'm not going to shoot you unless you do something stupid, okay?! Now, who the fuck are you?"

After several attempts, the man managed, "I'm... Alfredo...."

"And you do what for de Corazón?" One demanded.

"I'm... I'm his... computer... computer guy," Alfredo stammered.

Well, well...

By now the furious rage that had fomented within One after Kody's suicide had become more tempered and controlled. A lot of that had to do with the fact that he'd disposed of the rest of de Corazón's security force, but that had only slightly assuaged One's need for revenge.

In his core, One knew that what had happened in that office would leave an indelible, horrific stain on his heart and soul for the rest of his life, something he'd continually re-live as a series of "what ifs" and second guesses.

But he couldn't let that cloud his judgement and distract him from his needs of the moment. Not after all that had happened.

"You have all de Corazón's stuff on that laptop?" One asked.

The man gulped several times before saying, "No... it's not on here—"

One returned the barrel of the M4 to point at the man's face. "But you've got access to it all, right? Files, videos, plans, everything the Presagio cartel has and needs to operate?" One poked him in the chest quickly with the M4's barrel before re-aiming at his face, and growled, "Think really, really hard before answering – if not, you're of no use to me and, well, bullets don't cost much."

The young man goggled and shivered, nearly bouncing up and down in his seat.

"Oh! Yes! Yes! I can get it all for you, *señor*, yes!! Just... just don't kill me!"

Chapter 58

Epilogue

The day was incongruous.

It was pleasantly warm, with a light breeze ruffling through the nearby trees whose branches held a riot of autumn color – vibrant crimsons and burgundies, sunny yellows and golds, and oranges that ran a gamut of hues from pumpkin to mango. The grass was a verdant, earthly counterpoint to the autumnal display, marred only by the dark, open hole, four feet wide, six feet long, and six feet deep, and a pile of excavated soil, covered by a tarp of AstroTurf to camouflage its presence.

One stood with Garrett near the edge of the grave, looking at a simple, polished wood coffin sitting atop the straps of the lowering device. They were the only two present to mark the burial, unless you counted the two cemetery workers who hovered at a respectful distance, who were waiting for One and Garrett to pay their last respects before coming to finish their burial task.

Garrett was dressed in a black Brooks Brothers suit with a black tie over a bright white shirt, and polished, black dress shoes, while One was dressed in his Class A uniform, the gold oak leaves of his rank glowing in the late afternoon sunlight and the five rows of his ribbons – his "fruit salad" – were a brightly colorful contrast to their somber mood.

There was one new ribbon that stood out on One's uniform, because it was set above all the rest, alone –

A band of sky blue upon which were five, small white stars – signifying the wearer was the recipient of the Medal of Honor, the United States Army's highest award.

The medal itself was on a wide, sky-blue ribbon that One wore around his neck over the black tie of his dress uniform, so that the heavy gold, five-pointed star was displayed just above the bottom of the jacket's open V-neck.

It was a medal he'd been awarded after returning from the mission into Mexico, an award that had come to him due in large part to the teenager who they were here to honor today.

Garrett stole a glance at One, and saw tears on his cheeks as he stared, unblinking down at the small coffin.

Garrett's mouth formed a line of helpless frustration. He knew that One was not just grieving over Kody's death but held himself responsible for it.

A week after One's return to the US, Garrett still didn't know all the details of what happened in Monterrey, despite holding a relatively high position within the Defense Intelligence Agency. The records of One's mission and all its particulars weren't available to him on the Inter-Agency Database, being classified higher than his security clearance allowed, but he did know some of what occurred in the aftermath because he'd helped facilitate it.

After the shoot-out at the warehouse in Monterrey, One had called him and asked for him to arrange for someone to meet him at the border crossing at Las Carretas so that he could be escorted through customs with an HVT – high value target. There was no longer a need for a flight out, but rather One needed a fast return to the US because he now had an HVT who possessed sensitive intel with a very short half-life.

The HVT was Alfredo Vegas de Fuente, a 28-year-old CalTech Ph.D. computer genius that de Corazón had forced into his service through a combination of high pay and threats to literally crucify all his relatives if he didn't work for the cartel. He'd had this threat hanging over him for the last several years, and so did whatever de Corazón had demanded of him. He was the one person that de Corazón trusted – as far as a man such as he could trust anyone – to handle the cartel's sensitive IT and was the single person through whom all the cartel's business was funneled, which included its complex finances, the scheduling of drug and trafficking transactions and deliveries, cryptocurrency processing, and staffing and payroll.

The information de Fuente could provide to them on the Presagio cartel was an intelligence coup of monumental proportions, one that would virtually guarantee that the US could cut this cancer from the body of society in totality.

But only if they could get to work on it right away. Though they had the top IT guru for the cartel in hand, and he was willing to cooperate, his cooperation would last only as long as his family was safe. That meant forming several teams on the fly to insert into Mexico, retrieve his loved ones, and exfil with them to the US. The moment the cartel's mid-level capos discovered that Alfredo was missing, they'd assume Alfredo had fled with the cartel's records and a substantial amount of money – he was their sole cryptocurrency guy, after all – and would move to carry out their fail-safe orders, which were to kill all Alfredo's family members in retribution.

If that wasn't enough of a shock and surprise, One also told him that he was bringing the body of Kody with him. Garrett had naturally asked what had happened, but One pushed his questions aside.

Garrett knew this much: One had come to love the teenager. One's paternal instincts, coupled with his compassion for all that Kody had endured, clearly had made One realize how he truly felt, though it took Kody's death for One to fully understand his own, complex emotions and accept them.

In their phone call when Garrett had joked about picking up a son along the way, the tone of One's words in response held an undercurrent meaning that Garrett had immediately picked up. One might be a strong, extroverted, alpha male on the outside, but Garrett knew he was a caring softy on the inside, one who couldn't stand seeing someone in pain or in strife. He was the type of person that wanted to fix things, to make things right, and thus found a perfect way to do this working for the CIA's Special Activities Division.

Kody's plight had clearly pulled on One's heartstrings; their time together thereafter had intertwined One's with the teen's irrevocably. Despite having been together for less than a week, the bond they had formed – forged out of necessity, mutual need, trust, and love –

was palatable enough that Garrett could feel it through their phone conversations.

It was a bond that was still connected to One's heart; that much was clear by the tears on One's face as they stood graveside.

"He was a good kid," Garrett whispered, not knowing what else to say, but wanting to say something to get One to open up about what he was feeling – something One hadn't yet done.

"He was a *great* kid," One said with a sigh. "And I let him down."

Garrett reached and took One's hand in his. As he did so, he felt One tremble and heard a soft sob.

"You know… you can talk to me about it… if you want, and when you're ready," Garrett said with a reassuring squeeze of One's hand.

One's mouth curled into a sad, wan grin. He turned his head just enough to meet Garrett's gaze and nodded. "Thanks… but… but not just now."

Garrett returned One's nod, then looked back to the coffin. "I know it doesn't make up for it… but Kody was the domino that started the fall of all the rest… of the entire Presagio cartel."

That much Garrett did know. The information Alfredo provided – access to all the cartel's computers and data, its rosters of members, and the identities of all those who were on their payroll – gave the US intelligence community and its military the keys to the castle. Though the work had just started, there was no doubt that the Presagio cartel would be fully and completely obliterated. Its network of tunnels into the US, its drug caches and manufacturing sites, its money, holdings and property, its hundreds of thugs and scores of paid-off bureaucrats and police would be systematically removed from the chessboard because of the unprecedented access de Fuente had provided.

It would be the most far-reaching, most successful operation against the drug and trafficking trade that the US – indeed, the world – had ever seen, and would send a clear message that the US was winning the War on Drugs and the War on Human Trafficking.

It was an operation for which the President had awarded One the Medal of Honor.

"It was all because of that one decision," One said softly.

Garrett looked at One. "How so?"

One exhaled a slow, sad breath. "If I hadn't listened to the squad, if I'd followed protocol, we would have left Kody there, standing outside de Corazón's estate."

One finally reached up to wipe away his tears with the back of his hand.

"I argued against them, but... but inside I knew that I was going to take him with us... he looked so small, so helpless, drugged, standing there half-naked... even though I said to the team that we couldn't afford to take him along, inside, all I could think of... was if we left him... he'd either be killed, or worse... thrown back into the cesspool of sex slavery..." One paused, swallowing down his building emotions. "I thought... what if he was my son? How would I feel if... if a team of operators had the chance to rescue him... but didn't because of some stupid protocol?"

One sniffled, taking a deep breath to hold back the tide of sorrow that was hovering just beyond the edge of his control. "So I gave in, and we took him... then it was just him and me... and I got to know him... he was yearning, Garrett, wanting someone to trust, to care for him... it was so plain to me... but I couldn't... I couldn't bring myself to go there.... Instead, I played the Big Tough Soldier until the end... when he held the gun to his head, I tried... I pushed it aside and tried to be his friend... maybe even like a dad... but it wasn't enough..."

"Sometimes... people just can't be saved," Garrett offered. "Don't want to be saved..."

"He was the cost of one decision," One said, and sniffled again. "The cost of *my* decision..."

One went silent for a long moment, then said one final time in a hoarse whisper, feeling the weight of his statement and each of its words.

"The cost of One's decision..."

Garrett stepped in closer, pulling One to his side by their still-joined hands.

"Hey, hey! Look at me," Garrett ordered softly. When One didn't, Garrett pulled on his hand, jerking it hard to grab his attention. One looked to him reflexively, and holding his gaze, Garrett said, "This is *not your fault*. Do you hear me? *This is not your fault.* You did everything you could, jeopardizing your own life multiple times to give that kid a chance to escape with you, to get back here to safety – and I know that you found yourself loving him and... were planning on taking him in, with us, weren't you? After I told you he had no parents or family left.... so we could have the family we talked about?"

Tears came again, and all One could do was nod slowly.

"I didn't know him anywhere nearly as well as you, but despite that, I felt it all," Garrett continued. "You're a good man, and you did everything you could with the shitty hand you were dealt. It's not your fault this poor boy died... *it's de Corazón's fault*, plain and simple. It wasn't you, it wasn't Kody; but you both paid the cost for de Corazón's decision, for his actions – Kody with his life, and you with your love for him."

One's lips became a tremulous line, and he broke down into deep sobs. Garrett pulled him into a tight embrace, letting One cry out his anguish and sorrow.

When they finally broke their embrace, Garrett offered One a pack of tissues, and One took a wad of them with a grim nod of thanks, wiped his eyes, blew his nose, and then stuffed the soiled tissues into his pocket. Together with Garrett, he turned back to the coffin, which was burnished with reds and golds of the setting sun's light.

"He was brave, too, wasn't he?" Garrett asked.

His throat still tight with everything he was feeling, One simply nodded.

"Well... even though he's gone... I think he appreciated what you did for him, and what you've done here..." Garrett gestured with his chin toward the grave marker.

One nodded slowly once more, wiped his eyes, then looked up to the darkening sky, nodded toward it as if he felt Kody looking down upon him from heaven. He reached up and unfastened the ribbon from around his neck, took his Medal of Honor in hand, and then stepped to the coffin, laying it out so the award lay flat on the coffin, right above where he guessed Kody's chest would be within.

"You deserve this more than I do," One managed to croak from a throat raw with pain and grief.

Garrett was there then, wrapping his arms around One's waist and leaning his head against One's shoulder. They stood like that, looking down at the small coffin, until the final, scarlet glow of the setting sun disappeared, leaving them in purple twilight. Only when the stars came out in the post-twilight did they turn, arms around each other's waists, and walk away.

The attendants stepped to the grave after the two men were gone from sight, one wheeling a portable light on a dolly, the other carrying their shovels.

The one turned on the lights, and aimed it toward the grave.

They looked at the Medal of Honor on the coffin, then looked at each other.

Both had been working at the cemetery long enough to see people leave all sorts of tokens on coffins, each being something of special meaning for the deceased to take with them into the sweet hereafter. Both had also been in the military – the older serving in the First Gulf War, the younger in Afghanistan – and so both recognized what the Green Beret major had left on the coffin.

"Who was he?" the older attendant asked his junior.

The man took out a folded paper from his pocket, the blue copy of the five-part internment order. "Kody van der Byl," he answered. "Um... a 14-year-old boy."

"The major who was just here, his name plate was 'van der Byl,'" the older man said. "Damn, to lose your son... and one so young... geez, no wonder he was balling like he was."

"Do we leave it?" the junior asked, jutting his chin toward the medal.

"Yeah," the older attendant said and went to the release on the lowering device. Activating it, he stepped back and the two of them stood at respectful attention, as if honoring a fallen comrade, as the coffin disappeared into the grave. Once it was at the bottom, they undid the straps, removed them, pulled aside the AstroTurf cover on the pile of grave soil, and in time honored tradition, shoveled the soil into the open grave by hand. The groundskeepers would arrive first thing in the morning to compact and level the soil, then cover it with freshly grown turf.

When they were done, the two removed the grave marker from its wooden shipping box and hefted the white headstone into position at the head of the grave, sliding the end into the hole prepared for it. Once the soil had been tamped in around its base, the two stepped back to survey

341

their handy work in the light of hand lamps, and read the grave marker's inscription—

Kody van de Byl
Born: August 8th, 2009
Died: September 30th, 2023
He touched our lives and will stay in our hearts forever.

THE END

<—>

Afterward

Human trafficking and slavery are not something new; they have been with human civilization nearly since its beginning.

One would think that after the American Civil War, where slavery was abolished in the USA, and in a like manner, abolished throughout most other countries – which either followed the USA's lead, or had already made this practice illegal by their own impetus – that the world would have finally thrown aside this unjust, amoral and disgusting practice.

Unfortunately, there's always someone with selfish needs, someone who is stronger and crueler who can, and will impose themselves on someone who is weaker and more timid, regardless of the amorality and illegality of their actions.

Between 2008 and 2022, the number of human trafficking victims worldwide increased from roughly 31,000 to 115,300[1].

Furthermore, according to the United Nations Office on Drugs and Crime, the most common form of human trafficking is sexual exploitation[2], with approximately 79% of those trafficked falling into this category. Of these, 66% were women (18 years old or older), 13% were girls (under age 18), 12% were men (18 years old or older), and 9% were boys (under age 18).

---

1. "Total number of human trafficking victims identified worldwide from 2008 to 2022." Statista Research Department, 01 September 2023.

2. "Global Report on Trafficking in Persons." United Nations Office on Drugs and Crime, February 2009.

Human trafficking is often done hand-in-hand with illegal drug, substance, weapons, and/or contraband smuggling by criminal cartels who have discovered that flesh peddling – and the production of various types of adult and child pornography, as well as physical torture and mutilation of the victims for fetish-based multimedia production that comes along with trafficking – can be just as, and sometimes more profitable than manufacture and shipping of illegal substances.

This problem will not go away unless the world wakes up to the reality of the existence of human trafficking and just how broad a reach and scope it currently has. I hope that my story herein, the statistics I've cited, and the stark information in the Real-World Excerpts presented below, will help, in some small way, to motivate us all into addressing the scourge of human trafficking in our world today.

—Zayne Kulder, August 2024

<————>

REAL-WORLD EXCERPTS

INSIGHT CRIME (insightcrime.org; 23 September 2013) – *Drug Cartel Control Feeding Mexico Sex Trafficking*: Sex trafficking is increasing in Mexico and the victims are getting younger, according to a coalition of NGOs, as the diversification of organized crime fuels modern-day slavery...

Mexico's National Human Rights Commission (CNDH) has estimate there are between 16,000 and 20,000 victims of sexual exploitation in Mexico, said El Universal....

THE BORGEN PROJECT (borgenproject.org; 2 November 2019) – *10 FACTS ABOUT HUMAN TRAFFICKING IN MEXICO*: Mexico has the largest number of victims of modern slavery than any other country in the Americas... Those most at risk are women, children, indigenous people, people with mental or physical disabilities, migrants and LGBTQ individuals...

Out of 150,000 children living on the streets in Mexico, it is estimated that 50 percent are victims of trafficking for sexual purposes....

NBC NEWS (nbcnews.com; 29 April 2020) – *First drugs, then oil, now Mexican cartels turn to human trafficking*: MEXICO CITY – Organized crime is mutating in Mexico as gangs who steal oil and sell drugs try a lucrative new line of work trafficking people, according to a top official fighting money laundering...

...anti-trafficking justice efforts in Mexico have focused on sexual exploitation and been patchy....

YUCATAN TIMES (the yucatantimes.com; 29 April 2020) – *Mexican cartels turn to human trafficking*: ... Mexico is an origin, transit and destination country for human trafficking, a global business estimated to be worth $150 billion a year...

Human trafficking may be the third-largest illicit activity in Mexico, after drugs and guns....

MEAWW (meaww.com; 22 July 2020) – *Sex & Modern Slavery: US-Mexico border is a human trafficking hub for sex trade and forced labor*: Human trafficking is a pervasive problem across the world. It involves the use of force, fraud or conversion where people are forced into some type of labor of commercial sex act. Every year millions of people, including children, become prey to trafficking regardless of age, nationality or race... In the US, this humanitarian crisis is rampant at the Southern border. Powerful criminal networks and individual traffickers on both sides of the border traffic or recruit people for forced labor or sexual exploitation....

Thank you!

Thank you for reading *The Cost of One's Decision*. If you enjoyed it, a quick review over at Amazon and/or Goodreads would be greatly appreciated! Reviews help authors like me make a living and gives me the impetus to write more books for your enjoyment.

About the Author

Introduced in middle school to *The Hobbit* by some friends, Zayne found himself enthralled by the fantasy world that Tolkien had created. He soon read *The Lord of the Rings* and any other fantasy fiction he could find in the school's library.

With the advent of *Star Trek* on television, and being a fan of *The Twilight Zone*, *The Outer Limits*, and various Sci Fi movies, Zayne broadened his reading horizons to include science fiction, and then broadened it further to include techno-thrillers when he discovered Tom Clancy's *Red Storm Rising* and *The Hunt for Red October* as well as Dale Brown's *Flight of the Old Dog*.

Inspired by these and many more great works, and after reading over 1,000 of them, Zayne developed and settled on his own style of fiction writing – one that was sometimes edgy, dealt with controversial or uncomfortable subjects, and/or explored the human mindset and emotions, such as he's written here, in *The Cost of One's Decision*.

zaynekulderauthor@gmail.com

www.reesehaldenLLC.com

Made in the USA
Middletown, DE
26 August 2024

59352129R00205